CONCRETL

For my brother, in loving memory,
Winston Carl Dennis
1957-2025

FERDINAND DENNIS

CONCRETE DREAMS

A NOVEL

PEEPAL TREE

First published in Great Britain in 2025
Peepal Tree Press Ltd
17 King's Avenue
Leeds LS6 1QS
UK

ISBN 13: 9781845236021

EU GPSR Authorised Representative
LOGOS EUROPE,
9 rue Nicolas Poussin, 17000,
LA ROCHELLE, France

10 9 8 7 6 5 4 3 2 1

Supported using public funding by
ARTS COUNCIL
ENGLAND

CONTENTS

1. *Lucas buys a house, 1950s*

On a cold and overcast Saturday in January, sometime in the 1950s, Lucas Bostock, having done a morning's work on a Shoreditch building site, finished half-an-hour earlier than usual and travelled by bus to keep an appointment with an estate agent. The agent's office was sandwiched between the Brighton pub and Smith's grocery store and bore the legend "Burnham and Fosters, Estate Agents" in gold-coloured letters on the window. Lucas had a few minutes to spare, so he dusted down his donkey jacket, inspected his steel toe-cap boots, which still bore traces of concrete dust, and stomped his feet a few times before deciding that he looked presentable enough.

Lucas was a stocky 5' 7" and very dark. He was competent in several construction trades and had more than once boasted that he could single-handedly build a house but described himself simply and proudly as a carpenter. For a brief period, during his youth, the boxing ring had tempted him with promises of fame and fabulous wealth. Its legacy was visible in his broad shoulders, his way of entering a room as though he had stepped into a boxing ring, and was sizing up an opponent, arms crooked at his sides, and hands clenched into fists the size of a sledgehammer.

The estate agent, Joseph Liebowski, was seated behind a vast and untidy partner's desk and speaking on the phone. Covering the mouthpiece, he greeted Lucas in heavily accented English and invited him to take a seat, pointing with long pink fingers to a shiny oak captain's chair.

Lucas felt too restless to sit down. Hands clasped behind his back, he walked to the window and gazed at the passers-by, women carrying shopping bags and men in greatcoats and hats, their steps slow and weary, as if they were climbing a long and steep hill in the dusk. Only a few hours of daylight remained, and he wondered whether he would ever get used to these short winter days when the London daylight, weaker than a Jamaican full-moon night, covered almost everything in various shades of grey, even the red buses.

He heard Liebowski finish the telephone conversation and turned to face him.

"You're punctual, Mr Bostock," Liebowski said. "A man on time is a man to be trusted." He rose and walked around the desk; he was over six feet tall and had a slight stoop and a pronounced limp; one leg was shorter than the other.

"The buses running good," Lucas said.

"Now to the viewing, yes," Liebowski said.

Over the next few hours, with Liebowski as his guide and driver, the car, a Ford Prefect, toured the warren of streets north of the High Street. Lucas saw two-storey terraced houses which Liebowski, who clearly took pleasure in his knowledge of the area, called artisans' cottages. He was driven along narrow streets of Victorian, flat, white-fronted houses that reminded him of similar but more imposing buildings in Ladbroke Grove. He saw these houses in a new way when Liebowski pointed out cornices, quoins, Corinthian columns, Gothic window arches and Italianate styles; he made Lucas aware of the disadvantages of houses with valley roofs, and the danger to houses of long dry spells in a city built on clay; he dated the houses and spoke of the city's nineteenth century growth spurt, which swallowed what were once villages surrounded by fields outside the old city. "Then the twentieth century and two wars. Now the city must rebuild, yes. Men like you and me, we will rebuild it, yes."

They had viewed several properties, one as far as the Green Lanes Church Street junction, when they came almost full circle to Carlisle Road, which ran off Stoke Newington High Street. Liebowski had warned Lucas that this particular property needed much work. Its former owner, a widowed, elderly Greek-Cypriot, had returned home some years before and died soon afterwards. The only son had inherited the house and wanted to be rid of it.

Liebowski had not exaggerated. The four-storey house looked like a ruin. Clumps of moss grew on the low front wall. Pigeons exploded from its roof at the sound of the rusty creaking gate; the cornices above the first-floor windows were crumbling, and from one grew a brown, leafless shrub, a buddleia, petrified in the cold.

As they approached the front door, Liebowski apologised for his oversight and revealed that the house came with a sitting tenant – an old man who lived in the basement.

This disclosure upset Lucas far more than the property's dereliction. He had come to trust the estate agent since their first encounter weeks before; his confidence in him now wavered. Nonetheless, he proceeded with the viewing. He went into the back garden and noted the damaged drainpipe and the roof gutter hanging like a broken limb. Inside, he went from room to room, saying nothing as he turned on taps and light switches, tapped the walls for blown plaster, pulled back crumbling linoleum to inspect floorboards, swung doors to see if they were warped or hung properly, opened and closed cracked windows with rotting frames. The ground and first floors were reasonably dry. But the top-floor rooms had borne the brunt of years of neglect; they smelled of guano, their ceilings were disintegrating, and one wall was infested with a fungal growth that formed fantastic patterns.

Back in the first floor room overlooking the street, Lucas paced up and down for a few minutes, lost in thought. This was the largest but worst maintained house he had seen that day. Not only was it in a strange part of London, far from Ladbroke Grove, where he had lived since arriving in Britain, it required more work than he could afford. He needed a property that could accommodate tenants immediately, as well as his pregnant wife, Rhoda, and their nine-month-old son, Samuel. Yes, his family could occupy the ground-floor rooms, which would be a huge improvement on the single room where they currently lived, and the first-floor rooms could be rented out, but the top floor rooms were uninhabitable. The roof and ceilings would have to be repaired, the rooms dried out and redecorated. Then there was the old man in the basement; a sitting tenant was not part of his calculations. He returned downstairs and found Joseph Liebowski waiting for him in the hallway, a hand on the front door latch. "Now to the basement, yes," Liebowski said. He went outside and down to the basement. Lucas followed, hanging behind on the bottom step to scrutinise the brickwork and windows. The estate agent had to knock several times and shout through the letter box before there was any sign of life, which took the form of a sliding bolt.

The door opened and a tall, thin old man with a shock of frizzy white hair framing a narrow ashen face, and dressed in a three-piece green corduroy suit, stuck his head out like a feral creature, sniffing the air for danger. The weak afternoon light seemed to dazzle him and he blinked large rheumy eyes and retreated into the dark entranceway.

Liebowski said, "Mr Norton, I wrote to you last week about the viewing."

"The what?"

"Viewing, Mr Norton. We have a prospective buyer for the house."

"Oh, I thought you were Beatrice. Do you know Beatrice? No. What a shame. Still, you'd better come in."

Introduced to the old man, Lucas extended his hand, but Mr Norton refused to shake it.

Liebowski gave Lucas an apologetic glance, signalled with nod of his head that he should go ahead, and steered the tenant into the front room.

Lucas's inspection of the basement flat was hampered by the sepulchral light, stacks of cardboard boxes, and piles of books that spilled off crowded bookshelves. But he saw the peeling wallpaper, the rotting skirting board and discoloured ceiling, the newspapers taped to the broken windowpanes. In the damp, cold air he smelled or thought he could smell the odour of decaying and lonely age.

On his way out, he glanced into the room in which Liebowski had detained Mr Norton, then went back outside and waited. Liebowski followed minutes later. When he reached the top of the steps, he took out a handkerchief and blew his nose long and vigorously. They walked to the car and stood facing the house, its dereliction less visible in the fading light.

"You're probably thinking I'm trying to sell you a wreck and burden you with an old man in the basement."

"This place going to need plenty work. Plenty work. And the old man, if he's been living there a long time, must be paying far below the market rent."

"I don't mean to sound cruel, but forget about the old man. I doubt he'll still be alive in three, five years. Think about the future, think long term."

"Plenty work," Lucas repeated.

"Mr Bostock, when you walked into my office two weeks ago and I saw your hands, I said to myself, those are the hands of a man who's not afraid of hard work. I will find him a house. I showed you the other places to prepare you for this one. It's a bargain, but a bargain only for a certain kind of buyer. I believe you're that kind of buyer. And Joseph Liebowski is seldom wrong."

Lucas heard sincerity in these words. The other houses he'd viewed were either too small or too expensive, sometimes both.

"There's no hurry, Mr Bostock. Take your time. Think it over."

Lucas agreed to contact Liebowski within a week. He decided to walk to Finsbury Park tube and, trusting his sense of direction, he declined Liebowski's offer of a lift. As he walked, the brief dusk turned to night and the temperature fell. Lucas turned up his collar as he made his way through this unfamiliar neighbourhood where curtains were being drawn, children called inside for their suppers, and from somewhere ahead of him the roar of a football stadium punctuated the air.

He arrived back in Ladbroke Grove in a sort of trance induced by turning numbers over in his mind and weighing up the pros and cons of buying the house in Stoke Newington. He hardly noticed the gathering of West Indian men outside the station; some were dressed in their Saturday night suits, others in open-neck shirts and without overcoats – defiance, bravado and mischief in their laughter.

The smell of curry and the sound of music greeted him as he stepped inside the house where he lived. Sure signs that the two Trinidadian men who lived in one of the ground-floor rooms were entertaining. A slim, brown-skinned man with a pencil thin moustache and conked hair appeared in the corridor.

"Oh, is you Bostock," he said.

Lucas said a gruff good evening to Eric Drake, who had once told him he was a calypso singer.

"Thought it was Roy. He's supposed to bring a bottle o'rum. If he don't hurry, this party soon done. Come down for a glass later, eh Bostock. It have some nice skirts and we expecting more later."

Lucas frowned.

"Oh, I forget you is a family man."

Lucas shook his head and carried on. Drake's mocking laughter followed him up the stairs like the whirr of a bothersome mosquito, but its bite could not penetrate Lucas's hardened skin.

Hours later, with the party downstairs still going on, Lucas sat in the only armchair in the room watching Rhoda bottle-feed Samuel. She was sitting on the edge of the double bed that filled most of the cramped room; it was covered in a pink nylon spread. Mother and child, wife and son, and another child on the way: he had to find a larger space before the second child came. But he did not want to continue being a tenant, a paying guest in somebody else's property. He knew of other men who had become house owners. One was a fellow Jamaican with whom he had shared a room; he now owned a house in nearby Paddington. He, Lucas Bostock, could do that too. It was just a matter of finding the right property. Not some broken down old house with an old man living in the basement.

With Samuel now fast asleep, Rhoda put the child in his cot and said in a low voice: "Something troubling you, Lucas?" She was an inch shorter, and several shades lighter in complexion than her husband. She had a high-pitched, nervous voice.

"What make you think something troubling me?"

"You've hardly said a word all evening."

"Saw a house today, a mashed down place." He had not planned to mention the house in Stoke Newington because they had almost quarrelled the last time they discussed moving. One of Rhoda's cousins, Bertie Johnson, who had been in England since the war, owned two houses in Stockwell and had offered Rhoda rooms in one of his properties. But Lucas, determined to plough his own furrow, had rejected the offer. It was the only occasion Rhoda had disagreed with her husband.

"That reminds me. The landlord was here today, said 'im going to raise the rent by a shilling from next month."

"What the blood…" Lucas caught himself before completing the swear word, which would upset Rhoda. When they were dating in Kingston, she told him she disliked his habit of swearing and cursing at the least provocation. Since then, at least in her company, he took care to express his feelings in less offensive words; these he often did not possess, so he settled for furious and frustrated silence.

Long after Rhoda had retired to bed, Lucas remained in the armchair in the dark room, the faint sound of music coming from downstairs. His anger at the landlord and violent hatred of the room had subsided, but he reviewed the day again, focusing on the house in Stoke Newington.

Maybe he had allowed the old man's presence to cloud his judgement. Born in a remote mountainside village, he had craved city life from an early age. For many years, long after moving to

Kingston, his sights were set on New York, but London prevailed. Today he had seen the wretched side of city life: loneliness, despair, lunacy.

He returned to his calculations with a clearer mind and did something he had not done in several years. He placed his left hand on his thigh, splayed his fingers and tried to lift the middle finger, the nerves of which had been severed in an accident with a chisel back in Kingston. It could not move – would never move, the doctors said – independently of the index and fourth fingers. In the still and quiet and cold of that London night, he concentrated on that act, concentrated on it with such intensity that when Samuel bawled and Rhoda woke up to comfort and feed him, and ask again whether he was coming to bed, and returned to bed herself, he could not give an answer because he was in some far-off place fighting unwanted memories of a night many years ago. He remembered it with doubt because he could never repeat the act – when the injured finger defied the doctors' prognosis and gave the slightest twitch. It persuaded him to make the momentous decision to buy a piece of London.

2. *Lucas and a sitting tenant, some months later*

Lucas Bostock moved his family and their few possessions to Stoke Newington in late March. Among the items carried across London in a decommissioned military ambulance converted into a removal van were three battered cardboard suitcases, one of which once belonged to Rhoda's grandmother, who had acquired it on a decade-long sojourn in Panama in the 1920s; a wooden cot bought in Portobello Road market; and some brand new bedsheets given by Eric Drake. Lucas had accepted the gift with awkward grace but refused Drake's offer to help organise a housewarming party. There would never be a party at 72 Carlisle Road in Lucas Bostock's lifetime.

Throughout early spring, while still working on the Shoreditch building site, Lucas devoted all his spare time to renovations. On weekday evenings, he would return home from a day's hard labour, race through Rhoda's mountainous dinner of mashed potatoes and beef or pork drowning in gravy, bounce Samuel on his knees for a few minutes, then hurry upstairs as if he was late for an assignation with a lover. There he would work late into the night on those tasks least likely to disturb the neighbours: fitting locks on doors, hanging wallpaper and so on. At the weekends, after a morning on the building site, he worked from Saturday afternoon through to Sunday night, pausing only for meals and brief naps. On several nights he had succumbed to exhaustion and fallen asleep on the floor, a screwdriver or plane still in his hand, wood shavings a bed, his toolbag a pillow. He was most comfortable with carpentry work but did not hesitate to transform himself into a plumber, electrician, plasterer, painter and decorator, roofer, glazer, or floor-layer. The results were not always visually pleasing – years later he wondered who had painted a room pink and purple – but they were always effective. The pigeons nesting in the loft were driven out and the roof patched with a mixture of salvaged and new slates and bitumen to create a temporary but reasonably waterproof covering. The top floor rooms were fumigated, their walls washed down with white spirits and repapered. By late April, the rooms were ready. The first new tenants, a young St Lucian couple from Castries, fresh off the boat, moved in at the end of April, and by mid-May all the upper-floor rooms were occupied by working men and women who had swapped the intimacy of tropical villages for the indifference of a city where, according to the landlord, unless they paid their rent every Friday evening and kept noise to a minimum, shop doorways or park benches would become their beds, autumn leaves their blankets, and snow their source of water.

Lucas's direct gaze and forthrightness inspired trust and fear among these newcomers, but he found Mr Norton in the basement less tractable. He was a semi-recluse who received no social callers and only the most persistent ringing of the bell brought him to the front door. His curtains were often closed, though some evenings he could be seen through his living-room window seated in an armchair, a book on his lap, his frail figure, pale face and mop of white hair bathed in the light from a tall wooden lamp. He ventured beyond the front gate only on the last Sunday of each month to attend communion at St Mathias, the local Church of England church. The postman came several times a week, depositing a large number of letters. Every Saturday morning, a sputtering brown van driven by a pale, thin young man delivered a box of groceries, leaving the foodstuff on the doorstep. Mr Norton would usually drag it inside hours later, but it was not uncommon for it to remain there until Monday morning, when the charlady, Mrs Bradbury, who had a key, came to clean the flat.

She was Mr Norton's main link to the outside world. She posted his letters and, at the end of her working day, brought the envelope containing his rent in the form of a cheque to Rhoda, whose working hours at Homerton Hospital and child-care arrangements meant she was home by late afternoon most weekdays. In early May, Rhoda invited Mrs Bradbury inside for tea. She told Rhoda about some of Mr Norton's peculiar habits, the strangest of which was his habit of calling her Friday or Sancho Panza or Mrs Malaprop or many other unusual names, which, she suspected, came from the collection of novels he had been reading and re-reading over the years she had been in his employ. "He's not all there," Mrs Bradbury told Rhoda, "But harmless with it."

Rhoda's report coincided with Lucas's decision to turn his attention to the basement flat. He had noticed several worrying signs of damp there and resolved to treat them, less out of concern for Mr Norton's health, and more for the health of his property. But gaining access to the basement tested his patience.

One Saturday afternoon he spent an hour outside Mr Norton's front door, ringing the bell at five-minute intervals. Mr Norton finally came to the door and, without opening it, called out, 'Who is it, what do you want?' Lucas explained that he had been sent through Mrs Bradbury a list of repairs that were needed in the flat. Mr Norton replied, "Geoffrey Norton is not at home right now." A perplexed Lucas insisted that he was speaking to Mr Norton, but it soon became clear that he was speaking only to himself, because the figure on the other side of the door had retreated into the musty, dimly lit flat. To mitigate his anger, Lucas spent the remainder of the afternoon in the back garden sawing pieces of timber.

When he eventually gained access a month later and watched Mr Norton slowly negotiating his way round the crammed living room, Lucas had a rare moment of compassion. The work he had in mind would inconvenience Mr Norton. Would he survive having the floorboards lifted up? Yet the work was urgently needed; evidence of damp had risen to the ground floor bedroom where he, Rhoda and Samuel slept. Their health was at stake, as, of course, was the value of the property.

He would proceed with caution. He began by carrying out

a multitude of small repairs that made Mr Norton's life a little more comfortable. He fixed light switches, oiled rusty door hinges and replaced worn taps. Mr Norton usually stayed out of his way, but one day, as Lucas was repairing a broken bedroom window, Mr Norton remained in the room watching. He said, "And when you've finished that, Friday, you could see about the blocked kitchen sink."

Lucas ignored this refusal to address him properly, but when the old man called him Friday a second time, he said, "Who's this Friday you think you talking to, Mr Norton?"

"He's a character from a story written by a man who lived in this neighbourhood centuries ago. Daniel Defoe."

"And wha' this story call?"

"Robinson Crusoe. Friday was a cannibal who Robinson Crusoe rescued and turned into his manservant."

"So you think mi is you manservant?" Lucas had removed the pane of broken glass and was cleaning out the channels in the window frame. Mr Norton was sitting on the bed, his pale face lugubrious, the shoulders of his cardigan speckled with bits of dandruff as large as snowflakes.

"Well, mi nuh know nobody caal Friday. Mi name Lucas Bostock, Mr Norton, Where mi come from, when you tell a man your name and 'im refuse to caal you by that name and caal you something else instead, that man is looking for a fight." Lucas picked up the new pane of glass and began to leave.

"What are you doing? You can't leave the window like that."

"Can't I. Mi going to leave it like that 'til you learn some bumbaclaat manners."

"All right, Mr Bostock, I take your point. Please accept my apologies. Offence was not my intention."

"Accepted," Lucas said, and he finished the job.

Lucas was quite struck by Mr Norton's swift capitulation and graceful apology; maybe he had over-reacted to the eccentric ways of an old man. On his next encounter, Mr Norton was a model of politeness; on a subsequent visit he even insisted that Lucas call him Geoffrey, though on that same day he twice called Lucas Sancho Panza. That day Lucas also got a disturbing glimpse into Geoffrey Norton's mind. He had noticed an armed forces service medal and remarked that Mr Norton must have seen a lot of the world in the war.

"So much so that it killed me," Mr Norton said.

"Kill you. How? You right here talkin' to me."

"But you're not talking to the young man who went to war. He died. We still correspond from time to time."

Lucas gave him a puzzled glance.

"Look in that box." Mr Norton pointed to a large pine box in an alcove. "Go on, look."

Lucas removed some bric-a-brac from the box and saw that it was full of letters, neatly tied together in bundles.

"There are more in the wardrobe and under the bed. Not all from him, of course."

"Sorry, Geoffrey. Mi don' understan'. How?"

"It's elementary. All the letters I receive are letters written by myself to me, or to put it more accurately, letters written by my selves to my selves."

There was no trace of humour in Mr Norton's expression and Lucas realised that he was telling the truth. He was both sender and receiver of the copious letters that poured through his letterbox. Lucas left the basement convinced of his tenant's madness.

Further evidence of this came when a heat wave descended in late July. On an exceptionally warm night, with a sliver of moon in a cloudless sky, a piercing scream woke up the whole house. Lucas went to investigate and found the young St Lucian couple trembling in the stairwell and repeating, "Jumbie, jumbie in the garden!" The woman, Phoebe, unable to sleep, had woken up, opened the window, and seen a ghostly apparition wandering the garden. Her boyfriend, Cedric, had seen it too.

Lucas was a practical man. He believed in things he could touch, see, smell, taste and hear, the only exception being the Almighty, and even His existence he frequently doubted. He went downstairs and out to the back garden where he found Mr Norton sitting under an elder tree, his frail, white, stark naked body almost luminous. As Lucas stood there dumbstruck, Mr Norton began to recite: "I wish I had enough breath to speak with less effort and that the pain I feel in this rib would ease just a little, so that I could make clear to you, Panza, how wrong you are. Come closer, you sinner. If the winds of fortune, until now so contrary, blow again in our favour, filling the sails of our desires and carrying us safely to one of the insulas which I have promised you, what would happen when I, having won, make you its ruler?"

"Mr Norton," Lucas said, "you can't go wanderin' about in the garden at night without no clothes on. You scarin' the other tenants."

"Nonsense. I am merely speaking to nature without the impediment of clothes."

Lucas went inside and returned with a blanket to cover the old man and marched him back into the basement flat.

His explanation of the ghostly figure in the garden convinced Cedric, but Phoebe refused to believe she had not seen a jumbie, and a week later, they vacated the room with only a day's notice.

Their abrupt departure left Lucas anxious that Mr Norton's eccentric behaviour would give his house a bad reputation. Although the vacancy was quickly filled, he returned home each evening expecting news of some new outrage. Mr Norton gave him many other sleepless nights and it was on one such night that he rediscovered the resolve to treat the basement damp, regardless of the disruption the work would cause. Mr Norton did in fact survive the upheaval – the ripping up of the floorboards, the dust caused by hacking away plaster, the sight of his furniture piled ceiling high – but, in the middle of the following winter, Mrs Bradbury found Mr Norton's grocery on the doorstep, and he, inside, in a sleep from which he did not wake up.

3. *Lucas and his family, a year or so later*

Lucas Bostock, tool bag in hand, was standing at a bus stop in Kings Cross. He was tired and hungry at the end of a hard day and anxious to reach home, but unknown to him and the others waiting, a collision of several vehicles on Hyde Park Corner had reduced London's traffic to a crawl. Bored with looking at the traffic, he turned to sifting through his mind. Getting the basement flat ready to rent, the second time since Mr Norton's death, he had noticed that despite his earlier efforts to stem the damp, the problem would soon need attention again. Then there was Rhoda and the children: Samuel, Maureen and now Neville. He was worried about the future state of his finances because the family would soon have to claim one of the rooms currently occupied by a tenant. There was another far less tangible concern. Since giving birth to Neville in January, Rhoda often complained of tiredness, though she always found the energy to read the bible and pray before coming to bed. She now performed her wifely duty with such a lack of interest that he had rediscovered the secret and shameful pleasure of what he and his boyhood friends used to call milking.

It was more than the absence of sex that troubled him, it was something vaguer, but when he tried to focus on it and put it into words, he felt as though he was trying to identify an animal from a great distance, through a thick fog, or dense vegetation, and the more he tried to name it, the more blurred it became. Whatever it was, it seemed to him that this creature had always been a part of his life. Frustrated, he returned his mind to a project he had recently formulated – to concrete over the back garden – and instantly felt better to be back in a world where words and objects corresponded. His reverie ended when he heard his name called.

"Bostock!" a man said.

Lucas looked at the man and registered a shiny, crumpled zoot suit, the collar of his white shirt grimy, his shoes, once stylish, covered in scuff marks, his facial skin taut and dry. It was the toothbrush protruding from his breast pocket that triggered recognition and a name.

"Drake?"

"No less, no less." The broad, insouciant grin which used to infuriate Lucas was still intact, but it had lost some of its lustre. Drake inquired after Rhoda and Samuel and the new house, and Lucas revealed that he was now the father of three children, the youngest only a few months old.

Drake pumped his hand in congratulation, then said: "Funny I should run into you, cause there's a letter in the house for you. Been there almost a month now, but I couldn't post it on because I'd forgotten your address."

"Brown or white envelope?"

"Air letter. Jamaica stamp. It look like a woman's handwriting to me."

"How can you tell?"

"You know women, man. Fussy with their dress, fussy with their curls, plus I even think I smell a hint of perfume when it first came." Drake laughed.

The only woman who ever wrote Lucas letters was his cousin Jean, but he had long sent her his new address and had received letters from her there. Had Jean mistakenly sent it to his old

19

address? He found a pencil stub in his pocket and scribbled his address on a scrap of paper.

"Really appreciate it if you could send it on," he said.

"Sure, sure, man. Soon as I get home." Drake cleared his throat, moved closer and whispered, "By the way Bostock, I have a date later with a skirt – sweet, sweet-looking Norwegian, but things kind of tight right now. Real tight. If you get my drift…"

Lucas's reaction was one of astonished indignation and the shutters of his instinctive meanness came down. Anyway, he was still two days away from pay day; he could not help Drake. But when he remembered the bedsheets Drake had given him, the several letters he had forwarded in the first few months, his miserliness felt compromised

"I don't want to let this skirt down, man. She expecting me to wine and dine she. Soon as things turn round, I'll pay you back. Fact, I've got a new record in the pipeline. It going to be big."

Lucas pleaded that he was going through his own hardship, with Rhoda on maternity leave and him having to feed the household. He fished around in his pocket and found a half-crown. He handed it to Drake, and apologised, saying, truthfully, that it was the best he could do.

Drake took the coin and showered Lucas with such expansive gratitude that he thought the Trinidadian was mocking him. Just then, Lucas's bus came and the two men parted. Aboard the bus, Lucas looked back and saw Drake spin the coin in the air and catch it in his outer breast pocket, which also held his toothbrush, and skip toward the tube entrance.

When two weeks passed and there was still no sign of the letter, the calypsonian was reinstated in Lucas's rogues' gallery of the untrustworthy and treacherous. The letter waiting for him at his former address in Ladbroke Grove preyed on his mind like an untraceable odour, and when a stormy day made outdoor work impossible, closing the building site early, Lucas seized the opportunity to visit his old home and collect it.

He arrived at the house around mid-afternoon, thoroughly soaked; not even the old plane trees lining Ladbroke Grove could protect him. The door was opened by a stranger, who told Lucas, in a thick Barbadian accent, that he neither had knowledge of a letter addressed to Lucas Bostock nor a man called Drake, though he admitted that he didn't know all the other tenants as he had only been living there for a short while. He let Lucas in and invited him to knock on the door of someone who might know of Drake. It was opened by a woman in a floral dressing gown.

"I'm looking for Drake," Lucas said.

"Drake?" she said. "You'd better wait." She closed the door and after some minutes opened it and invited Lucas into the room. She was still in the floral dressing gown but she had tidied her hair and sprayed herself with a scent that permeated the room.

"So you looking for Drake?"

"Yes," he said. He told her about the letter.

"That's real funny," she said, "cause Drake don't live here for over a year. He comes back sometimes to collect his letters but it's months since I last see him. Last time I hear about him he was supposed to be sleeping in Hyde Park."

Lucas recalled the dishevelled figure and realised that Drake had used the non-existent letter as a softener in preparation for cadging money. The hole left in his pocket by that encounter grew all the larger. He was readying to excuse himself when he noticed a large suitcase with a name and familiar address: Petronia Brown, Constant Spring Road, Kingston. He had worked on a house on that road. He looked at the woman again and it registered on him that she was attractive, tall and slim and dark, with large clear eyes and full lips, much darker than the rest of her face.

There was a sudden and uncontrollable throb in his groin and he remembered the long-gone days back in Kingston when he would have acted on such a signal, but now there was Rhoda and the children and his tenants and the mortgage. He was leaving the room in obedience to those responsibilities but heard himself say: "Yuh from Kingston?"

"Born and bred," she said. "Ah going back next month."

"Mi work on a house near Shortwood Avenue back in '49; big house," he said.

"The Henriques place?"

"Same one."

She seemed to look at him with admiration, and there was a hint of playfulness in her eyes.

"That's something else. My uncle work there too. You must know him. Courtney Jones."

"Yes, me knew Courtney. Big guy, a plumber, come from Westmoreland."

It was clear that they shared a world, or rather an island and its city. They exchanged names, and when the rain escalated, beating a furious rhythm against the glass, she invited him to wait until it died down. He took a seat on a rickety dining chair and she sat on the edge of the double bed covered in a camberwick bedspread. While they continued to explore their shared island, she offered him a drink of rum from a bottle that a friend had brought for her from Jamaica, unaware that she would soon be returning because she found England too wet and cold and miserable. Lucas seldom drank alcohol because he disliked its loosening effect on his tongue, but with the rain lashing the misted windows of a room in which only the bedside lamp glowed and this lovely woman smiling at him with her fleshy dark lips and lively eyes, he accepted the offer of a glass of rum. It provoked memories of his younger, freer days that sometimes, especially on London days like this, seemed like a dream. Soon he could smell early morning mountain breeze on her breath, see the sea in her eyes, hear music in her laughter.

A heat, terrible and sweet, coursed through his body and he was aware of speaking more than usual but felt no need to censor himself. He hesitated at the offer of a second glass of rum. Rhoda, the children, the Victorian house with its tenants, entered his mind briefly, but they all seemed to belong to the life of another man. He accepted and, watching her pour the drink, he recognised that the raging heat consuming his body could only be cooled by diving into the sea.

The rain had long stopped when Lucas, adjusting his clothes, stepped out of his former home. It was after 9pm and the street lights glistened on the wet pavement and road. He bounded down the steps and made his way towards Ladbroke Grove, trying to remember when he had ever been touched, stroked and kissed with such passion. Had marriage, migration, children and responsibility destroyed the closeness between him and Rhoda? No, he decided, Rhoda had always been a little distant and aloof and those very qualities had made her attractive.

Nearing the corner of Chesterton Road and Ladbroke Grove, Lucas collided with a man, who fell from the impact. "Watch where you going," Lucas said. Picking himself up off the damp pavement, the man, speaking in an island accent filled with fear, said: "Don't go near the station. De white people dem gone mad. Dey attacking we. Dey attacking we cause we black."

While Lucas was still digesting this warning, two Caribbean men ran past. One called out, "Get inside man, white people looking to kill we!" The man who had crashed into Lucas turned and ran. Lucas clenched his fists, thinking I ain't running from nobody. But when two other men ran past, he thought again and decided to make his way out of the neighbourhood by an alternative route. He crossed over Ladbroke Grove and walked up Golborne Road, intending to weave through the backstreets until he reached Westbourne Park station.

The backstreets were indeed quieter. Lights blazed in the surrounding houses, and music and voices floated on the night air. When he passed two lovers locked in an embrace in a doorway, the night could not seem more ordinary. He relaxed a little, but still walked briskly, fists at the ready. A few yards on, approaching a corner, he saw a man whose halting, unsteady steps seemed to betray signs of drunkenness. It was a sight that filled Lucas with disgust. Men like him give us a bad name – lazy drunk, he thought. The figure passed under a streetlamp and was briefly illuminated. It was then that Lucas saw the blood. It was streaming over the man's hands and onto his clothes and the pavement. Lucas ran towards the staggering figure and reached him just as he collapsed. He knelt down and held the limp, damp body, which seemed oddly weightless, as if it had been hollowed out, leaving only the shell of a man.

4. *Rhoda Bostock's unhappiness, a year later*

After the birth of Neville, Rhoda Bostock had decided against having more children. She had left a home of elderly parents, one sister and countless cousins at sixteen, fled the quarrels over money, fights over the dinner table, long nights of empty growling stomachs and frequently-patched, threadbare, hand-me-down clothes that still carried the ineradicable odours of their former owners. The need to flee that overcrowded family house with all its unspoken secrets, and the more orderly life she experienced in the Kingston home of her kindly aunt – who one day admitted that her husband's premature death had been a blessing, otherwise she would have probably ended up with an oversized family – these features of her past predisposed Rhoda to tread a cautious, sensible path.

Rhoda had tried discussing "family planning" – a phrase she learned off a BBC radio programme – with Lucas, but he had seemed indifferent, as if the matter, like cooking dinner and bathing the children, was her exclusive province. Without knowledge of contraception, she decided to practise sexual abstinence. She developed several recurring minor ailments – severe headaches some nights, stomach cramps on others, which, for good measure, she sought to palliate by chewing garlic before retiring.

But in the week after Lucas, his clothes caked in blood, arrived home after midnight and recounted how he'd had to hold a man's throat to prevent him bleeding to death while he was being taken to Paddington's St Mary's Hospital, she relented. The incident reminded her of another night, years before, a night she and Lucas never talked about.

But even that night had not left Lucas looking so shaken.

For some days his rich dark complexion was ashen, his voice softer, less abrasive; he did no work on the house. She found this more vulnerable incarnation of her husband irresistible and one night lavished on him a loving inspired by both a desire to comfort him and sate her own hunger. A month later, her elderly, grey-haired Scottish GP, herself a mother of four, confirmed that Rhoda was pregnant again. She left the surgery feeling weighed down with a terrible sense of failure. Yet on reaching home, she closed the bedroom door, fell to her knees and thanked the Lord. Three children was practical, four divine.

It was, however, a difficult pregnancy. From the fifth month it became clear that she could not work up until the last minute, give birth, then, following two weeks' rest, return to work as if she had merely taken a fortnight's break. Three months before the due date, swollen joints and a persistent backache, far more painful than her imaginative effort at birth control, forced her to stop working altogether.

She was often alone in the house from mid-morning to early afternoon, with Lucas and the tenants at work, the children in school, nursery or with the childminder. At first, the house's stillness and silence disturbed her. She had never before been in an empty house or been alone with herself. But one day, around midday, she fried a plantain, one of several Caribbean fruits now available in Ridley Road market, and went to sit in a high-back East Anglian chair at the bedroom window, which overlooked the back garden, which bore traces of Lucas's handiwork. He had chopped down and uprooted the elder tree and several others, including a Conference Pear tree, in preparation for laying concrete. Only the wet winter and projects inside the house had prevented him from completing the task. She had protested, "You don't have to cover the whole garden with cement." She wanted to grow flowers and keep a kitchen garden. "Cement!" he said. "Is not cement I covering it with. Is concrete. When you mix cement and sand you get concrete. Mix it right and it will last forever."

"Concrete, cement, all the same to me."

"Bet you wouldn't say cake and flour is the same. Anyway, me nevvah come all de way a England fi keep jungle."

She had not protested further, blaming herself for failing to stake a claim on the garden earlier. But looking at the churned-up soil, the dying plants and the mound of gravel, she was angry with herself. But how could she have claimed the garden when she worked almost as many hours as Lucas *and* did all the household chores *and* looked after the children? Lucas was like concrete, as insensitive and hard as the cold, grey material he seemed determined to cover the earth with.

The colours outside and the smell and taste of fried plantain mingled to create a feeling of tranquillity, and Rhoda's mind filled with vivid memories of another time and place. One memory was so clear that she almost felt herself to be there. It is a bright, cloudless day and she is standing on the veranda wearing a flowery, sleeveless cotton dress and her mother is hanging out clothes on a line that runs from a veranda post to a flame tree in bloom. A gentle breeze billows the clothes and the air is filled with the aroma of fried plantain. Her grandmother sits a few yards away in a rocking chair, shelling gungo peas. Her younger sister, Irene, and several cousins are playing in the yard and on the veranda. Somebody, maybe her mother, is singing and her grandmother is humming softly.

These reveries fuelled her conviction that she had never been happier than when the mid-morning sun hovered over the house and her grandmother sat in her rocking chair on the veranda. Yes, there had been relentless hardship, but it was also a place of laughter and singing, a place of joyful celebration. How she missed it! Lucas would always ensure that she and their children would be housed, fed and clothed, but she doubted both his ability to make her happy and his own capacity for happiness. He seemed all restless energy and ambition. Birthdays, their wedding anniversaries, Easter and Christmas meant nothing to him. Although the family still only occupied two rooms, he was talking about buying a car, and maybe a second house. He was a man in flight from Egypt who lacked a vision of a promised land.

The fourth child was a boy and they named him Vincent. Rhoda returned to work only a month later, but the interlude left a lasting impression on her. During it she stood her ground more often with Lucas – and recognised with brutal clarity one of his several shortcomings. Her greatest victory was to win the case for the family taking over the basement, giving them exclusive use of two floors. Two rooms for the children and they would cease sharing the bathroom with their tenants. Long after conceding defeat, Lucas was still complaining about the revenue loss.

She concentrated on trying to recreate the home she had known. She sang to her children, taught them to sing, took them to church, and on their birthdays made sure there were flowers in the house and some kind of celebration – however muted by Lucas's solemn refusal to participate. It was far short of the ideal, but somewhat closer to what she had left behind in Jamaica, memories of which continued to be stirred by the aroma of fried plantain.

It was some years later, not long after Lucas had bought his second house – which he spent many hours repairing – that Rhoda's world was thrown into tumult. One Saturday morning, while choosing a piece of yam at a stall on Ridley market, with nothing more on her mind than finding the ingredients for a Saturday soup, she became aware of a woman staring at her. The woman was small, brown and wiry and had a pretty but pinched face. Rhoda wondered whether she'd mistaken her for somebody else. Disconcerted by the stranger's gaze, Rhoda returned her attention to the yams.

"Just off the boat from Jamaica, luv. Lovely yam." The stall holder was ruddy-faced, with a bulbous red nose. Looking away from him, Rhoda saw that the woman, a smile now on her lips, was still looking at her. The yam was too old, but she bought it and hurried away, feeling unnerved.

The next Wednesday, as she was feeding the children, the doorbell rang. A wave of agitation coursed through her when she saw the same woman from the market standing on her doorstep.

"I've come to see bout the empty room," she said.

"Empty room! There's no empty room here."

"Well, somebody tell me Mr Bostock have empty rooms."

"Oh, you must mean at the other house. My husband's not home yet. You have to call back."

"When he does come home?"

Rhoda guessed that the woman came from either St Lucia or Dominica. "Different times. He's probably at the other house now. You have the address."

"Yes. I does know it. But I have others things to do. Tell he Juliet Basquat come to see the room."

"Yes, okay."

"You'll remember, won't you? Juliet. Juliet Basquat. Make sure you tell he. Tell he Juliet Basquat," she repeated as she backed out of the gate, then walked away.

Rhoda thought the woman was strange, maybe even unbalanced. Her work in Homerton Hospital's geriatric ward had given her some insight into the peculiar pathways that the mind can take. The woman had not even left any contact details. Nonetheless, she made it a point to remember the name and pass it on to Lucas. He came home late that night, as he had been doing most nights recently. His entry into the bedroom stirred her out of a light sleep into a room filled with the smell of soap and toothpaste. She knew she wanted to tell him something but could not immediately recall what it was. Only after he was in bed did she remember.

"Somebody come looking for a room, this evening."

"Here?"

"Yes, a woman."

"A woman?"

"Yes, a woman. She say her name was Juliet Basquat."

Rhoda was suddenly aware of a tremor in the bed, as if an insect had bitten Lucas.

"Juliet what?"

"Juliet Beckett. Something like that."

"She say how to contact her?"

"No."

Lucas switched on the light, got out of bed and went to the bathroom. He was gone for what seemed like a long time. Rhoda had started drifting back into sleep when he returned and her last memory of the night was of Lucas lying beside her in bed, his left foot shaking, a sure sign of anxiety.

Her own anxiety was only just beginning. On her next visit to Ridley Market, this time accompanied by Vincent and Maureen, she saw Juliet Basquat again, standing among a group of young women on the corner of Colvestone Crescent. Her hair, recently pressed, was pulled back, making her gaunt orange-complexioned face seem leaner than before. It gave her a severe prettiness that seemed full of malice.

Rhoda hesitated and thought briefly of how to avoid walking too close to her, but with the children at her side and the crowd thronging around them, she had no choice but to continue and hope that woman did not see her. She seized the children's hands and pressed on. But Juliet Basquat stepped out from among the group of women and blocked her progress.

"Mrs Bostock, you tell your husband I want a room?" She stood akimbo and glared at Rhoda.

Rhoda gripped the children's hands and gathered herself up to her full height, towering over Juliet Basquat's diminutive but menacing figure.

"I told him, yes. But you didn't say how he could contact you."

The young women were paying close attention to the exchange, and Rhoda felt their eyes trained on her. Juliet Basquat turned to her friends and said, "You hear that? He don't know how to contact me. That Jamaican bastard don't know how to contact me, but he know where to find me when he need some brown sugar, eh."

Her friends erupted in salacious laughter. Stung by the bitter truth that she had spent days denying, Rhoda sidestepped the younger woman and carried on her way. Juliet Basquat shouted after her, "A real woman know how to keep she man." Laughter fell on her ears like stones and pursued her through the market as if she were a common thief being chased by a mob.

Rhoda avoided the market for several months. She shopped locally until Lucas, speaking as if addressing a recalcitrant apprentice on the building site, complained about the sameness and Englishness of her meals. Then she found shops in Lower Clapton and Finsbury Park selling Caribbean produce, and used them regularly, despite the inconvenience of the bus journeys there. Sometimes, as she journeyed to and from work or shopped at this greater distance, she could not help interpreting a lingering glance or a mocking smile from a female stranger as signs from Lucas's lovers. Once, when a woman looked at her longer than she thought proper for a stranger, she panicked, abandoned the basket of yam, plantain, pumpkin and dasheen she had gathered and fled, only regaining her composure on a bench in Finsbury Park.

When the malicious laughter and knowing smiles followed her into her bed, as she lay there alone at night, fearing Lucas's return from whatever repairs the second house supposedly required, and there was nowhere else to run, she wandered down to the basement where the children slept, crept into their dark rooms and listened for any signs of irregular breathing. After she'd silently adjusted their blankets for warmth and comfort, she returned to her own bed, her eyes first moist, then streaming with tears for the bountiful blessing of the Almighty. And when Lucas finally came home and lay beside her, she accepted his presence as punishment for her past sin, the secret that bound them together.

5. *Lucas alone, some months later*

One November evening, Lucas entered his house and noticed straightaway a damp patch on the hallway ceiling. He paused to gaze at it; it was shaped like a large island surrounded by chain of smaller islands. The stain puzzled him, as the weather had been cold and dry in recent weeks. Maybe a tenant had spilled water on the landing. He cursed silently and resolved to investigate after eating dinner.

In the back room, where the family usually gathered before dispersing to their individual spaces, he found the three boys watching television, the only light in the room. They mumbled good evening but did not avert their eyes from the flickering screen. It was the darkened kitchen that first struck him as unusual.

"Where's yuh mother?" he said.

Samuel, the eldest boy, looked at his father, and just then the television light flared, illuminating an expression that was both anxious and defiant.

"She's not here."

"And your sister?"

"She's not here, either."

"Unnu eat yet?"

"Yes. Mummy left some food for us."

"She not here when unnu come home?"

"No. She told me she wouldn't be here. I'd to let in Neville and Vincent."

"She tell you… What d'you mean…?" Momentarily lost for words, Lucas noted that the boy sounded more grown-up than he had ever heard him sound, as if the tasks Rhoda had entrusted him with had propelled him closer to adulthood in one day.

Lucas went into the kitchen and found a large pot of rice and a Dutch pot of bony beef stew. He stood over the stove and shovelled some rice, then beef into his mouth. The bittersweet brown stew of stringy beef, though cold, had an immediate impact on his stomach, which had been growling over the past hour; now it purred. Although he was still hungry, he went looking in the bedroom. There was an empty space above the wardrobe where they normally kept some of the suitcases they'd brought ten years ago from Ladbroke Grove.

Then he saw the envelope on the mantelpiece above the gas fire. He snatched it up, ripped it open and read: *Lucas, I can't take this life you have made for us anymore. Please look after our sons. I will be in touch when I have found somewhere to live. May God forgive me.*

Lucas's legs suddenly felt weak but a simultaneous explosion of rage kept him upright. He squashed the note and envelope into a ball and hurled it onto the bed. Head swarming with sulphurous curses, fists clenched, he stepped over to the wardrobe, which was large and plain with a reflective mahogany veneer that gave it a deceptive appearance of solidity. He raised and pulled back his right hand, the hand he had once thought would make his fortune in the boxing ring, and slammed it into the wardrobe door. It cracked, splintered and absorbed his fist into the empty compartment where Rhoda's clothes once hung. Jagged shards of wood penetrated his jacket sleeve, pierced his skin and sent a hot pain searing through his wrist. He yanked out his hand and unleashed another punch that was equally destructive and painful. Blood splashed on his face as he readied himself to deliver the final blow to his imaginary opponent who was, he knew, even in the most remote corner of his rage, himself.

He became aware of another presence in the room. He turned and saw Samuel, expressionless and still, standing in the doorway. He saw in the boy's face Rhoda's eyes and lips, his own nose and complexion. It seemed to evaporate his rage.

"What you want?" he said.

"Mr. George said to tell you that the light switch in his room isn't working."

The mundane challenge of this message helped to complete Lucas's recovery. He glanced at the wardrobe's two jagged holes, his bloodied hands, then at his son and said, "That damn fool. Probably just needs a light bulb. All right." He dismissed Samuel.

The boy left the room and Lucas set about gathering the pieces of wood strewn about the floor. When he'd finished, he went to the bathroom, tidied up himself, piled a mountain of food on a plate and rejoined the boys, who were still in front of the television. The dining table, positioned against the wall, could only comfortably accommodate two adults, and the seat Lucas chose faced the wall, with the children to his left.

He ate the bittersweet beef stew and rice in silence, the noise from the television barely impinging on his thoughts – curses directed at Rhoda and plans to cope with this crisis. When his hunger was sated he felt better disposed towards the world. He turned to look at the three boys and in that moment of brooding inspection he realised that he could cope, that he would have to cope.

He recollected his own childhood – the father he never met, the mother who died when he was eight years old, of carrying a paper parcel of his clothes on the long walk to the hillside house where a relative, Uncle Titus, whom he had never met, had agreed to take him in. The months of shame and humiliation inflicted on him by the high red mistress of the house, Mrs Fraser, and her son Horace, until Jean, the eldest child, stood up for him and demanded that they stop calling him "Kwaku" and "neygah boy" and "blackie shoe polish".

The boys, absorbed in their television watching, were his sons and he would bring them to manhood, woman or no woman. He stood up and said: "Samuel, take this plate to the kitchen for me, then put the rubbish out. Neville, go and wash the dishes. Vincent get the brush and pan and go into my bedroom and sweep up the wood. When you finish, go to bed!"

They turned in unison and looked at him as though he were a stranger. "Now!" he barked. They scampered off.

He collected a screwdriver and spare light bulb from the cupboard under the stairs. Mr George lived on the second floor and Lucas made his way there through layers of odours – the cooking from the tenants' kitchen, then the mixtures of perfume, aftershave and perspiration outside the tenants' rooms. He knocked on Mr George's door and was admitted into a room lit only by a bedside lamp. The bed, a single wardrobe, a mirrored dressing table, a single chair and a paraffin heater barely fitted into the room.

"Can't get any light from the roof," Mr. George said. He was small and dark with large bright eyes and a fixed smile which made him seem smug or anxious not to cause offence. On their first meeting, when he came to enquire about the room and revealed that he had been in England for less than three months, Lucas thought it strange that a middle-aged man had chosen to migrate, but Mr George had so far been a model tenant. He paid his rent on Friday evenings, as all the tenants were supposed to do, and generally kept himself to himself, an inconspicuous and quiet figure.

"You mean the ceilin', the ceilin' light," Lucas corrected him. With the help of the only chair in the room, Lucas changed the light bulb. As he had guessed, that was the problem; the switch was fine. The room, now bathed in light, was immaculately clean and orderly, without a trace of dust on any surfaces.

"You sure keep a tidy room," Lucas said.

"Ever since I was boy, Mr Bostock, ever since I was a boy. Even me grandmother used to tell me, 'Not even woman tidier than you, Everton Ulysses George'."

Mr. George's imitation of his grandmother caused Lucas to smile. "Anything else need fixing?"

"No. But I was wondering if I could ask you something?"

"Yes."

"If one of the large rooms become vacant, can I rent it for me and my wife?" He invited Lucas to sit down and he explained that he had arrived in London intending to stay only as long as it took him to fulfil a mission based on a death-bed promise made to his best friend. The friend's teenage daughter had, a year before, run away from home with her boyfriend. She had written once to her parents, revealing that she was in London, but they did not hear from her again, despite several letters to her London address. When the young woman's father fell gravely ill, Everton George, with deep affection for the dying man, promised to find her on his behalf.

Two weeks after the funeral, Mr George had left for London, and after a month of searching, he found the girl living in a Brixton bedsit, her third home in as many years. Mission accomplished, he readied to return home. Then one day, passing through Marble

Arch, he was so struck by the relentless energy and pace of the city – cars, motorbikes, vans, lorries, buses racing round, and people swarming about like ants – he decided to stay. He had been missing his village home – the sight of the sun setting over green hills, the gentle murmuring of a flowing river, the sound of rain falling on the roof – but as he stood outside Marble Arch tube station, he said to himself: "What a thing is this city." He felt he had to stay a while longer, and share this incredible thing with his childhood sweetheart and wife, who had blessed his journey but urged him to hurry back. Since his letters home told her about the wonders of London and how much he was missing her and wanted her to join him, she had changed her mind. But she had stipulated one condition: he had to find a home that included the numbers seven and two in its address. "You know how our country people superstitious," Mr. George concluded.

"Once you can pay the rent," Lucas said. He added, "Any children?"

"No, no, we don't have any children. Over twenty years we've been married. Tried for the first ten, then gave up. Still, she's the best thing ever happened to me. Best thing. And I miss her bad, bad." Mr George held his hands over his eyes, as if trying to hold back tears.

Lucas frowned and said, "Soon as a room become vacant, I'll let you know."

"Thank you, thank you, Mr Bostock. Thank you. Sometimes this London have me against the rope like Sonny Liston fighting Cassius Clay."

"That was a fight, eh," Lucas said.

"A fight? A battle more like."

Lucas had been readying to leave but Mr George's enthusiasm for boxing detained him. They talked for a long time about great boxing matches and champions. Mr George revealed an encyclopaedic knowledge of the sport that included all weights – Lucas knew only about the heavyweight and light-heavyweight divisions – all culled from American magazines that a cousin who had migrated to the US after the war had sent him.

It was after ten when Lucas left Mr George's room. He made his way back downstairs through the muffled sounds of televisions and radios audible on the landings and stairwell. His own part of the house was quiet; the back room where the boys had been watching television earlier had the stillness of a marketplace long after the traders and buyers had left. He carried out his usual security check, then prepared himself for bed. He took with him the *Evening Standard* and checked the performance of his shares – no movement since yesterday – then turned out the light. In the silence, with Mr George's open and honest longing for his own wife still fresh in his mind, his loss and his burden seemed, for a moment, unbearable. Yet something about Mr. George worried him. That he had sacrificed his home comforts out of loyalty to a friend struck Lucas as incredible. Friendship, loyalty, duty. These words, spoken by Mr George while recounting his London adventure, seemed strange to Lucas. He understood words like ambition, drive, purpose, work, discipline. They were the cornerstone of his life and their effects were visible in the two houses, car, and shares he owned. Had he chosen the wrong values to govern his life? No, if he had chosen to live a life without ambition, as Mr George had done, he would still be repairing houses in and around Portland or in Kingston. But should he, like Mr George, have been faithful to his wife, made of her a friend? He could not answer this question and his inability to provide an answer sparked the realisation that even if he had wanted to be true to Rhoda, he had not known how.

He continued to mull over these questions in his bedroom. This Lucas Bostock belonged to the night when, exhausted, he switched off the light and lay there waiting for sleep's sweet oblivion. By day, he remained crapulous, foul-mouthed, intransigent, belligerent, parsimonious, and priapic, bedding three women in the month following Rhoda's departure.

6. *Lucas brings up his sons*

A few days after Rhoda's departure, Lucas parked his Ford Cortina outside 72 Carlisle Road and took out several bags of groceries, bought in a frenzied shopping expedition on the way home from work. He locked the car door and brought the bags inside, where the three boys were again watching television. They jumped at his entry. Samuel picked up the broom he had put aside when the television commanded his attention, though he had no interest in horse racing.

"Sam, what me tell you 'bout cleaning out the place?"

"That you want to see it clean when you get home, Daddy."

"And is it clean?"

"No, Daddy."

"Bwoy, you know yuh problem? Yuh don't have no ambition. You wo'thless, wo'thless."

Head hung, Samuel began shuffling with the broom, like a novice ballroom dancer awkwardly holding an even less experienced dancer who expected him to take the lead.

"Neville, you wash de dishes?"

"No, Daddy"

"Then what de rass you waiting for?"

He turned to Vincent and said, "Come help me carry de rest of the shopping inside."

Neville scurried into the kitchen, and Vincent meekly followed his father outside. While they were removing the bags, a middle-aged Caribbean woman approached them. Large and brown with hot-iron-straightened hair, her stern expression, erect carriage and dark blue overcoat gave her a military appearance. She smiled at Vincent with maternal tenderness and patted his hair, as if comforting him.

"How you do, young man?" she said.

Vincent's lips moved but no words came out, and the woman smiled at him again, as if to signal that she understood the cause of his silence – his unspeakable and tragic loss. Lucas gave Vincent two bags and ordered him to take them into the house. The boy, weighed down by the bags, walked away slowly.

"Hello, Mrs Morgan." His tone was brusque and cautious. Mrs. Clarissa Morgan, a Jamaican from St Ann, had lived on Carlisle Road for the past five years and held a thrice-weekly prayer meeting in her living room. He had carried out minor repairs on her house.

"Mr Bostock, I was just passing by and, seeing you, I said to myself: nearly every West Indian on this road has been to one of our prayer meetings except you. Don't you think it's time you give your heart to the Lord, Mr Bostock?"

"I tell you before, Mrs Morgan, I don't…"

She interrupted him: "Mr Bostock, I know your wife has left you, left you with three young boys and I hallso know that no woman leaves a good man. Come and join us, Mr Bostock, join the way of Christ the Lord and mend your ways and find peace and happiness. For the sake of those boys, Mr Bostock, give your heart to the Lord…"

"Mrs Morgan," Lucas interrupted "yuh roof leak again?"

Mrs Morgan's eyelids fluttered and she seemed nonplussed for a moment. "No, the roof is fine. You did a good job."

"Well, you worry 'bout yuh roof, Mrs Morgan, cause as I tell you at the time, that was just a patch up job I did. You need a new roof. You worry 'bout your roof and I will worry bout my children."

"But they so young, Mr Bostock; and no mother. They need guidance."

Having missed lunch to do the shopping, Lucas was hungry. It ill-disposed him to this meddlesome but well-meaning neighbour and anybody else who stood between him and the food his stomach was crying for. He slammed the car door, locked it, picked up the remaining shopping bags and said, "Woman, come outta me way!"

Mrs Morgan stood firm and continued her lecture, now brandishing a much-thumbed prayer book in front of him like a sword. Stepping around her, Lucas said, "You damn feisty. Go bout you business."

"You're a sinful and wicked man, Lucas Bostock, a sinful and wicked man. That's why you wife leave you. I pray with hall my heart for the souls of your children. With hall my heart."

That same evening, after eating a chunk of bun and cheese and resting, Lucas cooked his first meal for his sons. It was a soup of mutton, yam, cornmeal dumpling, dasheen, cho-cho and fresh thyme, and its aroma made the boys restless. They devoured it and Samuel and Neville had seconds and then stole the bones from Vincent's plate, which brought howls of protest from the youngest son, who turned to his father for support but was told instead, "When you nyam with hungry dawg, mek sure you nyam fast." The boy looked at his plate, then his brothers sucking bone marrow and burst into tears.

"What you mean by nyam, Daddy?" Samuel said.

"In Jamaica we don't say eat. We say nyam. Me now, I'm a nyamer." Lucas then went and helped himself to a full second helping of the soup, while the boys looked on, astonished at his appetite.

"When is Mummy coming back?" Neville asked.

"She never coming back," Samuel said.

"How d'you know that?"

"She told me. She told me that when she finds somewhere to live, we can come and live with her."

"She didn't."

"Yes, she did."

Lucas looked up from his bowl. "She tell you dat, Sam?"

"Yes."

"Well, let me tell you this. Yuh mother not taking unnu anywhere. She can come back here and live, wash you clothes, cook yuh dinner, clean de house, but she not taking unnu. Damn wo'thless woman. Imagine just abandoning her pickneys. She w'orthless."

"Don't say that about my mother; it's your fault that she left." Samuel stood up, fists clenched, an angry scowl on his face.

Lucas pushed aside his bowl, burped, and said, "Bwoy, who yuh t'ink you speaking to? Better watch yuh mouth or I gwine pin you against the wall and punch out you raasclaat ribs. You hear me?"

Samuel buckled under his father's ferocious gaze and words, and resumed his position on the floor with his brothers. But in that moment, Lucas recognised that one day he and Samuel would fight. That day was some years away, but meanwhile he would not tolerate any rudeness. He had to show them he was the boss.

"Unnu not going nowhere. As long as my name is Lucas Bostock you will get food, clothes and a roof over your heads. When unnu finish school and start work, unnu can go and live wherever unnu want."

The rest of the evening centred on food. Lucas instructed Samuel and Neville to grate sweet potatoes, which he mixed with cornmeal, sugar, milk, raisins, cinnamon and vanilla and placed in the oven. While this pudding was baking, Lucas made a marinade for a huge slice of pork and placed kidney beans to soak for Sunday dinner. When the sweet potato pudding had baked and cooled down, he shared out large slices and Samuel made his brothers hot chocolate. The evening ended with the moment of tension seemingly forgotten, and the boys, stomachs bulging, staggering off to bed. Lucas dozed in his armchair, the television still on.

When he retired to his bedroom, he read the *Daily Telegraph's* economics pages, noted that a tenant in the second house was three weeks behind with his rent, and resolved to install central heating in the house. Between putting aside the newspaper and falling asleep, it occurred to him that he had never spent such a long time with his children. Although he found it oddly satisfying, he worried about the future; he needed a long-term solution. He had to either persuade Rhoda to return or find another woman. Might be easier to persuade Rhoda to return than find another woman. What woman would want to take on a man and his three sons? He thought of his present lover, Celia, whom the present crisis had prevented him from seeing. She was a St Lucian, fleshy and dark with a throaty laugh that exploded in the throes of pleasure. But in the quiet of night, he thought of her as not as a potential mother for his sons, but as a sanctuary from this bewildering turn of events. It had hurled him back to his bachelor days in Kingston when he had to cook for himself. What next? Would he have to wash the boys' clothes? Darn their torn socks? He cursed Rhoda and tried to summon an image of Celia, but, disturbingly, got instead one of Mrs Morgan. This took great effort to erase. Then sleep claimed him.

During the following week, Lucas telephoned Rhoda's workplace, Homerton Hospital. A female voice told him that she no longer worked there. So, on the second Sunday after her departure, Lucas, wearing his best suit, charged Samuel with looking after Neville and Vincent, and drove over to Stockwell to visit Rhoda's cousin, Bertie Johnson.

Slim and well-groomed, with a dazzling smile, Bertie lived with his English wife and their two teenage daughters. The children and their mother were, he explained, visiting their grandmother in Kent. Bertie was a few years older than Lucas but looked younger. He worked in a South London postal sorting office, and though his handshake was firm, his hands were soft, his fingernails clean and polished.

Lucas took in the living room, furnished with a beige-coloured three-piece suite, a glass cabinet full of books and a lacquered coffee table. Photographs of Bertie's family sat on the modern mantelpiece above a gas fire. A wedding photograph showed Bertie wearing top hat and tails and his wife, Maggie, in a flowing white gown. In others, their children, wearing school uniforms, beamed through missing teeth. There was a calm and orderliness to the room that made Lucas feel like an intruder.

"I haven't seen hide nor hair of Rhoda," Bertie said.

"But she don't know nobody else in London."

"She must have friends from work. You tried there?"

Lucas shook his head; it had never occurred to him that Rhoda might have made friends in her workplace; she never spoke about work. In recent years, all their limited conversation had focused on the children. When did they start living like strangers? Had he ever known her?

"Way I see it, Lucas, Rhoda doesn't want to be found. Way I see it, she knew I'd be the first person you'd come to, so she kept away from me. Mahn, what you do the woman that she just ran away like that?"

"Do? Me bring her to England. With my own money, me buy house. She and the children don't want for nothing, for nothing. That's what I bloodclaat do." Lucas clenched one of his massive fists.

"All right, all right, calm down, Lucas. You always did have a short fuse. Look, if she contacts me, I'll talk to her, for the sake of the children, try and make her see sense. For the children's sake."

"That's why me here – for the children's sake."

Bertie, spread his arms and turned his pink palms upwards.

"Look, Lucas, it ain't my business to tell a man how to live his life, especially a man who owns two houses and drives a car, but I been here since the war, and let me tell you this country ain't no different from Jamaica." Bertie got up, closed the living room door, and resumed speaking in a lower voice. "I used to think, after the war, that it was different. Mahn, after the war, drink, women…" He chuckled. "But you know, Lucas, after a time I say to myself that this city, all these miles and miles of concrete and brick and glass and metal and rubber ain't no different from where I come from because, just like over there, a man ain't man until he can find a woman to love and have children who will weep for him when he dies. But for too many of us coming from the West Indies… this confuses us."

Lucas was not sure that he agreed with what Bertie said, but he lacked the words to differ, so he settled for a phlegmatic "Maybe so." There followed a long minute of strained silence, which Bertie broke by remarking on the weather, and then a lengthy conversation about the difficulties of maintaining Victorian houses. Lucas was on firmer ground. An hour later, he left Bertie Johnson's home feeling warmer towards Rhoda's cousin than he had done in previous years.

This feeling did not last long. Damn fool, Lucas thought, reflecting on Bertie's remarks about what makes a man. He was driving across Vauxhall Bridge; a light fog hovered over the sluggish waters of the Thames, obscuring the view of Big Ben and the Houses of Parliament. Lucas understood perfectly well what Bertie had been trying to say, but he did not regard his occasional sexual affairs as any justification for Rhoda's disappearance. In keeping female friends, he was simply behaving like a man; in abandoning her children, Rhoda had done something unwomanly, something unnatural – a fact that no amount of highfalutin talk could deny. He would make sure he spent some time with Celia, whom he had not seen for nearly a month.

That same Sunday evening, Lucas, using his leather belt, inflicted a severe beating on his sons. He had, on arriving home, found them standing outside the house with other boys, looking like street urchins in the foggy dusk. By Christmas, he had administered another four beatings, the last, a week before Christmas, was accompanied by loud threats to place them in a children's home. This ended only because Mr. George knocked on the door. He had come to inform Lucas that the cooker in the tenants' kitchen was not working. He smiled when he realised that he had interrupted a flogging. As Lucas went upstairs to inspect the cooker, Mr George said: "Spare the rod, spoil the child, my granny always say."

They reminisced about the severe beatings they had received in their childhoods. But, though Lucas had no doubt that children, when they misbehaved, ought to be physically punished, he also recognised that, as he stood in the kitchen with Mr George, a month after Rhoda's departure, it had been tough for all of them.

With the advent of Christmas, he spared no expense on food, filling the fridge with a turkey, slabs of beef, pork and ham and fizzy drinks. There were no decorations in the house and no individual presents, but he bought two thousand-piece jigsaw puzzles – one of Buckingham Palace, the other of Piccadilly Circus – from Woolworths on Stoke Newington High Road, to keep his sons occupied. He noted their enthusiasm for the puzzles and resolved to buy others in the future.

On a misty Christmas morning he took the boys for a drive. The roads were empty, the pavements deserted, cold stillness hung in the air. He showed them Ladbroke Grove, where he first lived in London, then, as they drove back along Marylebone Road, he pointed to an office block he had worked on.

"You build that, Daddy," Vincent said, his voice filled with awe. He was seated in the back with Neville.

"Don't be stupid, Vince," Samuel said. "Daddy said he worked on it."

"That's right, son, me work on that office block. Me an' a whole heap a other men. Two years ago that was just an empty space. Now that building. Like de whole city, really. Long, long time ago, it was probably just trees. Swamp. Wild animals."

"Wild animals in London!" Neville exclaimed. "You mean lions and tigers and elephants?"

"Maybe. But one day a very rich man have a vision, you see. A mighty vision. He say he going to build a city. Cut down the trees. Put up mighty buildings."

"My history teacher, Mr. Jones, said the Romans built London," Samuel said. "He said the Romans taught English people how to build straight roads."

"Don't know 'bout that, son. Yuh teacher should know. So this man get together some surveyors and engineers and masons and carpenters and architects, and he say build me a city."

"What's an architect, Daddy?" Vincent said.

"Now that is a man, that is a man, yuh must respec'. Want to build a city? De first man he has to call on is the architec'. A man like me, me just work on the building. Me know how to use a hammer. Chisel. But the architec' now, the building coming from his head. Him sit down draw the whole t'ing first. Dat is the mahn, de maaahn."

"How come you're not an architect, Daddy?" Samuel said.

"Me? Most me can do is read a drawing plan. Yuh need eddication to be an harchitec'. Heducation."

"You mean education and architect," Samuel corrected him.

"No, me mean hexactly what me say. Cause you need heart and something in yuh head."

Samuel laughed.

Lucas shook his head, as if in awe, and silence filled the car as the boys looked out at the city racing past – Warren Street, Euston, Kings Cross, Old Street. Soon they were in the city proper, with its narrow streets and ancient buildings with Doric and Corinthian columns jostling with austere angular buildings. Lucas drove over Waterloo Bridge, then circled back, heading home. Every so often he slowed the car to look at a building and expressed admiration for its size. When they reached Shoreditch he said, "What you goin' to be when you grow up?"

"I'm going to be rich," Samuel said. "I wasn't born to be poor. I'm going to live in Hampstead Heath or Mayfair and drive a Rolls Royce."

"I'm going to join the army," Neville said.

"Not while I am alive," Lucas said. Neville fell silent. "And you, Vince?"

"I am going to be…" Young Vincent stuttered into silence, and Samuel and Neville erupted in laughter.

"Well, me hope you goin' to be something," Lucas finally said. "All of unnu, cause I ain't got time for people without ambition, for wo'thless people. Yuh mus' put something in yuh head."

"Heducation," Samuel said.

"Now yuh hunderstand me." Hearing the echo of his own voice, Lucas recalled his conversation with Bertie Johnson and recognised why he had not agreed with him. If his children did not make him feel proud of them, if they did not strive with all their hearts the way he had done to escape the island and claim a piece of this great city, they might as well piss on his grave.

When they arrived home, Lucas put the turkey in the oven and the boys attacked the ham, bread and fizzy drinks and played card games and worked on a giant jigsaw puzzle. Later that night, the doorbell rang and Neville, who went to answer, came back holding a small cardboard box, from which he pulled a black and white kitten and clasped it to his chest.

"Look, look, Daddy, somebody left a kitten on the doorstep."

"What? Who?" Lucas scowled.

"There was nobody at the door, just this kitten in a box."

"Me don't want no pets in this house. Put it back outside, right now."

"But it's freezing out. It'll die."

"Me say put it outside; mek it dead. Me no want it inna me yard."

Neville held the kitten closer, and stood unmoving, his eyes moistening. "Please, please," he pleaded, "let's keep it. I've even got name for it. We can call it Santa. I'll look after it. Please, Daddy." Vincent went over and stroked the shivering creature and added his voice to Neville's pleading.

At last Lucas gave in: "Alright, but unnu better make sure it don't shit up the house."

7. *Lucas and the Georges, winter to spring*

Throughout the winter, Lucas bullied, coaxed, bludgeoned, exhorted, lectured and cursed his sons into taking more responsibility for themselves. The acrid smell of burnt potatoes or rice greeted him less often when he came home from work; dishes were washed before bedtime; they cleaned and polished their shoes nightly; let him know when their school clothes were torn – Samuel had received a severe beating for wearing torn trousers to school, for bringing shame on him, Lucas said – and they made an effort to keep the home clean. Every two weeks he took their clothes to a launderette on the High Road for a service wash by an unsmiling Spanish lady.

But he did not always get his way. When he discovered that Neville shared his bed with the kitten and threatened to evict the creature, Neville put the animal under his jumper and ran into the back garden where, despite an icy fog, he remained until nightfall. With rough grace, Lucas conceded defeat on the condition that Neville kept the animal in its box at night.

Vincent's nightly raids on the food cupboard and fridge went unnoticed for several weeks and persisted beyond Lucas's threats, curses and a famously frenzied leather whipping, the futility of which became apparent to Lucas the night when he caught Vincent standing before the open fridge door chomping on a chicken leg, oblivious to his father's presence. Lucas could have sworn that the boy was still asleep. He did not disturb him. He returned to his own room where he rechecked the performance of his shares in *The Daily Telegraph*, mused on Rhoda's whereabouts, and – a new addition to his nightly reflections – imagined a not too distant future when he owned a building company called 'Bostock and Sons'.

Spring found the Bostock household still intact, and Lucas feeling confident that he had made progress in repairing a house that had been struck by a hurricane and shaken by an earthquake. On the Easter Bank holiday, he treated the boys to a long drive around the city and across the river Thames, ending with an afternoon at Battersea funfair. Watching his sons enjoy themselves on the big dipper gave him a novel pleasure. This strengthened his hope that the foundations and roof of the Bostock house would survive any future storms or seismic tremors.

It was around this time that Mr and Mrs Carter, tenants in

the large first-floor room, told Lucas that they had at last secured accommodation from the borough council. A quiet, reserved couple from Dominica, they had occupied the room for three years and never once complained or failed to pay their rent on Friday night. He accepted the news of the Carters' imminent departure with a tinge of regret, as if, coming so soon after Rhoda's flight, their going was somehow connected to that larger loss. But he found consolation in the fact that he could now fulfil his promise to Mr George. They had cemented their friendship over the winter, watching Saturday boxing matches on television, and on each occasion Mr George had correctly predicted the outcome based on the fighters' first round performances. Told that he could have the room, Mr George gushed with gratitude because, he confessed, his longing for his wife had often brought tears to his eyes.

Some days after Mr George moved into the room, and two weeks before Mrs Florence George was due in London, Lucas arrived home to find a large, green Jaguar saloon car parked in front of the house. Mr George was standing inside the gate looking admiringly at the vehicle. Annoyed that his parking space had been taken, Lucas parked several houses away and walked back to his house.

"Like it?" Mr. George said.

"A who car dat?"

"Mine." Mr George's chest puffed with pride.

"Dat's your car?" Lucas was so shocked he forgot that minutes before he had promised to give the car's owner a good piece of his mind for taking his parking space.

"Yes, mahn. Wait till Florence sees it. Her eyes going pop like ripe ackee."

"Didn't know you could drive."

"Now, that's something I want to talk to you about, Lucas. Driving lessons."

He agreed to give Mr George driving lessons, but advised that his Cortina would be better to learn in. Mr George thanked him, then walked to the Jaguar. Theatrically, he opened the car door, sat in the driving seat, and clasped the steering wheel, the size of which made him look like a child.

Lucas spent the first lesson telling Mr George about the controls: the ignition, brakes, the clutch, the gear. On his second lesson, Mr George moved the car a few yards, braked and began bouncing in his seat, shouting, "Me can drive, rawtid, me can drive." He was too excited to continue the lesson. The third lesson saw him drive round the block. Although Lucas had to park the car, Mr George was so excited at this achievement that once again the lesson had to end prematurely.

The fourth and final lesson ended abruptly when Mr George, told to turn left onto the High Road, not only turned right but drove on the wrong side of the road towards an oncoming double-decker bus. Lucas panicked, seized the steering wheel, shouting "Brake, brake!" The car ended up on the other side of the road, on the pavement, its fender a few inches from a greengrocer's window. Lucas could not find the courage for another lesson; he was too dependent on his car to take the risk. He advised Mr George, who was apologetic and understanding, to take lessons from a proper driving school.

Mr George did not pursue further lessons. Instead, he spent hours sitting in the car, occasionally revving the engine, but mostly simply holding the steering wheel. The woman, who arrived some days later, was tall and thin, wore floral nylon clothes and an ill-fitting wig with coarse hair which covered much of her forehead. She had several warts on a face that wore a permanent and severe expression of bewilderment. She spoke with a thick Jamaican accent, which even Lucas at times found difficult to understand. Something about her made him feel uncomfortable.

During her first month in the house, when Lucas returned from work, he often saw her sitting at the window looking out at the street, as if trying to decide whether to venture out. The tenant in the adjoining room, a Barbadian and a bachelor, confided to Lucas that he found her unsettling. On Sundays, husband and wife sat in the green Jaguar, Mr George at the steering wheel, his wife beside him, looking ahead like tourists driving across a landscape of breathtaking and sublime beauty.

Nearly two months passed without Lucas and Mr George spending time together as they had done over the winter. Lucas did not mind. Disaster had struck the second house. A drunk tenant had caused the bath to overflow, and the resultant flood had ruined the ground floor rooms. Lucas's insurance policy did not cover the cost of compensating the tenants affected – none of whom had personal insurance – nor repairing the damage. The tenant responsible had compounded his crime by absconding. Dealing with this crisis consumed much of Lucas's time and energy.

But in July, when there was a big fight on television, Lucas took some time out and Mr George joined him. At the end of a scrappy, mediocre bout – redeemed, in Mr George's opinion, only by a perfect example of how not to deliver an uppercut – he cleared his throat and said:

"Lucas, there's something I've been meaning to ask you."

"Yes."

"It's about Florence. She's getting bored and wants to start work."

"Well, plenty work in this city, mahn. Plenty."

"It's not that simple, Lucas. Florence has never worked a day in her life. What ah mean is that she's never worked for anybody. She's always worked where she lives."

"Making dresses, cakes, stuff like dat?"

Mr George cleared his throat again. "No, she's a fortune teller and a kind of healer. Herbs and thing. Very gifted. Back home, folks used to come from miles upon miles to see her. It's her calling. From she was a child, people saw she had the power."

The penny dropped. Lucas stroked his chin, shifted uncomfortably in his chair, and tried to find a reason for denying Florence George permission to practise obeah in his house. That the Georges wanted to conduct a business in a residential property was the only objection he could find, though he was aware of West Indian homes that doubled as bakeries, hairdressers, tailoring shops, nightclubs and churches. Did it matter that he, Lucas, had never made use of a miracle worker, believing that they were all fraudsters exploiting people's superstitions? No, he decided, but he would have to increase the Georges' rent.

Mr George pumped Lucas's hand in thanks and outlined his plan to install a telephone and place cards in newsagents on the High Road.

"You can be her first customer," Mr George said. "A free reading."

"Me? Nothing wrong with me."

"Nothing has to be wrong. Sometimes it's good to know what's waiting for you round the corner. Mind you, sometimes Florence can't tell; something about not being able to read everybody's energy. She's honest like that. Doesn't charge if she can't read the energy."

Lucas did not voice his scepticism.

When he next saw Mr George, Lucas was shown the card

his tenant had designed and printed. It read, 'Madam Florence, Spiritual Healer and Fortune Teller. Treatment for anxiety, love pains, loss, and incurable ailments. Available for consultation Monday to Saturday.'

Much to Lucas's surprise, Madam Florence, according to Mr George, was an instant though moderate success. Seldom a day passed when she did not dispense spiritual guidance or exercise her healing skills. She recommended herbs, brought with her from Jamaica, contacted departed souls, alleviated anxiety, predicted the future. Being out of the house most of the day, Lucas did not see her daytime customers, but he was aware that the tenants' front door bell now rang more often in the evening than in the past. The visitors, mostly West Indians, with a smattering of other nationalities, were ordinary looking folks, the sort that Lucas saw everyday going about their business, their expressions betraying nothing of the worries that so distracted them that they were willing to exchange their hard-earned cash for advice from a woman newly arrived from a tiny village in the depth of the Jamaican countryside.

One summer evening, as Lucas was standing by the gate, a man arrived whom he'd least expect to resort to Florence George's services. Lucas knew Lance Bedward by sight and reputation only. He was notorious, the sort of man respectable, law-abiding West Indians warned their children to avoid becoming. Over the years he had commandeered empty houses and transformed them into shebeens, brothels and gambling houses where violence and disorder flourished. A tall, powerfully built man with bowlegs and a horse-like face that belied his reputation with the ladies, Lance Bedward was wearing a blue crombie coat, matching trilby hat, shimmering gold-coloured two-tone trousers and an open-neck striped silk shirt.

"Madam Florence place this?" he asked. Some exceptionally tall men, aware that shorter people find their height intimidating, affect a disarming stoop and gentle mannerisms. Not Lance Bedward. This giant of a man revelled in his physical superiority and used his height to scare people into submission.

"No, this is my house," Lucas said.

"Sure Madam Florence don't live here?"

"That's a different question," Lucas said, his gaze fixed on Lance Bedward, who seemed shocked that a man over whom he towered had dared to obstruct him. Lucas opened the gate and said: "Ring the bell twice."

Lucas remained at the gate, allowing himself the rare pleasure of enjoying a summer evening without carrying out one of the numerous minor repairs awaiting him. He was still there in the fading light when, twenty minutes later, Lance Bedward came back out. The figure who emerged from the house and walked down the pathway seemed somehow shorter, his head hung low and shaking from side to side. Lucas opened the gate for him and Bedward left without acknowledging his presence. Shoulders down, he walked across the street, fumbling in his coat pocket for his car keys. He unlocked the car, got in, started the engine, then switched it off. He glanced towards the house, then bent over the steering wheel, his head in his palms, his broad shoulders heaving. Wide-eyed with disbelief, Lucas watched the car shake from the convulsive sobbing of its giant occupant. Tears streaming down his face, Bedward hesitantly manoeuvred the car out into the road, where it jerked and stuttered, then crawled away slowly in the dusk.

Presently, Mr. George joined Lucas at the gate.

"Florence working late," Lucas said.

"No choice. Fella rang and said he had to see her today. Wouldn't take no for an answer."

"Guess a bad man like Lance Edwards used to getting his way."

"Well, he was in a hurry to get bad news," Mr George said. He explained that Edwards had not only insisted on calling at an awkward hour, he had also pressed Florence to foretell his future, though she warned him that his energy was wrong for her type of reading. She had reluctantly taken his hand and after ten minutes of silent concentration, which climaxed with her sweating and shaking, asked him to leave because she was getting nowhere with his energy. But Lance believed she had seen something and demanded to know. Florence had said: "You'll be dead by the end of year." She had not known of Lance Edwards' reputation.

"You believe that?" Lucas said.

"Florence doesn't always get it right. She'll tell you that herself. But she gets it right a lot of the times."

Night had fallen and the two men went inside. Lucas found his sons watching television and gave them one of his milder lectures on ambition and their need to be prepared for manhood, which wasn't as far away as it seemed. This last point was particularly directed at Samuel.

Two months later, Lucas ran into a Jamaican acquaintance,

Canute Harris. They talked briefly and as they were about to part, Canute said: "Seems like hell's got a new recruit."

Lucas looked at him blankly.

"You haven't heard? Lance Edwards died last week. Drop dead. Cancer. Heart attack. Some people say poison. Nobody's sure."

Lucas agreed that Lance would not be missed. He hoped that the local paper, *The Hackney Gazette*, would give more details on the death, but the paper did not mention it. For several days, recalling Lance Edward's giant frame sobbing one summer evening, Lucas wandered among the ruins of his scepticism about Florence George's gift. Curiosity sprouted in the rubble and he finally accepted the invitation to a free reading.

It took place on a Sunday afternoon, almost a year after Rhoda's departure. Lucas entered the Georges's room expecting to see the fortune-teller wearing a turban and long gown and gazing into a crystal ball. Instead, he got plain Florence George, straight and thin, dressed in a red and blue nylon dress. She invited him to sit at a small round table beside the window. Mr George also sat at the table. Then she asked Lucas to place his hands on her outstretched palms. He complied and noted that her arms were as thin as sticks, her hands no larger than a young child's and her palms unusually warm. Florence closed her eyes and asked Lucas to do the same.

A minute of silence passed. Then Florence said, "I see leaves, plenty leaves, and flowers and saplings, and it's warm there and you're walking among the plants." Suddenly, she pulled her hand away, bringing the reading to an end. She apologised and explained that his energy was too resistant to a more detailed reading.

"Well, yuh didn't tell me anything me didn't already know. That I'll die happily in Jamaica."

"I didn't say anyt'ing 'bout Jamaica, Mr Bostock," Florence said. "And I didn't say, anything 'bout happiness. I only told you what I saw."

Lucas left the Georges's room with his scepticism fully restored. He and Mr George had often spoken of the day when they could retire to Jamaica, to its warmth and sunshine and greenness, its views of hills and sea. Now back in his own part of the house, Lucas scoffed at the gullibility of Florence George's customers and how coincidence – which was how he now regarded Lance Edward's death – can lead people into believing in nonsense.

8. *Rhoda and Maureen, a year later*

"I don't know what comes over these men, me dear. You and them sweet, then they come here and buy some broken down old house and before you know it they behaving like they is your lord and master. Fetch that, go there, don't go there, don't dress like that. Sister, when I finish with him he looked just like that blasted old house: a wreck. But my new man, he treats me nice, just right."

Rhoda was sitting in a launderette on Tulse Hill waiting for her wash to dry and listening to two women talk. It was a Saturday morning in February and the sky was a clear pale blue, the air outside sharp. The women, one a Jamaican, the other who sounded West African, had been keeping up a conversation around her for the past twenty minutes. They had tried to draw her in, as if her face betrayed membership of their club, but she had said nothing. She had smiled, raised her eyebrows and nodded in sympathy and understanding. The other customers, two English women and an elderly white man, appeared indifferent to this public lamentation.

"With mine it was gin. Everyday he drink gin. Morning he drink gin. Evening he drink gin. Middle of the night he wake up for gin. But it's different when you have children," the West African said. She was taller than her companion, had thick calves and her cheeks bore two scars which were animated by her mobile face and seemed like a second pair of eyes, narrow and opaque.

"I couldn't just walk out and leave my children. My sister, how I suffer for those children. Everyday I pray the man drown in gin. Drown, I tell you, yes. But God is truly Great. The council give me a flat for me and my children."

"So what happened to him?"

"Still there. Big house. I send the children to him for school shoes; he tell them he don't have money. No money. But he has money for gin. My sister, how I dey suffer-ooo. My mother die, my mother who dey born me, she die, I go to him for money to go for funeral..."

The spin-dryer rumbled to a stop and Rhoda, eager to get away, decided not to fold the clothes and bundled them into her bag. The West African's ululation rang in her ears as she stepped out into the biting cold. She crossed the road, walked along Water Lane, and turned into Josephine Avenue. Two young West Indian men dressed in baggy suits and talking excitedly walked past her. A Nigerian, wearing a voluminous but thin red gown and sandals in defiance of the cold, washed his Ford Zephyr.

She crossed to the other side of Josephine Avenue and had to stop because her arms and legs had lost all strength and she became aware of her shallow breathing. She placed the too-heavy bag on a low wall, took deep breaths, then resumed her journey, her energy threatening to vanish with each step.

The large middle-floor room she shared with Maureen was, as she expected, empty. Her daughter was at piano lessons. Dust motes danced in the mid-morning light streaming through the net curtains over the two windows. The room still smelled of the bleach she had used to clean the linoleum floor before heading off to the laundry. A double bed with a high mahogany veneer headboard, covered in a pink polyester bedspread, dominated the room. In the bay was a dining table, covered in red plastic. Three dining chairs were positioned around the room, along with two brown, mock-leather easy chairs with curved armrests. There was a paraffin heater, which Rhoda used sparingly and, on either side of the heater, two white wardrobes in alcoves. On the chimney breast above the gas fire hung a Constable print of a pastoral English scene, a horse cart fording a stream. Rhoda had inherited it with the room. The print of Jesus above the bed – palms pressed together in prayer, his heart exposed – she had bought in Woolworths.

She emptied the laundry on the bed and separated each item. She lit the paraffin heater. She walked over to the bay window, leaned against the plain green curtains, folded her arms tightly as if she were standing outside naked in the cold. She looked up at the pale blue cloudless sky, then at the street that she had just walked along, and held herself even tighter. She felt unbearably cold, a feeling she knew had a source other than the weather.

Rhoda was expecting a visit from her cousin, Bertie Johnson. She had made contact with him eight months after she left Lucas, when she and Maureen had lived in North Paddington and Harlsden. Fear, confusion and ugly memories had fuelled those nomadic months, and only the daily ritual of caring for Maureen had saved her from being swallowed by the vision of the house in Jamaica, the house shaded by the flamboyant tree, the house where she had known laughter and joy, the house where, as a girl, she had known an innocence she now yearned for.

Bertie had persuaded her to move to South London and found

her this room on Josephine Avenue. He had advised her to hire a lawyer to file for a divorce, seek custody of her sons, and claim a share of Lucas Bostock's properties. She had rejected Bertie's advice. She did not want to involve the courts. All she wanted was to be able to see her sons. Reluctantly, Bertie had agreed to act as a go-between, to arrange a meeting between her and Lucas.

Now, she saw Bertie's grey Rover arrive, watched him walk towards the house, and noted his grave expression. She met him at the front door, searching his face for any clue as to the outcome. When they were back upstairs, she asked, "You saw the boys? You saw Lucas?"

"No. I didn't see the boys. Think I heard the younger two. Bostock said something about the oldest boy being at a football practice."

"What did he say about me seeing them?"

"He said to tell you, you must come back to wash their clothes and cook their dinner."

"What did you say?"

"What could I say? I don't know what swamp that man crawl from. I don't think he has an ounce of feeling in his heart."

"But what did he say about me seeing them?"

"Said the two of you must meet and talk first."

"When? Did he say when?"

"Tomorrow."

Rhoda looked out of the window. She worked at St Thomas's Hospital and was due there on Sunday evening. On Sunday morning she attended the service at St Matthew's in Brixton. Should she miss the church service? The Lord would understand.

"You want me to be there?"

"No," she said firmly. A year ago she could not have faced Lucas alone and though she still feared him, her need to see her sons was greater than her fear.

"Rhoda, why are you putting yourself through this? This is England, a country of law. Let me find you a lawyer. It's the best way."

"No. Bertie. This is the best way. I don't want a fight with Lucas. I don't want his property. I just want to see my sons."

"But you have a right to a share of his property. Any court in the land will recognise that."

Rhoda stood up, folded her arms, looked away from Bertie and through the net curtains. The sky was clouding over, a feverish grey swirling over the pale blue. Men and property, she thought, they will kill and die for it. She had survived the months of confusion and found the courage to seek Bertie's help, but she did not have the stomach for a fight with Lucas. Besides, there was something else at stake, something that was as yet too vague for her to name, but she believed with an iron conviction that in time her self-restraint and patience would be rewarded, though she could not say what form or shape that reward would take.

"You don't know Lucas, Bertie. You don't know that man the way I know him."

"Sounds to me like you're afraid of the man. I have some pals from the army…"

"No," she interrupted, "he's my children's father. Anyway, maybe sometimes it takes more courage not to fight than to fight."

Bertie sighed exasperatedly. He agreed to call Lucas and give him a time, along with her address. Rhoda expressed her gratitude for Bertie's time and effort, which were all the more generous because he was experiencing his own troubles. His eldest daughter had run away from home to join a hippie commune in Camden Town.

"Any news of Pamela?" Rhoda said, eager to share his burdens, as he was doing for her.

"No. And I'm not looking to hear from her." She heard the hurt and anxiety in his voice she had sensed when he first told her about how his daughter, six months before her 'A' level exams, had failed to come home from a New Years' party. Rhoda heard Bertie retreating behind a fake wall of indifference to the child's fate, and as much as she tried, she had failed to scale that wall.

"Bertie, if there's anything I can do for you, anything, just say so."

"I'm supposed to be helping you, remember?" Bertie laughed, and for a fleeting moment Rhoda saw the confident, self-assured cousin she had met when she arrived in London many years before.

The next day Rhoda received Lucas in her Brixton room. Maureen, who had inherited her father's stockiness, was seated at the dining table doodling on pieces of paper. Without looking up, she gave a choked, barely audible greeting.

"Say hello to your father," Rhoda said.

"I said hello already."

"You don't see me for over a year and you don't have a smile for me?" Lucas said.

Maureen looked up now and burst into tears. Lucas attempted to hold her but she slipped out of his grasp and threw herself against her mother. Hands behind his back, Lucas walked to the bay window, parted the net curtain and said, "Me didn't know Brixton have big houses like this."

Rhoda did not respond. Instead, she told Maureen to dry her tears and go and play with Rita, a girl of her age who lived on the floor above. It would be best for her to be alone with Lucas and Rhoda had solicited the help of Rita's mother.

Rhoda offered Lucas some tea and he accepted. She came back with two steaming cups and found him in the middle of the room standing akimbo and pressing his weight on the floor.

"These houses built solid."

They sat at the table. Rhoda sipped her tea and Lucas clasped the cup but did not drink. A long moment of silence ended when he said, "So this is where you is. Remind me of our last room in Ladbroke Grove."

All these years in England and I've gone back to the beginning, Rhoda thought. For a moment she lost the certainty that she had shown Bertie about not finding a lawyer. She glanced at Lucas and noted his dark, ashen skin, his dirty nails, his powerful shoulders and the mound of his stomach. It seemed incredible that years ago, in a Kingston tenement yard, she had allowed this man to persuade her to share his dreams of migration and wealth. She had believed in him totally. But four children and several betrayals later, she wondered if the woman who accepted Lucas Bostock's marriage proposal and the woman sitting in the room were the same person. This thought disturbed her.

"How are the boys? How is Samuel? And Neville, and Vincent?"

"Dem fine," Lucas said, looking at her now. "But they need somebody to cook for them and wash their clothes."

It took all Rhoda's strength to hold in the scream. "When can I see them? I was hoping you'd bring them with you."

"Rhoda, stop this nonsense. The boys waiting for you at home, now."

"Home, Lucas. You call that a home?" She wanted to tell him that he did not know what a home was, that he was incapable of creating a home but, equally, she did not want to provoke him.

"When I met you, you were sharing two rooms with your aunt. Two rooms. That was your home?" Lucas's voice was even, with just a hint of disbelief that she had walked away from an entire house.

"I am not coming back, Lucas. Never. You need to accept that, and when you accept that, we can talk about the future. I'm never coming back."

Lucas repeated his case; their sons needed their mother. But Rhoda was unmoving. Eventually, he stood up and walked to the door and turned to face Rhoda. "All right, I can see you ain't coming back. Hear it your voice too. You can see the boys. I'll bring them this time next week. But hear this, they not spending a single night with you, not a single night, not while they're in my charge and they going to stay in my charge till they reach working age. You understand that?"

"Yes, yes," she choked.

"And that cousin of yours. He come telling me 'bout lawyer this and lawyer that. And army friends. You better warn him not to fuck with Lucas Bostock."

"I didn't ask Bertie to say anything about lawyers."

"Well, just in case you thinking of going to court, you better know this, if you don't already know, though I'm sure you do. What Lucas Bostock own, im own. You have to kill him to get it." Lucas jabbed his chest with his right index finger. "You know that. You know well, Rhoda. The same for my bwoys. Court or no court."

"And what about Maureen?" Rhoda said.

"Me no know what to do with a girl pickney. Me will take her for a drive when me bring the boys."

Tears streamed from Rhoda's eyes as the door closed. From the window she watched Lucas march across the road to his car. She folded her arms but that act could not stop the tremor that rocked her body. She had lost all conviction, all faith in her earlier stance and a wave of pity swept through her, not for herself or Maureen, but for the sons she had abandoned to Lucas Bostock because she lacked the strength and the courage to fight for them.

She walked away from the window and threw herself on the bed. The confusion was starting again, the memories resurfacing. Why oh, why, she wondered, on that full moon night in Kingston when Lucas rustled the guinip tree, their secret signal, had she stolen outside. If she had remained inside, she would not have seen his bloodied, swollen face, and heard him say: "Me just kill a man for you."

9. *Family visits, early 1970s*

Once a month, usually on a Sunday afternoon, Lucas drove his sons over to Josephine Avenue to see their mother. He did not enter the house. At first, Maureen would join Lucas in the car after half-an-hour or so. He would drive his daughter round London and try to interest her in buildings, but the one topic about which Lucas could speak with passion and humility was met with the bored and cold silence of a child enduring an ordeal that she knew would not, mercifully, last for ever. Soon, Lucas settled for receiving her in the car where he listened to her monosyllabic answers to his questions, gave her pocket money, sent her back inside, and waited alone until the boys' allotted hours with their mother ended.

In the early days of this arrangement, Lucas, behind his bluff facade, constantly worried that Samuel would decamp to Brixton, weakening his hold on the two younger boys. But Samuel showed no willingness to join his mother. In fact, it was Samuel who reported to Lucas that Bertie Johnson's daughter, Pamela, had become a heroin addict and lived in a Ladbroke Grove squat. Although Lucas had crossed swords with Bertie, he was grateful to him for effecting a sort of treaty with Rhoda. He took no pleasure in learning that Bertie had lost his daughter to the dark side of what his daily newspaper described as the swinging sixties.

Indeed, a week later, Lucas, reproaching Samuel for failing to clean the bathroom, hurled a volley of swearwords at his son and invoked Pamela's name as a warning against the fate awaiting the idle and purposeless.

"They say that people who swear a lot have a limited vocabulary," Samuel said.

"Limited what?" Lucas said.

"Words, vocabulary."

Samuel was almost six feet tall. He had not lost his direct gaze. He was nearing his final year of compulsory education and, despite the undoubted truth of his riposte, had shown little interest in school. Lucas thought about taking him out with a blow to his solar plexus but restrained himself. He settled instead for another volley of curses and Samuel backed down and completed his task.

Unknown to Samuel, he had wounded Lucas. Alone in his bed that night, surrounded by his newspaper, bank statements, and rent account books, Lucas allowed himself to feel the pain from the deep and raw gash that the truth can inflict. It had not occurred to him that in trying to get his sons to be better than himself, he also ran the risk of inviting their contempt. Yet he could see no other way to be a father. He remembered the day he was handed a brown parcel and directed to walk the twenty miles to the house where a distant relative, a stranger, had agreed to take him in. He was eight years old, had never known his father, and his mother had just died. He had walked those twenty miles in the blazing heat and the day ended in sacking arranged as a bed under the house's veranda, his sleeping place for many weeks. That painful memory soothed the wound caused by his own ambitions for his sons. Let them walk in my shoes, he thought, drifting into sleep, resigned to future confrontations, determined more than ever to be Lucas Bostock.

There followed a chain of events which left Lucas with little time to indulge in reflections on his flaws. The house, as always, required repairs, and the tenants demanded attention. Encouraged by Mr George, Lucas had abandoned his no-Jamaicans rule and had rented the largest top floor room to a young Jamaican woman, Esther Cummings. Within three months, Lucas was cursing Mr George's compatriot to him, because the new tenant had missed a week's rent.

"Maybe she thinks her beauty is her rent," Mr George said.

"Not inna my house."

"Problem is, when a woman's blessed with looks like that, she expects the world to come to her."

"Looks!" Lucas scoffed. "Is rent me dealing with. She mus' pay her rent, and she mus' bring it to me on Friday night, or she mus' guweh, tek her good looks to somebody else's house."

Esther had grown up in nearby Upper Clapton – audible in her cockney accent – and worked as a shop assistant in a West End department store. She was slim, the colour of sandalwood, and sported a modest-sized and immaculately maintained Afro hairstyle which framed an attractive oval face with large brown eyes and full lips that were never without a shade of red lipstick. The more ostentatious shades were reserved for Saturday nights when she abandoned her work uniform of smart blue or black skirt-suits, for fashionable mini-skirts and platform shoes. Her smile, marred only by a slight yellowing of her left incisor, was radiant and she had the confidence of a young woman who knew her own worth. Many young male admirers called at the house, doomed hope in their eyes, desperation in their car horns. None had so far got beyond the front door.

The next Friday she brought two weeks' rent to Lucas and apologised for failing to pay the previous week. The smell of her perfume reminded Lucas of the occasion when, as a young man, he had carried out repairs on the house of an elderly Kingstonian lady who kept a garden overflowing with flowers that produced a heady and sleep-inducing scent in the midday heat. Standing before Esther's young beauty, enveloped in her scent, Lucas became acutely aware of his ageing: the slackening muscles that had given him a double chin and a round stomach, the greying hair, the weariness at the day's end. He counted the money quickly, thanked her and resisted the temptation to reprove her. He was keen to get away from this terrible reminder of days he would never see again, but she detained him.

"Mr Bostock, I was wondering if I could change the bed in my room; you know, put in my own bed?"

"But the room come with a bed. Is a furnished room."

"Yes, but it's such an old-fashioned bed. All that dark wood and every time you turn on it the springs creak so loud the noise wakes me up. I'm not asking *you* for a new bed, Mr Bostock."

No other tenant had ever made such a request, so it took Lucas a while to work through the implications. He would have to break down the bed and put it in the basement room he used as his workshop and for storage, but he agreed and some weeks later, with Samuel's reluctant help, he moved the mattress, metal slats, and headboard of the bed into the storage room. This concession was swiftly followed by others, as Esther replaced the chairs, a dining table, and a dresser with her own, handpicked, brand new furniture.

He saw the newly refurnished room when Esther sought his help to hang new curtains. The new bed was monstrously huge, with an oyster-shaped plastic headboard that almost touched the ceiling, and the dresser, standing between the two windows, had a large mirror surrounded by twenty light bulbs. The new dining table was circular with two black, high-back chairs. A vase containing real roses sat in the middle of the table. Lucas did not consider himself an interior designer. He had chosen the original furniture for the room on the simple criteria of affordability and durability. The abundant Edwardian items found in second-hand furniture stores along the High Road in the 1950s had sufficed. But even to his eyes, there was an ugly clash between the grandeur of the furniture and the size of the room. A room occupied over the years by a succession of couples now seemed uncomfortably small. He assisted her in changing the curtains, which, he conceded, looked old and tattered compared to her pink velcrose.

Soon after Esther had hung her new curtains, Jasper Stewart became the first male caller to be allowed beyond the front door of 72 Carlisle Road and into her room. He did not own a car. He was shy, clean-shaven, handsome, and wore spectacles with thick black frames, which gave him a scholarly appearance. Indeed, he was rumoured to be a post-graduate student at one of the London University colleges, though his visits, some lasting entire weekends, became so frequent that the rumours seemed baseless. Nonetheless, it was obvious that Jasper Stewart was no working man. His subtly scented aftershave, brown checked jacket, neatly pressed navy-blue trousers, courteous manners, polished brown or black brogues and pronunciation – which seemed to give the name Esther a second 's' and several more 'rs' (Mr George confessed that he had always thought her name was Esta) placed him several classes above anyone who had ever stepped across the house's threshold in Lucas's lifetime.

Nine months after Jasper's appearance, Mr George, whose room was below Esther's, came to Lucas with a complaint.

"It ain't me," he insisted. "It's Florence."

"Can't be the floorboards. Me put dem down myself. Mus' be de joists," Lucas said. "Is a old house. Always make nuff noise."

"Poor Florence. She said she spent the whole night looking at the ceiling, said it looked like a sail in the wind one minute, then like a bowl the next and the ceiling lampshade was bouncing up and down like a yo-yo."

"But you didn't see any of this?"

"No, Sir. Fast asleep. But I am a man who slept through three hurricanes."

Lucas promised to speak to Esther on Florence's behalf. But when he next saw Esther, he could not bring himself to broach the subject. Later, he remarked that the house was not as solid as it seemed and hoped that she understood his meaning.

"Seems solid enough to me," Esther said. She was wearing an orange mini-skirt, a striped tank-top that exposed much of her shoulders, platform heels and smelled as sweet as a stolen mango.

"Bye, Mr Bostock," she said, beaming a smile that was genuinely innocent and puzzled; then she skipped away up the stairs, and Lucas, despite himself, inhaled her perfume's lingering trace and experienced a brief and disturbing moment of happiness, as if a share of Esther's joy released him from all his burdens.

It was Mr George who first told Lucas about the engagement and impending wedding. Esther Cummings and Jasper Stewart were due to marry late in summer at St Mary's Church in Stoke Newington. The two men had just finished watching an Edward G. Robinson film on television, having discovered that they shared another passion – 1940s and '50s gangster movies.

"Goes to show you can't judge a person by his class," Mr George said.

"Dat bwoy has class all right," Lucas agreed. "And taste, too."

"Looks like I am going to have to pay a pound to Florence. I bet her Jasper wouldn't marry Esther."

"Why?"

"Class, mahn, class. Is something England teach me. That young man come out of a Jamaica I don't know, will never know, except 'im pass me pon de road. It's as obvious as daylight. But Esther? Don't get me wrong, she's a damn fine-looking girl. Even Florence agrees with that and she's always telling me when she catches me looking at another woman that I don't know a damn thing 'bout beauty. Anyway, Florence agrees that Esther is a fine looking young lady. But the way I saw it, he ain't the right class for her and she for him. Guess I was wrong."

Over the next few months Esther Cummings was a picture of happiness. She was seldom seen without shopping bags from West End stores and would have replaced the wardrobe in her room if Lucas could have found space to store it. Two weeks before the wedding, Esther missed her rent payment again. Imagining that she was distracted by her wedding preparations, Lucas was patient. In the middle of the following week, Mr George brought Lucas the awful news. Jasper Stewart had disappeared, and Esther had not left her room in days. Florence had spoken to her through the door, which Esther refused to open, and heard the young woman crying.

Lucas trudged to the top of house, banged the door and shouted, "Miss Cummings, your rent is overdue." He heard a scratching sound and when he looked down, he saw a white envelope being pushed from the other side. He opened it and found two weeks' rent. On the way back down he passed Mr George and Florence. Florence's eyes were red and she was dabbing her cheeks with a handkerchief.

On the day the wedding was supposed to take place, the house had a stagnant and damp air of disappointment, as if it were weeping. The boys remained in their rooms. Lucas had long been meaning to paint the basement and ground-floor rear windows. But the tin of white gloss paint spilt while he was stirring it. Even this hard, unsentimental man conceded that it was a day for stillness and reflection. He retired to his bedroom. Between reading the newspaper and doing his accounts, he listened for the sound of movements in the house, the flow of taps and cisterns, water rushing down the pipes, the creak of floorboards. There was none. He sniffed the air for traces of cooking. There was none. Night stole over the house. Lucas slept, woke up, noted that it was nearing the hour of the Saturday night movie on BBC Two. But he could not find the will to rise in the mournful silence of Esther Cummings' betrayed dream.

10. *Vincent and the arrival of Horace Fraser*

That afternoon Vincent rummaged through the sideboard where he knew his father kept the spare keys for all the rooms in the house. He found the key he was searching for, slipped it into his pocket, and tip-toed upstairs.

It would be a disaster if Mrs George heard him. She would want to know what he was doing creeping about the house in the middle of the day when he ought to be in school. She had once chided him when he stood at the gate with his friend, Michael Farrell, chewing the fat. Michael had teased him about living in the same house as a witch. Vincent had risen to Mrs George's defence, extolling her virtues, such as the quality of her sweet potato pudding – which had exposed his father's efforts as a poor substitute – and her fortune-telling and healing gifts which attracted customers from all over London. If Mrs George was a witch, then she was a good witch. But his defence of Mrs George had been tempered by the discomfort she sometimes aroused in him when she looked at him with those large saucer-shaped eyes which seemed to express a pity reserved for him, as if she possessed some terrible knowledge about him.

But he doubted that Mrs George would interrupt his mission.

She was in her room with a visitor, a large, dark, fleshy-faced woman with an Indian nose, whom Vincent had watched waddle up to the house and ring the bell. If for any reason she saw him, he was armed with an excuse: a sore throat had prevented him from going to school. He had left something in Esther's room while helping his father prepare the room for a new tenant.

His stomach tightened as he neared Mrs George's door. He smelled a faintly sweet odour and turned and climbed the rest of the stairs. He inserted the door key, entered the room and closed the door behind him as silently as a burglar. The room's original furniture had been restored. Esther had taken with her the grand bed with its oyster-shaped headboard and fancy dresser. His father had told him that she'd had to sell everything.

He leaned against the door and slid to the floor. Clasping his knees, he closed his eyes and breathed in deeply, imagining that Esther was still there. He remembered the night, before Jasper started visiting, when his father sent him to ask Esther for the rent. Esther had invited him in and closed the door. It was lit by two lamps, one beside the bed, another on the dressing table, its surface a riot of cosmetics – tubes, jars, bottles and phials, and brushes of various sizes and shapes. The air was thick with a scent that made him feel giddy. Esther was wearing a plain golden silky robe and must have just applied lipstick because her lips seemed to glow. She turned her back on him while she searched for her purse. The folds of the robe flared out from her waist and flowed, shimmering and radiant, over her buttocks. He was transfixed, as if he was witnessing something forbidden and dangerous but wondrous, not of this world or any world he knew until that moment.

"Found it," Esther said.

She turned, causing the hem of the robe to swirl around her legs, and for a fleeting moment the cloth pressed against her thighs. As she came towards him, opening the purse and smiling, he felt as though he were falling from some great height, a feeling at once terrifying, exhilarating, and embarrassing because there was a sudden swelling in his groin.

"Better make sure you give every penny to your Daddy," Esther said. She threw her head back and laughed gaily, a musical sound that heightened Vincent's sense of having somehow crossed an invisible threshold and left everyday reality behind.

He reached for the money and as he took it, her robe slipped slightly and he glimpsed a smooth, golden-brown breast.

She adjusted the robe, tightened the belt, and gave another gay laugh, looking at him in a way that suggested he had seen something he ought not to have seen and they were now accomplices in some secret crime. He had backed out of the room and dashed down the stairs. From that night, Vincent tried to see her as often as possible, watched for her coming and going from the house, installed himself at the gate or in the hallway in anticipation of her passage, bursting with hope that she would bestow on him a smile, some hint of their shared secret. It aroused in his body a painful longing that found relief but never satisfaction in the bathroom.

Now seated on the floor in her former room, Vincent acknowledged the numbness and lethargy he had been feeling since Esther's departure. He leaned his head against the door and released a moan, soft and long.

Mission accomplished, he returned downstairs and, sitting at the dining table, tried to forget his loss in a history book about the Fire of London, borrowed from the school library. He was due to take a test on the subject at the end of the month. But his mind began to stray, and he was doodling with a silver and black Parker pen he had found on the street some weeks before when Samuel came in. He was not usually home so early and, as far as Vincent knew, he had not been home for a few days.

"What're you doing at home?" Samuel asked.

"I've got a sore throat." Vincent started chewing his left thumbnail, suddenly anxious.

"Sure you're not skiving? Dad's going to be mad when he hears you haven't been to school."

"I don't care. My teacher told me not to come in if I didn't feel well."

"You tell Dad that. It'd've been licks for me if I'd taken a day off school because of a sore throat. Nobody name Sick live in this house, he'd have said. Would've given me two cuffs. Anyway, least he can't blame me if you don't go to school."

Vincent feared, admired and loved Samuel and his censure aroused feelings of guilt. "I can't help it if I'm sick. It's the first day I've taken off school. Last winter my friend Michael Farrell took a whole week off."

"As I said, you tell that to Dad, mate." Then Samuel changed the subject. "See Neville's won a second boxing cup."

Neville was making a name for himself as a schoolboy boxer.

"Dad says there's no future in boxing," Vincent said. "He's told Neville to spend more time with his books. That's why Neville's left the cup in Mum's place."

"I know. I don't know what Dad expects. He and Mr George never miss a boxing match on the telly, and then he disapproves when one of his sons takes up boxing. Remember how he was always talking about thumping me. Did a few times too."

Samuel clenched his fists, turned them up and clasped his sides with his elbows. He released a flurry of punches followed by two karate high kicks which almost touched the ceiling. He had reached brown belt level. Vincent had watched Samuel training in the back garden, doing press-ups on his knuckles, and punching his stomach repeatedly. When Samuel's friends came to the house or stood outside the gate on warm summer evenings, cars, girls and karate dominated their talk. Vincent's interest in sports did not extend beyond football and even that game had begun to lose its appeal. His brothers' passion for enduring pain and inflicting it on others puzzled him.

Samuel's karate demonstration ended, and he went into the kitchen. When he returned, he looked over Vincent's shoulder and asked him what he was reading. Vincent told him he had to do a project on the Fire of London. Samuel laughed mockingly. Then he noticed Vincent's pen and said, "That's a nice pen. A Parker. Where did you get it?"

"Found it on the High Road," Vincent said.

"Liar. Looks nearly new. Bet you nicked it from Woolworths."

"I didn't. Michael Farrell and Terry Mattheson were there with me. But I saw it first. Ask them."

"Sure! Everybody knows that you three are as thick as thieves. Let me see it." Samuel snatched the pen from Vincent's hand, inspected it and said, "I need a pen. This'll do nicely."

Vincent protested in vain. Samuel left the room, laughing, and Vincent remained at the table, quietly writhing in impotent anger. It was not the first time Samuel had seized something of his, but none of his previous thefts hurt as much. He had grown fond of the pen and resolved to do better at hiding his belongings from his thieving elder brother in the future. He returned his attention to the book. But Samuel's act had destroyed his concentration. With a pencil, he tried to draw the family room, with its television on spindly legs in the corner, its ragged green sofa on which the cat, Santa, lay curled up sleeping. He had just begun this sketching exercise when the door-bell rang. Thinking it was another of Mrs George's customers, he ignored it until it rang again. He looked out of the window but only got a partial view of what looked like a man with a suitcase.

Just as the bell rang again, he heard Samuel, obviously annoyed, calling his name. Vincent went into the hallway and listened to the exchange between Samuel and the caller. He could make out the man's Crombie and the suitcase at his feet, shod in polished black loafers with tassels, but Samuel blocked his view of the man's face.

"I'm looking for Lucas Bostock," the stranger said.

"If it's about the vacant room, you'll have to come back later. My father should be home around seven."

"Ah, you must be one of his sons. And from your height and demeanour, you must be the eldest. Now, don't tell me, let me try to remember your name. Oh memory, you fickle friend, where are you when I need you? Got it. Samuel, yes."

"Yes."

"Good to meet you. Name's Horace Fraser. I'm sure you've heard your father talk about his cousin, Jean Fraser. I'm her brother."

The name Jean clearly meant something to Samuel and after some hesitation he invited the stranger in. Vincent ran back to the family room and waited for the stranger to enter. Horace Fraser, Vincent saw, was unlike anyone who had ever entered 72 Carlisle Road. Even Jasper, Esther's treacherous fiancé, would have looked and sounded like a hod carrier beside the newcomer. He made slow, languid movements, had a vaguely American accent, wore a grey, striped, double-breasted suit, had jewelled fingers, with a tapered nail on the smallest left finger.

"So this is where Lucas ended up, a long way from banana trees and remote winding mountain roads that take you from one obscure place to an even more obscure place. Now here he is, at the centre of the world. Even owns a parcel of it. The man has exceeded all expectations."

Horace Fraser told Vincent and Samuel that he and their father, having grown up in the same house, were like brothers. Only a few months separated them in age, and in his childhood Lucas Bostock had been a constant companion and loyal friend.

Vincent had often wondered about his parents' pasts, their

relatives. When his school friends referred to their grandmother or aunts, uncles and cousins, they made him feel he occupied a far narrower world. Only his mother spoke of relatives, her cousin Bertie, her sister Irene in New York. But his father seemed to exist only in the present, as if he had mysteriously entered the world fully formed, wielding a hammer and cussing and swearing, with no parents to account for his existence. Now, Vincent learned that he had two other cousins. One, the stranger who sat in his father's chair, seemed a unique individual. He could not wait to boast about him to his school friends.

For the next few hours, Vincent listened with rapt attention as the stranger, speaking with hypnotic eloquence – which was interrupted by a loud dry-cough – confirmed his suspicions that Horace Fraser was different. In response to Samuel's question as to whether he had just come from Jamaica, Horace laughed and said he had not been to Jamaica in over twenty-five years. He had left Jamaica to study law at Howard University in Washington but succumbed to a wanderlust which took him to many parts of the world and gave him more adventures than Sinbad the sailor. He had walked the Great Wall of China, gazed at the Taj Mahal, marvelled at the Giza Pyramid, gone walkabout with Australian aborigines and hunted armadillos with South American Indians. In 1957, he had fetched up in Ghana, witnessing that nation's birth. Then he lived in Nigeria for five years, in Lagos, using the city as a base from which he travelled all over the African continent. Then a few years in Sierra Leone before running a hotel in Dakar in Senegal, and when a business rival burned it down, he'd moved to Monrovia in Liberia. And now he was here in London until a business contract with the Nigerian government came through. "Just a matter of time," he said. Then a coughing fit seized him, and after it passed his eyes were bloodshot and bulging. Samuel brought him a glass of water, which he swallowed in one long gulp. Then he launched into a long recollection of sailing up the Niger, Zambezi and Congo rivers.

His father's arrival broke the spell. Vincent had expected to see his father smile, a rare event. Instead, he saw his father's face express surprise, then anger. After a shaking Horace's hand, his father turned to Samuel and said, "I want a word with you."

Vincent was left alone with the stranger, who fiddled with one of his rings and said, "Want to hear about the time I went hunting for okapis at night?"

"Yes, please," Vincent enthused, though he had no idea what an okapi was.

But just then, his father, his face still set in an expression of fierce disapproval, returned and ordered him to his room. Downstairs, Vincent found Samuel preparing to go out. He was ironing a pair of trousers.

"Uncle Horace's been everywhere in the world," Vincent said.

"He isn't your uncle," Samuel said.

"He is," Vincent insisted.

"Oh, yeah, then tell me why the old man just gave me a roasting for letting him in the house? Said I should've told him to come back later."

The scowl on Samuel's face reflected his mood. Vincent stood in the doorway and watched as his brother deftly passed the iron over the orange-coloured flares. He was using a damp handkerchief, which he moistened every now and again from a cup. When the hot iron touched the freshly moistened cloth it released a gentle hissing sound along with steam.

"What are you're doing?" Vincent asked.

"Doing what?"

"Using a damp cloth."

"Protecting the trousers, stupid. I don't want them to look all shiny. If you want to earn a tanner you could polish my shoes."

"No way," Vincent said. "Make it a half-a-crown,"

"Get lost," Samuel said. "I'll do it myself."

Vincent retreated to the room he shared with Neville. He had long regarded the ways of the adult world as a mystery and the presence of a man who falsely claimed to be a relative deepened that mystery, along with why it was a problem if trousers looked shiny. Later that evening, his father asked him to take some bedding up to Esther's room. Horace, it seemed, was staying the night.

As he lay in bed, Vincent wondered whether Esther's room would have a new tenant in Horace, and why there seemed hostility between his father and the stranger who claimed they had grown up like brothers.

★ ★ ★ ★

I am the narrator. No, I am not to be confused with the author, and I am most certainly not a disembodied, self-effacing voice selflessly recounting the lives of the Bostocks. I have my own story to tell. It concerns my troubled relationship with a young man whose behaviour almost prevented me from fulfilling my narratorial duties.

I had been living in a four-storey, flat-fronted Victorian terraced house on Selkirk Road since mid-December, occupying the upper two floors. I was still adjusting to my new home and neighbourhood when I became aware of the young man. His mother, brown-skinned, stout, with a round pockmarked face that bore several small scars, lived on the ground and basement floors. She had told me she had three children, two girls and a boy, and I guessed – from the small plastic play swing next to the rose bush in the back garden – a solitary yellow rose that defied the winter months – that she was also a grandmother and had once received regular visits from her grandchild or grandchildren. Now she spent little time in the house.

Her son first registered on my consciousness one early evening as I was leaving the house. The sun sat low in the sky and highlighted the white pediments and quoins of the houses across the street. The tall, slim black woman who lived almost immediately opposite was on the steps of her home talking with another woman, also black, but corpulent, with a jolly face.

The boy was short and dark; he wore blue jeans, brand-name trainers and a battle-green T-shirt, with the word 'Army' stencilled on the chest in red letters. The t-shirt, epidermal in its tightness, accentuated his tapered torso and bulging biceps. There was an exaggerated swagger in his walk, as if he had admired himself in the mirror for many hours, and was now demanding the world's unalloyed admiration.

He shouted something to the women. It was incomprehensible but its tone was unmistakably lewd. They turned their backs as if in disgust and contempt. I had been living long enough on the street to know that both women were mothers; the tall woman had a teenage son, and the other woman had two sons at primary school.

The boy smirked as he strutted past me. I looked back and saw he was going into the house that had recently become my home.

I did not see him again for several months. The countless small tasks required to transform my four rooms into a home preoccupied me, filling many pleasurable and frustrating hours browsing in second-hand furniture stores. Most urgent was concealing the traces of the former occupant. In my first week in the house, I'd removed biblical quotes scrawled on pieces of cardboard and sellotaped above the entrance to the flat: "Be strong and of good courage; be not afraid, be not dismayed; for thy Lord thy God is with thee whithersoever thou goest." This was repeated in the living room along with: "And he humbled thee and suffered thee to hunger and fed thee with manna, which thou knewest not, neither did thy father know; that he might make thee know that man doth not live by bread only, but every word that proceedeth out of the mouth of the Lord doth man live."

There were more sellotape marks on the bedroom walls but no biblical quotes. Concealing the adhesive marks in the hallway was not a priority, nor was filling in the circular indentation on the flat door's exterior, evidence, I surmised, that the police or fire service must have once forced entry into the property and nobody had bothered to paint it over. The interior was another matter. For the living room, I bought a canvas painting from a second-hand furniture store near Abney Park. Measuring 5 feet by 3 feet, its subject matter remained unclear until I had dusted it and recognised that it depicted an angel and a naked woman. Was it an interpretation of the Greek legend of Leda and the swan, as my good friend Irma Benjamin suggested on a visit? No matter; it served its purpose – my occasional visitors found it curious. In the bedroom I put up another less memorable picture – another temporary solution until I got round to painting the place.

I'd not had so much space for years, having spent the previous decade sleeping on friends' couches, on a park bench, in a hostel for the homeless converted from a former police station in Dalston Lane, then in a bedsit less than a hundred yards from a busy main road where my mornings were filled with the hissing sound of buses' air brakes and the smell of petrol.

My most enduring legacy from those difficult years – for which I blame nobody but myself – is an acute sensitivity to sound. This was the result of a curious condition called, to use the medical parlance, stress-related tinnitus. The constant ringing in my ears sounded variously like the tintinnabulation of distant church bells or a swarm of insects, such as you might hear in the tropics at night.

Sometimes it's just a single, high-pitched note like the sound of a whistle. It fluctuates in volume and tone depending on my mood and energy-level. It is the first sound I hear in the morning and the last at night. Whenever I lose control, I retire to bed for a few days until the cacophonous ringing subsides to a bearable level. If I try to ignore it, the simplest acts, such as crossing the road or shopping, become challenges requiring my utmost concentration – which in turn exacerbates the ringing in my ears.

When I first sought treatment for my tinnitus – *my* tinnitus – I long ago stopped trying to fight the condition; I now own it, and see it as a terrible companion forever cautioning me against excess. The Ear, Throat and Nose specialist at the hospital warned me that the condition was incurable but manageable. I was advised to abstain from alcohol, especially red wine and whiskey, tobacco, wheat, strong cheese and spicy meals. Regular physical exercise helped, as did avoiding stressful situations. I tried anti-depressants for six-months, to no effect. On the recommendation of well-meaning friends, I experimented with various alternative treatments: a concoction of bitter-tasting Chinese herbs which I drank for three months; a homeopathic infusion of tree barks; acupuncture combined with massage therapy; hypnotism and yoga. After a year, the rationalist in me prevailed, and I gave up on alternative medicine. My social circle shrank as I declined invitations to parties, dinners and drinks. I avoided crowded, noisy places, especially those with low ceilings, because simultaneous multiple voices confused me. I abstained from alcohol; if I succumbed to the temptation to accept a drink, I knew the price I would have pay: twenty-four hours of rage in my ears. I struggled with giving up tobacco, then settled for roll-ups, as thin as possible. I listened to calming music, solo instruments – the guitar, piano or flute. I developed a dislike of vocal music unless it was in a foreign language. In this way, my strange affliction, unknown to others unless I revealed it, was manageable. I may have been limping towards my fiftieth year, but I still had a sense of being alive, and was determined to get on with living.

The house on Selkirk Road seemed ideal. Early in the mornings, while drinking tea in the kitchen, I often heard the cawing of magpies, the cooing of pigeons and twittering of small, yellow-breasted birds that defied my limited ornithological knowledge. Over the winter, I had seen two foxes sleeping in the undergrowth of the neglected garden and, in Spring, cubs played on the back garden walls. There wasn't much of a vista from the south-west facing kitchen window, just the rear gardens and the windows of houses that backed on to it. Nevertheless, there was much to see. One morning in April, at the precise moment when the sunlight reached above the houses and lit up the highest windows opposite, I saw, in an upper stairwell window, a young woman with long brown hair dressed in a short satin robe, her legs and arms pale, seeming to float down a flight of stairs in slow motion. She was only visible for two seconds but she seemed like a revelation, and became a permanent memory. As Spring progressed, the neighbouring gardens disappeared from view behind an explosion of greenery. The north side of the adjoining house also had a neglected garden, visible in the winter, but concealed beneath a canopy of elder trees in the spring. When the elders flowered in May, the combination of lime-green leaves and white flowers was soothing and uplifting, stirring long forgotten dreams of becoming a painter.

My new neighbourhood with its village-like atmosphere was a mere twenty minutes' bus ride from Kings Cross, even less to the City of London. Ridley Road market was a ten-minute walk away and I soon acquired the routine of a weekly visit to the market to shop for vegetables and immerse myself in the market's atmosphere created by costermongers from the East End, Asia, Afghanistan, the Caribbean, Africa and Eastern Europe. On some trips I returned home with only a few items but had feasted my eyes on piles of plantains and yam and dasheen; had seen huge live snails tied together in baskets in African-owned shops, and heard the musical voices of the Yoruba women. I felt I had been to some foreign country and this mixture of the exotic with the quotidian reminded me that flight from the city to the countryside, however salubrious in its quiet, even if I could have afforded such move, was not an option.

As the upper two floors of one of the adjoining houses were unoccupied, the top-floor bedroom was a space of matutinal stillness and tranquillity. I often played music in those early months, as I believed the room below my living room was empty. Encounters with the occupant were rare; her letters piled up the hallway for weeks at a time. By now I recognised the pattern of her visits to the house: she mostly came every fortnight, to pick up her social security cheque.

Late that spring, our paths crossed in the hallway and she invited me into her home. We talked in her kitchen. I remained standing in the doorway, her flat door wide open, while she sat at a vinyl-covered round table. She told me she spent most of her time with her male friend over in West London helping to look after the man's ageing father. We established that we had Jamaica in common: it was her parents' and my birthplace; she was born in London and had only ever holidayed on the island. As I made to leave her place, I couldn't help noticing a varnished pine headboard.

"I thought that was your living room," I said.

"It's supposed to be," she said, "but when I moved in I couldn't get my armchairs in through my front door. Had to use the basement window. Turned out alright. I have some noisy friends. When they visit, the basement's the best place."

Exactly a week later I encountered her at the north end of Selkirk Road coming towards the house. She was dressed in black and wore high heels, and a rough and ready effort had been made to apply make-up, rouge and lipstick; the result gave her an air of grandeur and dereliction. A small man pulled a suitcase behind her. He had the same reddish-brown complexion and combined skinny limbs and a slight frame with a prominent stomach.

"He thinks I don't have a home of my own and he can treat me anyhow he pleases," she huffed. I gathered that her male friend had offended her and, assisted by her brother, who was pulling the suitcase behind her like an attendant to royalty, she was returning to her own home. Before the brother left the house that day, he weeded the front garden. It was covered in cement, but weeds – dandelion, oak seedlings – flourished in the fissures and cracks.

Then just as suddenly as she had appeared she disappeared.

It was one of my other neighbours who heightened my awareness of the woman's habits. Karen was a young mother with a daughter, Amanda, who had strikingly blonde hair, and three-year-old Tom in a pram. I frequently encountered Karen and we exchanged pleasantries. This time she asked about my absent neighbour.

"Does she still live there?"

I said as far as knew she did.

"She should do something about the garden."

Karen's kitchen was in the basement of her home and when the blind was up it was a most impressive sight, running the length of the house and fitted with state-of-the-art domestic appliances. Her husband worked as a journalist on *Capital News*, a weekly business publication. She was on extended maternal leave from her job as a human resources manager for a large corporation. Their garden was an immaculate space, with a small lawn and a sand area with a large pink and red plastic doll's house. Seen from the stairwell windows, the doll's house had an unsettling visual effect, like an optical illusion.

Karen's family was one of two obviously middle-class white families living on my stretch of Selkirk Road. The other family lived in the house directly opposite. The husband was a scarce figure but the woman – slim, dark-haired – skipped in and out of the house throughout the day. In the mornings she ferried the children to school in a silver-grey MPV; later she could be seen house cleaning, then in the afternoons she collected the children. At night fall, they closed the wooden shutters over the living room window.

The summer made my other neighbours more visible. To the left of the dark-haired woman's home, the house was divided into flats. The ground and basement floors were occupied by a tall woman, who, for no obvious reasons, I assumed was Irish. I often saw her in her doorway smoking, dragging contentedly on her fag. Once, when our paths crossed on the street, I smiled and said hello to her, but she ignored me. It was less clear to me who lived above her, though I once saw what looked like a naked figure in the frosted window on the top floor. Also on that side of the street was a large Sikh family. The father was small, with greying hair and always smartly dressed. The oldest son had the bulky chest of a body builder and drove a BMW car fitted with a powerful stereo, which could create an earth-tremoring sound. Fortunately, he did not play it too often. He was often on the steps of the house in the middle of the day and early evenings, as if he was the family sentinel. Back on my side of the street, towards The Selkirk pub, a lesbian couple lived in a basement flat. One of the women was shy and mousey, the other had cropped, greying hair and began to greet me with a smile and a hello as soon as it became clear that I was now a neighbour. Next to Karen's house was the corpulent, attractive black woman; she lived in the first two floors of the house. The upper part of that same house was occupied by a small, reserved red-haired woman who had two young, mixed-race girls and was carrying another child. The father was an occasional visitor. I guessed that he was an African, and this was confirmed when he greeted me one evening and I thought I heard a trace of the Francophone in his English.

The other visible figure was an old African man who on warm summer evenings sat on the steps of his house greeting passers-by. I guessed from the two small scars on his cheeks that he was a Nigerian and a Yoruba and my guess was confirmed when, passing him one evening, I said "Ekaro" and he smiled and said something back in Yoruba, puncturing my bi-lingual pretensions. I introduced myself and he told me his name was Mr Ablade. He had lived in Britain since the '50s and had been a landlord to many West Indians. Now he was waiting to go home, back to Nigeria, to a place called Ondo. He told me had almost made the journey the previous year but things had gone wrong when he asked some young boys to help him pack his cases and they had stolen everything from him. "Everything," he said emphatically. I commiserated and we agreed that young people nowadays had no respect for older folk.

With the long evenings, The Selkirk pub came alive with people sitting on picnic benches behind its iron railings and spilling out onto the pavement. I went in there one early evening and sipped a Scotch but when a woman said something about 'Niggers coming into our pub', I did not return. Months later I walked past the same woman on the street, and she smiled at me, and it occurred to me that she had probably just wanted me to acknowledge her existence.

The boy in question now became a regular visitor to the house. He usually signalled his arrival by making a whooping sound in the hallway like a child delighted at the sound of its own voice. Once he came with a reddish-brown pitbull terrier. I watched the dog hesitantly climb the steps from the sunken patio up into the garden, sniff the air, which must have been heavy with whatever odour foxes release, then scamper back inside. I didn't see the dog again. On several evenings, the boy locked himself in the flat and kept up an extended rap rant in which 'fuck' was the only distinguishable word. After one such session I met him as I was entering the house, and he apologised for disturbing me, saying, "I was just letting off steam. Bad day at work." This was our first exchange. His voice was deep and rough, belying his height: he was few inches shorter than me. Standing close to him, I realised he wasn't as young as I'd thought and now upped my estimate of his age by about five years, to his mid-twenties. He told me his name was Junior. He worked in the building trade.

There were no further encounters for about a month. One hot afternoon, sometime in August, I was aware of the boy's presence in the garden. Stripped naked to his waist, his biceps and abdominal muscles glistening with sweat, he was hacking at the dense undergrowth with a machete. From my kitchen window, I watched him for a few minutes, then went into my living room to read a book. Soon, I smelled something burning. I went back to the kitchen window, which was open, and saw that he was burning garden waste in a bin. Smoke and ash billowed from the incinerator and poured into my home. I went through the house and closed all the windows and doors but the smoke still penetrated. Eventually, I shouted from the kitchen window: "Excuse me, you should be doing that at the end of the garden."

He looked up at me, then at the rising smoke from the metal bin, then at me again and said: "It ain't much. Soon finish."

A few days later, I encountered him at the gate.

"I'm sorry about all that smoke the other day," he said.

I accepted his apology and jokingly said, "You couldn't have chosen a worse day to make a fire."

"Wasn't thinking. My mum asked me to help with the garden."

"It does need attention," I said. "Best to do that kind of thing in the autumn."

"Yeah, yeah."

A year passed, and Mr Ablade seemed to grow thinner and the Irish woman's daughter returned home with a baby girl whose father came to take her out on Sunday mornings. I had carried out a few of the planned home improvements. I had put up bookshelves in three alcoves, two in the living room and still looked forward to the day when I could restore the fireplace which had been removed, robbing the room of its central focus. Still, with two large, deep windows through which the sun streamed in the morning, it was probably the most pleasant room in the house. I settled into a routine of work, then home. My mornings began with a walk to the newsagent on Conrad Road, almost opposite The Selkirk. The shop was owned by a Grenadian whose mass of dark wiry hair suggested a mixture of African and Asian. If I arrived early enough and there were no other customers about, we fell into easy

75

conversation. His name was Zach and he told me he had arrived in London in the sixties, later studied for a master's degree, then decided that there was nothing to be gained by further study and opened this shop, which he had been running for twenty years.

"Going home, soon," he told me on another morning.

I was used to this refrain, "Going home soon". But with him it sounded like more than a dream, more like something he could effect.

He ran the shop with his wife, a woman with immaculately trimmed hair, protuberant eyes, and an elegant way of stretching out her left hand with long fingers and manicured nails for the money, giving the impression that shopkeeping was in her blood. She also came from Grenada. Their son and only child was a thin boy with an intelligent face; he had his mother's straight hair and a trace of his father's Africa in his full lips.

By the end of my second summer on Selkirk Road, the son, also called Zach, but affectionately known as Junior, became a more common sight in the shop, opening it in the morning and, after a break, during which his mother did a shift at the counter, returning at night. As with his father, Zach and I fell into conversation on quiet mornings. I discovered that he had just finished a master's degree in physics at the University of London, and, though he had been invited onto a doctoral programme, had chosen to take some time out to help his parents with the shop. One morning, I found him reading a news item about Iran's nuclear capability, and I said: "Whoever invented the nuclear bomb left terrible legacy."

"You can't blame the scientist for how nuclear energy is used," he replied. "In fact, we're going to need nuclear capacity in the future; one day we'll have to stop using fossil fuels."

"Yes, but we live in the shadow of the nuclear bomb. Doesn't it make you anxious?"

"No. How to make a nuclear bomb is now common knowledge. It's how to control its proliferation."

"Common knowledge?"

"Yes," he shrugged. "Basically it's about creating fission. You do that by splitting heavy nuclei like uranium by neutron. Most reactors need at least 3% uranium-235 and weapons grade uranium has to be enriched to about 90% U235."

"Is that your area of physics?"

"No," he said. "I'm into astrophysics. I wanted to work on the next generation of space probes, after Voyager II, but I'm not so sure now."

I said, "I think the sooner you get out of this shop and back to the physics lab, the better."

Late that autumn, I met the other Junior at the gate of the house. We had exchanged greetings since the smoke incident, and I had decided that there wasn't much to him. But he was a sort of neighbour and civility required me to continue being friendly.

"I'm moving in downstairs," he said.

"It's none of my business who lives downstairs," I said.

""Can't take it any longer with my baby mother. She's got another son and lets him get away with murder. Things aren't right. Know what I mean? Not right."

"Well, it's your family. You've got to learn to get along."

"Not right. She lets that boy get away with everything."

"Have you ever lived on your own?"

"Yeah, yeah."

"So you can cook and do your own laundry and so on."

"Yeah, yeah. Can't take it there anymore. Know what I mean?"

"Well, as far as I can see, your mother's hardly there. So…"

"Got to get away from those people. Look after myself."

"Guess it means you can do some gardening. The back garden looks like a jungle."

"Gardening? I cut it. But it just keeps on growing back. What's the fucking point. Know what I mean?"

I said no more.

And so Junior, as I knew him, moved in downstairs. The most visible sign of his presence was a huge black Yamaha motorbike, with L plates, parked in the front garden. On weekends he would rev it up noisily, then go for a short ride, return and rev up the engine some more before wheeling the bike back into the front garden, where it blocked access to the dustbins.

He had been there for some weeks when the 'baby mother' appeared. She was white with long, luxuriant dark hair and a pointed chin, and was always accompanied by her children, a boy of about nine with his mother's dark hair and pasty white skin and a younger boy, mixed race, of about four. Their voices carried up and in through the living room window. But I could not make out what she was saying above the boy's loud, gruff voice.

"That's right, I'm not coming back. And I don't need you coming round here bothering me. I am trying to make a fucking living and you're just fucking stressing me out."

Sometimes, when he didn't bother answering the front door, she would ring my doorbell. When this had happened several times I politely asked her not to do this as I had nothing to do with the person living downstairs.

I never saw the boy bring anything into the house because he moved around at night. In the New Year, though, it was clear that he had been bringing things in because his presence now filled the house. In the mornings, as I went to buy my newspaper, the odour in the hallway smelled of sweat. My living room, where I'd often sat and read or listened to music, became unusable when he was about. When he wasn't engaged in telephone calls filled with expletives, he was playing his stereo or some kind of keyboard instrument, which sometimes sounded like a piano and at other times like a moog synthesiser. His execrable efforts to make music were thrown into relief by other aspiring musicians on the street. Across the road was a schoolboy who practised the piano for an hour each evening and often played a fluent version of Dave Brubeck's 'Take Five'; farther up the road was a schoolgirl flautist who was just as disciplined and accomplished. I had got into the habit of retiring upstairs from about 7pm, so the noise, though unpleasant, did not trouble me initially.

One bleak January evening we met in the hallway, and I told him he was making a lot of noise and disturbing me. As he had done before, he apologised and said he wasn't aware that the sound could be heard upstairs.

"It's an old house," I said. "Stereo hadn't been invented when this place was built."

"Yeah, yeah, alright. I know I can only go up to 9pm."

"Look, if you have to make that noise, why don't you use the basement?"

"It's damp down there, innit."

I sighed and said, "And please tell your baby mother to stop ringing my bell."

"Yeah, she's a fucking pain that woman. Her and her fucking son. Gonna get my son from her. Used to give her protection; now she's giving me grief. Know what ah mean."

"What do you mean... give her protection?"

"Well, she's not from round here, is she. Comes from Essex. So

I protected her; let all dem bad youths know she's my woman and they mustn't fuck with her. Know what ah mean?

It was no clearer to me what he meant by protection. "You should get yourself a lawyer," I said.

"Yeah, yeah. Money, innit. Every fucking thing's money, innit. Know what ah mean."

"Then speak to somebody at the citizen's advice bureau. They give free advice. You'll probably find it's not that easy to get your son from her."

"Time, innit. Gotta work."

"Tell me," I said, "where's your father?"

"Dunno. I could do with a father. Yeah. Could do with a father right now."

He glanced to the ground, then silently and appealingly at me. A vague, inchoate thought ran through my mind, crystallised in the realisation that he was trying hard to be a man, but a man as defined by the rap musicians, and hard, rough-talking men.

"Anyway, there's no need to be so hard on her. She's just trying to look out for her son. More than money, she just wants to know that you still care about the boy."

"Yeah, thanks. Maybe you're right, thanks," he said. "It's good to conversate."

With that Americanism, we parted.

A few days of relative quiet were followed by more noise. The boy on his return in the evenings went straight for his keyboard toy and his stereo, stopping at 9pm. Some evenings he spared me the torture of his painful efforts to play music and rap and went out. But even those evenings were not without incident. Late at night, lying in bed, I often heard him talking on his mobile, his voice thunderous and angry. His loud music was getting to me but I also had some sympathy for his predicament. He was clearly under considerable stress and didn't need me adding to his burdens.

In mid-February, tiredly making my way to the shop on Conrad Road, having forgotten to pick up milk on the High Road, I passed him. He was accompanied by two boys – the oldest was about twelve, the other a few years younger – both brown in complexion but with straight black hair; they bore a vague resemblance to him. We acknowledged each other with a nod and I continued on my trip to the shop, wondering whether the boys were his sons. If they were, I had to revise my estimate of his age. Closer to thirty, I now thought. Back in the house, I heard conversation coming from the groundfloor flat. I had no doubt now that the two boys were his sons. I made a weak cup of tea, then went upstairs and took a nap. The sound of someone knocking on my flat door woke me, but I was far too tired to answer the door. I went back to sleep.

When I next saw the boy in the hallway, he looked at me resentfully and said, "You're a snob, a fucking snob, that's what you are."

"What are you talking about?"

"The other day I was with two of my sons. I've got three. See. I wanted them to meet you. Knocked on your door."

"Oh, they were your sons. Sorry, I was very tired. Went straight to bed when I got in."

"Yeah, sure… You're a snob," he repeated.

"If that's what you want to think, go ahead," I said. "And by the way, you're still making a lot of noise. Can't get any peace and quiet in my living room."

"Well, if you want fucking peace and quiet, go and live in the fucking countryside."

We glared at each other for a few seconds, then I said, "I don't take kindly to being called a snob. And cut out the noise." I closed the door.

I felt injured by his charge of snobbishness, but the feeling did not last, as he began to make me aware of the depth of the slight I had inflicted on him. His attempts at making music were now louder, and the rapping angrier. As he still observed the 9pm shutdown time, I refrained from complaining and now spent my evenings upstairs in the bedroom.

When we next saw each other, I said, "You are a noisy guy, aren't you." I said this as a joke and he received it as such, laughing. We talked on the steps outside and he told me that somebody had struck his eldest son on his head outside the boy's school.

I sympathised and said, "You should complain to the headmaster."

"Nah, no fucking point. They'll just say it happened out of school hours. Nothing to do with them. Know what ah mean?

"No, they'll listen, once you make your case calmly. You or the boy's mother should go to the school."

"Their mother! Must be fucking joking. She's a crack head, ain't she. Really fucked up. I'm trying to get my boys from her.

Get her mother to look after them. Her mother's white but she's alright. She's said she'll do it. But it's got to be done all legal, like. Know what I mean?"

"So the mother of your oldest two boys, the ones I saw you with, is mixed race?"

"Sort of. See her father is mixed race and her mother's white. All that mix up, mix up. That's why she's so fucked up. Know what I mean?"

I now understood why the boys I had seen looked so unusual, with their dark straight hair and almost Mediterranean complexions.

He continued, "It's not her alone. On my mother's side, we got Red Indian and German blood."

"Red Indian?" Quite unlikely. "Maybe Taino," I said.

"Taino?"

"Taino. They were natives of Jamaica before the Europeans and Africans and all the other people in Jamaica now. Most of them died out centuries ago." His mother's reddish complexion also made sense to me now and I promised myself to do some research on St Elizabeth, the parish his mother had told me her parents, his grandparents, came from originally.

"Really. Must tell Mum. It's good to conversate," he said.

We parted amicably and it seemed that the slight had been forgotten.

★ ★ ★ ★

11. *Lucas and Horace, 1970s*

Lucas was sitting up in bed trying to do his end-of-month accounts. From outside came whistling and explosive sounds. Guy Fawkes night was approaching. Horace was on his mind. He was still claiming to be waiting for a large contract from the Nigerian government. He had fallen behind with his rent and three days had passed since Florence George, alert to the most minute vibrations in the house – she even claimed to know the exact time he got out of bed – saw him leave home on Tuesday morning, which was unusual because up until then he'd never emerged from his room before midday.

Lucas's immediate concern was for the rent owed him. He

was not entirely surprised that this situation had risen. Horace's shocked expression when, after two weeks as a guest, Lucas had stated the terms for remaining in the house was still a vivid memory. And a satisfying one, too.

"After all Pa Fraser did for you?" Horace had said.

Lucas had reminded him that from the day he arrived in Pa Fraser's house, he had earned his keep. Besides, it was Pa Fraser, not Horace Fraser, who had taught him his trade. Horace had handed over the first week's rent with a reluctance that signalled to Lucas that his cousin, despite all his talk of having dined with presidents, kings, chiefs, emirs and sultans in Africa, was broke.

Horace was in some kind of trouble. A middle-aged man without a home, family, and no visible means of income. For Pa Fraser's and Jean's sake he would be patient. But how long would his patience last? After all, he and Horace had never been close. As boys, they had often fought, and Horace's betrayal had triggered Lucas's flight to Kingston. Lucas remembered the day well. Jean had won a scholarship to study in America and Ma Fraser had organised a party on the eve of her departure. Overwhelmed by the bleak prospect of the house without the girl who had rescued him from having to sleep under the veranda, bursting with powerful but secret feelings for her, Lucas could not bear the singing and laughter of the occasion. He walked up the ridge behind the house and there, thinking he was alone, released a torrent of tears. But he was not alone. Horace had followed him and guessed correctly the cause of his sorrow. The merciless teasing that followed climaxed when Horace told Ma Fraser about Lucas's feelings. A woman famous for her dislike of those bearing the "curse of Ham", she gave Lucas a stern lecture on having ideas above his station and said: "If my girl child ever brought home an ugly black brute like you, I'd die of shame, go and drown myself in the Portland Blue Hole." How Horace had laughed. He later apologised for his mother's outburst, and Pa Fraser told Lucas not to pay her any attention. But Lucas resolved to leave the Fraser's house at the earliest opportunity. Decades later, here he was, providing shelter for Horace.

His reverie ended when he heard the screech of car tyres and the slam of a car door. The gate, which he had been meaning to oil for weeks, creaked. All the tenants, and Samuel, were already home. He got out of bed, donned his dressing gown and waited until the front door opened before stepping into the corridor.

As he expected, it was Horace, unsteady on his feet, reeking of alcohol, his clothes dishevelled.

Horace cleared his throat, then a dry, raspy cough shook his body. Composing himself, he said, "Lucas the landlord." He made an arc in the air with one hand and bowed. "The man of property, ever mindful of nocturnal intruders."

"You is a week behind with your rent," Lucas said.

"Only a week! What's a week's rent between old friends like us, eh Lucas? Cousins who used to roam tropical bushes wearing cotton caps for pith helmets and searching for lions and elephants and wildebeest, while trying to dodge the natives' cooking pot?"

Lucas had a vague memory of such a game. It was a disturbing memory, bizarre in itself, but also a reminder that he and Horace had not always been enemies. But those days of friendships had been short-lived, he was sure.

"Me jus' letting you know, Horace. This ain't no Jamaican bush you in now. This is London. Here, a man has to pay his way."

"Lucas, Lucas. Your double negative is poetry to my ears. Lets me know that you're the same person. But don't worry, man. I know where I am, a city built to worship Mammon, and I've got a direct line to that god. When the contract comes, on that glorious day all debts will be settled. Might even buy a house on this street."

"We'll see," Lucas said. "But you still have to pay the rent."

"Yes, yes. Just going through a little cashflow problem. It'll be sorted out by next week. But now, dear cousin, I must sleep, must dream. What's a man without his dreams, eh?"

Lucas watched his slow, hesitant progress up the stairs. At the top of the first flight, Horace was arrested by a violent fit of coughing. The hallway light went off. The last sound he heard that night was Horace's dry, raspy cough.

The next day, on returning from work, Lucas learned from a distraught Florence that Horace was gravely ill. A doctor had visited and prescribed quinine tablets, which she had got for him. Lucas went upstairs and found Horace in bed in a gloomily lit room which smelled of stale tobacco and eucalyptus oil.

"Nothing to worry about," he told Lucas. "Florence over-reacted and called in a doctor. It's just a touch of malaria. Got it for the first time in Lagos. Never leaves your blood. It'll pass in a week or so." Sweat glistened on Horace's forehead, his face was drawn, the stubble on his cheeks seemed luminous.

"Looks to me like you should be hospital."

"No, no. The doctor says I'll be all right here. Just bed rest. Florence gave me some aloe vera tea as well. Give it a week. They used to call that part of Africa the white man's graveyard, you know. Us West Indians don't fare much better there, either. Too much European blood, eh?"

Lucas sat on a chair beside the bed. For the first time since Horace's arrival, he felt kindly disposed towards him.

"Oh, I forgot; you probably haven't got any. Those Maroons are pretty much pure Africans. Pa Fraser believed you had a touch of Taino, though. But it's all nonsense, of course. Blood. Africans aren't immune to malaria. It kills them, too."

"That's what Pa Fraser use to say," Lucas said. "Bout blood an' race an' colour. Used to say, never mind a man's blood, show me a man's character." Lucas remembered this with affection, the closest he had come to knowing a father.

"And he was proud of you, you know, Lucas. Yes. Told me once, after you had left for Kingston, that if he'd had the money he would have given you a proper education. But, as you know, the money in the family came from Ma, last in the line of Portland Blairs, old plantation family. Pa used to say Ma had only married him because he had the right colour."

"He did the next best thing. He taught me him trade. Me got no complaints 'gainst him."

"But you have complaints against me and Ma?"

"Me didn' say that. Besides, that was all long ago."

"One of the many things I learned on my travels, Lucas, is that the past doesn't go away. A man struggling to make his present and future does so with the past weighing on his shoulders. Nations, too. Seen that clearly in Africa. That's where Pa was wrong about blood not mattering. He was right, of course. But he was wrong too. It shouldn't matter, but it does. It was blood that gave me the advantage over you. I used to look at you setting off for work with Pa, carrying his tool bag, and think: I am me because I am not you. And Ma's inheritance was what separated us."

"Doesn't look to me like you make the best of the advantage you had over me."

Horace pulled himself up in the bed, and said, "You're still competing with me, eh Lucas. Still want to show that the black boy is better than the brown boy."

"Is clear to me that t'ings not all right with you, Horace. Don't think I'm taken in by all those fantastic stories you been telling my boys. Me waan believe it t'ings will come right for you. But at the moment, dem nuh right, t'ings nuh right. And me not talkin' 'bout yuh health. What beats me is how a man with your heducation can end up in London almost penniless, at your age?"

Horace chuckled, "Well, you always were plain speaking, Lucas. I don't fully understand it myself. But the little I do understand leads me to speculate that perhaps my ambition was not to acquire but to see. The curse of the islander. And by the time I had feasted my eyes on the world's splendours... Well. But I remain optimistic. The deal I am trying to pull off will happen soon."

Horace's remark about the restlessness of islanders touched something in Lucas, and he remained with him until late in the night, talking about the many childhood acquaintances and friends who had migrated. That night, Lucas retired feeling oddly grateful for Horace's presence.

Horace was bedridden for nearly three weeks. Florence George looked in on him during the day, and Neville and Vincent helped out in the mornings and early evenings. During this period, the coughing, which Horace said was unrelated to the malaria, was the first sound Lucas heard in the morning and the last he heard at night, a loud, rattling sound, as if the sick man was in danger of ejecting his innards. Some evenings Lucas came home expecting the worst, a second death in his house. Horace's coughing affected everybody. The tenant in the adjoining room, Cuthbert Thanes, a quiet, inconspicuous Vincentian, gave notice to quit because, kept awake for five nights, he had gone to work late for the first time in a decade and was in danger of losing his job and his sanity.

Mr George's complaint was of different order. The bronchial racket did not affect his sleep but he was unhappy with Florence playing the role of nurse. He told Lucas, "He only has to cough and she goes running upstairs with one herbal concoction or another, even at night."

"Sure you ain't jealous?" Lucas teased.

"A little maybe. It's all on account of a dream I had. Dreamed that Florence had run away with another man."

"I don't think you should worry about that."

"You think so? Well, just to be on the safe side, I am going to lock the door at night."

Horace's health underwent a dramatic recovery towards the end of November. He was away from the house for several days. On returning, he paid enough rent money to wipe out the arrears and put him in credit for at least a month. He also, Lucas learned from Florence, took delivery of a metal trunk, which needed two delivery men to carry it up to his room. Intrigued, Lucas visited Horace some days later. The room could not have been more different from the gloomy one where, weeks before, he and Horace had talked late into the night about the restlessness of islanders. Strips of brightly coloured thin cloth hung from the walls, silk rugs covered the floor, and there was a hookah pipe beside the bed. Horace wore a long, embroidered gown and a red fez.

"You could say, I have finally arrived in London," Horace said. He had lost weight and though his face was gaunt, he seemed more at ease than Lucas had seen him since his arrival.

Horace's recovery and settling of his debt restored order to the house in time for Christmas. Never happier than when the books balanced, Lucas floated through the festive season on a cloud of good will. Horace provided entertainment with African tales, which even the sceptical landlord found engaging. But as Christmas day drew to a close, with the boys retired to bed, Horace told Lucas that the Nigerian contract he had been hoping for had fallen through and he was stranded in London.

12. *Vincent sees new worlds in Horace and Lenai*

"A schoolgirl?"

"So Florence says. Says she can't be more than sixteen. Maybe it's his daughter."

"No, no. He hasn't said anything to me about a daughter."

"I don't think anything, you know, improper goes on. She stays for a few hours. There's a lot of laughing, music. Nothing more. So Florence says."

Vincent was in the kitchen listening to this exchange between his father and Mr George. Horace had been receiving a young female visitor since early January. He, Vincent, had once seen them leaving the house together. Like Mr George, he thought she was Horace's daughter.

"Not really de sort of thing me can bring up with him. You know my policy, pay de rent, no funny business in my house, and me leave you alone."

"As I said, I don't think there's any funny business going on. But you have to admit it's a bit strange: a man our age being visited by such a young girl and there's no relation between them."

"Me hear what you saying. Let's leave it for now."

Vincent went to his room, where, in an exercise book he used as an occasional diary, he made a note of this conversation. Horace had displaced Esther as the object of Vincent's curiosity. He understood enough of the world to know that adults spent their days away from home at work, with exceptions like Mrs George. But Uncle Horace, as he thought of him, seemed to spend most days in his room. Some evenings, on returning from school, Vincent found him standing at the gate, smoking a cigarette, a sad, worried expression on his face. And, despite his father's stricture not to spend too much time in Horace's company, he would stand with him for a while in the wintry dark, watching the street. Some evenings, he found a pretext to visit Horace upstairs and, in a room fuggy with tobacco smoke, listen to Horace's accounts of his African adventures. Here, in that room decorated with colourful cloths and Zebra skin, Horace was more relaxed, the lugubrious expression absent.

Two weeks later, during school half-term, Horace came downstairs and asked Vincent for some ice. The freezer compartment in the tenants' fridge was not working. Vincent obliged and Horace invited him to meet his friend.

It was early afternoon and light from a clear blue sky flooded the room, making its strange decor seem surreal. Horace's friend was the girl who had been the subject of his father's and Mr George's conversation. She was sitting in the room's only armchair. She rose, extended long, slim fingers, said she was pleased to meet Horace's nephew, and sat down again. Vincent took in her long, jeans-clad legs, feet bare but for stockings, and her small, finely chiselled face and long neck. Lenai Alongoha was the daughter of one of Horace's business partners, Peter Alongoha. She was a student at the School of Oriental and African Studies, Horace told Vincent; he had known her since she was a little girl.

Horace was on the bed, his back against the headboard. He was sipping Scotch and smoking menthol cigarettes while his guests drank coke. Vincent stole shy glances at Lenai. She made him think of a giraffe, though he had never considered that creature beautiful, but he had no doubt that she was beautiful.

"Destined to become the first female president or prime minister in her country. Isn't that so, Lenai?" Horace said.

"You once told me you don't believe in destiny, Uncle Horace."

"A figure of speech. Yes, we make our own way in the world; there is no supernatural guiding force predetermining our future, only the burdens bequeathed us by our parents, and others' expectations."

"In which case I will probably become a housewife. An African woman is not expected to go into politics. Besides, I find politics boring. Who wants to become a prime minister or president?"

"Your father didn't send you to all those expensive English public schools for you to become a housewife."

"My father is not in a position to object to what I do with my education," Lenai said, and folded her arms.

"Your father was a good man, Lenai. He wanted the best for you. Much blood has been spilled over the centuries to get us to this current situation."

"Where Europe and America rule the world?"

"Would you prefer Russia and China where a person isn't allowed a private life? Dream, child, dream of making a difference. The chaos in your country isn't inevitable. The difficult art of governing a nation is new to your people. And don't say we were governing ourselves before the Europeans came. That doesn't cut any ice with me. The entity called the nation is entirely new to the continent. Whether it succeeds will be down to educated people like you."

"What does a president do?" Vincent said.

Horace and Lenai laughed, and Vincent felt embarrassed.

"Good question," Lenai said. "Not much, except loot and steal."

"Now, now. Lenai. Don't corrupt young Vincent with your cynicism. A president leads, Vincent. Heads the government."

"Oh, can't we talk about something other than politics?" Lenai got up and went to the record player.

Horace was elaborating on the role of a president, but Vincent was not listening. He was watching Lenai sift through a handful of records, pulling each one out and holding it up to the light.

"You have some strange records," Lenai said.

"Careful with those things. They have followed me through many countries."

"Can I play one?"

"Only if you'll dance with me."

Lenai put on a record and tinny music came from the player. "You need a proper stereo."

"There are many things I need, but at present I wouldn't say a stereo is one of them."

Lenai went to stand beside the door, the largest open area in the room. Extinguishing his cigarette, Horace got off the bed and went and held her. She was not as tall as Horace.

"This is Miles," Horace said, as he swayed gently with Lenai. "Know anything about music, Vincent?"

"Some reggae."

"Our island music. That's not a bad place to start, but music's as big as the world and one of the stops you have to make is in Miles Davis's territory."

"Will you stop talking and dance," Lenai said.

"Sure, baby."

Watching the two figures, Vincent felt out of place and feared that his father might walk through the door and order them to turn off the music because only worthless people and jigaboos listened to music in the middle of the day. The homework he had waiting preyed on his mind. Before he had made his decision, the music stopped and Horace asked him to put the stylus back to the beginning. Vincent's musical appreciation was limited to the bouncy rhythms of reggae and the breezy lyrics of pop music. Horace's collection of jazz and blues produced a less familiar sound, sad and slow. When Horace asked him to play a record by singer called Nina Simone, Vincent felt consumed by a sweet sadness when he heard the mournful voice sing, "What is love but a prelude to sorrow/I got the blues, what can I lose?" In the grip of this sensation, he saw the faces of his father, his mother and Uncle Horace, Esther and many of the adults he saw daily on the streets.

"Yep, nothing truer," Horace said as the music stopped. He bowed to Lenai and returned to the bed, she to the armchair.

The atmosphere in the room had changed. Each of them seemed focused on private thoughts and feelings.

"Do you like this music, Vincent?" Horace asked.

"It's not very happy."

Horace roared with laughter, which turned into a coughing fit. Recovering, he said, "Now what makes you think life's about happiness, young man? Only a child is truly capable of being happy."

Lost for an answer, Vincent shrugged his shoulders.

"Who's the cynic now?" Lenai said.

Her intervention sparked a new discussion which eventually returned to the state of African politics. For the next few hours, she and Horace talked and listened to music. Vincent gave no further thought to the homework waiting for him downstairs.

With the light fading, Lenai said she had to leave. Horace offered to walk her to the bus stop and invited Vincent along. On the High Road the clamorous traffic noise and streams of pedestrians disoriented Vincent for a moment, as if, immersed in the music and talk, he had forgotten that he lived in a noisy, crowded city.

They walked down to Dalston, past the market where the traders were packing up for the day. Horace and Lenai kept up a lively conversation. Vincent heard only isolated words, but enough to know they were still talking about politics.

At the bus stop, as the number 38 approached, Lenai pecked Vincent on his cheek and said goodbye. Her arms around Horace's neck, she hugged him lingeringly and Vincent saw him patting her back, as if he was comforting a child. He stood beside Horace as she boarded the bus that would take her back to her student hostel.

As they walked back, Vincent asked, "Are you and Lenai going to get married?"

"Lenai is a child, Vincent. And every child deserves a future." He said nothing more. Vincent wondered why he heard in his words the same sad mood he'd heard in the music.

Vincent tried to catch up on the reading for his school project, but his concentration was poor, still thinking that he had caught a disturbing glimpse of the adult world awaiting him. When school resumed, his friendship with Michael Farrell and Terry Mattheson began to decline. Somehow, they seemed very young, mere children really, ignorant of the ways of the world.

Vincent did not see Lenai again, though he was aware that she continued visiting Horace until mid-March, when Horace went away for almost three weeks, his longest absence from the house. Vincent gathered that his father thought that Horace would be away for only two days, and Vincent heard his father curse Horace daily for again falling behind with his rent; he even threatened to change the front door lock, issue the tenants with new keys, and throw Horace's belongings outside.

When Horace came back in early April, Vincent was sent upstairs to collect his rent.

He counted out fifteen pounds. "Give this to your father."

Still in his Crombie coat, though the weather was mild, Horace was sitting in the armchair. Vincent noticed that his fingers were bare; his rings had gone, only their imprint remained, bands of grey skin. But the usual odour of tobacco and lime was in the air. He sensed that this was not a time to linger but Horace said:

"How have you been, Vincent?"

"Busy. School's breaking up next week. I've got a project to finish by then."

"Good, good. You keep that up, son."

"Is anything wrong, Uncle Horace?"

"Vincent, I've lived so long, I've seen so much, lost so much, loved so much that I'd started thinking life held no more surprises for me. But I was wrong. We were supposed to go away together. She didn't turn up. Now I don't know where to find her."

Was this about Lenai, Vincent wondered, but Horace's sombre mood didn't encourage him to ask.

When he took the money to his father, Lucas counted it and declared "Dis not enough."

"He said he'll talk to you tomorrow, Dad."

"That man! I'm going to get him outta me yard."

Vincent did not hear anymore complaints about Horace for a while. An uneventful Easter passed and one day, before school resumed, Vincent persuaded Neville to come with him to visit Horace. Neville's left wrist was encased in plaster, the result of a hairline fracture from his boxing training. Reluctantly, Neville accompanied Vincent upstairs. Horace was pleased to see Vincent and he made a great fuss of Neville, calling him a pugilist and the next Mohammed Ali. Vincent asked if he could play some records and while the soaring horns and mournful singing still excited him, Lenai's absence robbed the room of the atmosphere from which he had emerged feeling that he had learned something important about life.

Horace entertained them with further accounts of his African adventures, and then he said, "You boys will soon be men. Has your father spoken to you about the facts of life yet?"

"Make money," Neville said. "As much of it as you can because only people with money get respect."

"Dad didn't tell me that," Vincent said.

"Well, that's what he told me. He said to make it honestly."

Grinning, Horace said, "Well, that's pretty important, Neville. I wouldn't want to say otherwise. But money comes and goes; it doesn't come often but it goes quickly. By the facts of life, though, I meant something more basic. Primary. Want to hear a story?"

"Yes, yes," Vincent said.

"When I lived in Africa," Horace, began, as he often did, "my great friend David Opolu bestowed on me an honour; he invited me to accompany him to his village. How could I decline such an invitation? We drove for a whole day, sometimes on proper roads, sometime on dirt tracks and we had to leave the car in a town. We slept there that night, then the following morning, later than we planned, because David Opolu was a great drinker and was nursing a hangover, we travelled for another day by foot. We crossed rivers, walked through forests along tracks used by animals at night and men by day, all the while climbing higher and higher. The village was in the mountains and there wasn't a road leading up there. The village was located on a plateau and called Tudun Wada. David Opolu's father was the chief and so we were greeted like distinguished visitors. The ceremony had already started. A group of young men were being initiated into manhood. They had spent many nights and days in the forest hunting and had returned with their kill, a mountain lion. When we arrived, the initiates were celebrating their success in a hut specially reserved for them. There was much banging of drums and bells and drunken shouting and singing. On the following day, the young men were gathered in the village centre, and there they were encircled by young women holding pieces of foliage. On command from the village witchdoctor, the drums started and the women, some no more than girls, fell on the young men, thrashing and beating them, playfully at first, but as the drumming increased in volume and tempo, the beatings became more severe. This was to determine which of the young men were ready take wives, because only a man who is capable of tolerance is ready for marriage. Some of the initiates were clearly not ready; they seized the switches, broke them and threatened their assailants, then walked away. Others, some with blood flowing down their arms, took their beatings. These were the ones rewarded with marriage. But the initiation was not over. The lucky young men retired to their huts with their wives for three days and there they were pleasured by women who were skilled in the arcane arts, handed down from one generation to the next, of pleasing a man. On the morning of the third day, the men were driven from their huts to till the fields and hunt in the forest. If the wife, lost in pleasure, failed in this task, her mother performed it. She drove the men out of the hut with vile curses. 'Our people,' my friend told me, 'have a saying: A woman's tongue is as poisonous as a serpent's bite and as sweet as mother's milk.'"

"I don't understand that proverb," Vincent said.

"Neither did I, not straightaway, though I thought I did. It was only some days later, as I watched a mother nursing her infant boy that its meaning came to me. The infant was crying, bawling like a bull elephant. How did the mother stop him? She lowered her head and pleasured him into silence."

"I know all about sex and love," Neville interrupted.

"I didn't say anything about love, Neville. I'm talking about something else. You see, sex is pleasure and pleasure is close to death. The two are soul companions. Love, though, is uplifting; it can hurt, but you're never more alive than when love is in your life. And sex within love? Well, you'd have to sit on a rock overlooking the Atlantic Ocean and listen to the beating of the waves to understand the elemental power of that combination. Now, there are some women who are so skilled in pleasuring a man that they can render him senseless with pleasure. Senseless. So, watch yourself on that front. No, sex – the sooner you get that out of the way, the better. In fact, I know, a good place in Kings Cross, where you boys can learn the practical ABC of sex. We could go there one afternoon."

Just then the door, which had been ajar, flew open and Vincent saw his father standing there, his face distorted with anger, his massive fists clenched.

"Horace, what you telling my boys? Neville, Vincent, downstairs right now."

They scrambled up and scooted out of the room. The last thing Vincent heard was his father saying, "Horace, you way out of horder, you hear me, way out of bloodclaat horder. Yuh waan corrupt me pickney. Yuh bloodclaat, yuh."

13. *Samuel Bostock and Sylvia, mid 1970s*

In the summer before his nineteenth birthday, Samuel Bostock finally acknowledged that he had left his father's house. He had drifted through several jobs since leaving school with a single O-level. These included working for six months on a building site as a general labourer before he decided he couldn't take January's icy cold. He now lived above a grocery store on Seven Sister's Road, equidistant between Manor House and Seven Sister's tube stations. He had last visited Stoke Newington in mid-January to collect a favourite jacket – rather than any desire for the company of his father and younger brothers.

Lying in bed on a July Sunday morning, with daylight bleeding through the the the curtains, with his woman, Sylvia, sleeping soundly beside him, he reflected on the almost imperceptible transition from son to lover, child to man. He recalled the Saturday night at Mingles in Bruce Grove, when he asked a tall, rangy girl wearing electric-blue hot pants – which made her long legs seem even longer – for a dance. One dance segued into another until they tacitly agreed that they needed a more private space to truly, truly dance. The following afternoon, he discovered that she had a whining nasal voice and a salacious sense of humour as she reached under the bedsheets to seize his tumescent prick and cry out, "I've caught a whale!"

Sylvia came from Bequia, a Caribbean island of a few thousand people who subsisted on whaling, extracting oil from the great beast, and meat which they cured and spiced and kept in jars as a pungent measure of a family's wealth. Two years older than Samuel, she had arrived in London as a fifteen-year-old after discovering that the woman she knew as her mother was in fact her aunt. A few years after joining her real mother, who had started another family and lived in a small, terraced house in Edmonton, she'd struck out on her own. For a while she tried modelling. Her height, narrow hips, small breasts, and dark terracotta complexion secured her some work, but the closest she came to fame was modelling for the LP sleeve on an album of traditional Caribbean songs called *Big Bamboo*. Unlike the migrant tenants with whom Samuel was familiar, Sylvia harboured no nostalgia for the tiny island of her birth. She hated the sea. "In Bequia," she once told him, "you can't get away from it. It's everywhere. All that emptiness, that never ending emptiness that threatens to swallow you up. Close your eyes and you can smell it, raw and strong. Plug your nostrils and you can hear it, roaring and wailing. Close your eyes, plug your nostrils and your ears, and you can taste it, feel the sting of the salt on your skin." Sylvia loved the city.

When, a few months into their relationship, Samuel revealed he had made several unsuccessful attempts to gain further educational qualifications, Sylvia persuaded him to stop working and concentrate on his studies. She would take care of him. And she did. They were never short of money because Sylvia supplemented her income as a receptionist with occasional work in a West End nightclub. Some nights she would return home late, rouse him and insist that he hold her, just hold her, because the journey home through the night had been long and cold and lonely. Then, on the following Saturday, she would take him shopping for clothes at Lord John or Cecil Gee on Oxford Street, insisting, when he baulked at the prices, that nothing was too good for her man. On the one occasion when he asked her how she could afford such lavish spending, she replied: "A girl's got to do what a girl's got to do." He didn't ask again. He concentrated on his studies.

Now, Sylvia stirred, put an arm round his waist, pulling herself closer to him. He turned and held her and a great feeling of peace washed over him, but it was short-lived and he was soon out of bed.

"What's the time?" Sylvia murmured, her voice thick with sleep.

He told her it was just after seven, as he readied himself to do the fifty press-ups he always did to begin his day.

"Jesus, it's Sunday morning, Sam. We got in after one a.m. Come back to bed."

"Told you once, told you a hundred times, I can't sleep much beyond seven. Habit."

Sylvia's own sleepiness silenced further protest.

Samuel finished his press-ups, then donned his running gear and set off for Finsbury Park. He jogged at an easy pace, raising his long legs high, his elbows tucked in. He ran inside the park's perimeter, keeping on the orbital road, which sloped at this point, lined on both sides with old plane trees for about a hundred yards. Then the road began to rise steeply, and his thigh and calf muscles hurt, but in a good way. He felt relieved when he reached the peak, where he turned left and ran beside the boating lake. This he circled and rejoined the outer orbital road which now sloped towards the Finsbury Park gate. There, he veered left into the park on a gentle but long incline. From behind came the sound of an intercity train. He was running comfortably within himself and he felt strong. He mentally intoned the mantra, "I want a house. Want a car. I want to always be able to dress well. I want to be rich."

After a third lap, he jogged to the south-facing summit, and ran on the spot below a plane tree, looking towards the Arsenal stadium and beyond to the city, the peaks of its tallest buildings visible through the morning haze. Over the next half hour he practised *catas*, high sideways and frontal kicks and ended his exercise with one hundred sit-ups and another fifty press-ups.

Samuel had not always shown such dedication to keeping fit, but two years beyond the school gate had impressed upon him that London's streets were dangerous. Three friends had been stabbed at nightclubs, and he and a group of friends had been attacked by a gang of white boys on the Mile End Road, where they had gone in search of a nightclub famous for soul music and girls. Six foot-three, slim with narrow shoulders, he was vaguely aware of something called race but gave it little thought. He had a youthful optimism, energy and an irrepressible desire to roam the city of his birth; he could not countenance the existence of weighty baggage that he had not himself created.

His exercise finished, Samuel left the park through the Manor House gate and bought a *Sunday Mirror*. As he walked, he read the front-page story of a political scandal.

Back in the bedsit, he made a breakfast of scrambled eggs, toast, and tea and roused Sylvia. He tried talking about this story with Sylvia, but she was not interested.

"What're you doing today?" she asked.

"More exams in December. Gotta keep reading those books."

"Why don't we visit your mother over in Brixton? You can work on Monday."

"No. Gotta put in some hours today. Besides, my mother's probably working today."

"But your sister Maureen will be there."

"Maybe next Sunday."

On their way to a nightclub in Camberwell, Samuel had brought Sylvia to meet Rhoda, and they got on well. But having just escaped from his father's house, he was not eager to spend too much time with another parent. He could not tell Sylvia that his feelings about his parents were confused. He knew he was ambivalent about his father, seeing him sometimes as a mean, violent monster whose sexual greed had stolen his childhood, burdening him with responsibility for his younger brothers. Sometimes he saw him as an unwelcome presence in his mind, exhorting him to excel; sometimes he thought of him with warm affection as the man who had mothered him. His feelings towards his mother were less complicated but by no means straightforward. He loved her unquestioningly, but it was a love refracted through Lucas's insistence that he should make his way in the world without leaning on either parent. On his last visit to Rhoda, he had not wanted to leave, but Lucas's voice, never far from his mind, was telling him he had overstayed.

After finishing her breakfast, Sylvia knelt on the bed and embraced him from behind and kissed his neck.

"All right," she said. "I guess that's why I love you. You're different; you really want to get on."

"And you think that's good thing?"

"You don't?"

Samuel thought for a moment. "Yes, but sometimes I think it's a curse. Sometimes I think it'd be nice to go dancing every night, wake up at midday, make love through the afternoon. But I can't; that could never be my life. But equally, I don't know that wanting to get on is going to get me anywhere at all. And that's scary."

"Well, you have to want to achieve something."

"That's the scary part. I don't know what I want to achieve. Just to pass these bloody exams would help, I guess."

Sylvia tightened her embrace. "Samuel, I'm with you, wherever you want to go, I'm walking beside you. You must know that in your heart."

Samuel put aside the newspaper, turned, held Sylvia and they fell back on the bed and worked their way under the covers.

In late August, Samuel got his exam results: five passes out of six subjects. "That's fantastic," he shouted, hugging Sylvia. "Great, great, great."

They celebrated on Saturday night, went to the All Nations club in Dalston and danced until early morning to hits by James Brown, Al Green, Smokey Robinson, The Temptations, The Supremes, Delroy Wilson, Jimmy Cliff, Tommy McCook, Don Drummond and others. They walked home in the early morning along streets where rose bushes spilled on to the pavement and released an intoxicating scent. Around mid-afternoon, they strolled over to the park and sat looking towards Alexandra Palace and, beyond, to the flat expanse of Hertfordshire.

The next weekend, he and Sylvia spent, on her insistence, an entire day in bed.

"I can't believe I just did that."

"What?"

"Spent a whole day in bed."

"Wow, and you're still alive."

"Yeah, just about. I gotta feeling I'm going to be punished for it, though."

"Only person's going to punish you is Samuel Bostock."

"Yeah, s'pose you're right." He was resting on his elbow and gazing into Sylvia's eyes. He had been wanting to say something of importance to her for some time, and now he said it.

"That part-time job you do, Sylvia."

"Yes."

"I don't want you doing it anymore. I'll take care of you, of us."

"Ok, Sam," she said. "I was only doing it for you, anyway."

"I know, and I can't thank enough." He kissed her forehead, and she hugged him.

Some weeks later, the summer already a fading memory, the horse chestnut trees yellowing, the air crisply cool, Sylvia met Samuel after work in Knightsbridge, where she was working in Harrods Department store. They walked to Hyde Park, went as far as the Serpentine, then turned towards Hyde Park Corner where they intended to catch the Piccadilly Line back to Finsbury Park.

"Sam," Sylvia said, placing her arm through his, "there's something I need to tell you."

"Yeah?" Samuel was thinking about the evening classes he had registered for again.

"I think I'm pregnant."

"What?" They stopped and Samuel felt weak at the knees.

"Sorry, I didn't say that right. I am pregnant. Two months. I had a test last week and the result came through today."

"What're we going to do?"

"I don't know."

When they reached home, Samuel looked around at the bedsit with its cooker, sink and bed a few feet apart and was suddenly struck by how cramped and squalid the room looked. The neatly made bed, the rose, picked one night in summer and now shrivelled and dry in its mock-Grecian copper vase, the grease-stained poster of the Desiderata – all useless efforts to turn the room into a home. It now looked like a prison, not a place to bring a new child. Terror seized him and he made a conscious effort to breathe deeper, as he had been instructed by his karate teacher when faced with danger. The breathing exercise helped, but the fear remained, a pulsing current radiating from the pit of his stomach through his limbs.

They spent a sombre weekend discussing their options. Not wishing to burden Samuel with responsibility for a child, Sylvia offered to have an abortion. She knew two girls from work who had made that choice. Samuel agreed to this on Friday night, changed his mind on Saturday morning and again on Saturday evening. Then, on Sunday afternoon, his head cleared by a running session in the park, he told Sylvia, "It's not my body. I'll walk beside you, whatever you decide to do."

The following Sunday, with Sylvia having chosen life, Samuel walked to his father's house, passing though Clissold Park. It was a glorious day, the sun making a last defiant stand against the encroaching winter. As he walked, Samuel rehearsed the request he would make to his father. He knew he had disappointed Lucas. He had rejected his father's offer to secure him an apprenticeship in one of the building trades, opting instead to remain in school for an extra year in a bid to secure GCSEs, and failing disastrously. Lucas had repeated his offer, and Samuel had again declined.

"A father at your age!" Lucas exclaimed.

"It wasn't planned, but we're close. I love her."

They were sitting in the living room, a room Samuel had rarely sat in when he had lived there, and which in recent years had been redecorated and refurnished to receive visitors. The brown three-piece suite – probably Lucas's first brand-new purchase – was comfortable. Samuel was pleased to see that the stereogram, bought from a neighbour, showed signs of being used. On top there was a sleeve of an Otis Redding album, though he could not imagine Lucas listening to the languid sound of Otis's music. On the mantelpiece were photographs of Samuel and his brothers. In the centre of the room was a glass-top circular coffee-table with a vase of pale pink plastic flowers. His father was making an effort to create a home, but something was lacking, some vital spark.

"What you know 'bout love?" Lucas said.

He looked at Samuel in his challenging way. It was the prelude to a quarrel, but Samuel did not want to fight. He wanted help.

"I don't know, Dad. I'm still learning."

"Glad you know dat."

Get it out, Samuel thought. Ask him now. "Dad, look, where we are at the moment is very small, just a bed sitter, really. I was wondering if you could help."

"Help how?"

"Rent us a room here or in the other house."

"Me rent you a room? Bwoy, me been watching you for de past two years, you know. Watching you hard. Sure, you paid me rent right up until this May, but what me see, and what me been seeing for a long time, is your superior attitude. Nothing here was ever good enough for you. Not until you leave and find out how tough it is; then you come running back, lookin' for help. How long you know this girl?"

"About a year."

"And you've never once brought her here. Me know you took her to your mother's house."

"That was, that was…" Samuel did not know what to say. His brain raced furiously but every excuse he could think of seemed implausible. How could he justify a trip to Brixton with Sylvia and not the short walk to 72 Carlisle Road?

Lucas stood up and held out his palms. "See these hands, these hands work for everything me own. Dese hands so tough I can strike a match on them. See these two fingers…" he held the two dead middle fingers, "lost all feeling in them when I was twenty. But that don't mean I don't have no feeling in my heart. Yes, me Lucas Bostock, I feel."

"It wasn't deliberate, Dad. We were in Brixton and…" How feeble he sounded to himself.

Lucas slapped the back of his right hand into left palm. "Bwoy, let me tell you this. If you big enough to live with a woman and breed her, then you mus' be big enough to find somewhere for both of you to live."

"We have somewhere to live, but it's too small. You've got two houses. All I'm asking you for is a room. We'll pay."

"All you asking? What Lucas Bostock own, 'im own. I alone decide who gets to live under my roof. When me dead and gone, you and you brothers and sister can share it. Until then, there's nothing else I have for you. You go out there and get your own house."

Samuel felt a great anger swell inside him and all the hours of karate training that had taught him the importance of self-restraint meant nothing. He felt like fighting this mean bastard, not just for this refusal, but for all the threats and punishments he had inflicted on him over the years. He snapped out of his chair, clenched his fists and glared at his father.

Lucas assumed a classic boxing stance, fists before his face, arms and elbows guarding his stomach. "So, you come to fight me now," Lucas said, swaying. "Me see this moment coming for years. Come, Ah gwine give yuh de beating of yuh bloodclaat life. Wait, lemme just take out me dentures. Paid plenty for them." He slipped out his dentures and placed them in his pocket.

Just then the living room door opened and Vincent pushed his head round it. He froze for a moment and in that moment Samuel regained his senses. What was he doing? It had gone all wrong. He'd come to ask for help, not this madness.

"Forget it, Dad," he said. "I'm sorry I asked for your help."

"So, you're backing down now. See, you can't take me, eh. Yuh know Ah woulda whip yuh bumbaclaat."

"Dad, I don't want to fight you. You're right. I'm going to walk out that door and you can just forget I asked for your help."

"Go on, then. Get the raas out of me house."

As Lucas began swearing, and without speaking to Vincent, Samuel left the house. He walked to the park as if in a trance and when he reached the lakes he could not recall the various twists and turns he had taken to arrive at this point. The park was emptier now, the sky clouded over, a penumbral light playing on the grass. Now he felt like running until he'd exhausted the anger and confusion raging inside him. The lakes behind him, he turned into the park and sat facing Green Lanes, under a horse chestnut tree he had often climbed as a boy. He remained there until his agitation subsided. When he rose to make his way home, he walked with the purposeful strides of one determined to be courageous.

Near the door, Samuel heard female voices and assumed that one of Sylvia's friends was visiting. He rubbed his face, concentrating on his eyes, which had felt moist in the park, stiffened his carriage and entered. He saw Sylvia standing by the window, then realised that the person sitting on the bed was his mother.

"Mom, what're you doing here?"

"It's weeks now I've been meaning to visit you and Sylvia," she said.

14. *Lucas, Vincent and Horace*

The confrontation with Samuel did not trouble Lucas. Indeed, he took it as a positive sign that his eldest son had at last reached manhood, a crossroads he had reached at a much earlier age, when he recognised that a man needs the courage to ask for what he wants, the strength to fight for it, and the humility to accept that life guarantees nothing. They finally understood each other now. He expected that in years to come, looking back, they would both laugh at the incident.

But two weeks later, when Lucas learned from Neville and Vincent that Samuel had moved in with Rhoda, optimism turned to anger mixed with self-recrimination. Moving in with Rhoda was a backward step, and a wounding act of disloyalty. It left him questioning whether he had failed as a father.

"Don't be so hard on yourself, Lucas," Mr George advised as they watched television together. "This is a different country, different times. What made a man fifty-odd years ago on our piss poor island ain't what makes a man today, here in London."

Lucas was not so easily consoled.

Over many weeks, he reflected on where he had gone wrong. The years had eroded his dream of starting a building company, Bostock and Sons. Samuel had refused to take an apprenticeship. Neville, against his advice, had neglected his schoolbooks and seemed determined to box professionally. Vincent – fond as he was of the boy – was timid and had a worryingly dreamy air about him; he would not survive a day in the building trade. He had tried to rear men, instead he had produced strangers.

With this cloud of failure hovering above him, Lucas turned to the problem of Horace. Since the day he had listened at the door to Horace offering to take them to a brothel, he and Horace had barely spoken. Then he had received a long-distance telephone call from Jean Fraser in Jamaica. She had thanked Lucas for accommodating her brother. He had not mentioned the difficulties he was having with Horace, but took the rare opportunity to find out about what was going on in Jamaica. Then Horace had come to the phone, and when he finished talking, Lucas thought he recognised a look of smug triumph on Horace's face, as if Jean's call ought to have reminded Lucas that blood and a long past bound them together.

Since then Horace's payments had become even more erratic. He was now at least two months in arrears. Wanting to explain this unacceptable situation to Jean, draw her attention to her brother's unreasonable behaviour, and warn her of the action he was about to take, Lucas tried telephoning Jamaica both directly and through the operator, but neither attempt yielded a result. He would go ahead, anyway. He had taught Samuel an important experience in manhood; he saw no reason why Horace should be spared a similar lesson; consistency demanded no less.

"Me can't carry you no further," he told Horace. "Yuh have a month to quit the room."

"Lucas, I am trying to put together another deal. I need more time."

"That's all the time I'm giving you, Horace. I've run out of patience with you."

"But Lucas, this deal is as certain as day follows night. The money I owe you is a pittance. I'll clear the debt."

"Me giving you time, one month, no more. And truth be told, is not just the rent you owe me. Me don't want you in my house. You is a bad influence on my boys."

"Come, come, Lucas, I thought we'd settled that matter. You made your position clear at the time, though it's not one I agree with, and since then I've refrained from talking to your sons."

"For now, yes. Anyway, me nuh have nothing else to say. Four weeks, Horace, then I want my room back. There's no shortage of honest hardworking people lookin' to rent rooms."

The following week, Winter signalled its arrival with a succession of bitingly cold days. In the mornings, a blanket of frost covered the pavement and cars. Horace settled part of his debt, then took to his bed and his loud coughing once again filled the house. Lucas was working in Wembley, on a high-rise office block, and the long drive back on the North Circular did not inspire generous thoughts. Horace was malingering, playing sick to win sympathy and continue the almost free ride he had so far enjoyed. He willed himself to ignore Horace's racket. And, as he expected, the coughing in time stopped.

A few days before the deadline in late November, Lucas received a rare visit from Florence George. Smelling of rose water, she had come to appeal on Horace's behalf. They sat in the living room.

"The man isn't well, Mr Bostock. Give him some time to recover before you evict him."

"That's what 'im want you to think, Mrs George. But 'im ain't foolin' me. I suppose he's had you running up and down the stairs."

"It's no trouble to me. And it's not every day I meet someone with Mr Fraser's experience of the world."

"Experience of the world! So, I must let him live rent free in my yard because 'im have experience of the world!"

"Me not saying that, Mr Bostock. Me just saying, give him a bit more time."

"Mrs George, you been living here for many years. Anything goes wrong – electricity, water, the windows – me fix it. You notice that. That's my deal with you. Pay me the rent, an' rainwater won't fall on yuh in yuh sleep. Me can't make hexceptions to that rule, hexperience of the world or not."

Lucas stopped talking when he noticed the look of pity on Florence's face, her watery eyes. He felt defeated.

"All right, Florence, let me think about it. Maybe I'll give him an extension. Let's see what happens on the deadline. But don't say anything to him."

"Thank you, Lucas. Thank you, Mr Bostock."

Lucas remained in the living room, cursing softly. He thought about the old rooms in Ladbroke Grove, and the nights and weekends of backbreaking work to repair this house. It seemed unfair, wrong, that Horace should enjoy the benefits of his sacrifices without abiding by the simple and reasonable rule to pay the rent. He was still brooding on the misfortune of being burdened with a freeloader, when Vincent came in. His face was solemn and he carried a bundle of cloth.

"What you want, Vincent?" Lucas said, weary and exasperated.

Vincent stretched out his arms, saying, "I want to give you this." Before Lucas could take it, the cloth fell from Vincent's hands, and coins – pennies and half-pennies mostly, with a few silver pieces – scattered on the carpet.

"What dis? Where did you get dis?"

"It's from my penny jar. It's for Uncle Horace, so he can stay in his room."

Lucas shook his head and ordered Vincent to pick up the coins. He was about to launch into a lecture when his tenderness for the boy and recognition of the futility of the exercise held him in check. He settled for saying, "Pick up yuh money and put it back in the jar. Don't worry 'bout Horace. He's a big man. He'll be all right."

Feeling besieged, Lucas retreated behind an even gruffer facade than usual. He was relieved when Horace, some days before the deadline, came to see him and announced that he would be moving out. A friend, an old Africa hand, had offered him a room. He asked Lucas to look after his trunk until he found somewhere more permanent, which, he said, was likely to be back on the African continent. He felt confident that the coming year would bring a turnaround in his fortunes.

"I hope you have no hard feelings," Lucas said.

"None at all, Lucas. In fact, these last few weeks I've been thinking about Pa and, if it had been his house, what he would have done, and I came to the inescapable and sad conclusion that I would have been out on the streets months ago. This feels like a good time to be moving on. I feel rested, rejuvenated."

"Good. I'm glad we understand each other, Horace."

They shook hands.

The room was let to a young Dominican couple and a woman selling souse from an iron pail started calling at the house, the spicy smell of her wares leaving a trace in the stairwell on Friday nights.

That Christmas, there were no tales of journeys up African rivers, character sketches of Freetown creoles, memories of dining with emirs and chiefs. With order restored, Lucas felt he had survived a war of some kind and in his quiet moments, surrounded by bank statements, newspaper and the accounts notebook, he wondered if he had conducted himself in a fitting manner. Had he done the right thing? He resolved to sit Vincent down and have a serious chat about money.

With the New Year less than a week old, Lucas got an answer. One evening, still tired from work but sated by his evening meal, he answered the door and found two uniformed policemen on the doorstep. Beyond them, under the streetlamp on the other side of the street, snow swirled like a swarm of fireflies in a glass jar.

"Is there a Lucas Bostock living at this address?"

"Yes, that's me."

"I wonder if we could come in. It's a rather delicate matter."

Lucas's immediate thoughts settled on Samuel; he feared the boy had committed some crime and his sense of paternal failure, quiet recently, flared up again.

In the family room, they told him they wanted him to identify the body of a middle-aged Jamaican whose corpse had been found at low tide at London Pool with Lucas's name and address in an empty wallet. Lost for words, Lucas looked around the room and then at the ruddy-faced officers, the first whites in the house since Mr Norton, and a tremor shook him.

"It looks like suicide," one of the officers said.

The other officer said, "Happens a fair bit this time of year."

"Suicide!" Lucas exclaimed. Then he remembered the trunk in the storeroom, the black and red tin trunk belonging to Horace.

Lucas got his coat and followed the police officers outside. He had forgotten his flat cap and, on the brief walk to the police car, huge flakes of snow fell on his head. He could not remember ever feeling so cold in England.

15. *Rhoda, Maureen and her alter-ego*

Snow fell for two days, and when it stopped the temperature dropped and Brixton's backstreets became treacherous, slippery with ice. That Friday afternoon, Maureen Bostock negotiated her way home from college through the dark, shut herself in her room, snuggled up in bed and listened to BBC Radio 1 until she had thawed out. Feeling warmer, she looked up at the posters of Marc Bolan and David Bowie and tried to decide which most deserved her adoration. As usual she was unable to decide and her thoughts drifted away and settled on the new domestic arrangements. She and Rhoda had been living in the two-storey house for less than a year and, after their one room on Josephine Avenue, she had begun to enjoy the space: the long narrow kitchen, the through lounge, her new room – the second largest bedroom of the three – the back garden. She didn't care that the house hadn't been decorated for years. Then, without consulting her, her mother had spoilt everything. Samuel's and Sylvia's presence had forced her into this tiny bedroom, just large enough for a single bed and wardrobe. The house was not large enough for four adults. And Sylvia was expecting twins. How would they all live there?

She listened to the silence in the house. Her mother was working the night shift. Samuel and Sylvia usually came in late on Fridays. Maureen got out of bed and pulled out a pink and white polka-dot dress she had bought for a snip in a second-hand store on Brixton Hill, a pair of white high-heels and a plastic bag. She stripped down to her underwear, put on the dress, which fitted perfectly, and squeezed into the shoes – they were about half a size too small and uncomfortable. She parted her hair in the middle, covered her head in a nylon, knotted at one end to create a cap, and pulled out a shoulder-length blonde wig and put it on. After applying blood-red lipstick, blue eyeshadow and rouge, she admired the transformation in the wardrobe mirror. She did not like her unadorned chest and covered it with a flamingo pink boa, bought at Brixton market.

"Well, Mary-Jane," she addressed the mirror, "let's go for a walk." Often left alone and instructed to lock herself in her room when Rhoda was working nightshifts, Maureen had conjured this friend, Mary-Jane, from an imagination nourished on television movies, comics and Gothic horror books she'd borrowed from the Brixton Tate Library.

She admired the skill with which she had applied the make-up, turned on the transistor radio to hear Rod Stewart, another of her idols, singing "Maggie May". Clasping her shoulders, she swayed in a dancing motion. She did not like the DJ's next choice, so turned the radio down and sat on the bed, her feet outstretched. Resentment flickered like a flame. Why had she been born into this family? She pulled up the dress and noted her thick thighs and calves, inherited, her mother said, from her father. At least you've got rid of him, Mary-Jane said, and Maureen drew strength from that achievement, which she knew would not have been possible without her alter ego's help. Could she do it again? Get rid of Samuel and Sylvia? Of course you can, easy as baking apple pie, Mary Jane answered. Let me remind you of a moment of sweet triumph.

It was in July. Lucas had got into the habit of taking her shopping. They would go to Oxford Street, and she would drag him from one boutique to another in search of clothes she felt would define what she wanted to be. Lucas would wait outside until she had chosen the items, then he would come in and pay for them. Contrary to her mother's assessment of him as a miser, a man meaner than a star-apple tree, she found him generous, though he often complained about her slowness in choosing the clothes. On one shopping expedition, when he had come into the shop and urged her to hurry up, she'd responded to his impatient prodding with a wailing flood of tears so intense that a shop assistant mistook him for a molester and threatened to call the police unless he left immediately. On another occasion, when he again tried to hurry her, Maureen had walked out of the shop, leaving Lucas holding several cotton skirts and blouses.

The final rupture came at the end of a particularly gruelling trek along Oxford Street. A light drizzle was falling when they reached Oxford Circus, but Lucas did not hurry her. She had taught him that a shopping teenage girl was best cosseted with patience and tolerance. They had returned to the car, parked off Edgware Road, with Lucas laden with bags. Lucas had thrown the bags onto the back seat and took his position at the steering wheel. She noted that he gave off an odour of lime and sweat and dampness. They had been getting on well that day and her conscience pricked her for having subjected him such a long expedition. Then Lucas asked if Maureen had a boyfriend.

Emboldened by her apparent success in training him in the art of shopping, she gave an honest answer. She produced from her scruffy denim handbag a photograph of a long-haired, moustached young man who looked like a rock musician.

Lucas frowned and said: "What work 'im do?"

"Nothing at the moment. He used to work on a farm. But he's packed it in and come to London to look for work."

"You don't think you can do better than that, Maureen? Me didn't come hall de way from Jamaica fi see me only dawta marry a farm worker."

"I'm not going to marry him, Daddy. He's just a friend. Anyway, it's none of your business who I go out with."

"Might not be my business, but is my duty to advise you."

"Your duty. That's rich. You caused me and Mum to spend years living in one room. Now you're telling me about duty?" Her voice had risen. "Well, I'll show you what I think about your duty." She opened the car door, emptied the bags on the wet pavement and stamped on the cheesecloth blouses and cotton skirts. The two pairs of open shoes that had taken most of the afternoon to find, she hurled into the road. "I've never needed anything from you anyway," she shouted, walking away through the falling rain. She had not seen her father since that day.

Now, sitting on her bed, communing with Mary-Jane, Maureen fumed at the intruders. Her mother ought to have sought her agreement before offering shelter to this modern-day Joseph and Mary. The audacity of this thought delighted her. Mary-Jane applauded and reminded her that she had forgotten to put on her false nails, the long, crimson ones she had bought in a little boutique in Victoria. It all comes down to this, Mary-Jane said, as Maureen went about the business of attaching the inch-long extensions, which looked like bloodied talons. It all comes down to this. How far are you prepared to go? Far enough, Maureen thought. Far enough. I'll show you.

Then Maureen left the house and made her way through Brixton. Wearing dark glasses, and a headscarf over her blonde wig, she walked up Effra Road, and along Water Lane to Brixton Hill. Her white highheeled shoes pinched her feet, but the pain spurred her on. So, too, did the remark "Freaky-deaky chick" hurled at her by a group of Black boys milling about on the corner of Dumbarton and Brixton Road. A Black girl in a blonde wig walking through Brixton was fair game for taunting, but Mary-Jane was impervious to abuse from boys who lacked imagination and were trapped in the ghetto of their skin.

Her destination was the third floor of a 1930s block of council flats near the summit of Brixton Hill. In the doorway of number 46, she hugged and kissed Harold Cross, pressing herself against him forcefully. The smell of incense, cannabis and beer wafted from the living room, where his flatmates gathered. She told him she did not want to join them and he led her up to his room. There, she pushed him onto the bed, threw herself on him and said: "I've missed you so much, Harry. I'm bursting inside."

"Steady on, luv." Harry said. He was a slim, with long, greasy shoulder-length brown hair and a Frank Zappa style moustache – which did not entirely conceal his rather feminine face. He wore blue jeans and a grubby white T-shirt.

"You're no fun." Maureen said. "I haven't seen you for three days. We're supposed to ravish each other like in the movies."

"Is that what you call it?" Harry said. "Well, I'm no Cary Grant and you're no Marilyn Monroe." He stood up in the narrow room, produced a pouch of tobacco and rolled a cigarette.

Maureen removed her coat and shoes and sat cross-legged on the bed. She could not say what she saw in his bedraggled figure.

Of the many boys, all white, she had formed crushes on at school, none had thought her attractive enough to return her affection. But Harold Cross, noticing her in Brockwell Park the previous summer, had approached her. On their third meeting, satisfied that he would only go as far as she allowed him to, she had asked him for a photograph and declared herself his girlfriend. Despite the seven-year difference, Maureen felt herself to be more mature, more worldly-wise, than this erstwhile Shropshire farm lad, a self-confessed fugitive from the land in search of adventure in the city.

"I got the sack on Friday," Harry said.

"What for?"

"Nothing. Not enough orders for glassware. Rest of the workforce's on a three-day week."

"What you gonna do?"

"Find another job. Go down the social on Monday. Couldn't have come at a worst time, though, a few months before my mother's birthday." He lamented that he would not now be able to visit his elderly mother. Maureen realised that she could turn Harry's misfortune to her advantage. Mary-Jane spoke to her again, asking, *How far are you prepared to go?* And Maureen responded, *I'll show you.* She stood behind Harry and held him round his slim waist. She worked her hand up to his chest, stroked the curly mat of hair, which she had once said made him look like Tom Jones, and said, "Have you got a condom?"

"Told you before I don't like using those things."

"Don't be silly, Harry. I'm not going to get pregnant at my age." She tweaked his nipples.

He squirmed, said "Ouch!" but did not pull away.

She had tested him several times before, sensed his excitement at the gift she was offering him, sensed, too, his fear of accepting the gift. She had not been serious on those previous occasions, merely playing, probing. In the months between first allowing him to finger her and now, her confidence in her ownership of Harold Cross had grown. Now, she needed his help. She pushed him back on the bed, knelt down, unzipped his pants, lowered her head and opened her mouth after hesitating at the urinous odour, seized his penis and ever so gently asserted her ownership.

As Harry lay limp on the bed, Maureen said, "Harry, I know where you can get some money."

"Oh, yea?"

"My house. I can tell you exactly where my mother keeps her savings. You could be in and out in under five minutes."

"What, you want me to burgle your house?"

"Well, it wouldn't exactly be a break in. We just have to make it look like one."

"Do what you just did again and I'll think about," Harry said, trying to sound commanding.

"Sure, honey chile," Maureen and Mary Jane said in unison.

Three weeks later Maureen ran away to Birmingham.

16. *Rhoda and Constable Macfarlane*

One evening, two weeks after Samuel and Sylvia had moved into the house, Rhoda returned home and found the backdoor wide open. She immediately went to her bedroom, lifted up the corner of her mattress and, just as she feared, discovered that all her hard-earned savings were gone. Sylvia found that her small jewellery box containing gold bangles and earrings was missing. Rhoda reported the matter to the police.

She was reflecting on the meaning of the burglary as she waited for the police to arrive. Seated at the dining table, her Bible opened before her, the weak morning light at her back, at first she saw it as an omen, a forewarning of a worse disaster to come. Her daughter was threatening to leave home. But then she reflected that her first-born child was living with her again and, the Lord willing, she would soon become a grandmother. Maybe the burglary signalled the end of a phase, marked a new beginning, and this more positive thought caused a fleeting smile.

A policeman arrived, and after inspecting all the windows and the back and front doors, he joined Rhoda in the dining room. Constable Neil Macfarlane, as he introduced himself, told Rhoda that he had not found any signs of forced entry. He was middle-aged, tall, burly and had a craggy face and thinning brown hair; he spoke with a faint Scottish burr. He quizzed her about missing items and money (fifty pounds), members of the household and their routines, the number of keys, and so on. He jotted down Rhoda's answers, then put his notebook away.

"Opportunistic burglary. Seems to me that someone left the door open and somebody just walked into the house. Under a mattress is the most obvious place to look for money. I suggest you change the lock on that door, on the front door too." There was a weary note in his voice, as if he had investigated too many similar crimes before.

"You mean you can't catch the person who did this?"

"Mrs Bostock, this is Brixton. We get hundreds of burglaries every month. Sometimes, when items like jewellery or electronic goods are stolen, we can link a suspect to a particular crime. But there's no way of tracing cash."

"All my savings."

"I'm sorry."

"But who could've done this? Just walk into my home and take everything."

"Who knows? You're probably not going to like what I'm about to say, but I've been stationed in Brixton for twenty years and I've seen some things. Years ago, it was just the rude boys with their flick knives, the shebeens and gambling houses and drug dealers, now there's something else going on. Something I don't understand. You only have to walk down Railton Road any time of day to see it."

"I never walk down Railton Road," Rhoda said. "It's a sinful place, sinful." She pictured the men milling about, the women in indecently short skirts, the large fancy cars. Railton Road was the quickest route to the market, but she had long decided that the longer route, along Effra Road, was less offensive to her eyes.

"You and many decent people think like that. We know who the main guys are. The pimps, the dealers and the gamblers. They don't worry us. It's the kids who've started hanging out there. Fifteen, sixteen. They all claim to be Rastafarians. It's as if they're all pouring out of school and joining this cult."

"Rastafarians? But they are madmen." Rhoda recalled the half-naked man with thick matted hair who used to walk up and down Maxfield Avenue back in Kingston. "Madmen."

"Maybe so. That's not for me to say. What I can say, though, is that when a criminal stands before a judge and brandishes the bible and tells the judge he doesn't recognise his authority, there's trouble brewing. None of the fair cop lark we were used to."

"You saying one of them Rastafarians broke into my house?"

"No, I'm not saying that. It's possible, but I'm not saying that. I found no evidence. He rose, glanced down at the bible, and said:

"I see you read the good book. Great book that. All the wisdom of the ages. Methodist myself."

Rhoda thought and said, "Christian." She was vaguely aware of the many denominations of Christianity but did not understand the differences. Since coming to England, she had worshipped in Catholic, Methodist, Baptist and Anglican churches, sometimes out of the need for instant relief from her burden, at other times simply because she liked the building. Mostly, she had sought comfort, strength and wisdom in private, from the book which taught her that life and hardship and strife were inseparable and had to be endured.

"Yes, we're all that," he said.

"I try to read it every day," Rhoda said.

She accompanied him to the gate. He lingered on the pavement and Rhoda sensed a subtle shift in his demeanour. For a fleeting and intense second she saw through the stranger in a uniform, saw a man of flesh and blood, saw there was desire in his eyes, in the play of his lips, in his seeming reluctance to leave. It brought a smile to her lips, triggered a long-forgotten feeling, a rare acknowledgement of her womanhood, a reminder that she, a mother of four and a grandmother-to-be, could still elicit admiration from a man.

"You can call the station if anything regarding the burglary occurs to you. Ask for PC Mcfarlane."

"Yes," she said. The moment had passed, the normal order restored; they were victim and policeman again.

His visit had lasted much less than an hour. She did not have to be at the hospital until six pm and it was just approaching mid-day. Feeling peckish, she poured some vegetable oil in a frying pan and ignited a ring on the gas cooker. There were three plantains in the vegetable rack; she selected the ripest, its skin coloured black and yellow, peeled it and cut it into long thin slices. She sprinkled salt on the slices, then placed them in the hot oil.

As the aroma enveloped her, she remembered how once before she had prepared plantain for herself, alone in an empty house. It had been a secret pleasure. Her mind drifted back to the policeman and she wondered if she had imagined his admiration. She chided herself for her vanity. Those days were gone. It seemed that she had stepped straight out of childhood and into motherhood, without the intervening period of freedom that she knew many of her acquaintances in the factories and hospitals where she had worked had enjoyed. They had seemed so much more confident. They spoke of their husbands as friendly rivals whose wiles they were aware of and without whom life would be like unseasoned meat.

The plantain slices, now golden brown on both sides, were ready. She put them on a plate, and brought it to the dining table. While waiting for the plantain to cool, she corrected an earlier thought. Her memory had robbed her of the six years between leaving her grandmother's house and giving birth to Samuel. She must have lived those six years without a sense of adventure, and so they had passed without memorable incidents. She had not been brave. The plantain had cooled and she began to eat. She ate slowly, tasting first a slightly salted and bitter flavour, followed by a sensation so delicious that if gold were edible it would taste just like fried ripe plantain.

She recalled the Kingston house that became her home when she was sixteen. It was on Linden Road, off Maxfield Avenue and fronted a compound, behind which were other, smaller properties, occupied by Aunt Milly's quarrelsome in-laws who never forgave her late husband for leaving her the property, she a woman who had borne him only one child. Wooden, with a rusting zinc-roof, its three small rooms were used mainly for sleeping because life was lived mostly in the dusty, ochre-coloured yard. This was swept morning and evening, and in the dry season sprinkled several times a day to keep the dust down. Breadfruit, ackee, mango, soursop and guinep trees surrounded the house, and elsewhere were patches of callaloo and okra. The guinep tree, famous throughout the neighbourhood for its plentiful fat fruits, had low thick branches, one of which, on windy nights, often brushed against the window where she shared a room with Bridget, four years younger than she was and known to everybody as Bridy.

Bridy always slept through the scraping sound of the guinep tree, but it took Rhoda almost two years to rid herself of the belief that duppies were trying to enter the room. Rhoda saw little of Kingston in her first two years. She cared for Bridy, and sometimes helped Aunt Milly bake bread, gizzadas, and puddings that brought in a small income. Then she got a part-time job as a maid to a Syrian family on Molynes Road. She left her Aunt's house only for work, to go to the market, and to attend church.

Aunt Milly, six feet tall, dark and fleshy and, like Rhoda and her mother, straight as a pole, warned her against certain types of men.

"Never mind how dem smile pretty and them clothes fancy, look for a man with working hands. Plenty girls come from country, fall for pretty man and soon find dem fall for heartbreak. Wuk man no pretty but 'im will mind you and you pickney."

The shy, brown country girl with her height, erect posture, and slim build attracted many unsuitable admirers who retreated when they met her ferocious aunt, but not Lucas Bostock, who lived in a compound opposite. Rhoda rightly took Aunt Milly's silence as approval of the confident Portlander with the immense rough hands, smooth and black skin.

It was under the guinep tree, late one night, that Lucas revealed his ambition to leave the island, to find work in America. Coming to Kingston had been a gigantic leap for Rhoda; she did not expect to journey any further. She lacked the courage and the curiosity that had taken her grandmother to Panama. Even after all these years in Kingston, Rhoda still left her Aunt's yard with trepidation. Kingston's bustle and noise, its swaggering men and loud feisty women unnerved her. America! Lucas's boldness, his self-belief, the sheer magnitude of his ambition simply overwhelmed her. It was under the guinep tree that she promised herself to him. And it was there, too, months later, that he told her about the fight in which he had killed a man.

Over the next few weeks other people told her more. Trinity Gordon, Lucas's opponent, had goaded Lucas into a fight by claiming that he had been intimate with Rhoda. She had only met Trinity twice, once in Half-Way-Tree when Lucas had introduced him as a workmate. Her only memory of the man was his reddish complexion, towering height and broad angular shoulders, like a swimmer's. Another time, he had followed her and Bridy through the market and told her, "Brown girl like you should be with a man like me. Not dat likkle black man." Bridy, as spirited as her mother, had chased him away.

It was the empty claim of a jealous man, she and other people told Lucas. But Trinity persisted with his boastful lie until Lucas could take no more. He challenged Trinity to a fight, which was to be held on waste ground near the Jewish cemetery. On the eve of the fight, she pleaded with Lucas to withdraw.

He said, "And walk with my head down for the rest of my life? Me can't do that. The man is a blasted liar and I am going to shut him up for good."

"We can leave Kingston, go to Manchester, even Portland."

"Me on a one-way journey. Me leave country and me nah go back a country. No man driving me back there."

The midnight fight, eyewitnesses told her, attracted hundreds of spectators, including uniformed constables. Bets were made, women set up stalls selling roast fish and breadfruit and bammy and roast corn and coca-cola. A man on stilts and wearing a Jonkunu mask walked among the crowd on stilts, blowing an abeng horn. Other men beat drums and hollered, "Fight of the century! Fight of the century!" Young women in stiletto heels clung to their escorts lest they trip on the stony ground. Someone on the fringe of the crowd, a soap box preacher, bellowed: "An eye for an eye."

Lucas was four inches shorter than his opponent and the odds were against him, but from round one it was clear that his technique more than compensated for his lack of height. Feet planted firmly, eyes fixed on his opponent, the Portland Puncher, as the bookies called him, jabbed and parried and commanded the centre of the makeshift ring. Both men were bleeding by the third round and the fight remained evenly matched until the sixth round, when Lucas's right hand landed a mighty overhead punch that staggered Trinity and had men in the crowd claiming they felt it too. Trinity's knees buckled but he managed to remain upright. The crowd was braying for Lucas to deliver the final blow, but he held back, giving his opponent time to recover and cling to him until the bell went. Within seconds of the next round, Lucas had floored Trinity but he rose unsteadily and kept on coming at Lucas, who repeatedly pummelled the man until he fell on his knees, blood gushing from his nose and mouth, his eyes mere slits. For a frozen second, Trinity did not move, and Lucas hovered over him shouting, "Tell them a lie you tell." Trinity raised his bloodied face in slow motion then he fell backwards, as if a breeze had blown him over. The referee declared Lucas the winner and there was much noise and commotion as bets were settled. It was some minutes before Lucas learned that Trinity was still unconscious; the water thrown on his face had not brought him round. A group of men carried the defeated man to Kingston Public Hospital, where he remained in a coma for three days. When he came round, he could neither speak nor move. He was all but dead.

Lucas had exaggerated on the night when he roused Rhoda by shaking the branch of the guinep tree. Nonetheless, he was persuaded to leave Kingston earlier than planned. A month after he left, with Trinity now in the care of his parents somewhere beyond Irish Town, there came rumours that his breathing and open eyes, his only signs of life, had ceased, and Rhoda felt unsafe because people said Trinity's family would be seeking revenge, and in Lucas's absence she felt unsafe, as the target of their wrath. Fortunately, Lucas, three months after leaving, sent the money for her passage to London.

She would have stayed with him. All she'd asked of him was loyalty and respect. Looking back, she saw that she had allowed herself to be swept along by the irresistible currents of his restless ambition. She'd been a child, but no more.

17. *Rhoda and Neil Macfarlane, a year later*

An overcast, chilly spring afternoon and Rhoda Bostock was on her way to work at the geriatric ward in St Thomas's Hospital. She was waiting at a bus stop on Brixton High Street. Buses came and went but not hers, a contra-flow of pedestrians swirled around her, car horns stabbed the air, and snatches of conversations in a medley of accents darted past her ears. She had become a grandmother to Sam and Sylvia's twins the previous summer and their crying over the last three nights had disturbed her sleep, leaving her feeling out of sorts: ultra-sensitive to sound, light-headed. She longed for the hospital's ordered urgency and routines. Hurry up, bus, she thought.

She was pleased that Maureen had returned home, though she had still not spoken a word to Sylvia. Maureen was hard-headed like her father, but she'd come round. But that positive belief was overshadowed by what she had recently heard about Neville. He had not only left his father's house under a cloud, he had changed his name to something like Kimani – it was not a name that stuck in her memory – and declared himself a Rastafarian. Neville, so gentle as a child, now wearing dreadlocks? A sign of madness. How, in heaven's name, did that come about? And neither he nor Vincent had become the regular visitors she expected them to become when Samuel moved in with her. Indeed, she found Vincent distant, silent and sullen.

"Mrs Bostock," a voice called, ending her reverie. She did not recognise him immediately. The off-white Macintosh, the trilby hat, the white shirt and striped tie – he had replaced one uniform with another. "Neil Macfarlane," he said quietly, as if mindful of the other people at the bus stop. "PC Neil Macfarlane."

She laughed as she remembered the burglary and the visit from the two constables. Samuel and Sylvia's arrival and the birth of their children had transformed that incident into nothing more than an irksome accident that had conferred on her membership of a large club, putting her in a position to sympathise with at least two work colleagues who had suffered a similar mishap.

"Sorry we didn't get back to you," he said. "That's the way it is with most break-ins."

"I wasn't expecting to hear from you again. You said as much at the time."

"Och, did I? That was a dereliction of duty. We're supposed to leave people with the hope that the criminals will be apprehended. Justice done and seen to be done and all that."

Rhoda said nothing, and Neil McFarlane remarked on the awful weather and her agreement formed a bridge onto other matters that they walked across – with, for Rhoda, surprising ease. He told her he was on his way to St Thomas Hospital's cardiac unit, which he had been visiting for the past three months. Rhoda was curious to hear more but the bus arrived.

It was full, but there were few seats on the lower deck and Rhoda claimed one, while Neil McFarlane remained standing. When the passenger next to her got off, the constable sat beside her, a silent middle-aged white-man, but one whose gaze had made Rhoda aware that she was not just a mother and divorcee, not just a frumpily dressed West Indian woman.

On the way to the hospital, she learned that he was a widower with two sons, both grown men, one in the navy, the other in the army. At the hospital entrance, as they readied to part, Neil Mcfarlane again hesitated and gave Rhoda a look that reached beyond the various selves she had accreted since her teenage years. "Mrs Bostock," he said, "that was a pleasant journey with you. I was wondering if I could invite you to dinner."

"Me!"

"Yes, you, Mrs Bostock."

Words refused to come to her mouth and she shook her head.

"Can I at least call you at work?"

"Yes, no, yes."

"Which one?"

"Yes, yes."

And so it started. The idea of going out to dinner was so foreign to Rhoda that their first rendezvous happened in a Wimpy bar opposite Victoria Station, because its red moulded plastic seats resembled those in the hospital canteen. She found it easier listening to him than speaking about herself. To his questions, she gave hesitant, evasive answers born of the belief that nobody, least of all a man like him, could possibly find her interesting. Fortunately, he was eager to tell her about himself: the Hebridean island he was born on; his uneventful war-time experience; the boredom of civilian life relieved by joining the police force; the long journey to London through a series of transfers, each one taking him closer to the city; the loss of his wife; his puzzled concern that neither of his sons had as yet shown any willingness to start a family. Responding every so often with an exclamation, or a sigh, or an "ah", Rhoda kept him talking for over three hours and when he'd finished, she realised that her suspicions were baseless, her fear unnecessary. She decided that she liked Neil Mcfarlane, liked his quiet voice, his humbleness, his simple and honest declaration that he was lonely.

They continued to meet – always at Neil's initiative – through the spring of that year, and a tacit understanding developed between them that theirs was a private relationship to be ended when either party decided. In mid-summer, they began meeting on Wednesday or Thursday afternoons in a hotel room with curtains imprinted with yellow carnations. It was for Rhoda a period of withdrawal, of respite from the demands of work and the mounting tension at home between Maureen and Sylvia. Although that unfolding drama was never far from her mind, she did not speak about it to her lover.

Neil did not seem to want anything more from her than those few quiet hours of secret and unhurried love and she wanted nothing else from him. She laughed in that room, never loudly, for as Neal pointed out the walls were as thin as cucumber slices. She cried, too, when she imagined how different her life could have been if she had met someone like Neil – gentle, quiet and unassuming, a man satisfied with his lot. She would not have left Jamaica. She told herself that regrets were foolish; this was her life now: four children, two grandchildren and, in her early forties, a secret lover. But far from stemming her tears, this summary of her blessings caused her to weep more.

"Something troubling you, Rhoda?" Neil asked, his breath minty. He touched her bare shoulder.

"Just this life," she said. "I wish I could understand it."

"Understand what about it?"

"Everything. Me, you. The journeys I have made and not made. The turnings I have taken."

"What's there to understand? We're born and we try to make ourselves useful, and somewhere along the road to death we hope to find a little love, a little peace, a glimpse of beauty, knowing that none of those things will last forever, otherwise we wouldn't be alive, not really alive."

"You don't think it can be understood?"

"Not by the likes of me and you. What I do know, though, is that you filled a hole in my life, Rhoda. You may not think it's much, but you've given me something to look forward to. It makes the times when we're not together bearable."

"And you me." She knew she was not being entirely honest but did not wish to hurt his feelings.

"You know, Rhoda, I know a place, quiet and peaceful, where we, you and me, could make a home. The island where I was born. Truth is, I'm tired of London. As a young man I thought there was nowhere else to be. Maybe a big city really belongs only to the young, when you've still got energy. Sometimes, I wonder what's keeping it all together; what's holding in all the anger and frustration you see every day on the streets; how come it doesn't explode. I've got a good pension coming. I could take early retirement. Maybe even get a transfer. It doesn't have to be Scotland. I hear Cornwall is lovely. Devon. Somerset. We could make a go of it elsewhere."

Rhoda concealed her shock, thought for a moment, and said, "No, Neil, I can't leave London. I've got too much to do here, too much unfinished work."

"Think about it."

Neil was good for Rhoda. He illuminated her life and lightened her burden. She payed more attention to her appearance, bought clothes with a subtle hint of style, though always appropriate for her age. She treated herself to regular sessions at a hairdresser on Coldharbour Lane and received advice on the best dyes for concealing the growing streaks of grey. She even bought a pair of shoes with heels higher than she had ever owned, a fact approved by Maureen, a long-time critic of her mother's sartorial backwardness.

Neil was quite capable of ranting about politics, declaring himself a floating voter who had, over the years, voted both Labour and Conservative. He made her aware of the differences between the main two parties and their leaders, so that when she listened to or watched the news, it made some sense, though she retained her habit of voting for the candidates with the warmest smile. There were days when her duties or routines were stalled by a wistful memory of a moment of Neil's tenderness, leaving her wondering if that was what people meant by love, and if that were so, why it had taken so long to enter her life.

Nonetheless, she refused his invitations to go on daytrips and any other activity that entailed meeting outside the hotel room. "Are you ashamed of me," he asked once. She reminded him of their early agreement, fell silent, then said, "If only I had known…" But she could not continue because she could not put into words her worries as a mother that insisted on maintaining their secret. So, she cried instead, and he comforted her with a renewed promise to uphold their agreement.

18. *Rhoda prepares for Irene's visit*

In the same month that Neil confirmed his intention to retire and leave London, Rhoda received notice of a visit from her sister Irene, who lived in New York. Pushing Neil to the back of her mind, she threw herself into preparing the house. On the day Irene was due to arrive – Samuel was meeting her at the airport – Rhoda carried out a last minute inspection.

She started in the bedroom, straightening for the umpteenth time the blue nylon bedspread, bought specially in Bon Marche in Brixton. Unable to decide whether the room looked better or worse in the full Spring light, she half-closed the curtains, but then decided that the reduced light gave the room a gloomy, uninviting feel, reopened them again but noticed that the increased light exposed a patch of flaking paint in a corner of the ceiling. She settled for a compromise position, which balanced privacy and cheerfulness.

Before leaving the bedroom, she inspected herself in the wardrobe mirror. She regretted she had not had time to dye out the white streaks that made her hair look like a zebra's coat and hoped she would be able to steal away to Mrs James's kitchen hair salon sometime over the next few days.

She would have liked more than the month's notice that Irene had given her. How was she expected to receive her properly with such short notice? It was typical of Irene; the years in America hadn't changed her. She was still self-centred, inconsiderate and bossy, believing she only had to click her fingers, and Rhoda would do her bidding.

Rhoda took a duster from her apron and wiped the mirror. She walked to the open door, sniffed the air, walked back to the dresser and raked over the pot pourri of pinecones, rose petals and lavender. She went through the other bedrooms. In the bathroom, with its sparkling taps and brilliant white ceramic and enamel surfaces, she surrendered to a moment of hubris and congratulated herself but quickly recovered and muttered a prayer in repentance. She would give Irene a tour of the house, so every room had to be perfect. It was a good thing Maureen was away – she was working and studying in Birmingham – otherwise there would not have been enough space for a guest. Even so, it was going to be a tight squeeze. She would have to sleep on the living room sofa, and there was a foldaway bed in case, as she hoped, Maureen visited. Sylvia had offered to take the twins to her own parents' home, but Rhoda had baulked at the proposal. The prospect of having her sister, her grandchildren and her own children under one roof, if only for a day, filled her with unbearable anticipation. She would sit up all night in a chair or sleep in the garden if necessary.

She made her way downstairs and into the living room. It was tidy enough. The new net curtains with rounded hems were beautiful, the light streaming through them clear and clean; Samuel had done a good job fitting the curtain rods. Having him and his family live with her was truly a blessing. She had almost repaid Bertie Johnson's loan and her savings had grown. The bed-sofa, less than a year old, the tall wooden lamp with its high hat, the large brass-fronted gas fire, the thick carpeting throughout the house – these were all Samuel's purchases. Irene would be impressed, she thought.

She could not resist running the duster over the cabinet containing Neville's boxing trophies – cups, platters and medals. Of her many secret worries, Neville's so far successful boxing career was one of the greatest. She had refused the first trophy he brought to her, told him to take it to his father, but relented when she saw the hurt on his face. She hated the sport, Lucas's passion, and still remembered the warning that the Gordon family were vengeful people with long memories. She feared for Neville's life. Where would she find the strength if the worst happened, if what had happened on that fateful Kingston day many years ago reached into the present and claimed one of her children? Standing beside the cabinet, she prayed again.

In the kitchen, she inspected the tops, the fridges and the stove. A hitherto unnoticed crack in a cup caused panic. She hid it under the kitchen sink, and set about scrutinising all the other cups, glasses, plates and utensils to make sure she had not missed some defect, some smudge that would betray her home as being anything less than perfect. Her final act was to mop down, for the second time that day, the kitchen floor with a mixture of Dettol and rose water. When she finished, she looked at the clock in the living room. Irene would be here soon. She felt tired but was reluctant to sit, or take a nap upstairs or on the living-room sofa. She chose instead to sit at the dining table and wait.

Irene Washington (née, Mason) blew into Rhoda's home like a transatlantic gale. The sisters hugged and cried and laughed in equal measure. They stayed up most of the first night catching up on news about cousins flung far and wide from the village. It was a night of fond reminiscences, marred only by a disagreement over their different memories of the day they wandered too far from the house and were chased to their gate either by a ghost dressed in an all-white, three-piece suit – Rhoda's version – or the elderly planter and widower who took pleasure in scaring children because his wife had long run off to Panama with a field hand and died there – Irene's version. Rhoda, as she used to when they were children, defused the row by conceding that Irene was probably right, though, secretly, she thought her version was the better story.

The few years' gap between the sisters seemed much wider because of Irene's immaculate grooming. Her hair was a slick and stiff black helmet, created by the latest scientific breakthroughs in straightening kinky hair. Her cosmetics bag was the size of an overnight suitcase, and her clothes – trouser suits, pencil skirts, plain but brightly coloured blouses with rounded or pointed collars, shoes for different occasions in their stylishness – put Rhoda to shame. Irene was a middle-ranking hospital administrator, Rhoda little more than an auxiliary nurse. Irene's husband, who was an insurance clerk, was currently camping with their thirteen-year-old son in what Irene described as some kind of strange American initiation rite.

When Irene recovered from the flight and the long night of talking, they ventured out into London. These were not always successful ventures for Rhoda, particularly as the first outing happened on a morning when Irene complained that Rhoda's armchairs were too small, saying that her own armchair back in Brooklyn could not get through Rhoda's front door. This slight was compounded by Irene's disdain for everything in Brixton – the tiny fruits in the market, the narrow dirty streets, the incomprehensible stallholders, the idle young men hanging about on street corners. But when she saw Buckingham Palace, St Paul's Cathedral, the Tower of London, she saw the London that she came expecting to find and a sort of peace was restored. As they left the Tower, Irene said, "Gee, Rhoda, this city makes me feel so ignorant about history. I think I'm going to take some night classes in the fall." And though the Tower of London was also a lesson in history for Rhoda, she felt flattered that something about her adopted city had impressed her sister; she swelled with pride as if the city was a mere extension of her living room. She began to enjoy the reunion again.

The following weekend, Rhoda found herself with the full house she had hoped and prayed for. Maureen came on Friday night and, having travelled with her sleeping bag, was content to sleep on the living-room floor, though Rhoda found her habit of referring to Irene by her first name disturbing – rather than the polite Auntie. She blamed herself for telling Maureen, in the years when they lived alone, too much about their often stormy relationship. Irene, though, did not seem to mind; indeed, aunt and niece got on so well that Rhoda felt a twinge of envy because her own relationship with Maureen had never quite recovered from Samuel's presence.

Around noon on Saturday, while the house was still waking up, Neville arrived with his girlfriend Shirley. Bertie Johnson had visited that morning and, as he was leaving, Vincent stepped into the house with all his hesitancy, shyness and vulnerable good looks. It prompted Irene to exclaim within minutes of their meeting: "I'd take him back to the States with me any day."

The kettle was filled and refilled, frying pans sizzled with eggs and plantain, bun and cheese sandwiches were made, bottles of pop fizzed and overflowed like champagne, and cans of lager for the young adults were snapped open. The twins tottered through the house, getting under everyone's feet, whooping and crying in turn. Rhoda ruled the kitchen, with Sylvia and Maureen her handmaids, bestowing food and smiles on everyone. Her heart was a drum that pounded with ecstatic joy. What did it matter if her armchairs were small; here was a home.

Early that evening, Irene pleaded exhaustion and gave Rhoda a look that expressed her gratitude for the lengths to which Rhoda had gone to make her feel such a special visitor, and retired to her room. Weary herself, Rhoda went into the living-room where her children were – Neville in the armchair, his bulky body looking less than comfortable; Samuel stretched out on the floor in front of the fireplace, Joseph's head on his stomach; Vincent sitting on a dining chair beside the record player; Maureen, Sylvia and Shirley and the other twin on the sofa. She sat down with them, the better to enjoy this rare and special day. Maureen made space for her. Vincent turned down the music.

"I'll probably go into retail management," Maureen was saying. "These chain stores are always looking for graduates. But right now, I'm not looking that far; I'm just enjoying student life. It's brilliant. The lecturers treat you like adults and I live in a great house; everybody gets on really great."

"What about you, Neville?" Samuel asked.

"If I win my next fight, I'm going to turn pro."

"Course you're going to win," Sylvia said.

It pleased Rhoda to see how easily Sylvia fitted in with the others.

"You haven't lost a fight yet," Samuel said.

"Haven't I? I took some blows against that Russian kid in my last fight. I don't know how I got the verdict. That guy really hurt me, I can tell you."

"It was a cold war fight," Vincent said. "There's no way the judges were going to vote against you."

"That's unfair to Neville," Samuel said.

"I don't know nothing bout no cold war. Guess, I was just lucky."

"Anyway, Vincent, what about you? What're your plans?"

"Me?" Vincent stood up and said with great pomp, "I'll probably go into politics. Serve the people and the nation. And if I do go into politics, I aim to become foreign secretary or president."

"Don't be a fool," Samuel said sharply.

"What?"

"First of all, Britain has a prime minister and not a president."

Everybody laughed.

"My mistake. I meant prime minister."

"Sure, Vince. And secondly, you're a Black man in a white country."

"What's that got to do it?"

"Stop dreaming, Vincent; get real. Set your sights on something more realistic."

Vincent looked agitated; Rhoda sensed an argument brewing.

"I can dream if I want to. Who're you to tell me what I can and can't dream?"

"Vincent, you've never been out there, the way I have," Sam said. "This is a white man's country. I ain't saying that we shouldn't aspire, but you've got to recognise that there are only so many spaces they're going to allow us to enter. And becoming prime minister isn't one of them; that's absurd."

"I agree with Sam," Sylvia said. "I work as a secretary and I can tell you some of them white people look at you as if you've got no business being behind a desk – that you should be in the canteen or mopping the floor. Sometimes, they make me feel so stressed out. No wonder so many black people are in mental hospitals."

"Who'd want to be prime minister anyway?" Maureen said. "He has to go to the bloody Queen – sorry Mum – before he can take up office. I mean the Queen... she doesn't do a day's work, sits about drinking tea and taking her corgis for a walk, and this poor bloke, after he gets elected by the so-called people, he has go and see her."

"Well that's just tradition," Vincent said. "And anyway there's a strong republican current in this country that would like to abolish the monarchy, and adopt a written constitution like America."

"And when you get elected as the first Black prime minister, you're going to do away with the monarchy, are you Vincent?" Samuel made the words seem so ridiculous that the room exploded in laughter, and even Vincent joined in, though he was the first to stop laughing, and his face assumed a expression of concentration, as if he was searching his mind for a response.

"You gotta go in the ring to win the fight," Neville said in the brief lull. Nobody responded.

Rhoda had never seen Samuel so obviously enjoying himself. She had often thought that premature fatherhood had made him grave and serious, but among his brothers and sisters, he seemed transformed, as if being with them shaved years off his age. And how Sylvia had changed: no more hot pants and short skirts; she looked like somebody's wife.

"Hey, Vince, and what's going to be your first *act of parliament*?"

It seemed that Samuel only had to speak, stressing certain words, and the room would laugh, even Neville, who had seemed to be on Vincent's side.

Rhoda saw that Vincent felt hurt and said: "Samuel, leave Vincent alone; and don't forget the story of David and Goliath."

"Mummy, this is England, I'm trying to make him see reality. Vincent's problem is that he hasn't spent any time in the real world. He lives too much in his head."

"It's okay, Mum, I can speak for myself," Vincent insisted. "Samuel's just talking crap." But the quiver in his voice betrayed his wound to the room.

Rhoda nursed her own hurt silently. She felt Vincent was resisting her, putting up a shield against her affection. If only he knew how, in the dismal days when she decided she had to leave Lucas, she had agonized over whether to take him, the youngest of her children, as well as Maureen; how she had stood over his bed on several nights trying to make that decision. But dragging two young children around London would have been crazy. At the time, it made sense to leave him with his brothers. She had no regrets about leaving Lucas, but she had not reckoned on losing her youngest son. She would try harder to win him back.

"Yeah, you carry on, Vincent, until you knock yourself out against a door marked 'No blacks allowed' – by Act of Parliament. Hahahahahahaha!" Samuel rolled about on the floor in laughter.

"Gotta go in the ring to win the fight," Neville said again.

"You haven't got any imagination," Vincent said.

"How about corgi walker, by act of Parliament?" Samuel said.

"Yeah, yeah," Maureen shouted, "or royal tea maker?"

"Gotta be in the ring to win the fight," Neville said again, and at last his words registered on the others and there was another round of laughter.

Rhoda decided that it was time for dinner. As she left the room, Vincent turned up the music and she sensed her intervention had not helped him. With Sylvia and Maureen's help, she served plates of rice and peas and chicken, plantain and green salad.

They ate in the living room and Rhoda remembered the early years when a squabble among her children was a sure sign of hunger; food had the power to restore peace and harmony.

While they were eating, Irene came back downstairs looking refreshed, a vision from a different world, stirring in Rhoda a mixture of pride and envy. Her permed hair, stylish clothes – ten days into her stay she had not worn the same clothes twice – contrasted with the faded wallpaper and worn carpet – and with Rhoda's own still mostly unadventurous clothes.

"Gee, you Bostocks sure know how to have a family gathering; I ain't heard so much laughter since I went to see Richard Pryor at the Apollo."

"Let me get you some food," Rhoda said, heaving herself out of the sofa. She left the room but did not go immediately to the kitchen. Instead, she went upstairs to the bathroom, locked the door, and wept with joy for this rare gathering of her children and her sister; she wept, too, for the lover she was about to lose because she could not follow him.

19. *Lucas meets Jean, again, 1979*

Relations between Lucas and Mr George cooled when the Conservatives, led by Margaret Thatcher, swept to power. They had stayed up on election night, following the results with the same fervour that they would a boxing match. Mr George, a Labour voter, had found offensive the victorious leader's remarks about white Britons feeling swamped by immigrants, a below-the-belt remark. Lucas, a die-hard Conservative voter, attached little importance to it, dismissing Mr George's objection as a loser's nit-picking.

They had parted amiably enough but some days later, encountering Mr George in the front garden, Lucas attempted to strike up a conversation and found him cold and distant. The next Saturday night, when BBC2 showed a James Cagney movie again, a film they had twice watched together over the years, Lucas was a solitary viewer.

Lucas would not admit that he missed his friend's company; instead, he busied himself with work on the two houses, work that now took longer than before because the autumnal temperature made his knees and wrists stiff and painful. Seeking relief from this arthritic pain, he consulted Florence George. She, refusing to be drawn into the fallout between Lucas and her husband, prescribed bay rum, and a thrice-weekly drink of constitutional bitters brewed from aloe vera, cerassie, pimento and a secret ingredient.

Lucas's latest lover, Mavis Banks, gave him a weekly massage with the bay rum. She was a short, round and dark woman whose husband had returned to Jamaica. She lived alone and had five children scattered around London. Lucas had often considered inviting her to live with him, but the prospect of her grown up children visiting his house was unappealing. He was disappointed with his own children's lack of loyalty; ashamed of Neville's boxing career; disgusted by the knowledge that Samuel – who had not even bothered to visit with his grandchildren – was living with Rhoda; and angry with Maureen for abusing his kindness. It made him reluctant to take on another family. Then, that November, Mavis Banks became a grandmother when two of her children became parents and said that her grandmotherly duties were far too demanding for the physical intimacy they once enjoyed, which she now called 'nonsense'. He accepted her massages, grudgingly given, and resigned himself to the inexorable end of their relationship.

Christmas came and his only visitor was Vincent, now attending university in Yorkshire. Though he was fond and proud of the boy – the only one of his children with whom he had never quarrelled – Lucas derived little pleasure from his company. Vincent always had his head buried in a book, seemed to speak another language and he held some puzzling views. When, in an attempt to start a conversation, Lucas told Vincent he was considering buying a third property, his son looked up from the book he was reading – Lenin's *State and Revolution* – and opined superciliously, "I agree with the thinker who said private property is theft."

"What the raas you talking bout, boy?" Lucas replied.

"I wonder what the etymology of the word raas is, Dad. It's interesting that among your generation it's a profanity, but in my generation, spelt, 'Ras', it's a sacred term, an abbreviation that serves as a title, denoting belief in the divinity of Emperor Haile

Selassie. The contested meaning of the word both confirms and questions the universal and timeless validity of binary opposites…"

Fortunately, the Queen's Christmas message came on the television at that moment, rescuing Lucas from what he thought a torrent of gibberish, and transporting him back to a familiar and reassuring world. Nonetheless, after Vincent's departure he felt even lonelier. So, it was with some excitement that he received, in early mid-January, a letter from his cousin, Jean Fraser, with whom he had last communicated when he made arrangements to ship Horace's coffin back to Jamaica. The letter, brief and to the point, informed him that she would be visiting London in early February, and staying at an address near Baker Street. He had not seen Jean in over thirty years, and was keen to make a good impression. He bought a new and expensive double-breasted check suit, new brown brogues and, noticing the discolouration of his fingernails – they were almost as dark as his skin – made vigorous but futile efforts to improve their appearance. He wanted to show her the man he had made of himself, a man of substance, a property owner with a portfolio of shares.

On a still, grey afternoon, with snow flakes floating down and evaporating as soon as they touched any surface, he drove to the address in his Rover. He found the building, a redbrick mansion block, and Jean admitted him via the intercom. In the small rickety lift, he adjusted his tie and examined his nails. The lift stopped on the third floor and refused to go any higher. An elderly gentleman with a magnificent nose, and the stub of a cigar between his lips, was waiting for the lift.

"Doesn't go any higher," he said. "Have to walk to the fourth floor. Should be no sweat for a young man like you."

"Young?" Lucas expanded with indignation.

"Relatively, relatively," the elderly gentleman said. "At my age, everybody's young. Are you the workman working at number ten?"

"No, I'm a visitor," Lucas said.

The elderly gentleman got in the lift, and Lucas stiffly climbed the stairs.

The door to number eight was ajar, but he knocked anyway, and a woman's voice told him to come in. He entered a hallway whose deep-pile brown carpet was soft under his shoes. He wondered if he had to take his shoes off. Paintings in gilded frames hung on the corridor walls.

Jean appeared, and though he recognised her, he was struck by the years inscribed on her long face, her sagging cheeks and the deltas of fine lines around her eyes. Light brown in complexion, she had once been regarded as a great beauty, and he had been one of her greatest admirers. They shook hands, then hugged awkwardly.

"Lucas, Lucas; Lucas Bostock," she said, pushing him and holding him by his shoulders, looking into his eyes, smiling.

Lucas smelled a faint trace of alcohol on her breath. The weakness in his knees told him that the not so secret feelings he had once felt for Jean had survived the decades. The image of the ageing woman he had first seen on entering the room was replaced by that of the slim brown girl who had shown him kindness in a cruel house, taught him his letters under the light of a kerosene lamp, chased him up and down hillsides planted with banana trees, and swum with him in a warm sea at night. He knew about the failed marriage, no children, her years as a schoolteacher, then a civil servant in the island's ministry of trade. He knew she had rubbed shoulders with the good and great in Jamaica, but none of that mattered. Her warm greeting spoke of something before the failures and successes of her adult years, long before age had claimed her beauty.

She brought out a tray with biscuits, poured tea for Lucas, and herself a generous measure of vodka. She sat at one end of a Chesterfield, Lucas at the other. He had said little since entering the room, perplexed between the woman she had become and girl he had once known.

"So, Lucas, England is treating you good," she said.

"I'm doing alright. Could be better, though."

"Same old Lucas. Still striving. Even your English is better."

"Better Hinglish! Me nuh pay too much attention to dat. Hinglish people understan' me, and me understand dem."

He did not want to say that he had been feeling weary and unmotivated, as if he had spent all his once famous energy.

"I've been meaning to write you a long letter to thank you for sorting out that terrible business with Horace. But with the work at the ministry and going through my second divorce, I just couldn't seem to find the time."

"No need to thank me, Jean. It was terrible business. Terrible. Did you say second divorce? I thought you'd only married once."

"Once? Three times wedded, three times divorced. Oh, let's talk about happier times, Lucas – me and you. Remember when you first came down off the mountainside? Walked all the way from Maroon Town to Port Antonio with your little brown parcel. How the dogs barked when you came into the yard but you just stood still. You were not afraid at all."

"Me had two rockstone in me hands," Lucas said. "If dem did try anyt'ing, me woulda defend myself."

"Oh, they were just mongrels, Lucas."

"Mongrel dawg bite nuff people."

"Nowadays in Kingston you need at least a Dobermann or a rottweiler to guard your property. Anyway, I was probably the first to see you. I was standing on the veranda wondering who's that little boy? Isn't he afraid of the dogs? Remember the time Horace got stuck in the Indian mango tree, trying to pick the only ripe one high, high up, and you had to climb up and help him down? Remember how just before dusk, we'd make our way home along the hillside, and you could smell wood fire burning, yam or breadfruit roasting, and maybe you'd catch a glimpse of the sea; and before we got home the fireflies would be out, zipping through the dark? Oh childhood, eh Lucas? Those were some days. Now it's all gone – Ma Fraser in sixty-one, Pa Fraser five years later. Did you know we sold the house to a Chinese family?"

"No, me didn't."

"I regret it to this day. Kingston's not a place to retire to."

"But you nowhere near retirement age," Lucas said.

"Nearer than you think. All those blasted marriages to useless men. The first, to an Englishman with an excessive fondness for dark rum; the second, to a real estate dealer from Florida who was just looking for a Jamaican connection; the third, the biggest disaster of all, to a Jamaican who had all the vices of the first two and none of their redeeming qualities. It takes a lot out of you to keep on failing, picking yourself up and trying again. I don't have it in me to try again, not at my age. You haven't thought about marrying again, Lucas?"

"Sometimes the loneliness gets me, but you know me, Jean."

"And you have the children, of course – your sons, the daughter. Tell me about them."

"Nothing much to tell," Lucas said. "The youngest, Vincent, is at university. I don't see much of the others. Far as I know, they're getting on with it."

"But Lucas, that's a marvellous achievement – a son at university.

Education. Education. Education. That's what Pa Fraser always used to say." Jean refilled her glass with ice and vodka.

Lucas started seeing the middle-aged woman she was, and the sadness etched in her face. A teetotaller, he was alarmed at the rate at which she drank the vodka, but it did not seem to affect her. Her magic was wearing thin.

"Oh, Lucas, Lucas," Jean said, "we were given freedom and we made a perfect mess of it. As a nation and as individuals."

"Nobody gave me freedom," Lucas said. "Mi had to fight for it, my ancestors, too."

"Yes, I forget. Your Maroon ancestry, your proud Maroon ancestry. Do you tell your children about it?"

"Is not something dem need to know. Is all in the past. What dem need to know is that yuh haffi fight for anything worthwhile in life." Lucas felt she was mocking him, heard in her voice an echo of Ma Fraser's contempt for his ancestors, when she dismissed them as capturers of runaway slaves.

"I agree. The past can be a chain. But sometimes you have to confront it to go forward. That's partly why I'm in England. That last divorce left me exhausted. I needed time to reflect on how and why I'd gone wrong again and again and again."

"Have you found out?"

"Not yet. In fact, coming here has made me think about Horace more than anything else. I went wrong there, too. He was always reckless, wild. I should have kept him closer to me."

"How could you have done that? Horace was a man, not a bwoy."

"Oh, Lucas, Lucas. Some boys never become men. Yes, their voices deepen and they start shaving, but they remain boys. Remember all those boys' adventure stories Horace used to read? Pa Fraser used to send to England for them. Horace used to sneak under the house at night with the kerosene lamp to read about Tarzan and Biggles and god knows who. He was still reading them right into his teens."

"Yes, him use to try to interest me in dem, too. But after a day working with Pa Fraser, me always too tired."

"And you know, I told him more than once: Horace, those are English people's stories. Told him: Horace, you are a subject of empire, not an Englishman. But he wouldn't listen. Got vexed. Ran away. And as soon as he could, he went searching for adventure. Abandoned his studies at Howard University, went traipsing around Africa. Got himself mixed up with all sorts of evil people. Smuggling diamonds, gold, people even. Did you know he was running guns? My little brother."

Lucas sat forward in his chair and said, "But him hardly have money when him came to the house."

"Yes, he was mixed up with some foolishness. I can't imagine how much money passed through his hands over the years. It all went on high living, gambling, women, investments that didn't work out. His associates ripped him off. In one letter, he admitted that in Africa you had to be white or belong to a tribe, and he wasn't either, so that made him vulnerable. Yet he stayed. My little brother running guns in Africa. Something went wrong with a deal, and he had to run, had to go underground. That's how he ended up in your house. My little brother."

Jean stood up, glass in hand. The long dress she was wearing clung to her meagre frame. Lucas noticed the large brown spots on her arms, the skin there loose and leathery. He recalled that Ma Fraser, who had been paler than Jean, often walked with a parasol. Jean had probably never taken such precautions against the tropical sun.

"You keep calling him you little brother, Jean. But he was a man. As a man he was responsible for himself."

"You would say that, Lucas." She leant towards him, her glass angled in such a way that he feared she would spill her drink. Her speech had slowed, become more emphatic.

"You know he used to envy you?" she said.

"Me! I was the hewer of wood and fetcher of water in that house. Not'ing to envy about my lot."

"Yes, but you did it without complaining. He admired your stoicism, the fact that you were a doer. He wanted Pa to show him how to plane and saw and hammer. He was tactile, loved doing things with his hands. But, you know Ma; her son was going to get an education. He wasn't going to become a carpenter."

"But it was good enough for me," Lucas said.

"Is that why you threw him out of your house, Lucas? You know, he tried to make contact with me during that period, but, as I said, I was going through a rotten phase myself. Threw my little brother out on the streets of London, threw him out for him to wander into the Thames, because you envied him his privileges, his education."

"I tried to contact you too, Jean. And me nevva exactly throw him out. 'Im didn't paid the rent in months. We, me and Horace, we agreed that the situation couldn't continue. And the gun running business! That's news to me. I knew something was wrong, though."

Jean raised the glass to her lips and took a long draught. The ice cubes clinked against the glass. She lowered the glass and a shiny film remained on her lips.

"He was still my little brother, Lucas. Yes, his involvement in Africa's tragedies was unforgivable, but I think I understand the paths he followed to end up doing what he did. What I don't understand is you, Lucas. What happened to you? How could you have been so merciless, so lacking in compassion? It must have been obvious to you that he needed help."

"'Im was a man, damn it," Lucas said. He got up suddenly.

"And because he was a man you could not show him kindness, could not indulge him a little, give him time to pull himself together? He was a man on the run, after all. People were after him. Tell me, Lucas, was it us, the way we treated you that made you so mean? Or was it London, was it this city that filled that beautiful island of Jamaica with slaves and the cruelty of the slave plantation?"

"Me nuh know what you talking 'bout. Me was renting out rooms. Still am. Me give him plenty chances. And I had me sons to think about. He was corrupting them with all his blasted fancy talk about sailing up rivers and walking across deserts and hacking his way through jungles. Even offered to take them to a brothel. Imagine that! I had my bwoys to think about."

"When you were a defenceless boy, unable to look after yourself, we, Pa Fraser and me, we showed you kindness. Didn't we? Tell me, Lucas, was it the way we treated you that made you so mean? Or is it London? They say big cities do that to people. Tell me so I can understand, tell me, Lucas."

"I was less than ten years old, Jean. Ten years old, and as me tell Horace, from the day me get to that house, me was working for my keep. Horace was a grown man. But you don't want to see him as a grown man because if you did, you'd have to see that 'im mek 'im own bed and 'im have to lie in it."

"No, Lucas, I knew he was a man. But he was still my little brother, and he came to you for help and you turned him away, turned him out before Christmas. You know, he was sleeping rough under Waterloo Bridge; that was his last home; my little brother, my sweet, sweet little brother who I held in my arms when he was less than an hour in the world."

Jean's glass fell from her hand and the ice cubes bounced off the leather sofa. She held her hands to her face.

"You'd better go, Lucas," she said softly. She was shaking.

"Jean…" Lucas appealed.

"No, go now, Lucas."

Lucas adjusted himself in his suit, which suddenly felt too large for him, and began walking out of the room.

"And Lucas," Jean said, "If and when you come to Jamaica, don't bother coming to my home. I wouldn't like to have set the dogs on you. And they're not underfed mongrels this time."

20. *Samuel Bostock and a meeting, early 1980s*

Samuel Bostock had turned his life around. Studying as a mature student, he had secured a history degree from Goldsmiths' College, and now worked as a housing officer for Southbridge Council. He lived with Sylvia, twin sons, Joseph and John, and Rhoda, in a smart 1930s house off Tulse Hill. They had been living there for less than a year and though Rhoda had initially expressed some misgivings about its greater distance from her beloved Brixton Market, she had mostly seemed happy there. This was important to Samuel who felt indebted to her for the security and stability she had given him when he was still searching for a direction and facing the prospect of unplanned fatherhood in the narrow confines of Sylvia's Finsbury Park bedsitter.

This Saturday morning, Samuel was thinking about his car as he flicked through *The Guardian*. It was in the garage and he'd been promised he could collect it around midday. He drove a 1960s Citroen saloon, an expensive vehicle to maintain, and he managed this largely through his friendship with Bigger Moore, a Trinidadian mechanic who ran a garage in a mews off Railton Road, who was unfazed by the car's complex hydraulic system.

Rhoda was gathering the ingredients for a cake she planned to bake that day. Sylvia was taking her weekly soak in the bath, and the twins were watching *Sesame Street*.

"The boys will love this fruit cake," Rhoda said. "I'll bake a cornmeal pudding as well. You'll have some, won't you, Sam?"

"Yes, Mummy," he said, only half listening. He was reading a film review, and thinking he had not been to the cinema in years. He had enjoyed the luxury of a year's full-time study in the last phase of his degree programme, and had participated in student life, joining the film club, attending debates. He had watched continental art house movies, visited art galleries and theatres. One legacy of that year was his participation in union activities at work.

Now, his return to full-time work and the pressing need to start paying back Rhoda and Sylvia for their support had blocked his access to the satisfactions he'd discovered at university. There was promotion to fight for at work, especially because his superiors seemed reluctant to acknowledge his experience and competence. But he was not sure that promotion, much as he would welcome it, would appease the restlessness he felt inside.

"Morning, Mrs B," he heard Sylvia say.

"Morning Sylvia," Rhoda said.

Samuel felt Sylvia's hand on his shoulder. She smelled of ylang ylang bath oil, which he liked.

She had gone up from a size 10 to a size 12 over the years and this fleshier appearance suited her. An array of skin moisturisers kept her complexion looking as smooth and radiant as the day they first met. She, too, had started studying and had moved from receptionist to benefits officer in the DHSS office.

"You're not baking again, are you Mrs B? We haven't finished the last cake you made."

"Oh, that's stale, now. No good."

"But you know I don't want the boys eating all those sweet things. Rots their teeth and makes them hyperactive, especially Joseph."

"That's not so," Rhoda said. "I always used to bake for my children. And they loved it. Isn't that so Sam?"

Samuel had anticipated this appeal in what was becoming a source of tension in the house. "I'll eat the cake, Mummy, but put it in the highest cupboard so the boys can't reach it."

"Sam, I'm trying to control the children's diet. You know they'll search the cupboards once they know there's cake in the house. They'll just use a chair."

"A piece of cake won't do them any harm, Sylvia," Rhoda said.

"Sam can I have a word with you, please?"

"I'll be there in a minute."

"Now, please."

Samuel glanced at his mother, excused himself and followed Sylvia upstairs to their bedroom.

"You're always encouraging her, Sam. You know what the dietician at the surgery said."

"Okay, okay, calm down, Sylvia. I happen to agree with Mummy; a slice of cake isn't going to harm them."

"You always agree with her, Sam, always. The mushy vegetables she cooks, the endless dishes of rice and peas. I feel I'm fighting with her over that kitchen. We're not in the Caribbean now – there're so many other meals we can try. If I have to eat another dish of mushy cabbage and carrots with all the vitamins cooked out of them I'll go mad, I'm telling you."

"All right, Sylvia. I'll have a word with Mummy. But understand her position. She cooks what she knows and likes. Look, I've got to go and get the car from the garage."

Sylvia told Samuel that she was going over to Edmonton with the boys, to see her parents.

It was rare for him to have a free Saturday afternoon; he often took his sons to museums or to exercise classes. So, having seen off Sylvia and the boys, and said goodbye to his mother, he stepped out into a mild spring afternoon feeling like a free man. He admired a magnolia tree in bloom and noted the fat buds at the tips of rhododendrons. Sun bathed the street, but the air was cool, so he zipped up his brown leather bomber jacket as he turned down Tulse Hill.

He was relieved to be out of the house. It was not so much the tension between Sylvia and his mother – he was used to that – but the space to think about a solution. They needed a larger house, ideally one with a granny flat so Rhoda could have her own kitchen. He had to speak to his line manager. Promotion was now an imperative.

He passed the George Canning pub and resisted the temptation of the tall glasses of lager he saw people drinking outside. He was trying to cut back on alcohol and so settled for swallowing saliva to quench his thirst. This need to restrain himself concerned him. When he reached Railton Road, the sight of two Rasta youths, their dreadlocks peeking through woollen hats, their springy stylised walk, made him think of Neville.

He felt a smidgen of guilt that, preoccupied with his own

matters, he had missed Neville's last fight. The truth was he hated boxing, the braying crowds, the violence boxers inflicted on each other. It bothered him that his interest in karate might have encouraged Neville, though when he last saw his brother, he was glad to see he seemed happy, despite the four children, the three they'd had so rapidly, and Shirley's first-born. Really, he ought to make the effort to visit them more often. He thought about their council flat, chaotic and tiny, and he wished he could do something to help, and that wish brought him back to the need for promotion at work.

He was so lost in thought that he almost walked past the mews entrance where the garage was. The mews buildings were dilapidated with broken windows and rotting green doors. The garage was the only business operating there and it, too, looked as if it had seen better days. Samuel's Citroen was sandwiched between a Ford Capri and a Cortina, a hopeful sign, as the car had been moved from where he'd left it. The smell of petrol, grease and burning metal filled the air. He called out and a small man with wispy white beard, wearing a peaked cap, eventually came out of the garage.

"Nothing happening, man," he said.

"You mean you haven't fixed it?"

"Exactly. Sent off for the brake shoes but they haven't arrived yet. Give me till Monday evening. Promise you."

Samuel was disappointed. He had been hoping to take the family for a Sunday drive to Brighton or Southend.

From behind a makeshift wall came the sudden clanging of metal. Bigger excused himself and Samuel heard him shout, "Boy, what're you doing? You come here to work, not to play."

Bigger returned and apologised. "Don't know what's wrong with these youngsters. Boy's using my blowtorch to make a sculpture, when he should be working on a customer's car."

Samuel smiled. The sound of police sirens cut through the air. He turned and caught a glimpse of two marked cars speeding past the mews entrance.

"More trouble on the Frontline," Bigger said.

"There's always trouble there," Samuel agreed.

"True, but most times the police stay away. They say is just Black people fighting among themselves. Lately, though, they've been going in three, four times a day. That place will soon blow."

"Like Bristol."

"Exactly. Only a matter of time. Those youths don't think they have to obey the law. Openly dealing, buying and smoking drugs on the street. Only a matter of time, believe you me. Some days they come running in here trying to hide their drugs. I have to chase them out, yes. Man, I don't know what's happening to us in this country. When I was a boy back in Trinidad, we didn't carry on with this nonsense. You were looking to advance yourself. That's what I grew up hearing. But these kids – is like they want to go backwards with all this talk about Africa and Haile Selassie. What the hell we travel across the ocean for? They're lost. It don't make no sense to me."

Samuel was familiar with Bigger's lament. The garage was on the edge of the Frontline, a strip of shops and houses notorious for illicit trading. He listened to Bigger a while longer, extracted from him another promise to have the car ready by Monday evening, then decided to walk down to Coldharbour Lane to get a haircut.

The police sirens must have scared away the drug-pushers, because the road was empty. The desolation ended as he neared the junction of Railton Road and Coldharbour Lane and Brixton market's atmosphere spilled out onto the streets.

As he walked past the Atlantic pub, his willpower failed him, and he entered the pub and bought a pint of lager and took a window seat and gazed at the middle-aged Caribbean women laden with shopping, the teenage girls who had taken advantage of the warmer weather and wore short skirts that exposed plump thighs, and the young men with sharp haircuts and a swagger in their steps.

Most of the drinkers were middle-aged Caribbean men, and he heard the sound of ivory tiles slammed on wooden tables, eruptions of whooping and swearing. Somebody selected a dolorous country and western tune on the jukebox and a thin, emaciated man started dancing, alone, holding himself to suggest that he was dancing with a partner, turning her with loving delicacy to the music.

These were men who had been seized by the idea of escaping villages where they tilled the soil for a living, of crossing an ocean to England. No doubt they had known disappointments, but what an intense moment they must have lived through. He had no longing to be anywhere else, but he yearned for the intensity born of an absolute conviction about a goal. He wanted to be able to say, "This is what I want", and to throw himself into its pursuit. For a moment, he felt humbled by his fellow drinkers, these men with their large, rough hands, easy camaraderie, and boisterous laughter.

He finished his pint and walked to the barbershop a few yards along Coldharbour Lane. The relentless banter of barbers and customers helped to lift his spirits, and the gentle vibration of the shears over his head, and the oil massaged into his scalp – the feeling of being pampered and polished – raised them further.

Outside again, the air felt cooler. He turned up his jacket collar, plunged his hands in his pockets and walked on. On Monday he would press his case for promotion. He was a prepared to negotiate or confront. He would take the matter to the union if necessary.

He walked past the Tate Library and crossed the road a few yards beyond St Matthews Church, passing a large 1960s housing estate. As he approached a road leading into the estate he heard a cry for help. He looked down the road and saw a woman on the ground, her jean-clad legs thrashing wildly, and two men trying to wrestle her bag from her hands. He shouted, "Hey stop that!" and ran toward them. The men released the woman's bag and looked at him fearfully and defiantly.

"This is none of your business," the larger of the two men said. Samuel saw that he was a youth, despite his size, hairy chin and bloodshot eyes.

"What's the matter with you guys? I'm making it my business. Leave her alone. Get lost. I should warn you I'm a karate black belt."

The two youngsters turned and ran. He made as if he intended to chase them but took only a few steps. He walked back to the woman, who was now standing and dusting herself down. She was slight in build, with brown hair cut in fashion that he associated with an earlier decade. The multi-coloured bag was fashionably ethnic. On the ground around her were handbills. Samuel asked if she was all right and when she turned to face him, he realised that she was nothing more than a girl, a teenager.

"I'm fine." She laughed nervously.

"I don't know what's wrong with these kids," he said.

"It's not their fault," she said, stooping to gather up the handbills that had survived the skirmish.

"What do you mean it's not their fault?" He saw that she was unhurt but shaken, and admired her tenacious hold on the bag, even on the ground. She had certainly given them a fight.

"Just that," she said.

"What're you doing around here anyway? Don't you know this is not a good place?"

"It's a free country. I can walk where I want. I'm delivering leaflets for a CND demonstration next Saturday. We're trying to get a greater variety of people involved, not just white middle class."

"And you think you're going to get people living on a Brixton council estate to attend a CND demo?"

"Why not? They have a right to know about the Tory government's reckless and irresponsible nuclear weapons policy."

Samuel laughed, and then became aware that she was standing akimbo, as though she was ready to wrestle with him too.

"Now that *is* irresponsible," she said. She stuffed the handbills into her bag and turned to walk away.

"Hold on, hold on," Samuel said. "You're right, you're right. Was it Burke who said 'It's necessary only for the good man to do nothing for evil to triumph'?"

"Or woman," she fired back. "And it wasn't Burke, though it's often attributed to him."

"You seem pretty certain, so I won't argue. Point is, I hear what you're saying."

"Good. And I wouldn't go as far as calling this Tory government evil, just wrong."

They had reached Effra Road and Sam realised she was going in his direction. He said, "Maybe. Anyway, look, I'm heading up to Tulse Hill. By the way, my name's Sam."

"Elena. I'm meeting some friends in the George Canning pub."

They fell into step with each other and talked until they reached the pub. As they were parting, she said: "Me and my friends meet in the George Canning every Thursday night. Why don't you come along next week and meet them."

"I'll see how it goes," Samuel said, and continued on his way, thinking she wasn't as slight and small as he had first thought, and wondering how he had managed to retrieve the quote from his usually unreliable memory.

21. *Donnette Bostock arrives* at *Heathrow*

Donnette was standing in the immigration queue at Heathrow, UK passport holders only. She felt nervous. She had invested all her savings and spent months practising for exactly this moment. She could not afford to fail again.

The line moved forward and Donnette was facing the immigration officer, a toothy blonde, who looked first at the passport, then at Donnette and back at the passport and riffled through its pages. Donnette's heart raced, her stomach tightened; she smiled her best smile and hoped for the best.

"Thank you," the immigration officer said, holding up the passport, which Donnette almost snatched from her hand.

"Thanks," Donnette said. She tried to express a modicum of petulance, to suggest her absolute right to enter the UK.

Her nervousness came in waves. The next hurdle, customs. Keeping her head up and eyes straight ahead, she passed through a line of officers standing under the 'Nothing to Declare' sign. She had started to think she was through, when she came to the inspection area. Several passengers from her Jamaican flight had been stopped, their suitcases flung open on shiny steel surfaces, and customs officers were pulling out bottles of rum and fruit.

A middle-aged male officer beckoned her. "Shouldn't keep you long," he said as he hoisted her suitcase onto the table. Donnette realised for the first time that her case was conspicuously flat, unlike the bulging suitcases of her fellow passengers. A quiet panic seized her, and she thought: I should've packed more clothes.

She stood stiffly as the officer probed the contents of her case. He lifted her blouses, her jeans, her knickers, his expression impassive.

"What, no white rum?" he said, smiling.

Donnette's mind raced furiously. Should she have brought a bottle of white rum? Was this part of her condition of entry into the country? Fool, he's being friendly. She reached for her best English and, in a voice intended to convey understanding of his humour, she said: "I don't drink."

"Not missing much, luv," he said. He shoved the suitcase aside and Donnette slowly pushed the clothes back in, zipped up the case, placed it back on the trolley and joined the stream of travellers heading for the exit. She had made it. She had to stop herself leaping into the air. On her second attempt – the first had ended ignominiously two years ago when an immigration officer at Gatwick saw through her pretence of being a student.

The bright lights of the concourse and the crowd of expectant faces and hugging people disoriented her for a moment. Then she saw Lester's tall figure in ankle-high trainers and baggy pants, a patchwork shirt over his trousers. Their eyes met in mutual recognition and he smiled, revealing a gold tooth. As she had been instructed, she hugged him, long enough to suggest kinship but not intimacy. She smelled a stale trace of musk.

"You get through," he said.

"Nuh, must," Donnette said.

He pushed the trolley towards the car park, all the while complaining about how long he had been waiting and the awful food he'd had to eat. The plane had arrived several hours late.

As his car, a BMW series three, descended into the tunnel leading out from the airport, Donnette allowed herself to relax and savour her achievement. She could not remember when she had not dreamt of getting to England. Her late mother had often told her about the marvels of London shops, and she was here at last. She had a father to find and an address in her bag. But this success had its price. Her patron, Cornelius Lane, was expecting her to make more trips. He had warned her not to think she could disappear once she reached London. She belonged to him.

Lester interrupted her thoughts when he said, "You bring everything through?"

"I'm not no petty drugs smuggler," Donnette said.

"Cool, cool, just checking, you know."

They were on the motorway now, among a steady flow of cars. Lester reached under the dashboard and pulled out a large spliff and said, "I've been thinking about this for two hours." He lit it and the sweet cloying odour filled the car. Donnette cracked open the window.

When she refused his offer, he said, "You must be one serious soldier."

"You know why I'm here," she said. "I've got to keep a clear head until it's over."

"My head's only clear when I've a fucking spliff in my hand," Lester said, laughing dryly.

Donnette did not reply. They were now on an elevated stretch of the motorway and on either side, as far as she could see, the city glittered.

Four hours later, Donnette was lying in a double bed in flat in Ladbroke Grove. The laxative Lester had given her had been effective and she was free of her cargo. Let me find some way to stay here and make a life, she thought.

She did not know she was a only few hundred yards away from where she had been conceived and, unable to sleep, she recalled how her mother, Patsy, stricken with cancer, which claimed her six months later, had finally revealed the name of Donnette's father. For years she had maintained that this man had abandoned her as soon as he discovered that she was pregnant. Later, Patsy had told her the truth, described London in the fifties as a place where strangers encountered each other on the streets or in illicit nightclubs, and struck up relationships that relieved loneliness but had no permanence. With this man it had been sheer chance. He had called at her rented room looking for someone else. Rain had fallen, they got talking and drank a few rums... Everybody was in transition, looking for work, testing London, prepared to try their luck further afield in cities like Bristol, Birmingham, Wolverhampton or Leeds if the capital did not yield the work they sought. She, fearful of having to bring up a child alone, and acknowledging her attempt at migration was unsuccessful, had returned to Jamaica, only to discover that she was pregnant for a stranger, Lucas Bostock, and she wasn't even sure that was his real name. Donnette wondered how she would find her father, if the address she had been given was still current, and what she would say to him if she found him.

Donnette stayed in bed in the empty flat until the next afternoon, when Lester returned with a take-a-way meal. She was famished and ate hastily. When she'd finished, Lester asked her if she wanted to go for a drive. He drove her down Harrow Road and stopped outside a parade of shops on the Stonebridge Estate. This huge housing complex of prefabricated blocks and a maze of walkways dazzled Donnette who had known only the rundown houses and tenement yards of downtown Kingston.

Lester pointed to a housing block and said, "You can earn yourself five grand, for another job."

She laughed and said, "Five thousand pounds. What do you want me to do, kill somebody?"

"No. You leave that to us."

Lester explained that Cornelius had set up a man called Juba Morgan in London, furnishing him with a false identity, British passport, contacts, and supplies of grade A ganja. Juba had taken delivery of this large consignment but Cornelius, still then in Kingston, had not seen any returns. Reports filtering back to him suggested that Juba had gone solo, found a new supplier, and was boasting that he'd made a fool of his former employer. Cornelius wanted revenge. Donnette's task would be to befriend Juba and get him alone. He and others loyal to Cornelius would do the rest.

Lester pointed to a group of youngsters standing outside a betting shop. "His soldiers," he said. "Black fucking Brits. They're the ones Juba trust. Nobody from yard can get near him. Not anymore." He said Juba, surrounded by his cronies, visited the Lafayette nightclub in Harlsden every Sunday night.

"Cornelius didn't say anything about this to me," Donnette said.

"So what you saying, you not up to this? Is five fucking grand we're talking about. Minimum. Five times what you made for this trip. If we get rid of Juba, we can control this estate. Thousands a week. We'll look after you, too. Trust me."

"I'm not saying that. I wasn't expecting anything like this. It's one thing to bring in a bit of coke, it's another thing to kill somebody."

"I'm not asking you to kill anyone. Just get him alone. You're a nice looking gal. Show him the fucking punani; me know Juba, 'im can't resist. Trust me. Think about what you can do with that money. Open a shop in Kingston, buy a house in the country."

"Take me back to the apartment; I need time to think about this."

"Alright. But remember is we bring you here. And we can send you back any fucking time. Trust me."

Lester turned the car round and they drove in silence until he said, "Me like you, you know. If we can control Stonebridge, I'll make you my queen. Trust me."

Donnette did not reply.

Back in Ladbroke Grove, Donnette closed the bedroom door. What had she got herself into? She was no killer, just someone desperate to leave Jamaica and find this Lucas Bostock, her supposed father. She had fallen in with ruthless men. But how could she get away? She knew only one other person in London, Petronia Jones, a distant cousin and ex-schoolfriend. The address she had for her was so old, she was not sure she would still be there. Donnette clasped her hands together and prayed, "Lord God, please help me get out of this."

She slept fitfully, woke up in a dark room, and heard male voices coming from the living room. She got out of bed, tip-toed across the room, pressed her ears to the door and heard Lester say, "First we take Stonebridge, then Bristol. We have a few guys operating in Nottingham. Nuff potential there; nuff fucking potential…"

"We gonna need more soldiers for that," the other person said.

"Nuff fucking soldiers here already, star. Is a matter of recruiting them, training them up. That's what Juba recognised. He doesn't fucking need anyone from yard. Cornelius can't see that from yard."

"Cornelius just wants his fucking money."

"He'll get it. Im send me a sweet t'ing; she thought she was just making a delivery, doesn't know anybody in London. All I've got to do is persuade her to go through with my plan. I need a bit more time with her. You know, taste the punani. She's desperate enough. Me can smell it pon her."

"Fuck. Look like you aiming to become the don."

"Then why the fuck you think me come a fucking London. You know dem way deh?"

The men laughed.

Donnette crept back to the bed. She opened the case and counted her money. She had a little over five hundred pounds in cash, half her payment for the job. She would collect the rest when she got back to Kingston. From a small, secret slit in the case, she pulled out a soiled piece of paper and read: 'Lucas Bostock, 72 Carlisle Road, Stoke Newington, London, United Kingdom'. Was he still at that address? What if he rejected her? Would she be able to find Petronia Jones?

22. *Maureen and Phil, a backstory, 1983*

Maureen Bostock was putting her ten-month-old son, Andrew, to bed. She had learned, earlier that day in November, that she was pregnant again; she was looking forward to telling her partner the good news. Phil worked at the Natural History Museum and that morning he had told her he would be meeting his friends, Ian and Simon, for a drink in a pub in Notting Hill. She had not approved, but then she didn't approve of anything Phil did with those two reprobates.

As she tidied Andrew's room, she imagined Phil and his two mates sitting in a smoky pub, glasses of real ale between them. Ian would be rolling shag into a matchstick-thin fag that would become soggy with saliva and expire after two puffs, Simon would be ogling the girls with his puppy-dog eyes and giving a post-match analysis of Birmingham City's latest defeat, while Phil would try to steer the conversation away from football to something serious, like the riots earlier in the year, or the Falklands war or the Third World Debt crisis. Why Phil continued to hang around with those two layabouts was a mystery, but she was prepared to admit that she did not understand male friendship.

When Andrew's breathing became steady, Maureen dimmed the light even lower, left the room and went downstairs to the usual mess. She was not a house-proud housewife, not even a wife as she and Phil were not married. The hallway was strewn with shoes, wellington boots and trainers. The kitchen just about passed muster, only two bowls needed washing, but the living room was a disgraceful mess. The sofa's cushions were on the floor, along with Sunday's newspaper and the ashtray overflowed with cigarette butts.

Their neighbours, another young couple, had visited the previous evening. Records had been played, wine drunk, a joint passed around and Maureen, called away by Andrew's crying, had turned in early, leaving Phil alone with their guests. There was a precariously balanced stack of LP jackets, inner sleeves and vinyl discs on the floor below the stereo.

She turned on the television, and heard, "The question is, was the sinking of the Belgrano a legal act of war?" Bloody hell, she thought, they're not still going about that. She began the labour of tidying up the pile of records. Coming across the Bob Marley and the Wailers album, *Get Up, Stand Up*, she smiled because it connected to her first encounter with Phil. It was at a reggae concert, the first she had ever attended, in a Staffordshire field, and there was Phil, a lanky white boy, pogoing to 'Get Up, Stand Up', limbs flailing wildly, brown hair plastered to his forehead with sweat.

All that energy for music that left her cold – she was only there to accompany her friend Janet, a flesh and blood version of her long abandoned alter-ego, Mary-Jane. Janet was a self-declared neo-punk with spiky black hair and a ghostly pallor; she'd initiated contact with Phil's friends, dragging her into a circle of whites, where she was the only Black, and was uncomfortably conscious of that fact. The journey back to Birmingham, the messy students' house, the subsequent days tripping on magic mushrooms, the parting that gave no intimation that she and Phil would meet again years later in London and start going out together – all these memories came rushing back as she held the album.

She put the disc into an inner sleeve, inserted that into the album jacket and continued working her way through the pile. Several albums later, she came across Carole King's *Tapestry*. She could not recall playing it and decided that Phil and their visitors must have played it after she'd gone to bed. She placed the record on the turntable, selected the track, 'Will You Still Love Me Tomorrow', and instantly regretted her decision, as other memories came rushing back.

It had started as what they called the Geisha game. She and Janet would frequent pubs in the Birmingham city centre, and allow middle-aged businessmen to pick them up. These men would buy them drinks, meals and unburden their worries – the wives who did not understand them, the ungrateful children, the company cars that never reflected their importance, the thwarted secret ambitions to become painters or musicians and give expression to their sensitive souls. At the end of the meal or the rounds of drinks, they expected sex and that was the thrill of the exercise, how to enjoy the evening without paying the ultimate price. She and Janet derived great pleasure from these encounters, dissecting the shortcomings of their respective partners with merciless wit.

Then Maureen met Stephen Clarkson.

He was in his mid-forties but looked closer to thirty, lean, with thick, jet-black curly hair and fine, chiselled features. He was a married man and father of three children. She knew she had fallen for him when she accepted his invitation to spend the night in a hotel, but did not know how far she had fallen. The following morning, as he drove her to her Balsall Heath flat, he played a homemade compilation cassette of Carole King songs.

Over the next year, she seemed to be always on the verge of tears, tears of longing for Stephen, tears of joy for being with him. She did not tell Janet about the affair. Instead, she pretended to be bored with the geisha game. She and Janet fell out, stopped being best friends and when Janet announced that she was moving back up north, Maureen merely wished her good luck. She had little time for anybody but Stephen, though she only saw him once a week, and sometimes for only a few hours. There were days when she had to fight to concentrate on her work at the insurance company, evenings when she sat with the telephone in her lap waiting for the call that never came, nights when insomnia kept her staring into the dark.

She tried her best to conceal her hopelessness from Stephen, to keep up the pretence of being a big girl, able to play in the adult world. But she could not deny her need and begged him to spend more time with her.

"I can't," he said. "My wife and I have an understanding. I'm a very lucky man. I'd be pushing it to see you more often. She gives me a very long leash. I can't abuse it. That's part of the understanding."

"But do you want to?"

"To what?"

"See me more often."

There was moment of silence before he said yes.

"Does she know about me?"

"Oh, she knows I'm sleeping with somebody else. She probably has a lover, too. We never discuss the details."

She wanted to let him know how she felt, admit her pain, but she held back. She wanted to believe that she had walked into this with her eyes wide open.

He touched her and said, "I'm sorry."

It was his pity that triggered her sobs. "It hurts, Stephen, it hurts."

"Do you want us to end it? Would that stop the pain?"

"No, that would only make it worse."

But once, driven to distraction because he had cancelled their weekend, she had telephoned his home. A calm female voice answered.

"Stephen is away and won't be back until Tuesday. Can I take a message?"

"Yes, if you could tell him that Maureen called."

"Oh, yes, Maureen. Yes, I will do that, Maureen. Goodbye."

When they next met, Stephen rebuked her, not for calling his home, but for disbelieving him.

Some weeks later she decided she could not take it anymore and found the strength to end the affair. Stephen was understanding. But two weeks later she was on the phone again, calling him at work, just to hear his voice. Then one Saturday afternoon, determined to fill the void caused by his absence, she went into the city centre intending to shop. And there, on Corporation Street, she saw him, a family man with his wife and children. Husband and wife were holding hands, fair-haired children skipping in front of them. She knew then that she had to get away, leave Birmingham and return to London. It was six months after this, recovered and angry with herself for being so weak, that she ran into Phil Smith on Kensington High Street.

She filed the record and her memory away. Well, almost. She thought of Janet and her departure from her life. She had been such fun. It was a shame they had lost touch. She would call her parents' home, arrange a reunion, where they could catch up and reminisce about their student days and the wicked times that followed. These thoughts were interrupted when the doorbell chimed with the annoying sound of the opening of Beethoven Fifth symphony – Phil's handiwork.

She was not expecting callers and opened the door to the shock of seeing her mother standing there, a large suitcase beside her.

"Mum! What are you doing here?"

"Help me with this," her mother said.

Maureen helped her to bring the suitcase into hallway.

"I can't live there anymore. Not one day more."

Maureen ushered Rhoda into the kitchen. There, as she filled the kettle, Maureen realised that what she had wished for over a decade had finally happened. She watched Rhoda fussing with her hat in her hands, her knees drawn up.

"What's going on Mum?"

"Every day it's the same thing. You overcook the vegetables, you put too much salt in the food, too much sugar in everything. You cook too much meat. I can't take it anymore. Took it for years. But no more. I want my own kitchen. I want to be able to cook what I want, how I want."

"Is this about the kitchen, Mum? You've left your home because of the kitchen?"

"It's not just that, Maureen. It's big part of it, though. Sylvia just doesn't want me living there. Said as much."

"But what about Sam? What does he want?

"Sam! Sam hardly lives there anymore. Can't remember the last time he spent a whole day with his family."

Rhoda went on to recount Samuel's comings and goings. In the last year he had thrown himself into attending union and political meetings. Either he was on a demonstration or he was attending a meeting where they were planning demonstrations. He was planning to become a local councillor and gave ever more time to that project. He was often home around midnight, and several times had spent up to a week away from home on residential training courses. On the evenings or weekends when he was in the house, he was often on the phone for hours, receiving or making calls. Sylvia had suggested that he install a separate phone line for his political work. But no, it was not Samuel who was responsible for making her leave. After all, most of the time she had been living with Samuel and Sylvia, he had been a scarce figure, the years of studying taking up all his spare time. No, she blamed Sylvia. She had not spoken a kind word to her in months. Complaint after complaint had climaxed the day when Sylvia told her, in the twins' presence, to get out of the kitchen. That humiliation was the last straw.

Maureen quizzed her mother for more detail. She had imagined that Rhoda and Sylvia got on well, like – though she had never dared to think the simile before – mother and daughter. Sylvia was house-proud in the old West Indian way, with a fondness for flowery things, embroidered antimacassars on the armchairs and sofa, plastic coverings for the dining table, even vases with plastic flowers – all signs that despite her age she was closer to Rhoda in taste than she, Maureen would ever be.

"What are you going to do, Mum?"

"Well I need somewhere to stay for now. Neville said I can come and stay with him, but you know he doesn't have no space and he always gets upset when I don't remember to call him Kenya or Kanya or whatever."

"You can stay in the spare room. I'm sure Phil won't mind. But you know how small it is."

"Thank you, Maureen."

"Meanwhile, I am going to call Sam. That house is your home. You helped them to buy it."

"I don't want any trouble."

Maureen exploded. "Mum! Trouble! You're always running away from trouble. This is the second time in your life you've done this. You allowed my father to bully you out of the house, and now you're allowing Sylvia and Sam to do the same thing."

"Sam has got nothing to do with what Sylvia is doing. I don't want you bothering him."

Rhoda's insistence that Sam was blameless baffled Maureen. She remembered her own powerful resentment when he first moved into the house. Was her mother trying to atone for leaving her sons with their father? She thought of her son sleeping upstairs and thought of the saying, 'You can't beat the firstborn'. Was that true? Would she feel the same way about Andrew?

"But Mum it's as much your house as theirs. If you want to leave, fine, but Samuel has to find you somewhere else to live."

"I don't want any trouble. The Lord will make a way."

Just then, Maureen heard the front door open. Phil was home, smelling of beer and nicotine. He entered the kitchen. "Maureen, whose suitcase... Hello, Mrs Bostock," he said, his surprise visible.

Phil always addressed Rhoda formally. A working-class lad from Swindon, he was the first in his family to attend university, from a family in which you showed respect to older people. Brought up in London's apparently déclassé environment, Maureen had mistaken Phil's mother's acceptance of her as an invitation to address the elderly woman as Rose. Phil had rebuked her for that social gaffe, telling her that even if his mother invited her to call her Rose, she was to refuse. Phil, speaking with a passion that he normally reserved for his collection of rocks, made her feel that she had exposed her immigrant roots. He told her that in his mother's generation, respect for age was second only to respect for seniority in rank, and she needed to recognise that the stiff British upper lip wasn't a thing of past. He often had to resort to it in his work in the museum when the bunch of public-school tossers who were in charge play-acted at being cool and trendy, but betrayed their inborn belief in their own superiority as soon as an outsider like him dared to suggest anything innovative. Phil was frustrated at work, but time and experience had shown her that he was not entirely wrong.

She made up the bed in the spare room, and when they were alone, she told Phil her good news. They were still discussing names when the telephone rang. It was Sam.

"Is Mummy there?" Sam said.

"Yes, she's here," Maureen said. "Came in a taxi. She's in bed. Sam, how could you allow your wife to persecute Mum to point where she feels she has to leave? How could you?"

"Take it easy, Maureen. I've been a bit distracted lately. I didn't know things had deteriorated so much. I mean, I knew they didn't always get on, but I had no idea Mummy was going to leave. She didn't say anything to me."

"So what're you going to do?"

"Can she stay there for a while? I'll sort something out."

"You'd better, you bastard," she said, slamming the phone down. Maureen instantly regretted this, but it was too late.

"That was a bit harsh, Maureen," Phil said.

"They've all used her. First Dad, now Sam. Those fucking bastards. And the thing that gets me is she just keeps on smiling and saying the 'Lord will make a way'. I can't believe it." Maureen sobbed, tears running down her cheeks.

"She can stay here as long she likes, you know that."

Still crying Maureen said, "No way. She'll drive me mad."

Phil held Maureen in his consoling arms, and she began thinking about Mary-Jane and Janet.

★ ★ ★ ★

The Narrator: writing circa 2020

The boy soon resumed his noisemaking.

By the time summer came around again, my patience with him had worn thin; his seizure of my living room in the evenings and at weekends was forcing me to live in one room, a situation I thought I had escaped when I moved to Selkirk Road. Weekends were the worst. Some weekend mornings I would stand at the living room window, see the sky a cloudless blue, and watch people going about their business – the slim dark-haired housewife skipping in and out of her house, Mr Ablade sitting on the steps, the red-haired woman pushing her newborn baby in a pram, her two other children walking behind her – while the boy's voice filled my living room and the floor beneath my feet vibrated with bass-driven music. Sometimes stomping on the floor brought the music to an end but it would resume soon afterwards. Was he using the music to fashion a persona for whatever rave the Saturday night held for him, or the paternal role he had to play?

After one particularly unbearable Saturday when the noise started at 7 a.m. and was still going on in the early evening, I telephoned his mother, whom I had not seen in months. I had tried treating him as man but his behaviour was now too extreme. A child answered the phone, and I asked for Carmen Hillman. I thought I heard the child call out, "Grandma, it's for you" but the line was fuzzy. Then the call was terminated. I redialled and again got a child's voice. After a pause of a few seconds, another person came to the phone.

"Is that Carmen Hillman?"

"If you're calling about my son, he was with me all night."

"Is that Carmen Hillman?" I said again.

"Who's that?"

I gave my name.

"I don't know anybody by that name." She sounded haughty and indignant. "You've got the wrong number. Don't call it again."

She hung up.

It was her, and her response told me I was not alone in whatever difficulties I was having with her son.

Some days later I had to visit a friend on a campus at Oakwood, and though it was within walking distance of the station, I chose to wait for a bus – the soles of my feet were aching from stomping on the floor. Ten minutes passed, then another ten. I lit a cigarette and paced up and down. Lost in thought, I carelessly flicked the butt on to the pavement. Within seconds, a uniformed couple confronted me; the man was Asian and the woman West African.

"Excuse me, sir, you've just violated the council's litter law."

"Have I?"

"Yes, you just dropped a cigarette butt."

"When did dropping a cigarette butt become an offence?"

"Enfield Council has a zero-tolerance policy for litter bugs. It's been all over the news. You've just incurred an eighty-pound fine."

"I don't live in Enfield, I live in Hackney. I didn't know." Just then the bus rolled up and I made to board, saying, "I'm sorry, now that I know, I won't do it again. I must get on this bus; I've been waiting for ages."

"We can't allow you to do that, sir," the woman said. "We need your details: name, address,etc." She was holding what looked like a mobile credit card machine.

The penny dropped. I resignedly watched the bus drive away as I gave them my details and watched in amazement and ire as the woman punched in the information I'd given her. The machine issued me with something like a receipt, and the two enforcement officers politely said, "Have a good day, sir," and strolled away. She had such a beautiful smile.

Even after a convivial lunch and having my account listened to with incredulity and sympathy by my friend, I was still smarting

– it would wreak havoc with my bank balance – as I made my way home. But it occurred to me that maybe there was something to be learned from the incident: I had been too tolerant, too easy going.

Before I could implement *my* zero-tolerance approach, a group of squatters moved into the northside neighbouring house. They were friendly, energetic and young. For a few weeks they kept up a racket as they replaced the floorboards in the upper part of the house. But once they had finished, the noise ceased. They cut down the elder trees, which initially seemed like vandalism, but their absence made such a difference to the light coming into my kitchen that I soon thought otherwise. Now other back gardens were visible. I had heard the sound of children playing beyond the elder trees but never seen them, now I could see a garden with a trampoline, on which three brothers played with dizzying energy.

To signal to the boy downstairs, I bought a mallet in the Jewish-owned woodwork store on the High Road, and as soon as the music started, I banged the floor repeatedly. This seemed to work and for a few weeks I enjoyed relative peace and quiet. I wasn't against the boy playing music, just the volume at which he did it. He seemed to understand that, and now whole days went by in peace. If a group of squatters could take over the house next door and occupy it with consideration for their neighbours, maybe this boy could do the same?

One evening as I was standing on the steps, the boy came up and said: "I've forgotten my keys at work."

"That's careless," I said.

"Yeah, thing is, I can get into my place through the window with a ladder. But I can't leave the ladder there all night. Know what I mean? Can you help me? Do you have a stepladder?"

"And what about tomorrow morning?"

"I'll leave through the back and climb over the gardens."

I had a long enough ladder, bought in anticipation of the day when I would tackle the painting and decorating of my flat. The boy placed it on the concrete incline before the groundfloor window. When he had entered the house through the window, I removed the ladder. In the hallway, I shouted to him, "Do you have food in there? Are you going to be okay?"

"Yeah, I'm alright. It's just tomorrow I'm worried about now."

I said, "Do you think you can reach my stairwell window at the back? It's quite low?"

"Course."

"OK, well tomorrow, I'll open that window, and you can leave the house that way. You don't want to go climbing over people's back gardens early morning."

"Thanks."

He told me the time he planned to set off for work, and the following morning I woke at 5.30am, and opened the stairwell window for him. Looking out the window, I realised I had underestimated the drop. But with one leap, he grabbed the window ledge and hauled himself up. He thanked me and I watched him go off to work, wondering how one person could combine such a puzzling mixture of immaturity and braggadocio.

But within days, I was again banging on the floor with the mallet. Then in mid-July, the boy again started to park his bicycle in the narrow hallway. A red and expensive looking thing, I had to squeeze past it to get in and out of my flat. After two weeks of this, I said to Junior, "I hope you don't intend to leave that bicycle there. You've got a big back garden or can you park it in basement shed at the front."

"No. No. It's just for now."

"The sooner you move it the better," I said. "I'm not a young man; I don't want to have to squeeze past it every time I leave or come into my home."

He looked at me defiantly, then walked away.

The bicycle disappeared, but after two days it was back. That Sunday, as I was leaving the house to meet a friend for lunch, my right trouser leg snagged on the pedal. I opened the front door of the house, left the door ajar, then returned and knocked on Junior's door: "You said you were going to move the bicycle."

"I am. I am just cleaning up."

"Look, son," I said, "I'm quite fed up with you. You take over the front garden with your big motorbike, and now you want to take over the hallway. You never asked me if it was all right to park your things in these spaces."

He stood akimbo and said, "I thought it would be alright, innit."

"Well, you thought wrong. Move the bicycle."

"I can put what I want in the hallway. Suppose I want to put a pram there. You can't do anything about that. You know what it is: familiarity breeds contempt, because you helped me out the other day. That's what it is."

"I've tried to be reasonable with you. I saw that you were in difficulty; I gave you sympathy, and I tried to advise you. Now I am tired of you. If you don't move the bike and stop the noise you're always making, I am going to bring in a third party to tell you what is allowed and not allowed. Got that, son?"

"Don't fucking call me son. You can go to whoever you fucking want. Nobody knows I live here. As far as the law's concerned only my mother lives here." In his laugh I heard a trace of malevolence.

"I'll see about that," I said. "Meanwhile, move the bike."

The bike was gone when I got back that evening, but I still thought it was necessary to bring in a third party.

The following evening, sitting in my kitchen, I heard the boy's voice at the front of the house. He was saying to somebody, "I'm going to box him down."

He was talking to Clive, a tall Black man who lived across the road with his Portuguese wife and their three children. I thought: Does this guy expect me to walk in fear of him in my home? I donned my shoes, went outside and, palms showing, walked towards the boy and his friend, saying, "Here I am; box me down."

The boy said, "I didn't say that."

"I heard you very clearly. I want you to know that I am not going to be coming and going from this house in fear you. So if you're going to box me down, do it right here and now."

He came up to me and put a finger under my chin. Our eyes locked. I kept calm and said, "Go on, son. Box me down. But you'd better make sure I never get up and go and explain your actions to the law."

He pulled his finger away and stormed off into the house.

I returned to my flat and allowed myself to feel the fear that I denied when he threatened me. I am not, I should say, a particularly physical person. Schoolboy football, stints of jogging in my twenties – nothing more than that. While most of my peers were learning martial arts or boxing, I hung out in the local library. The only time I ever raised my hand to another man was entirely in jest, and I instantly regretted it because of the fear in his eyes. Physical violence is a foreign country to me.

I'd never registered a complaint against anybody with the police, but I did that summer. An officer at Stoke Newington police station took down my account of the altercation outside the house and promised to get in touch. As I walked home, it occurred to me that

I would have to involve the young man who was with the boy at the time. I also contacted the local council as the landlord of the house.

A young Black woman from the anti-social behaviour unit told me that the boy should not be living in the house, implying that he was known to them. The estate manager came to interview me and I explained that Miss Hillman did not actually live in the house, that she was at best an occasional visitor. He promised to interview Miss Hillman at a later date.

On the day the estate manager came to interview Miss Hillman, I saw the boy scampering away from the house around midday, an hour before the estate manager arrived. Later, I found a note under my flat door. Roughly written in ink, and unsigned, it read: "My son has nowhere to live. I am all he has. Please show him mercy."

I filed the note away, and in a telephone call to the estate manager learned that he was satisfied that the flat remained Miss Hillman's principal home.

The motorbike was now parked out in the street.

Some days after I'd received a log sheet for recording noise incidents from the anti-social behaviour unit, I noticed a rusting meat cleaver in the front garden. Was this a message from the boy? I kicked it into the dustbin shelter and tried not to think about it.

The boy must have been interviewed by the police because, weeks later, he was in the back garden swearing and shouting up at my kitchen window. He was standing among a broken shattered mirror, discarded broom handles, plastic bags and other refuse.

"What do you want?" I asked.

"You went to the police. What if I get my friends to beat you up?"

"Grow up," I said, and closed the window.

I kept the log of noise incidents for a month. During that period, I encountered the boy once or twice in the hallway.

"I am not doing anything wrong, just listening to my music."

"You're denying me the use of almost half of my home."

"I could turn this place into crack house, bring in all sorts of bad people."

"You can try."

"What have you got against me? I'm not a bad person."

"I've got nothing against you; you just need to acknowledge that this is an old house. It's not a music studio or a disco."

"You got no respect for me; that's what it comes down to. But I'm going to make you respect me."

"What's respect got to do with it? It's something you earn. You come in here playing man with me but your mother has to come and appeal to me for mercy for you. Grow up. Stop hiding behind your mother's skirt."

"What if I burn the fucking house down?" he said, banging the inner wall of the hallway. "This fucking house is hollow, innit. Burn like fucking paper."

"You know, you really should stop making threats, and learn the difference between trying to inspire fear and earning respect."

"Ah, you're just a fucking idiot," he said and stormed off.

I would like to say I was untouched by the boy's threats, but this was not so. One autumn night in late November, as I made my way along a back street, I saw three young Black men standing beside their bicycles. Were they watching me? I hastened as I entered the Somerset Grove estate. I looked back and the boys were mounting their bicycles. I panicked and broke into half-run. I had to reach the other side of the estate where there was a cab office, corner store and West Indian restaurant. I looked and saw the boys riding towards me. Were they his friends? I reached in my pockets for something sharp to defend myself with. There was not even a pen. I turned into a parking lot and saw the mini-cab office. A few drivers were standing outside smoking. If the boys caught up with me there I could shout for help. I resumed walking, my breathing laboured, my brow moist with a sweat. A few yards from the mini-cab office, I looked behind; there was nobody following me. But after that incident, I thought twice about being out at late at night.

My efforts to involve the authorities paid off, and after Christmas the boy fell quiet. He was unemployed again. His white baby mother visited the house many times over the winter. Mostly he ignored her, refusing to answer the door, but sometimes he went outside and for a while they would argue bitterly and loudly on the doorstep.

★ ★ ★ ★

23. *Neville's final fight, 1983*

It was the night of Neville's third professional fight as a heavyweight under the nickname Killer Kumba. He was in his corner with his trainer-manager, Dragon Caine. An ex-soldier in his late forties,

Caine still jogged up and down the steep footpaths of Springfield Park wearing heavy hobnail boots and carrying a backpack filled with bricks. He had persuaded Neville to turn professional.

"Don't let him rush you. He's gonna be looking for a quick knockout. That's his style. He's gonna be looking to get under your defences. You gotta hurt him in the first round. Really hurt him. Let him know what to expect if he gets too close. And don't let him dazzle you with all his fancy footwork."

Dragon had been giving him the same pep-talk for the past month, so he was only half-listening. But he heard clearly enough: survive the first three rounds, take the fight to the distance. His opponent, Rufus Jones, also known as Rocket Rufus, was an East Londoner. He was the same age, weight and height as Neville, but had a quarter-inch advantage in reach. He had a reputation for quick knockouts and an entertaining patter, but he had never fought twelve rounds. Neville's reputation was quite the opposite; he had demonstrated a talent for taking punishment, for being able to absorb the other fighter's blows until the man had exhausted himself, then he struck with combination punches, which had given him three knockouts and earned him the name Killer Kumba.

There was a lot riding on this fight, not just the purse, the biggest so far in his career. Victory would mean a giant step towards getting a crack at the British heavyweight title and an even bigger purse; defeat would mean returning to fights in provincial cities, in near-derelict leaky halls, and booing home crowds who had no appreciation of the art and techniques of boxing, who cheered at the sight of blood or seeing a man floored. This happened to him in Huddersfield when he slipped and fell; the half-empty hall erupted in raucous applause that nearly kept him pinned to the canvas. Despite Dragon's efforts to insulate him, he was aware that the boxing cognusen... what's that word that Dragon always uses? Cognisc... fuck it...the punters, didn't believe he was ready for a fight at this level, saw him as a no-hoper chosen by Jones's ambitious manager for precisely that reason. But he believed in himself, Dragon believed in him, and he had mouths to feed.

"Hurt him in the first round, really hurt him," he heard Caine repeat. "Let him think twice about getting too close."

But Neville's thoughts were on the world beyond the fight. There was the home and family he had created with Shirley, four children now, and if he wasn't mistaken – though she hadn't said anything – he thought she was pregnant again. She was not among the spectators; she hated the sport, and after each fight she tried to persuade him to give it up. But what else could he do? Unlike Samuel, Maureen and Vincent, he didn't have the patience for studying. He had wasted years hanging around a sound system, he'd watched his friends throw bricks at policemen. There'd been madness in the air and he realised he'd drifted into bad company. He had to re-focus on the one activity at which he excelled. In this other world – of the thwack of leather against skin, beefy men skipping with balletic grace, the rhythmic sound of men beating a ball, of the grunts, ecstatic and agonized, of men pumping iron, of swaggering men with bulging biceps and muscle-packed stomachs – he had found a trade as respectable as any other. Many people, including Shirley, saw it as a brutal sport, but they were wrong. It was his livelihood, and one day, when he had enough money in the bank to look after his family, he would retire. He would open a shop or gym or a cafe, even buy a farm. Yes, he could see his children among those rolling green fields he had seen outside London – that other England visible from trains or cars, on his way to and from fights; see them in a farmyard of cows, pigs and chickens, and a dog. But that was a long way off, he had to do his shift tonight. Do it right. A clean job. No mess.

"Don't let him rush you!" Dragon Caine called.

He heard the bell, the preliminaries having passed as though he had been sleeping, and he leapt off the stool and threw some punches in the air, limbering up. As he always did, he aimed to dominate the ring centre, keep his opponent circling. He tried to manoeuvre into that position and felt a stinging blow on his cheek. Hands too low, adjust stance, crouch. Another blow struck him in his left kidney and another in the right; he tucked his elbows in, and locked his eyes on his opponent to let him know he wasn't hurt; he would have to do better than that. He released a left jab which struck air and propelled him forward. He grabbed at Rufus, held him in a clinch, with Rufus working his kidneys and whispering: "I'm gonna send you to the moon, bro, gonna send you to Mars and Venus and you ain't coming back." Rufus was famous for his speed and his tongue. Neville gave no reply; he wasn't a talker, wasn't a fancy dancer like Rufus. His head jolted backwards from a sneaky uppercut but he rode the blow and held on to his opponent. The referee stepped in and separated them but before he had fully moved aside, Rufus rushed at him and released a flurry of combination punches which struck his abdomen and head and sent him reeling backwards onto the rope. He was in pain, a whole new continent of pain, and became aware of the crowd and Dragon shouting "Get those fists up, get your elbows in!"

He felt a blow to his left temple and another slipped past his right elbow and connected with his abdomen, sending a tremor through his entire body that almost seemed to lift him in the air. Punches rained on him from every direction; the rope was cutting into his back, and he imagined he heard voices saying, "I told you the kid wasn't ready."

The referee again parted them, and in that fraction of a second, Neville found a new strength which kept him on his feet, poised and ready for the next onslaught. He had to stop Rufus from hurting him; he had to regain the ring centre, be in control there. But he wasn't in control; he could only defend and all the defensive techniques he could remember were useless against punches that rained from above, below and both sides.

The bell went. For a moment he couldn't tell where his corner was until he recognised Dragon's red and green T-shirt. The few steps to his corner seemed to take forever, but as he sat down and felt the cold sponge on his face and the water running down his body, he felt hope returning. He had survived the first round, when Rufus was at his most deadly, but he hadn't delivered the hurting punch, the deterrent that Dragon talked about. Maybe the next round. Definitely. The next round.

"You're doing alright, Kumba," Dragon said, massaging his back, "but you gotta hurt him. Slow him down. You can't take that kind of punishment much longer. Let him know what's in your bag."

Rounds 2 and 3 repeated the opening round, with Neville often clinging and praying for the bell to end the storm of punches. In round four, Neville finally delivered the blows Dragon had been urging: a left jab followed by an over head punch as Rufus came forward. In the split-second pause, an expression of painful shock was on Rufus's face, as if asking 'What was that and where did that come from?' The Rocket rocked.

This would be his round. He went for Rufus, picking through his defences with left jabs to the head, right hooks to the body, an upper cut that didn't quite connect but did some damage. Blood oozed from a gash above Rocketman's right eye.

The bell went and Neville sauntered back to his corner, confident he had earned his opponent's respect. This fight would go the distance. The cheering crowd, some blurry faces nodding, impressed, Dragon's animation: "You're in with a real chance now. Rocket's felt the deterrent effect. Remember, he ain't never been, can't go, the distance. You can. Wear him down."

Neville took the next round, but in round 6, as Rufus got a second wind, Neville's shortcomings were once again exposed. He was too slow, his footwork was plodding, his defensive techniques poor. Strength, courage and resolve could only carry you so far in the fight game. He fought on, nonetheless. By round eight, both men were exhausted, but Rufus's greater experience and technical know-how meant he was picking up points with stinging jabs and combination punches. Towards the end of round eight he struck an overhead punch which whiplashed Neville's head, sent him staggering backwards, feeling for the rope, but grasping thin air, and collapsing. Before he kissed the canvas he heard Dragon shouting, "Take the count, take the count."

In those eight seconds many thoughts swarmed in his head: Shirley and the children, his mother who had known so many upheavals, the father whose respect he craved, the farm he wanted to own with all its cows and chickens and ducks and geese, and maybe a slow moving stream or a river nearby where he could take his boys fishing, Uncle Horace holding court from his bed, and the difficulty of talking, putting sentences together so they made sense, like Samuel and Vincent could do, and Maureen, his sister – the sister he didn't know but whose feistiness he liked.

Then he was up on his feet, his knees shaky, though he was trying hard to control them. The referee held up three fingers and he took a guess and got it right. When the referee stepped aside and Rocket, now a blurry figure, rushed forward, Neville held him in a clinch which thwarted his opponent's attempt to deliver the final blow but couldn't stop the left and right punches to his kidneys. The bell went and some autopilot took over. Still dazed, he found his corner only by following Dragon's voice. He crashed onto the stool and did not want to ever, ever again feel such pain. His lips were swollen and throbbed, blood streamed from a cut above his right eye. While Bill Pierce, one of his cornermen, attempted to staunch the cut, he heard Dragon say: "You don't have to go back out there, kid. We can call it a day. Throw in the towel. Just say the word."

But it wasn't Dragon's voice he heard. It was his father's saying, "You gotta finish the job. Start it, you gotta finish it." And he knew that finishing the job wasn't just about winning anymore, it was about going the distance, surviving the twelve rounds. It was all about heart now. Courage.

At the end of round twelve, Rufus's camp rushed into the ring, lifted their man shoulder high, and started shouting "The future world champ!" There was no celebration in Neville's camp, only dismay that he had somehow found the reserve to survive. He thought it strange that he felt as if he could go another round; his swollen eyes were mere slits, his lips felt distended, as if they were touching his chest, and the ringing in his ears added to his sense of disorientation. He felt hands kneading his shoulders and biceps, the sting of iodine on the cuts, the cool of vaseline being applied.

A sudden uproar in the ring confirmed what he already knew. Rufus had got the verdict.

"Close," Dragon said, his voice coming from a great distance, though he was kneeling beside Neville, unfurling the bandage from his right hand. "Close," he said again. "Rocket ain't gonna be in no hurry for a rematch, that's for sure." He slapped Neville's right shoulder and said: "Better patch you up. Get you home to your lady, your kids. You're gonna to need them."

Rocket Rufus came over and hugged Neville and raised his right hand in a magnanimous gesture to the first of his opponents to survive beyond round three. "You'll be back," he whispered consolingly.

Neville's post-fight medical gave him the all-clear. He returned home where Shirley and the children, friends and neighbours pampered and further consoled him, tempered the bitter taste of defeat with music and laughter and post-match analyses that examined every punch, and identified round four as the moment when he came within an inch of winning the fight. But this only made him feel he had experienced far more than defeat, something closer to tragedy. Two days later, as he sat in the livingroom at home – his face still a mass of swelling, his body throbbing with pain, the blood in his urine still visible, the ringing in his ears still audible – a slow darkness began descending on him and he felt himself falling forward. He heard Shirley's alarmed voice asking: "Neville, what's wrong, what's wrong?"

"He's off the critical list, but he'll never box again," Shirley told Lucas. They were standing outside Homerton Hospital. Lucas had been a frequent visitor to the hospital over the past month.

"Good," Lucas said.

"You're a heartless man, Mr Bostock," Shirley said.

"Heartless man? You know how many times me tell that boy nuh fi tek up boxing. You t'ink me did that because I don't have a heart. The boy's a damn fool. You tell him that from me." Like all the other visitors to Neville's bedside, Lucas had up until then shown only concern for his health. But now that he knew his son would survive, he saw no reason to mince words. "Damn fool," he said again to Shirley. And for months afterwards he would say "Damn fool" when he thought of Neville.

Vincent came back to London several times to see his injured brother and stayed with Lucas, who cooked for him and over dinner recalled with fondness the days when they – Samuel, Neville, Vincent and he – had muddled along. On one of Vincent's visits, he found Lucas low and thoughtful; he confessed that his greatest regret was his failure to keep his family together. Vincent took this confession as an expression of desire for more frequent visits, because a fortnight later he was back again, and chose to spend Saturday night on the living-room sofa. Lucas did not object. But that same night, Jean Fraser's harsh condemning voice woke Lucas up. Then, as he lay in the dark, an image of Neville on his hospital bed, eyes closed as if dead, played on his mind. The memory seemed to become a vision of his own future. He put on his dressing gown and went to the living room. He switched on the light, saw Vincent and demanded, "What you doin' here?"

"I told you I was staying the night; you said it was okay."

"No, you come to see how close me is to death so you can claim my money. That's it, isn't it?"

"Don't be ridiculous, Dad."

"Yes, I know you... you and your brothers and your mother. You all waiting for me to die. Well, let me tell you, Lucas Bostock ain't dead yet. Far from it. Me intend to go the distance. So don't hang around. Go out there and make your own."

"Dad, let's talk about this in the morning."

But the morning brought Lucas stillness and peace and no urgency to talk. Vincent left, and did not return for several weeks.

It was around this time, late summer, that Mr George told Lucas that he and his wife were going home. Relations between the two men had improved to the point where they talked in the front garden but no longer watched boxing matches and late night movies together. Neville's accident had dampened their interest in watching the sport. Mr George cited the inner-city riots of the previous years, and the Tory government for his decision, and admitted that Florence feared meeting old age in London. In better times Lucas would have greeted this news with visible disappointment, but he refused to show any emotion.

"What about you?" Mr George said. "You not thinking of heading home anytime soon?"

"In the next few years, in the next few years," Lucas said, expressing for the first time what would become a regular reply.

Over the next few months he became aware of the Georges' preparations. He ran into Florence on Stoke Newington High Street pushing a shopping trolley and carrying plastic bags. He came home and found cartons containing a fridge, electric cooker and television in the corridor. In late September, he found a huge wooden crate in the front garden. On its sides were written: 'Mr & Mrs George, Me-Soon-Come, St Thomas, Jamaica, West Indies'. The crate was there for a week. The evening, when Lucas came home and saw that it was gone, it left a blank space like a recently fallen tree that had long served as a landmark.

A week before the Georges were due to depart, Lucas was startled by a slamming door and shouting. It was the first time he had ever heard the Georges quarrel. Minutes later he found Mr George at his door, his face contorted in something between exasperation and anger. When he regained his calm, he said: "After I book the flight, buy up half of London and ship it back to St Thomas, she's now telling me she doesn't want to go home."

"It's a bit late now for that, isn't it?" Lucas said.

"That's what I'm trying to tell her. The thing is, it isn't that she doesn't want to go home. She does. She doesn't want to go by plane. She's dreamed about balls of fire falling from the sky. She's afraid of flying. God didn't make human beings to fly."

"But she flew here, didn't she?"

"That's just it. She didn't. Florence must be one of the last of us to come here on a banana boat."

"So, what you going to do?"

"Mr Bostock, you know I am a peaceful man. You know how I love and care for Mrs George, but I swear to god if she doesn't get on that plane next week Sunday, not even her voodoo mumbo jumbo can save her. So you will pardon us the noise while I go and sort out this thing once and for all."

Everton George pulled up his trousers, tightened his belt and straightened himself up to his five-foot height, and with a grim expression excused himself. Some minutes later Lucas heard a mighty roar as if from some unimaginably gigantic creature, and then there was silence. Not a sound was heard from the Georges' room for the rest of the day.

On the Sunday morning, Lucas saw Florence George, dressed in white and walking with unusual stiffness, a Bible in her hand. She was on her way to the nearest Catholic church and went there every morning until the eve of their departure. To supplement her faith, she drank a homemade infusion designed to keep her mind blank, empty of the portentous vision of balls of fire plunging to earth.

Lucas had agreed to drive them to Heathrow airport for a modest fee, and on the morning of their departure he helped Mr George put their suitcases into the car. Mr George then went back inside and returned with Florence, who was dressed in a red trouser suit, wore dark glasses and walked with dignified rigidity, as if she were a centenarian. She carried a small potted plant, which she presented to Lucas, before taking her seat in the back of the car, where she sat, grim and silent. Mr George sat in the front with Lucas. As they neared Hammersmith, he said, "You know, I'll miss London."

Lucas said, "Tell you something; this city won't miss you. You can bet that before you land in Kingston, before you even catch sight of the Caribbean Sea, there'll be another ten immigrants to take your place. Yes, sir, young and old. The young bursting with energy and dreams. The old looking for a last shot at the title. It's that kinda place. It don't miss anybody. Not this city."

"I'll still miss it," Mr George said. "If we'd come here at a younger age, we'd have had a hell of a time, a hell of a time. Ain't that so, Florence?" He twisted in his seat to look at his wife.

"Then what you think you putting me through now?" she said.

Mr George had explained to Lucas his strategy for getting Florence onto the plane. He had rehearsed their movements right up to the departure gate. Beyond that point, he admitted, he was as ignorant as a boxer who had never gone beyond ten rounds. Florence would be the last to know that he was as scared as she was, because he planned to slip her a powerful sedative at a suitable moment.

Lucas said a restrained goodbye to Mr George and respectful farewell to Florence. She nodded almost imperceptibly, but remained silent and rigid, her eyes hidden behind her dark glasses. Lucas watched as Mr George guided her to the departure gate, saw her hesitation, her attempt to turn back thwarted by Mr George's grip on her elbow, while handing over their passports and tickets to the attendant. Then they were gone from view. They had not looked back.

Cap in hand, Lucas wandered around the terminal, marvelling at its scale and wondering if the future inhabitants of cities would lead all their lives in immense buildings like this one. He drove back into London at a leisurely pace. The house seemed quieter than usual. None of the tenants seemed to be moving about. He ate a simple meal, watered the plant Florence had given him, then went upstairs to the empty room. There, as he paced up and down, he admitted to himself what he had not admitted to the Georges. He would miss them, was missing them already.

He would miss Mr George's Saturday night visits and their arguments over who was the all-time greatest boxer, Mohamed Ali, Joe Louis, Jack Johnson, Rocky Marciano. This always ended without agreement because Florence would call her husband to bed. He would miss Florence too, her invisible presence, the shuffling sound as she moved about upstairs, the clatter of pots and pans as she prepared her husband's meals, the lavender-scented water she used to disguise her own natural odour, which, on the rare occasions when he smelled it, evoked memories of parched, arid land on which rain had recently fallen. He would miss their silent and inexhaustible intimacy, their devotion to each other. It was as though he had lived in and through their marriage, derived consolation for his own failure from their success.

Feet still on the floor, he lay on the bed and drifted into a light sleep in which he dreamt of wispy clouds drifting across a mountain on which sunlight played, creating alternating shades of green and blue. When he woke up, he felt sad and confused, uncertain of his location, until he glanced through the window and saw the terraced houses on the other side of the street. He was still in London, forever in London.

A few months later Lucas received this letter:

Dear Lucas, I would love to able to tell you that Florence and I arrived safely in Jamaica and Me-Soon-Come, but that is not the case. Where to begin? When I booked the flight they didn't tell me that it was an indirect flight to Jamaica via Miami. Florence was now fully awake and upset that I'd drugged her with a mild tranquillizer. She gave me a difficult time. Said it probably wasn't the first time I had drugged and taken advantage of her because she had woken up some mornings with memories of a dream in which she was having to fight off a beast. I managed to calm her down and get us through US immigration. On the way to our connecting flight, she said she needed to use the ladies. After about fifteen minutes I realised Florence was taking a very long time. I could hardly go into the ladies to hurry her up. I found an airport official and explained the problem. The kind lady went to look for Florence and came out saying she wasn't in there. They called out Florence's name several times on the PA system. Still no sign of my beloved wife. I couldn't go without her, so the flight took off without us. Then it occurred to me that Florence had done a runner to avoid having to board the plane. I remembered that she had a cousin in New York and wondered whether she was trying to get there. I am now in New York searching for my beloved Florence, been here for about a month but there's still no sign of her. I have cried myself to sleep many nights, but I won't leave here until I find her.

Your former tenant and firm friend,
Ulysses George.

It took Lucas a while to recover from this news. When he did, he threw himself into a frenzy of work. He repaired windows and painted the exterior of both houses, restored the original basement flat where he'd lived, installed a new bath in the second house, where he also erected a new fence and finally concreted over the back garden. These projects cost him pain because the arthritis in his knees and fingers was worse than ever. But there were nights when exhaustion and aspirin tablets failed to deliver the temporary oblivion that he sought and he was forced to reflect on his life.

One night found him dismissing Jean's condemnation of his treatment of Horace as female hysterics born of grief and the need to blame somebody for Horace's death. On another night, he realised that he had married Rhoda because she resembled Jean, a few shades darker, and less refined, but they could easily have been mistaken for close relatives, if not sisters. It was a moment of self-knowledge that sent him staggering towards a morning that seemed reluctant to arrive. Yet he refused to blame himself. Nobody had instructed him in how to be a man in the world. He had groped his way out of the dark, out of the bush, had always lived within the law and tempered his aspirations to his ability and means. He knew of no man worthy of respect who had not fought tooth and nail for what he owned, his property or his children. Yet he remained troubled. Unable to find peace, he retreated further into the rugged mountainous interior of the island that was himself.

25. *Samuel, Elena and Sylvia, a year later*

Samuel, on his way from work, was stuck in a traffic jam near Herne Hill. He loosened his tie, stretched his back and spread out his right arm, feeling the tension accumulated from work – a tension that also anticipated what he had to do that evening. Tight muscles reminded him he had only recently resumed running; too many evening and weekend meetings. The traffic started moving but stopped after a few yards.

He was a busy man, juggling several balls with the ease of one who relished responsibility. He had long achieved his promotion and was in the middle of buying a house in Streatham for his mother. His immediate concern was his marriage. He rehearsed, for the umpteenth time, his opening gambit: "Sylvia, we need to talk." Hardly original, but then what he wanted to talk about was not original, though he'd never been there before. If anyone had predicted two years ago that a woman, then a teenager, whom he'd saved from a mugging would have so shaken up his life; that his mother now lived in a tiny room in her daughter's house, a situation he was determined to end; and that he was about to leave his wife, he would have laughed derisively. Yet that was precisely his position.

For some months after meeting Elena Harris, Samuel had fallen into the habit of going to the George Canning pub on Thursday nights when Harry Stephenson, Elena and others gathered, forming a lively, informal political discussion group. Harry Stephenson was well into his seventies. He had been politicised as a teenager when his father, a trade unionist, took him on the Jarrow March in 1926 and he claimed to have participated in and organised political marches under every government since Neville Chamberlain's appeasement debacle. A bearded, pipe-smoking, ex-communist party member, now a stalwart of the local Labour Party, he was a master raconteur with an inexhaustible store of anecdotes about the second world war – he had served in Burma – fighting fascists in the East End, protesting against Eden's invasion of the Suez Canal, marching against the Vietnam war. "You've got to keep the bastards, on their toes" was Harry's catchphrase. On Thursday nights, Samuel would walk back up Tulse Hill feeling merrier and vaguely reconnected.

One Thursday night in August, Harry did not turn up and Samuel found himself with Elena, Pete Compton and Dave Mills, the latter leaders of a squat on Railton Road. The evening was no less lively for Harry's absence, but at closing time Samuel noticed that Elena seemed a little lost; she usually left with Harry. He asked if she wanted a lift home. She declined, pointing out that he had been drinking and suggested that if he wanted to walk for a while, he could walk her towards Clapham Common and turn back whenever he chose. As they walked down Effra Road, they talked about Harry, who was not well. Elena spoke of her experience of going to the women's anti-nuclear protest at Greenham Common. Samuel talked about the Conservative government's plans to weaken trade unions. Before they knew it, they had passed the Town Hall and were half-way to Clapham Common. He declined her invitation to come in for coffee, but as he made his way home later that night, his lips were still moist from a kiss that he, up until then a faithful husband, understood was an invitation.

Elena lived on the north side of Clapham Common, in a house behind tall, creaky, wrought-iron gates, in a basement flat reached by stone steps worn smooth by time. His early visits, at night and lasting no more than a few hours, brought delicious and heady feelings of transgression, far stronger than any guilt that he was having an affair and his lover was several years his junior and white. But Elena was more than an erotic object, more than exotica.

Distributing CND leaflets on a Brixton housing estate had not been the passing display of impetuous youth. The granddaughter of a Yorkshire suffragette, Elena had abandoned university after her first term to travel the world for a year, and returned to London with an almost evangelical zeal for political activism. She was a Labour Party member, a CND organiser and collector of signatures for countless petitions. An inheritance gave her a modest but comfortable monthly income. That she enjoyed such an enviable privilege was not evident in her clothes – most were bought from charity shops.

Samuel's visits to Elena were as much for the opportunity to talk about politics and ideas as for sex. After each visit, he returned to Rhoda, Sylvia and the children and found himself irritated with his mother's fondness for quoting the bible and frustrated with Sylvia's lack of interest in anything outside the home.

Still waiting for the traffic to move, he remembered visiting Elena a week after the Brixton riots. Elena had said, "They have no political representatives, nobody speaking for them. You should be out there, Sam." He'd laughed and said, "Me, I agree with old Harry, I don't trust politicians."

"But Harry's distrust is part of his radical activism. Yours is naive."

Samuel bridled at being called naive but he settled for asking her to elaborate.

"We live in a democracy. Somebody's got to do that job. When most people think of freedom, they only think of individual freedom, the right to do what you want, so long as it doesn't harm anybody. But political freedom's just as important, and with political freedom comes the right and the duty to take part in politics. You can't separate the two."

"And you're saying that I separate individual and political freedom?"

"I'm saying that you enjoy one, and take the other for granted. I am saying you could be more active, Sam. There isn't a single black MP in Britain."

"I'm sure they'll come along eventually."

"If you're so certain, what's to stop you becoming one? Remember that Saturday afternoon in Brixton? What do you think those boys ran away from?"

"A good beating. They were out of order."

"True, but they also ran from your authority. You had the

courage and authority tell them that what they were doing was wrong. Another person might have ignored what was going on or they might have been attacked. Not you. It's something that Harry pointed out to me. He thinks you've got what it takes. Says he'd enjoy keeping you on your toes."

He'd mulled over that conversation for weeks. On a morning run round Brockwell Park, he thought about what it meant to be a citizen, the duties and rights that accompanied that status, thought about his parents' journey to England, their narrow immigrant lives in London. He became aware that his past had blinkered him, encumbered him with too great a readiness to settle for the safe and mundane. He laughed at his career achievement. How could he have been so unoriginal, so lacking in imagination? He regretted mocking Vincent, who now seemed set on an academic career, when, years before, he had tried to introduce politics into their lives. He realised, as he ran, that he had never really exercised choice, only drifted. Now, nearing thirty, he felt he could and ought to choose. Samuel Bostock, statesman; Samuel Bostock, MP; both had an authentic ring, an echo of destiny.

Now, he was set on becoming a local councillor, the first step in what he hoped would be a political career. Never in his life had he been so sure about what he wanted. He wanted political office, and he wanted Elena, who had given him this vision, to be his wife. What stood between him and these ambitions was the family life he had built. He could see no alternative but to destroy it to move forward. But, he reasoned, it was already smouldering rubble; only hypocrisy and denial fostered the delusion that it was still solid, intact and habitable. Constructing something new required acknowledgement of that reality, however ugly, and the courage to walk among the debris and salvage the salvageable. The children. Sylvia's cooperation – he would have to live with her bitterness.

When the traffic on Herne Hill finally started moving, Samuel prepared himself for the most difficult evening of his life. He was almost deflected from this course when he got in and Sylvia told him that Vincent had called twice in the past hour. Samuel said he would call back. At a little after nine o'clock, he was alone with Sylvia in the living room.

"It's like this Sylvia; I've thought about it long and hard, and well, it's like this…" He could not go through with it. But when he shifted in the armchair and felt Elena's keys to her flat in his pocket, his resolve returned and he spoke quickly. "It's like this, Sylvia, I want a divorce."

The house was quiet, the children were in bed. They had not spent any time together in months. There was a stunned expression on Sylvia's face and Samuel's gaze darted between her face and the varnished floorboards.

Sylvia got up, arms folded, and stood before the television. She was wearing an African-style, tie-dye smock with a round, gold-coloured embroidered neck. "I don't understand," she said. "Where has this come from? Is it because of your mother?"

"This has got nothing to do with Mummy. Look around you, Sylvia. When was the last time I was home this early... six, nine months ago? We're living a lie."

"It's not my fault you've been at your political or union meetings. Years ago, I said I'd stand by you in whatever you wanted to do. Sure, I'd like to see you home earlier, get help with the children."

He remembered Sylvia's exact words when they lived in a bedsit north of the river. He felt wretchedly sick, hated himself for what he was doing. He clasped his hands and covered his mouth.

"Look at me, Samuel, damn it. What're you trying to tell me?"

He looked at her and felt a warm affection for the mother of his children, but the lover he'd known seemed to belong to another lifetime. They had been so young, so unknowing. Her pressed hair, her painted nails, her cheap gold earrings – he had never noticed these things before and he was struck by how much his wife resembled the secretaries and receptionists at his office. He wondered whether he had ever loved Sylvia, whether she had merely been a convenient interlude until he found the destiny he was convinced was his. The thought deepened his wretchedness and self-loathing. As if he was running and determined to keep going for one more mile, he steeled himself in anticipation of her tears. He looked at her directly, and said, "I'm in love with somebody else, Sylvia, and I want to marry her and she wants to marry me." I ought to have started there, with that admission, he thought.

"You, you... how long has this... Who is she... how long?"

"Sylvia, please, don't make this more difficult than it has to be. I've not taken this decision lightly." He hoped his voice carried the right tone of appeal because he wanted her to know that he was appealing for her to release him.

"Samuel, you've got two young boys upstairs. They're

depending on you. You're not just leaving me. How can you…"

"You and the children will not go wanting. You'll be looked after."

He saw her eyes moisten and he wanted to comfort her but restrained himself and felt sick again. Then, to his surprise, Sylvia, eyes fixed on him, inhaled deeply and said in almost a whisper, "I think you'd better leave, Sam. Take your clothes and go."

He went upstairs to the bedroom and put some clothes in a holdall. He looked in on the children, walked to their bunk bed in the dark room, which smelled of stale socks, and touched them lightly. He thought they were both sleeping, but Joseph was awake. He asked, "Dad, when is Granny coming back?" They had lost their grandmother and now they were about to lose their father and he was responsible. Go, he told himself. Get out now.

"We'll visit her soon," he said. "Everything will be all right."

He left the house and threw the holdall in the back of the car. He sat for a while, feeling confused, as if he had forgotten how to drive. He saw the living-room curtains part and Sylvia's face, ghostly and disembodied, framed by the window. I can still go back, he thought. It's not too late. Fear seized him for a moment and his breathing felt shallow. He turned the ignition key and felt the Citroen's suspension system kick in as the rear of the car started to rise. The living room curtains closed.

26. *Vincent and Sam, advice rejected, 1984*

"So, you've abandoned the thesis?"

"Quite a while now."

"Remind me what it was about."

"That was the problem. I couldn't decide. Something to do with race, modernity and post-colonial subjectivity. Something like that."

"Right. Haven't a clue what you mean by that, mate."

"Neither have I. As I said, that was the problem."

"Anyway, so what have you been doing?"

"Just hanging around, mostly up north, had a few casual jobs."

Vincent and Samuel were sitting in the Morningside Cafe in Camden Town. They had last met at Neville's bedside. Samuel had chosen the date and time of their meeting – mid-afternoon.

He had an appointment in the neighbourhood. Vincent had chosen the venue – a greasy spoon cafe incongruously decorated with Aubrey Beardsley prints – for the view of the busy junction where pedestrians, cars and cyclists couldn't resist trying to beat the lights. He watched a male cyclist, forced to dismount by a carelessly driven blue Mercedes saloon, shaking a fist at the disappearing vehicle. Time was when he would have interpreted such an incident as an instance of class conflict. These days he was reluctant to make such hasty interpretations; he was searching for a fresh way of looking at the world, trying to decide whether he had witnessed urban spatial dissonance or urban spatial dysfunctionality.

Vincent had followed a degree programme that spanned the humanities and social sciences. Within weeks of starting it, though his precocious political dreams had begun to fade, he was introduced to thinkers who fired his imagination. The works of Karl Marx, Sigmund Freud and others inspired him with a new dream, to become an academic. Then, it was the works of Althusser, Foucault and Derrida – and also Fanon, Dubois and Marcus Garvey. Having to decide whether he was a positivist, rationalist or realist on the great epistemology debate gave him many long, feverish nights, which ended only when he recognised that this project inevitably led to the cul-de-sac of infinite regress, so he settled for the position favoured by the pragmatist philosophers: we know what we know in relation to the problem we pose.

"Vincent?" he heard Sam say.

"Oh, sorry Sam. I was a little distracted for a moment."

"Distracted. Distractedness seems to be your default mode. I noticed you at Neville's bedside in the hospital and his home. You didn't seem to be there most of the time. You seemed so preoccupied. Physically present but mentally absent."

"The hospital. Oh, come on Sam, it's not everyday you see one of your brothers rigged up to some fantastical electronic contraption designed to measure and maintain every possible electrical current and pulse in a human being. I was puzzled by the meaning of my brother's condition, wondering whether, strictly speaking, he was a whole new life form. Everything about him challenged the orthodox notion of a living organism. I felt as though I were looking at the future…"

"Vincent, cut the crap. Neville had a subdural haemorrhage. He's lucky he lived so close to Homerton Hospital. Thank goodness he's continued to mend. Look, we're all very concerned about you. Me, Mummy, Dad, Maureen and Neville. We had no idea you'd abandoned your studies."

"Neither did I initially. Thought I was just taking a break, but things just dragged on. After a while, I just didn't see the point in returning to all those long hours in the library trying to get my head around opaque, impenetrable, torturous prose."

"You'll regret it," Samuel said. "If you've got a doctorate, somebody somewhere will employ you."

"You're assuming I'd have got the doctorate. That was never guaranteed. Anyway, I'd really just had enough of that life. Maybe I'll return to it when I can find a subject to sustain my interest over the long haul. In fact, I've been lucky already; got a strong chance of getting a bedsit in Finsbury Park."

Samuel smiled and said, "Near where Joseph and John were conceived. What are you going to do by way of work?"

"I'm trying to decide. There's a possibility of some part-time teaching, but I am trying to avoid having to take it. A friend of mine works for a small magazine. Maybe I'll see if I can contribute to it; something different."

"How you can throw away all your education?"

"Spare me that line, Sam, please. I've heard enough of that from the old man. There was little point trying to explain my, let's call it, existential crisis."

"Existential crisis! Vincent you're Black. Black people don't experience existential crises. We can't afford to despair."

"An existential crisis isn't synonymous with despair, Sam. It can be quite the opposite. I need a new direction, that's all."

"Sounds like despair to me. Sounds to me as if you're lost."

"Lost? Despair? Sam, I'm beginning to find your line of conversation quite irritating and bordering on the offensive. I've been out of London for several years exercising responsibility for myself and returned reasonably fit and healthy. I don't appreciate your big brother crap, or your misguided insistence on trying to place me in a straitjacket called 'black person', because, if pressed to define such a person, I'm sure you'd soon find yourself staggering around some dark labyrinth without a thread to guide you back to your starting point, and some mythical beast waiting to gore you to death. Remember when Aunt Irene visited, and I told everyone I wanted to be prime minister and you said it was an impossible dream? Because of the colour of my skin. It's ironic, isn't it, now you're a local councillor."

"And you resent me for that? Is that why you're being so awkward?"

"Resent you? Why should I resent you for waking up to the possibilities around you. On the contrary, that you've settled on an ambition I once held is a source of pride to me. Yet another reason for you to back off with your big brother crap."

"Okay, I was wrong then. I couldn't see what you saw. Our world seemed so limited. But I'm realistic about what I can achieve. I'm not dreaming of becoming prime minister or foreign secretary. In fact, I'm not dreaming at all. There's a long queue of Black people wanting to be MPs and I joined the queue, very late. Right now, I am happy to serve as a councillor. What worries me is that you don't seem to see any future for yourself."

"Sam, the realist, eh. Where I go from here is my problem, not yours. You were wrong in the past, and you're wrong now. I was given a chance to do post-graduate studies; I seized it, then realised my heart wasn't in it. It's not a nice admission to make, partly because I denied the space to someone with a stronger commitment. But that's the truth." He had been visiting a friend in Sheffield and, unable to sleep, at about 2 a.m, he'd dressed and wandered out into the back garden to have a cigarette. It was a cold, frosty night; the sky was clear and velvety black and full of stars. Then from somewhere in the dark came the faint sound of a trumpet blowing a note that was so sweet and pure and full of grace that it compelled him to concentrate. The music seemed to float slowly, then soar, like some wondrous nocturnal bird riding on a vector of warm air, cutting a golden path through the darkness that stretched across to the Derbyshire moors, visible in the daylight from the back garden. It was there, below Orion's belt, within earshot of a pure graceful trumpet sound, that all his doubts, present from the outset, about continuing to study coalesced, and he decided that while his ignorance was as vast as the universe, he knew enough about one academic discipline, understood the self-questioning nature of knowledge, knew what it was to know. From that night on, he began to drift, slowly but ineluctably, away from academia.

"Fair enough. So long as you recognise that the future's still yours to make," Samuel said.

"There you go again. Now you're trying to patronise me."

"There's no need to be so defensive, Vince."

"Then speak to me as you would to an independent adult, not some whining little brother."

"Sorry. Maybe you're right. It's not easy to change the habit of a lifetime."

"A bad habit. Try harder."

"Okay, okay, fair enough. Look, what I'm trying to say is that it's a good time. Britain's changing, especially for us, especially since the riots. Believe me. You had your head buried in books when they were happening. I felt the change immediately afterwards. There's a massive social engineering programme going on designed to include us, the second and third generations. That's my reading of the situation, one shared by many people."

"I'm not entirely sure that I want to be socially engineered."

"Now who's being arrogant?"

"Actually, I was being facetious."

"Or facile?"

"Very good, Sam." Vincent resisted the temptation to ask Sam if he knew the multiple meanings of the word.

"Look, Vince, let's be serious. We're all concerned about you."

"I am serious, Sam. Thanks for your concern. But I intend to do with the rest of my life what I choose. I am not going to do anything just because it satisfies your committee of concerned relatives, including Mom."

"Goodness, Vincent. What is the matter with you? Is that the problem? You haven't got over Mom leaving you, us, with the old man. Haven't or can't forgive her? If that's so, then you have a lot of growing up to do."

"Okay, it was an unnecessary remark. Look, the main point I am trying to make is this: I'm an individual. You're speaking to me in a way that denies my individuality because you're clinging to the cosy assumption that you and me, being Black, being brothers, being the children of immigrants must, willy-nilly, want the same things from life. Supposing I don't share your life aspirations?"

Sam sighed exasperatedly, and said, "Do you even want life?"

"Even that, Sam, dear Sam, is my bloody choice to make."

"Okay, okay, Vince. I really don't know where you're coming from with that kind of talk."

"It's called freedom, Sam."

"Okay, Vince. I can't really go there with you. The point I'm trying to make is that we, the family, are more than willing to help you. That's what families do."

"I hear you, Sam. Loud, but at this distance, less than clear."

Vincent knew that Samuel was going through his own travails, the divorce from Sylvia, the house hunting for their mother, who still lived with Maureen, who blamed Sam for causing Rhoda's homelessness. But nothing about Sam's bearing suggested he was drowning in his troubles. His blue wool suit and crisp, starched, white shirt, his glowing skin, pearl-white teeth and neatly trimmed thick hair heightened Vincent's awareness of his own receding hairline, his dull, ashen skin and time-worn clothes. A stranger might mistakenly see him as Samuel's elder, or some distant relative fallen on hard times. Samuel possessed some secret reserve of strength, vitality, resilience, no matter what was thrown at him. Vincent regarded him with a mixture of brotherly love and admiration – from an unpromising beginning, by discipline and determination, Sam had transformed his life.

Their conversation became less tense when Samuel told him about his efforts to find a house for Rhoda and how he and their father had made something of a reconciliation over Neville's hospital bed. "It's a start, but I don't think we'll ever be bosom buddies, but at least you're close by. The man thinks he's invincible. But seeing him at the hospital, I saw how much he's aged. He's going to need you."

"Dad! Need me?" Vincent said. "If that day ever comes, I'm sure he'll decide his time's up, and top himself."

Samuel laughed and looked at his watch. "How're you doing for money?"

"I'm signing on. Meaning…"

"You don't have to tell me, Vince. I've been there. Many times. Take this. It's not much, but it's all I can give right now. Check me at the end of the month. Come to dinner. Elena bakes a mean lamb casserole."

Vincent took the money and said he would contact him later in the month. Sam called for the bill, and outside, above the din of the traffic, he said, "Chin up, Vince, remember you're a Bostock. You'll be all right. We'll be fine."

"Yeah, sure," Vincent said.

They shook hands, hugged and parted.

Vincent was staying with a friend near Seven Sister's station. As he walked there, he reflected on the curious effect Sam had on him. In spite of his almost epiphanic moment of certainty that academia was not for him, his aggressive rebuttal of Samuel's right to question his life choice had been a masterly piece of dissembling; he had far less confidence in the future than he'd pretended. By abandoning his postgraduate studies, he had committed one of Lucas Bostock's cardinal sins: failing to finish something he started, and he'd felt a sense of shame that kept him living in Leeds. He'd drifted from one casual job to another – a bakery, a steel foundry. For a time, he'd even belonged to a commune whose members were all university drop-outs who spent most of the day high on cannabis while discussing utopian ideals. It was Neville's boxing accident that persuaded him he should return home to London. Neville had come close to death; he had merely abandoned a doctoral programme. Failure, he recognised, need not be a source of crippling shame. Maybe he'd grown by failing. But he still feared he'd be plunged into a swamp of uncertainty, miasmic and insalubrious. There was that night in the back garden when a musical note borne on the night breeze had inspired him to seek a different path. When that memory came to him, clear and strong and pure, like that trumpet sound, he relished the challenge of making himself anew.

As he walked, Samuel's parting words rang in his ears, "You're a Bostock. You'll be all right. We'll be fine." He recalled Aunt Irene's visit, how Samuel had ridiculed him. Perhaps Samuel had played a part in bringing him to this impasse? Then this idea seemed too close to a failure to take responsibility for himself, and it threatened his love for Samuel. In his first year at university, when he was most missing home, Samuel and Neville were always in his mind. And when failure came, it was the shame of facing them that kept him away from London. But he was not about to lose his elder brother to envy and rancour. He agreed with Samuel that there was a different mood in London. There were more black faces on television, a new Black newspaper; even the music had changed: the lamentation of Rastafarian reggae for the assertive urban music of rap or hip-hop, a music devoid of nostalgia. Hope had been born out of the violence and destruction of the riots. Better, he thought, to applaud Samuel for seizing the moment, even if it was one he had himself once entertained and which was now out of the question because Samuel had staked a claim to it – as he had claimed the front seat in their father's car on their Sunday drives around the city.

Nevertheless, "You're a Bostock, we'll be fine", seemed a strange thing for Samuel to have said. Had he been speaking to himself, as if he conflated their futures? As if he was denying him, Vincent, the right to be an individual, separate and apart from the family. If so, he could see only one winner in such a relationship: Samuel. He did not have Sam's calm, confidence and energy; he might be swept along like so much debris in the surging river that was Samuel's career and life. He was not sure what the future held for him, but whether it was failure or success, he had to keep his distance from Samuel. Distance would enable him to continue loving him.

27. *Vincent meets Donnette, a few months later*

That Christmas, Vincent moved into a bed-sit on the top floor of Phoenix House, a brown, cube-shaped block on Seven Sisters Road. Originally built as an hotel, the building had been converted by the borough council into housing for single people, who did not always remain single, so it was not unusual to hear children playing in the corridors. Among other tenants, he became acquainted with Martin, a thin, impecunious, white blues musician who subsidised his benefits cheque with busking and occasional gigs in North London pubs; Mr Krishna, a retired mathematics teacher from India, who always wore a beatific smile; Vernon, a Jamaican van driver who worked for a bakery called Mixed Blessings; Angus, whose background was vague, though he intimated that he had once been on the stage; and Paul, a Nigerian schoolteacher and devout Catholic. These men formed the core of the Phoenix House Tenants' Association, and they provided Vincent with information about his new home and neighbours – the failed fathers and single mothers, the asbestos in the former ballroom, now home to pigeons and feral cats who entered through its broken windows. And if he ever doubted their description of Phoenix House as the biggest whorehouse in Europe, he had only to leave his room at night to see and hear the drug dealers and prostitutes in the stairwell, where children played during the day.

It seemed fitting to Vincent that he lived in such a place of impermanence and transience. He subsisted on a modest and erratic income from freelance journalism, writing record and book reviews for small and obscure publications run on shoestring budgets. Many afternoons, his meagre work done, found him walking around the park or sitting at his ninth-floor window looking towards the city as though it was some intractable and fiendish puzzle – like the jigsaw puzzles of his childhood, Buckingham Palace, Tower Bridge, and so on. He was aware that the greater conundrum was not how the city fitted together but how he fitted into it. If he solved that puzzle, maybe he would be able to move on.

It was in late May, on his monthly visit to his father's house, a twenty-minute walk across Clissold Park, that Vincent discovered he had another sibling. "She's got my stamp all right," his father said and Vincent assumed that she was result of a relationship that predated his parent's marriage. Lucas asked Vincent to show her around; he was intrigued but reluctant. He lived a solitary life, kept a small circle of friends who, like him, subsisted on the lesser pickings of the city, and his longest regular journeys beyond Finsbury Park involved going to collect the records and books from the offices of the publications that gave him work. He was hardly the best guide.

"What about Neville or Samuel?"

"Neville's just getting back on his feet. And Samuel, well he seems like a busy man to me."

Vincent agreed that his father could give her his telephone number. Her name was Donnette.

Some days later she called, and they met in a cafe on Blackstock Road. He recognised her straightaway. The smooth dark complexion, oval face and high cheek bones, the dimple in her chin, the brown eyes with their direct gaze. He saw a variation of Maureen and Neville, and perhaps a female version of himself. The doubt he had expressed to his father vanished. He tried to guess her age but drew a blank and simply assumed that she was older than Samuel.

"Gosh, you look like your father," she said, after they shook hands.

"So do you." They laughed together. His laugh was shallow and brief, Donnette's lasted longer, as if it was beyond her control.

Shy, reticent, and more at ease with roaming his own mind than expressing his feelings and thoughts, Vincent was a natural listener. Donnette was ebullient, talkative; she seemed, even on this first meeting, to want Vincent to know everything about her Jamaican childhood: the man she thought was her father who disappeared when she was around five years old, her mother's deathbed revelation and hearing for the first time the name Lucas Bostock. She started accounts, digressed, forgot why she had gone down particular avenues and apologised for her digressions. She laughed a great deal, sometimes so loudly that other people in the cafe looked at them, causing Vincent to wince in mild embarrassment. When she had exhausted one topic, she would start with a question like, "And did I tell you about the time a scorpion bit me?" And she would be off again, describing a world of heat, dust, whole families sharing single rooms and privacy an unknown luxury. What astonished Vincent was that he did not hear any anger or rancour in her recollections.

"You're so lucky to live in England," she said. "To have everything a person could want: work, somewhere to live, buy good clothes. It's like God gave everything to England and nothing to Jamaica, just sunshine and poverty. Hardship everywhere."

"I'm not sure God had anything to do with it," Vincent said.

"You mean you don't believe in God, Vincent. How come? Say that in Jamaica and people will stone you."

"Sorry, I shouldn't have said that. It's difficult to explain." He was still trying to decide whether he was an atheist or an agnostic. "Anyway, that's not the point. Many West Indian settlers would say England's a bit like a mirage to a thirsty person, an illusion. Are you getting what I am saying?"

"No. Tell me, Vincent. There's so much I don't know and want to know. I've seen things on the television and on the streets that don't make sense to me. Help me to make sense of them. Be my brother." Donnette reached across the table and laid her hand on his.

Moved by her appeal, he allowed her to touch him for a moment, then pulled his hand away and lit a cigarette. He felt trapped and anxious.

"I'm not a teacher or a guide, Donnette. I'm still trying to work out what it's all about." Yet, in Donnette's presence he was seeing himself in new and unexpected ways. He had never given much thought to his privileges, had seen himself as the unfortunate child of a broken family who lacked the fight and energy to secure a comfortable niche in the city for himself. But here was Donnette, the wide-eyed newcomer, expressing envy of him, seeking his help.

"Oh, God," Donnette said, terror on her face. She slid lower in her chair. "I think I just saw Lester. I've got to get out of here. God, I hope he didn't see me."

"Donnette, calm down. Who's Lester?"

"Let's get out of here now, please."

Vincent tried to remember how he had left his room. It was capable of descending into chaos. He went to pay the bill, and when he got back to the table, Donnette had put on sunglasses, though it wasn't sunny outside, and a floppy canvas hat. They left the cafe and when Vincent tried to turn left, Donnette pulled him to the right, saying: "He went that way, if it was him. He went that way."

They hurried along Blackstock Road and turned right on Seven Sisters Road. "You live near here, don't you. Can we go there?"

She did not comment on the mess as Vincent went about tidying up. She stood by the window, smoking a cigarette with short rapid puffs.

"I'm sorry, " she said at last. "I just lost it there. I swear it was him. Lester."

"Who's Lester?"

"Oh, just some guy. A guy who helped me to get here."

She removed her shades and hat and shot him a glance which made him feel naive; yet though he had never encountered anyone like Donnette, he felt at ease with her.

"If you want my help, you'd better tell me what's going on."

"You know where I've come from. How do you think I got here? England doesn't want any more Jamaicans, unless they're educated. Yeah, my English isn't too bad, because my mother always listened to the BBC world service, but I don't have any education, Vincent. I got here using my wits. As we say in Jamaica, I had to try a t'ing."

"Meaning?"

She told him about buying a fake passport with savings and borrowed money and that she had been expected to work for the syndicate until she had repaid her debt, but she had absconded. When she finished, he felt complacent and idle and self-pitying. He had never been in trouble with the law.

"Did you tell my father?"

"You mean our father, don't you?"

"Yes, I'm sorry."

"How could I? It took me such a long time to reach him. Lester and his people had me trapped. Over a year. I wasn't going to tell him that the daughter he didn't know about had entered the country on a fake passport, carrying drugs, arranged for by gangsters in Kingston."

"He's a tough old guy and more wise to the real world than me. But you probably did the right thing not telling him. So, what now?"

"I'm trying to earn enough to pay off my debt. I just don't want to work for Lester. The man's a killer."

"A killer?"

"A gunman."

Vincent felt his hold on reality warp and slip. Guns and killers belonged to movies, the London underworld, and the world's war zones. Now here he was with a half-sister who spoke casually of killers and gunmen, who effortlessly moved between Jamaican patois and Standard English.

"Those are my people. He comes from yard, from Kingston."

He realised that he had not fully grasped what she had told him in the cafe.

"How old are you, Donnette?"

"I don't normally tell men my age, but as it's you... I'll be twenty-six on my next birthday."

"Me too. What month?"

"June."

"Me too."

"What date?

"The seventeenth."

"Mine's the sixteenth"

They looked at each for a long while, Vincent trying to digest this coincidence, to think through its implications. He shuffled dates in his mind and thought of the rupture between his parents and his mother's sudden disappearance.

Donnette asked him for a cigarette. He lit it for her and she inhaled deeply and said, "We're twins, sort of." She released a long loud laugh. Vincent smiled wryly and shook his head.

She showed no desire to leave and he, unusually, did not want to be alone. He prepared eggs in the kitchenette while she lounged on the sofa bed. When they had finished eating, Donnette asked him to tell her about growing up in London. He told her about life in house of tenants, about the separation between his parents, the years of being driven across London to see his mother and sister. Donnette said she was an only child and pressed him for details of his siblings. She wanted to meet the others – Samuel, Neville and Maureen.

"I'll tell them about you, but don't hold out any hopes. Neville, maybe. But I doubt that either Samuel or Maureen will want to know you. I'm just being honest." He saw the hurt on her face and wanted to retract what he had said.

"Why not?"

"Maybe I shouldn't presume to speak for them. We don't meet up often. I wouldn't say we're close. But I know they're out there somewhere."

"What're you afraid of, Vincent?"

"Me, afraid?"

"Yes, I was watching you prepare the eggs and noticed fear on your face. I saw it earlier in the cafe, too."

"I'm not aware of being afraid."

"Where I come from in downtown Kingston, you learn to watch people, to see how far they'll go. Their eyes tell you everything. We have a saying downtown, "Born fi dead". You can tell when a person truly believes that because that person's not afraid of anything – policeman, soldiers, customs and immigration officers – nobody."

"Like you?

"Yes."

"And my eyes tell you I'm not like that – that I'm afraid?"

"Sometimes, and I wonder what you're afraid of."

"Maybe it's not fear on my face, at least not a simple fear. You see, Donnette, until a few years ago, I thought I knew exactly where I wanted to go; now I'm not so sure. And you know what's really scary? I don't think I care." This admission surprised Vincent in its brutal clarity. He had hoped that by returning to London, the flame of purpose would reignite and propel him to towards a meaningful future. But now he felt he had expended the energy of a lifetime against some overwhelming force, and this had left him too exhausted to achieve anything of much significance.

"That's a dangerous place to be," Donnette said.

"Look who's talking! What about the guy you're hiding from?"

"Lester. He's just some power-hungry mad man. I can outwit him. I have faith in myself. But it sounds to me that you're holding a gun to your own head."

"That's a slight exaggeration."

Donnette lit another cigarette, and Vincent was aware of her watching him with their father's eyes, eyes that seemed to look at life as a challenge to be relished. There was something calming about her and he wondered why he, with all his advantages, felt so much weaker, so lacking in spirit.

"Maybe God decided to balance things out," she said, as if reading his mind. "Gave you London and gave me faith."

"As I said, I'm not a believer, at least not in any simple way."

"You know, wherever I am, no matter how bad things are, I always make time to pray. Pray to the Almighty, yes. Maybe that's what separates us."

"Then you're luckier than me." He was aware of the flippant tone in his voice, but wondered whether faith in God or a god was necessary for self-belief. She reminded him how much he lacked confidence, trapping him between the past his parents had made and a future he could not make.

Vincent felt weary. Donnette's candour, her direct questioning, had caused him to talk more in six hours than he had done in the last six weeks. Yet he did not want her to leave. She was the clearest mirror he had ever looked into, giving back a reflection that helped him to understand his inertia. He liked her womanly presence; the jewellery, perfume and lip gloss. He had missed Maureen as a child, and now she remained a stranger.

He asked Donnette to make space for him on the sofa; the chair at his desk was uncomfortable. She shifted to one end and he sat down.

"You want me to leave?" Donnette said.

"No, no. Stay." He touched her fleshy, soft, dark arm and recalled her pleading gesture in the cafe earlier. "Help me to understand," she had said. He could not bring himself to repeat her words. He had read many books, and numerous grand abstractions swirled in his mind. And yet he felt an overwhelming urge to ask this half-sister, who seemed so knowing and at ease with herself, to answer the question: *Where do you find the courage and daring to be yourself?*

"Stay," he repeated. "Tell me more about Jamaica."

She told him about the seasons, the vegetation and landscape. After a pause she said, in almost confessional tone, "I have a ten-year old daughter, Korah. She goes to a boarding school in Kingston and stays with an aunt when school's closed. What I'm doing is all for her. I want her to have an education. It's her only chance."

"Did you tell Dad about Korah?"

"Yes, he wrote me a cheque. He was very generous. He said it wasn't for me, it was for the child because I was a big woman who should know how to look after myself."

"Sounds like him. Still, you're lucky. Most people only see his mean, hard side. You must miss her, your daughter."

"Miss her? Vincent, every minute of the day I think about when I can hold her in my arms again."

"And Dad… you'll see him again?"

"Yes, but I don't want to bring the world I move in to his doorstep."

She said she had to go, and she got up off the mattress and gathered her belongings. When he said there would not be any public transport at this hour, she told him that her car was parked a few blocks away.

"A car!" Vincent exclaimed. He could not drive.

"You don't think I'd walk around at night with all these dangerous people on the streets," she said, laughing.

Their exit from Phoenix House went without incident. The block's nightlife could be filled with furtive and menacing figures; tonight, it was having a quiet night. They walked to a road parallel with the main road and stopped beside a dark blue BMW series five. Vincent refrained from commenting. They hugged and she whispered, "Thank you. I'm glad to have a brother like you." She said she would call again.

"Same here, a sister like you."

He walked back to Phoenix House feeling a little light-headed. Another sister, very different from Maureen, and he liked her. But he could not help worrying that he was making a mistake inviting her into his life. She had entered the country illegally. How was she surviving? He feared that he knew the answer to that question without hearing it from her lips. He felt confused. His father had fathered a child who almost shared his birthday and age; he had driven Uncle Horace out of the house, leading to his suicide. Should he deny his father? Should he deny Donnette? No, he loved his father. And after one evening in her company, he was sure he admired her and could one day come to love her, too. Back in his room, as he readied for bed, something glinted between the sofa's cushions. He pulled it out and saw that it was a gold bangle, plain but with a solid weightiness; it had to be Donnette's. He placed it on his desk and went to bed.

On a cool summer night, Vincent was gazing out the window as he waited for Donnette; he had not seen her in over a week. She had telephoned earlier in the day appealing for help but refusing to say what kind of help, her voice breathless, urgent, pleading. He had reassured her that he would give whatever help he could. It seemed unnecessary for her to ask. They had seen a lot of each other since their first meeting. She often telephoned him late in the evening and could arrive at past-midnight; she always brought food and drink. They would stay up for a few hours playing cards – she was a convincing poker player – and talking. They had slept together on the sofa-bed, the mattress on the floor, observing their close blood relation by forsaking sex, though one daybreak found their limbs entangled, and Vincent found himself rushing under the shower.

Her visits had revitalised him and he became more involved in the Residents' Association. Along with Mr Krishna and Vernon, he put out a questionnaire for tenants on how to improve the block. Now they were agitating for greater security, a children's play area, and a launderette.

He was writing more for a weekly called *Urban Lines*. The pay was awful but regular, his all-white colleagues friendly. He had ventured beyond his usual fare of reviews and written a twelve-hundred-word feature article on the docklands area. Researched over two weeks and written over three agonising weeks, the article explored the impact of urban regeneration on the local community. Tramping around the dusty streets, gazing at the cranes, piledrivers, earthmovers and men in hard hats and steel toe-capped boots was an adventure. He was witnessing what seemed like a massive rebirth of the city. One October night he persuaded Donnette to drive around docklands; he explained the names of sites like the West India Docks and Jamaica Street, signs of their people's own much earlier presence in the city. Then they walked along the Thames at night. Donnette said the sounds from the river were scary – which made Vincent laugh heartily because she had betrayed the limit of her prodigious courage.

His sense of the city's wonder was still with him as he waited for Donnette. She arrived half-an-hour later with a bulging large navy-blue suitcase. She wore black leggings, a light blue denim skirt frayed at the hem, a thick wrap-around brown cardigan and an amber necklace. She seemed upset, and told Vincent that, in the lift, an elderly man with a walking stick had offered her five pounds for what he described as temporary relief from the strangulating loneliness of old age. Vincent laughed, reminding her of Phoenix House's reputation, and told her she had probably met Mr Krishna, who lived on the eight-floor.

"What's with the suitcase?" he asked.

"I need somewhere safe to stay. I think Lester knows where to find me." She had been found by Pedro, one of Lester's henchmen, in the Walthamstow flat where she was staying with a group of girls whose position in London was just as precarious as hers. One of them had brought Pedro to the flat, inadvertently exposing her to danger. She had begged Pedro not to tell Lester of her whereabouts. He had agreed because, he admitted, he did not have any faith in Lester's plan to displace Juba, the Stonebridge don, and was beginning to suspect that Lester was losing touch with reality. But she did not trust Pedro to keep quiet; she knew too well the importance of loyalty among soldiers.

"You should go to the police about this guy Lester."

"I'm an illegal immigrant, here on a fake passport and false name. Only you and a few other people know who I am, know me as Donnette."

"Yes, sorry. But you can't spend the rest of your life running from the guy." Vincent remembered their walk by the Thames, Donnette's fright at the river's murmuring and slapping sounds. His laughter now seemed misplaced. Perhaps that night Donnette's mask had slipped, and he had seen not just fright, but the real Donnette beneath the alias.

"I don't intend to; I just need a bit more time."

"For what?"

"This and that."

He would not to quiz her. He sensed that their intimacy, the energising influence of her presence and the palpable sense of wholeness that she gave him would not survive if he knew the details of her daily movements. Both Samuel and Maureen had refused to meet her and forbade him giving her their telephone numbers, though he had only told them that she was in the country, not how she got here, and not her age. She had met Neville, but with his large family and fledgling mini-cab business, he had little time and space for a new sibling. So, Vincent saw her as his responsibility.

On the occasions when his conscience troubled him, he sought refuge in history's unfairness and smothered his qualms with the undeniable fact that he was in love with Donnette.

While Donnette took a shower, Vincent prepared something for them to eat. He found a plantain so ripe its skin was completely black and speckled with mould. Another cupboard yielded a bottle of red wine. Soon the pungent aroma of fried plantain filled the room. On the bed, over the bottle of red wine and dish of plantain, Vincent expressed scepticism about her fears.

"Those guys are real," Donnette insisted. "They're out there right now, dealing and scheming. They'll do what ever it takes to build bases here."

"I don't know how you could get yourself mixed up with people like that."

"Because they offered me a way out. You wouldn't understand that, Vincent. Most people think of Jamaica as paradise. Why would anybody want to leave paradise? Cornelius understood. Cornelius said he could do it but he didn't tell me the price and when he did it was too late. My heart was already committed."

"You mean Cornelius was a lover?"

"Vincent!" She shoved him playfully. He seized her and they struggled for a moment, with Donnette laughing and telling him that English boys were rude. He subdued her, or she allowed herself to be subdued, and he rolled on top of her and pressed his lips against hers. Her lips parted and she held him tightly and he plunged his tongue into her mouth and tasted the residue of wine, sharp and sweet.

"Get off me," Donnette said, pushing him aside with surprising force. "You're my brother."

"Only half," Vincent said. "Anyway, go on, tell me about Cornelius."

"I guess he was a kind of lover, but not in the normal way."

Donnette was lying on her back and Vincent, stretched beside her, rested on an elbow. She had met Cornelius when she was working as a chambermaid in the Rivers Hotel in Ocho Rios. He had been a guest there and had returned to his room while she was cleaning it, and they'd struck up a friendship. His plaited hair, gold rings, chains and bangles, and high-pitched laugh convinced her that he was harmless, though she later learned that he had seventeen children between Jamaica, New York and Port-au-Prince. When Cornelius offered to take her for a morning drive she accepted. They drove up into the hills above the resort. On a road that became little more than a dirt track they stopped beside a pool. Massive ferns grew on the bank. Cornelius stripped naked and waded into the stream and called Donnette to join him as though they were children playing. She hesitantly followed. The water felt so wonderful she forgot she was naked before a man she had known for less than forty-eight hours. He did not try to touch her; they lay on the rocks with water rushing over their bodies.

When they'd dressed, he told her he wanted to show her something special. They drove along an overgrown path and then she saw it: a field of ganja, about hundred yards long with plants seven to eight feet high. Taking off most of his clothes again, Cornelius explained that this was one of his sources of income, how he could afford to take a break in a holiday resort used by foreigners. He took some items from the car, including a shower cap and wraparound sunglasses which he put on. He told Donnette to wait. She watched as he set off running between the rows of plants, the leaves stroking his near naked body. He returned to the car and gave her what looked like a spatula and told her to scrape his skin, from his shoulders down to his ankles, removing a thick resin. When she'd finished, she had created a small, sticky brown ball. Cornelius repeated his run through the field until they had harvested a fist-sized ball of resin. He held it and said: "Now that is worth hundreds of dollars on the streets of New York. That is what I deal in." He invited her to look him up when she was next in Kingston.

"He opened my eyes," Donnette said. "And once they'd been opened, I couldn't shut them again."

Vincent tried to imagine Donnette's life in Jamaica, its lack of choice, her hopes for her daughter, her discovery that she had a father in England. In comparison, he was a spoilt child, agonising over a cornucopia of choices. He regretted doubting her and told her so and she accepted his apology with grace. He regretted, too, that first kiss, so playfully given. After all, she was his half-sister. Yet, some days later, when Donnette initiated the next kiss, he could not resist. And thus began something that over the next three months filled him with guilty feelings of moral transgression, but also indescribable pleasure. They were like children, their bodies toys.

For a few weeks, their favourite nocturnal game was swapping sexes, with Vincent wearing Donnette's clothes and Donnette wearing his. After pulling him down on the bed, she rolled on top of him and kissed him with her hands up his skirt as he removed her trousers. Donnette told him that she liked watching him put on her clothes, but he admitted that the sight of her in his clothes did nothing for his libido.

Then Donnette started venturing out again, returning late at night and one evening in July, Vincent returned from work to an empty room. This was not unusual as Donnette often arrived around midnight. Late that evening the telephone rang.

"Where are you?"

"I'm in Harrow Road police station."

"What?"

"Listen, Vincent, listen please. They're going to deport me."

"I'll get you a lawyer."

"No. I've seen one already. She explained everything to me. There's nothing you or anybody can do. Please don't tell our father. Don't worry. I'll be all right. I'll call you from Kingston."

The following day, Vincent visited her at the police station. He quickly wished he had not gone there. Seeing her in that tiny, windowless basement cell, a policeman waiting outside, unnerved him. She seemed resigned and accepting of her fate and tried to reassure him that she would be all right. Before they parted, she whispered to him, "Remember, it's not me, Donnette, they're deporting. I'll be back."

He returned home, feeling inconsolably sad. Only the need to finish an article for the magazine that was going to press the next day held him together.

But when press day had passed and he was at home again, he had nothing but his loss to occupy him. Several times he picked up the phone to call his father to ask for help, but each time Donnette's appeal not to involve him stopped him. Sometimes he felt relieved that she would no longer be there; they had committed a great wrong and it had to come to an end. But this moral clarity came to him like flashes of lightning in a gathering storm of desire and pleasure and painful loss. Exhausted, he went to the window and looked over the city. His breathing became shallow, and he began gasping for breath. He opened the window, and the cool air thrashed his face but brought no relief. I can't go on, he thought. I can't. The city lights, the night sky, the precipitous height – all seemed to conspire in tempting him towards a sweet, terrible and irreversible oblivion.

Then the telephone rang; he snatched it up and heard his mother say, "Vincent, you've been on my mind all week."

29. *Rhoda, at around the same time*

Rhoda's years of shuttling between Brixton and Acton – between the discomfort of sharing a house with Sylvia and Maureen's reluctant hospitality – ended when she bought a house in Homerton, near Hackney Marshes. Her cousin Bertie Johnson found and recommended the property and squashed her misgivings about moving back north of the river, living so close to Lucas, by pointing out that there was enough distance between them for their paths never to meet. She would be closer to Neville and his children, and to Vincent. Soon after moving in – in the winter of '84 – she discovered he was right. She could walk to the shop in Chatsworth Road, or a little farther, Mare Street. Neville's mini-cab company was nearby, as was his home. Finsbury Park, Vincent's home, was a short bus-ride away.

But her greatest discovery was the neighbourhood's Black church, the New Church of God, on Chatsworth Road. From being a believer, she became a regular worshipper, never missing a Sunday service. There in the noisy gathering, she prayed for her children's souls. Samuel, who had funded the house purchase, was, she believed, all right now: she had seen him with Elena, noted his stillness in her company, so different from when he was with Sylvia, when he always had a distant look in his eyes. Sylvia had been all wrong for him. There was no point Sylvia blaming her for Sam leaving – as she had done in one of their many bitter exchanges – saying that Rhoda didn't think she was good enough for her son. And Maureen? Age and motherhood would redeem her. There only remained Neville and Vincent, and towards them she directed feverish prayers for their redemption, prayers for them to recognise and receive her love, denied in their childhood by Lucas Bostock.

To prepare for the long hours in church, she would retire to her bedroom early on Saturday night. There, without fail, she would receive a phone call from Neil, from the Shetland Islands. Over the years she had received calls from him from different parts of the world: mainland Scotland, and Australia and New Zealand, while visiting his children. Once, he had called from the Everglades in

Florida where he had gone orchid hunting, one of many passions acquired in retirement – gardening, watercolour painting, learning to play the piano. His telephone conversations were filled with the details of hobbies discovered then abandoned.

One month before the calls stopped altogether, he revealed that he had found a new interest, cloud spotting, and he reeled off a list of impossibly long names for clouds – cumulonimbus, cirrocumulus, translucent cumulus and so on. She'd insisted, "But Neil, a cloud is just a cloud."

"No, Rhoda. They're all different, and the Paquot tribe in South America believe that clouds are the spirit of the dead. When I die, I'm going to come back as an altocumulus lenticularis."

"Neil, why're you suddenly talking about death?"

"I'm not. I'm talking about clouds."

When Neil did not call, Rhoda phoned his house and was told by a woman who described herself as his niece that he had lost his year-long fight against cancer. Year long! Since then Rhoda had worn black on Saturdays, and often looked at clouds and wondered if Neil's wish had been granted.

That autumn, while Rhoda was still grieving the passing of her secret friend, she received a telephone call from Maureen.

"On the M1. They had to cut Phil out of the car. His left leg is badly injured. The doctors are talking about having to amputate it."

"Phil! Amputate!"

"Yes, Mom. Amputate. Mom, I can't believe this is happening to me."

Rhoda said she would make her way to Acton immediately, and with the help of Neville's mini-cab company, reached there later that day. The house was quiet and the only light came from the television screen. Andrew had opened the door and he returned to the living room where he had been watching a video with his sister, Kate. She sat cross-legged in front of the screen, sucking her thumb, a habit Rhoda thought she had abandoned at the age of three. Asked where their mother was, the children both glanced up at the ceiling. A great believer in the comforting effects of food, Rhoda made sure the children were not hungry before making her way upstairs.

She found Maureen in bed, the bedroom curtains drawn, the lights off, the room smelling of tobacco. Rhoda switched on the light; Maureen protested; she had just come back from the hospital.

Rhoda saw that Maureen had been crying, her face puffy. It was almost two weeks since she had last seen her and Maureen had cut and restyled her hair; usually permed and glossy, it was now low on her scalp and consisted of shiny little twists.

"Now is not the time to take to bed," Rhoda said. "Tell me what happened."

Maureen did not have all the details. She did not know what Phil was doing on the motorway when he ought to have been at work. She described a figure swathed in bandages from head to toe, his legs in traction, and all sorts of tubes stuck into his body. Since telephoning Rhoda, she knew that amputation was definite; his left leg had been crushed to a pulp.

"When are you going back to the hospital?"

"I don't think I can go back there, Mom. I can't, don't want to see him like that. His mother's at the hospital. She can look after him." Maureen sobbed. "I need a cigarette."

"We need to pray to the Lord. We need to pray to the Lord for Phil, Maureen."

"The Lord! I need a fag, Mum." Maureen snatched up a packet of Silk Cut and, with shaky hands, pulled out one but did not light it. Instead she swallowed two paracetamol tablets. Then she lit the cigarette. "Sorry, Mom. I know you don't like me smoking, but I'm so stressed. I just can't believe this is fucking happening to me. Can't. Jesus wept!"

"Maureen, your mouth is filthier than a pit latrine."

"Sorry, Mum."

"Anyway, it's Phil who's going to lose a leg. Not you."

"Oh, you don't understand, Mum."

Rhoda took charge of Maureen's house. The following morning, after seeing the children off to school, she cajoled her daughter into visiting the hospital. Maureen had not exaggerated about his appearance; he had suffered third degree burns and was swathed in bandage, with only two small slits for his eyes.

His bed was surrounded by a jumble of machines, and a mass of tubes stuck out of him like the tendrils of an old banyan tree. He could not speak but was clearly glad to see Maureen, who kept her distance from the bed, a petrified expression on her face. Rhoda, at ease in the hospital environment, touched Phil, more precisely his bandaged hand, in a comforting gesture, which elicited a strangled murmur. Despair clawed at Rhoda to see the father of two of her grandchildren in such a pitiable state. He had always shown her kindness and hospitality, a loyal man who had helped Maureen to settle down and abandon some of her wild ways. Refusing to surrender to hopelessness, she took out the small bible that accompanied her everywhere, seized Maureen's hand, pulled her to the bedside, and began praying. With Maureen standing beside her, as meek and obedient as a child, she intoned the Lord's prayer and called on the Almighty to heal Phil.

Rhoda went with Maureen to the hospital for three consecutive days. Maureen was grave and silent on these visits. It was left to Rhoda to talk to the doctors and Phil's family. They met Phil's mother, Rose, several times. A slim woman with pinched features and thinning, heavily lacquered hair, swept backward in a vain attempt to disguise its sparseness, Rose spoke obsessively about Phil's happy childhood, as if she were resigned to losing him.

Rhoda offered comfort to Rose, too. When she expressed the view that Phil's ordeal would test his and Maureen's relationship, requiring them to show loyalty and strength, Maureen heaved and coughed and excused herself, saying she was going to be sick.

Later that same day, when they were alone, Rhoda asked Maureen if there was something she wanted to tell her.

"Like what?" Maureen bristled.

"You're not behaving right. Your husband is at death's door and it's…"

"He's off the critical list, mother," Maureen said, with some of her usual aggression. "And besides, you know me and Phil are not married."

"You have two children and you're living together. You're as good as. Why the two of you aren't married, I don't know. You young people and your modern ways! Now is the time for you to show your commitment in marriage, because he's going to need to know that you'll stand by him."

"Mum, you're as bad a Mother Teresa. I appreciate all the help you've given me, but I won't be converted to your way of thinking."

"These are the Lord's matters, Maureen. You and Phil have been living in sin and that's why Phil had that accident. It's the Lord's punishment."

"Phil's accident had nothing to do with sin," Maureen said. "If you really want to know…" Maureen stopped.

"If I really want to know what?"

"Nothing, nothing. You wouldn't understand."

"Maureen, are you seeing another man? Is that what's going on? Is that why Phil drove his car into a wall?"

"Who told you that?"

"The nurses talk, Maureen. One told me that the accident report said no other vehicles were involved, and so either Phil lost control of the car or he drove it into the wall."

"No, Mum. I'm not seeing another man. Can we leave it, please? My head is hurting." Maureen massaged her temples and went to the medicine cabinet, from which she got a huge container of Paracetamol.

Rhoda had lost count of the number of times Maureen had popped those pills. She did not press any further, but her suspicion grew that something was awry in Maureen's home.

That night Rhoda retired to Kate's room – Kate was sleeping in Andrew's room – weighed down by what she knew and did not know about her children. She felt as though she were trying to put out a fire. She knelt and began praying.

Just then the door creaked open, and she saw Kate silhouetted in the doorway. Holding a small teddy bear, she was rubbing her eyes and sniffling.

"What's the matter, baby?"

"Granny, can I sleep with you? Andrew says he doesn't want me in his room and I don't want to sleep there because he's got cheesy feet, and Mummy's door is locked."

Rhoda hugged her, smelling the soap she had washed her with earlier that evening and said, "We can't both sleep on your little bed, sweetheart. I'll sleep in the living room."

"You can't sleep there, Granny." Kate said, whispering. "That's where Daddy sleeps. When is Daddy coming home?"

"Your father will be home soon, sweetheart, the Lord willing. Now tell Granny, how long your father's been sleeping in the living room?"

"I dunno," Kate shrugged. "Maybe since Sandra moved in."

"Sandra. Who's Sandra?"

"She's our new neighbour. She's Rochelle's mother and me and Rochelle are best friends. She's much more fun than Andrew. And Mummy and Sandra are bestest friends, too. I saw them kissing."

Rhoda shook her head. The sleepy child had to be mistaken. "Hush now, child," she said. She put Kate to bed, and got a blanket from the linen cupboard and went downstairs to the living room.

Stretched out on the sofa, a storm of bemusement mixed with biblical passages about the abominations of the world raged in her tired mind. Before falling asleep she decided that whatever was going in this household, she would refuse to see it; she was there to help with her grandchildren and nothing would prevent her doing so.

30. *Donnette and Vincent, two years later*

"Did you miss me?"

"Yes."

"You're a liar. Bet you brought in another girl the very next day. How much did you miss me?"

Vincent and Donnette were sitting under a sprawling copper beech tree in Finsbury Park on a warm Saturday summer afternoon. Vincent searched his mind for an apt phrase that could capture his empty, bleak days of longing following Donnette's involuntary departure. But he remembered instead his mother's telephone call, which helped bring him back to his senses, and his slow recovery as he threw himself into work on *Urban Lines*.

"Like missing the last night train to London from a village deep in the English countryside."

"Doesn't sound as if you missed me much."

"You ever been to a village deep in the countryside?"

"No."

"Well, there you are. But I imagine being stuck in any village in the world must be nightmarish."

And the train had come, though in her absence he had been enjoying his work at *Urban Lines* and had made some good friends, their camaraderie heightened by the journal's unrelenting financial struggles and its radical reputation in conservative times.

He had been so absorbed in his work that when he heard Donnette's voice on the phone it took him a while to realise that this call wasn't coming from New York or Atlanta or Boston or Kingston; she was here in London again. Now here they were, sitting in Finsbury Park, his head in her lap, trying to find words to describe his feelings.

"Well, I missed you, Vincent. Thought about you every day when I was in prison in New York. All those weird things we did together. At the time we were doing them, I was just playing along with you. But nobody I've met since has made me feel, so, so nice."

Nice? Those long summer nights when the desire for pleasure plunged him into feelings of gnawing guilt? 'Nice' seemed too feeble a word for what they had known together. But he did not want to revive those brief, intense and unforgettable days. And now the Donnette on whose lap he was resting his head with genuine affection was different. Her voluptuous figure had turned to fat, which bulged out of the waist of her skirt; her legs and thighs, once sturdy and shapely, were now simply thick. He wondered if his memory was deceiving him.

"Me, too," Vincent said vaguely. But he'd moved on, found new playthings. The cruelty of his thought shocked him because he did not doubt that he still had strong feelings for Donnette.

"You know, Vincent, this is my last run. There are only so many times you can come into the country on false papers. I took the risk because it's worth it. I've got a bit of money put away. Korah was awarded a scholarship after she won the island-wide spelling bee contest. I've been thinking that I've got to go legit. And I've got an idea. Lignum Vitae. It's the heaviest wood in the world and it grows in Jamaica. I've seen some beautiful carvings and things made from it – bowls, candleholders. I know some guys in Ocho Rios who carve it for the tourist market. I'm thinking of investing in a workshop, finding buyers in department stores here and stateside."

"You were always a businesswoman, Donnette."

"But I need a partner, Vincent. And me and you, we're so close; it's like me and you are one. Why don't you come to Jamaica with me? Nobody need know we're related."

"That's not what you said before."

"I hadn't seen what I've seen since. You know, when I was in prison in New York, I felt down, not because I'd been caught – I knew the risk I was taking and I wasn't going to allow my conscience to drag me down, I was down because I felt lonely, and I felt lonely because I'd known the peace of real companionship with you. That's precious, Vincent. Let's not lose it."

Vincent squirmed inside. How could he tell her that he had changed? "I'm hungry," he said. "Let's go find something to eat."

He stood up and extended a hand to Donnette. With her tight denim skirt restricting her movements, she rose awkwardly. He watched her pulling the skirt down over her thighs and noted her heavy breasts and fleshy face. She remained a handsome woman, but he saw her becoming a stout middle-aged Caribbean woman, the sort seen on old tourist pictures – chequered bandanna and skirts and a beaming smile while carrying a bunch of bananas on their heads. As they walked out of the park, Vincent was conscious of Donnette tottering beside him on high-heeled shoes more suitable for a younger, slimmer woman.

"Well, what do you think?"

"It's a great idea, Donnette."

"You haven't been listening to a word I was saying. I mean about coming to live in Jamaica?"

"I was. But that's a heavy thing you're proposing. I'm still trying to get my head around it."

"If it doesn't work out, Vincent. We can come back here. Or try the States."

Tell her, he thought. But tell her what? The truth, the truth about your feelings. And just what is the truth? Get yourself together, man. She's serious. Jamaica. Bloody hell, I'm uncomfortable on the other side of the North Circular. Just the truth. But it will hurt her and I don't want to cause her pain.

As they walked, Donnette elaborated on her plans. Vincent half-listened and murmured encouragingly. They walked past groups of men and women idling on the grass. The sun had brought out the neighbourhood's winos and dope dealers. A man, skinny and dark, with a dense grey beard drunkenly approached Vincent and said, "Give me a money, star."

His smell – beer, tobacco, something vaguely cloacal – triggered a reminder of one of Vincent's many fears. Destitution, vagrancy. He reached into his pocket, pulled out some coins, and thrust them at the beggar.

"Shouldn't have given him anything," Donnette said. "He's only going to waste it on drink."

"I know." He touched Donnette's elbow, signalling that they ought to hurry along.

Donnette did not want to eat in any of the many greasy spoon cafés in the neighbourhood. He followed her from shop to shop as she bought ingredients for a meal, including from the greengrocery shop where his old schoolmate, Terry Mathessen, worked. The badinage between them centred on Arsenal's prospects for the coming season. As they walked from the shop, Donnette said, "I didn't know you were a football fan."

"You can't grow up in this corner of London without being one. I don't go to matches but I follow the team's progress. Whenever I see Terry, that's what we talk about."

They crossed Blackstock Road and went into the Pakistani-owned butcher's shop. While Donnette haggled over the price of mutton with the butcher, an ever-smiling man with an extravagantly flared, waxed moustache, Vincent went outside. He felt impatient and recalled vague memories of shopping trips following his mother through Ridley Road market.

Back in his room, while Donnette prepared the meal, Vincent's thoughts turned to her proposal. He looked around the room: at the futon on the floor, the shelves of books, many unread, most bought in a charity shop on Blackstock Road, the framed print of Dali's *Metamorphosis of Narcissus*, the files containing the essays written while he was at university, one containing the year's desultory research on his abandoned doctoral thesis. He was nearing thirty and all his worldly possessions were in this eighteen by twelve-foot room. What had happened to him? What had caused this stagnation in his life? Where was the person who, defying all expectations, had sailed through school and onto university and won a post-graduate award? Was it Locke who defined the self as a continuous consciousness over time? Who was the Vincent Bostock who once strove and achieved? It seemed to him that at some indefinable point he had suffered some discontinuity within himself, some rupture. Was he seriously now deliberating on whether to run away to Jamaica with his half-sister? As this last question echoed, he realised that his thinking had shifted. He had evaded giving Donnette an answer earlier because he did not want to hurt her. Between now and then, the prospect of a radical change, a seismic upheaval, had inveigled its way into his consciousness, taken shadowy form, which every passing second became more solidly attractive.

Donnette called him to help make a salad, and standing beside her in the small, curtained recess which served as the kitchen, their bodies touching with every movement for lack of space, Vincent urged himself to live in the moment. He cared for her, of that he was certain, and he ought not to allow the past or the future to spoil this intimate act of preparing a meal together.

They ate at the little oak foldaway table Vincent had bought in a secondhand store near Holloway. He had polished it with real beeswax and replaced the hinges on the wings. Seeing the meal – curried-goat, plain rice, an assortment of vegetables and salad – spread out on its dark-brown surface, alive with the swirls and knots of the wood, he felt proud of this minor achievement, tangible evidence that he had not spent all of the last eight years wandering around the labyrinth of his mind. Maybe he had missed his vocation – working with material things, transforming them into things of beauty and utility.

He looked up Donnette, saw her broad face with its hint of his own and his father's features. She returned his gaze, a slight smile playing on her lips and he noticed for the first time that her eyes were amber-coloured. And the longer he looked at her eyes, the more he felt a falling sensation, a precipitous and spiralling descent.

When they finished, the table cleared and stowed away, they went on to the bed.

"Well, have you thought about it?" Donnette said.

"I'm still thinking."

"All right. I'm going back in a few months. Come back with me for a visit, see for yourself." She moved closer and kissed and hugged him and said again, "Just a visit."

The long-drawn-out July dusk was coming to a close when Vincent woke up. Leaving Donnette asleep, he went to the window. A train pulling into the overground section of the station drew his attention; he watched the carriages fill up with shadowy figures; the train pulled away and was swallowed by the night. The station platform was empty, but then he thought he saw a solitary figure standing under the light at the farthest end of the platform. A passenger who had missed his or her train? He watched cars move smoothly along Seven Sisters Road towards central London, as if drawn into some vast and complex centripetal machine. What's keeping me in this city, he wondered. He lived on its margins, he couldn't afford to shop in the West End, frequent its nightclubs.

I'll go with her, he thought. See a new place. There's nothing keeping me here. I've never travelled. Maybe in travelling and being with Donnette I'll find a new self, a new me, one less prone to anxiety, one who could connect with other people.

He returned to the bed and, finding Donnette awake, wondered how long she had been watching him.

"Okay, I'll come," he said. "I'll come with you to Jamaica. Just a visit, though."

She threw aside the blanket, sat up and hugged Vincent with

such force that he knew for the first time what it was make another person happy. In that moment, wrapped in her fleshy arms, all his worries and solemn meditation vanished, as he sank into the oblivion of happiness.

31. *Vincent heads to Heathrow, two months later*

Vincent was sitting on the westbound platform of the Piccadilly Line at Finsbury Park station. Beside him was his sole piece of luggage, an olive-green nylon holdall, its main body secured with a combination lock. An outer pocket held his passport and money. The bag contained mostly clothes bought in Camden Town market with money borrowed from Neville – to whom he had spun a yarn about a moment of betting madness which left him owing money – from Samuel, his mother and several friends. Although Donnette had assured him she had enough for them both, he felt he ought to pay his way. He was useless with money, but he was not a ponce.

Donnette had spent her last week in England in Nottingham and would meet him at the airport. Sitting there, the platform filling up with office and shop workers, he wondered what she would be wearing. He hoped she would wear a skirt and the white v-neck blouse with the simple lace trimming.

A gush of warm air signalled that the train was approaching. Vincent got up, hoisted the bag onto his shoulders, and glanced at the electronic notice board: Heathrow. He boarded an almost empty carriage and took an end seat. Then there was a sudden stampede of passengers, and the carriage quickly filled up. Not having ridden the tube at rush hour in many years, he had forgotten the uncomfortable physical closeness of strangers. The hand of the male passenger next to him – hairy, suntanned and wearing a gold wedding ring – was less than eighteen inches from his face. An Asian woman opposite him was looking into a compact mirror and applying cosmetics to her face with such concentration she could have been performing this act at home. Some passengers had their heads buried in paperback books, others looked straight ahead, their faces blank.

He thought about his flat and how long it would take the landlord to realise he was no longer living there. Fond memories of his years on the ninth floor came to him: seeing a rainbow over the city, the fiery sunsets, the stillness and quiet of high-rising living; the eerie sense of dislocation he'd experienced after days of staying in his room, then venturing out onto the crowded streets. In years to come, would he indulge in the sort of nostalgic conversations he'd overheard between old Caribbean immigrants? He shifted slightly and felt the keys to his former home press against his thigh. He had not decided what to do with them. He imagined tossing them into a bin at the airport.

The train stopped at the Arsenal; nobody boarded, nobody disembarked. It rushed on. The woman opposite was now applying her lipstick, cherry red in colour. Somehow, she occupied the narrow space as if her home was not bricks and mortar, furnishings or other people, her home was herself.

The passenger next to her was reading *The Daily Telegraph*. It reminded Vincent of his father and visiting him the previous evening. They had talked boxing for a while. Then his father had expressed concern about Vincent's drifting. "At your age and with your start you should be long settled into a career and have some responsibilities, a wife, children," he had said.

He had not risen to the bait; he had recognised the rueful tone in his father's voice, which betrayed that it was his own errors he wished to speak about. He had laughed and said: "Not everybody is cut out to shoulder responsibilities," or something to that effect. His father had assumed a sour expression and fallen silent. Fearing that somehow, despite the care he taken not reveal his plans, his father suspected something, Vincent had left earlier than planned. He had tried to make it seem like just another farewell, had said, "See you soon." He had walked home brooding on his failure to live up to his early promise, and his unwillingness to pay a visit to his mother.

The train stopped at Holloway and the passenger opposite lowered his newspaper and seemed to stare at Vincent, who averted his gaze. He felt his bag being pressed against his chest by a standing passenger.

He tried to stop thinking and, between Holloway and Kings Cross, largely succeeded. As the train pulled out of Kings Cross, Vincent began to feel uncomfortable. It was the crowd, the legs and waists and briefcases and handbags, skirts and trousers swaying in front of him. He was sweating heavily; his back felt damp, his underarms clammy. He tried to read the tube map, but swaying figures blocked his view. He guessed at the number of stops before his destination: between eighteen and twenty-two.

Once we get through Central London, I'll be all right, he thought. He clutched the holdall and closed his eyes. Sweat fell into his eyes with a saltiness that burned. He rubbed his eyes, and his bag slipped off his lap and rested against a man's legs. The man, young, clean-shaven with slick jet-black hair, his gold cufflinks sparkling, looked down with what seemed like a mixture of disdain and aggression. Vincent mumbled an apology but could not hear his own voice above the noise. He retrieved the bag and held it close to his chest. The man next to him reading *The Telegraph* shifted; his hand was now a few inches from Vincent's face. Vincent felt he was suffocating. He inhaled deeply but breathed in only warm stale air. The veins in his temples began to throb, his stomach heaved, and a rancid taste filled his mouth. Russell Square, Covent Garden, Leicester Square, Piccadilly, Green Park – these stations blurred into one unending journey. At Hyde Park Corner, he had to force himself to remain seated and ignore the powerful urge to get out of the carriage, to breathe fresh air again. But as the train broke out of the dark and entered the light of Knightsbridge station, he could no longer control himself. He stood up suddenly, his head striking the arm of the passenger standing above him. The train braked and he lurched into the man, who said: "Excuse me." Vincent said sorry and pushed his way to the door, and stepped onto the platform, brushing against passengers waiting to board.

He was now part of a stream of people flowing along the platform, and did not know where he was going. He seemed to be colliding with everybody; the ceiling seemed to lower, filling him with even greater urgency to be above ground. He threw the bag over his shoulder and barged through the crowded platform. The ground beneath his feet seemed to be moving upwards, throwing him forwards, and he realised he was on the escalator. He clung to the moving rubber bannister; seeing the descending passengers, still as mannequins on the other side, made him feel giddier.

He was out at last, on Old Brompton Road, the Knightsbridge traffic rushing by, car horns honking, indicators blinking, the colours on the traffic lights changing at frenetic speed. Vincent leant over a railing and retched, but all he released was thick, bitter-tasting mucus. Then he gulped air. Feeling calmer, still leaning over the railing, he muttered to himself: "I can't do it. I can't do it."

He didn't know this part of the city, with its opulent shop windows, a long way from Finsbury Park. When he saw a 19 bus, with Finsbury Park on its front, he ran after it but missed it and had to wait at the bus stop. It began to rain, a steady warm rain from which the bus stop afforded him no protection. Another 19 bus soon came and, damp from the rain, he boarded it and took a seat on the upper deck, apologising for his bag as he sat down.

Barely conscious of the journey, he thought of Donnette. It was mid-morning; she would be at the airport by now, wondering where he was. They had talked on the phone the night before. What had they talked about? He could not remember.

Somebody sat next to him, but moved away. He became aware of the odour emanating from him, a cocktail of damp and sweat, a hint of petrol. Somewhere along Piccadilly, another passenger, a man, took the seat. Vincent, clutching the holdall, shifted. The bus moved and the man said: "Can you move over?"

Vincent tightened his grip on the bag and shifted again. He couldn't move any further. Donnette was waiting for him at Heathrow and he wasn't going to be there. He felt the man's shoulders and thighs pressing against him, and his chest tightened with a burning sensation, and he felt as though he was drowning.

"The problem with you people is you want all our space," the man said.

Vincent glanced at him, saw his wet blonde hair plastered to his forehead, his scabrous red face. Of all the days to meet someone like this, a caveman, a dinosaur. He stood up and squeezed past the man, and the thought occurred to him to tell him to crawl back into whatever cave he had been sleeping in. But between the thought and its utterance, some slip occurred, and he heard himself say: "You want space? Take it, take the fucking the seat, go on take it, rip it out, take it home with you. Who wants to sit next to a cunt like you anyway."

He walked away as the man returned a salvo of swearwords and racial epithets, demanding that he come back and fight. Staggering down the aisle, his bag brushing against shoulders, Vincent was thinking "What will I do if he comes after me?"

Then he was off the bus and walking along Shaftsbury Avenue. The rain, heavier now than when he boarded the bus, penetrated the cotton clothes he'd planned to wear on his journey to Jamaica. He caught the number 29 bus outside St. Martins College and arrived back at Phoenix House early in the afternoon. He entered his ninth-floor room, locked and bolted the door and disconnected the telephone. He closed the thin curtains, blocking out the grey light. He washed his face and rinsed his mouth. He undressed down to his underpants and T-shirt. Then he got into bed, curled up like a foetus, and tried to erase from his mind the vision that had been pursuing him since Shaftsbury Avenue: Donnette, dressed in the mid-thigh-length denim skirt he liked, her favourite high-heeled clogs, her fleshy midriff gently folding over her waist, the oval-shaped malachite necklace; Donnette who was only Donnette to him because she was travelling on a false passport, Donnette standing alone in the airport terminal with the rain falling on her.

★ ★ ★ ★

The narrator, 2020s

The squatters next door were evicted in late January. They went without any trouble. But within weeks another group arrived. These were different; they brought their belongings in an Audi estate car, wore Gothic-style clothes, and spoke in a foreign language that I couldn't recognise, but thought was from Eastern Europe. They were not friendly; even their clothes seemed designed to discourage a friendly approach. They were noisy, too, playing loud music in the room to next my bedroom. Fortunately, they didn't last long. The property had been designated a building site, so it was easier to remove them; this happened in mid-March, with the police in attendance. I watched this from my living-room window. I was surprised by the number of people who had moved in. Some I had not seen before; one was a strikingly beautiful woman with beehive-style black hair, who was dressed entirely in black lace. The men seemed protective; one of the squatters was drunk and swore repeatedly at the policemen, who remained impassive as they went about their duties.

Spring came, and the first group of squatters' work in the back garden was evident in the kitchen. It was now flooded with light, and that made the need for a coat of paint more apparent. Outside, the gardens began to explode with greenery, and the three brothers played on their trampoline from as early as 7.30. The youngest boy sometimes only wore underpants and seemed to take great pleasure in urinating while standing on the edge of the trampoline;

he did this with the other two boys playing around him.

The boy downstairs had been quiet all winter. I had reflected on the antagonistic relationship that had developed between us and wondered whether I had been too harsh on him. He had gone the entire winter without work. I felt for him; he had children. It occurred to me that because he was some kind of construction worker, his skills probably included painting and decorating. I could give him some work painting my kitchen.

I knocked on his door and said: "I notice you haven't worked for a few months. I can give you some work painting my kitchen, if you're interested. I'll buy the paint."

He grunted something incomprehensible and said, "Let me see the job."

I led him upstairs to the kitchen. Hands in pockets, he surveyed it, then said with brash confidence, "Two days' work. One to prepare the surface, another to paint it."

"So you've done this kind of thing before?"

"Nuff times."

He gave me a price and as I had decided that whatever price he gave, if it was reasonable, I would accept, and I did.

"But I got no gear," he said.

I looked at him blankly.

"No tools for the job, like. No brushes. Know what I mean?"

The next day, we met at the Homebase store in Green Lanes and, following his advice, I bought brushes, sugar soap, paint and sandpaper.

He set about the job with alacrity and diligence, using a sponge to wash the ceiling, walls and skirting boards with the sugar soap. The kitchen ceiling was high, but he reached it effortlessly, perching on the top rung of the stepladder with the ease and confidence of one who was used to scaling heights.

As his working day came to an end, I gave him half the money he had requested, and we got to talking.

"You seem comfortable doing that. What is it you do? I know you're in the construction business."

"I'm a banksman, innit. Direct traffic on the building site. Trained as a brickie as well. But I can do a bit of everything. Plastering, carpentry, electrics. Could do your kitchen tiles as well, if you want. Extra work. More money. Know what I mean?"

"I'll think about that," I said, scrutinising the white kitchen tiles around the cooker and sink. Here and there the grouting was yellowing, but otherwise they seemed fine to me. "How come you don't have any tools?"

"I do. They're at my baby mother's place."

"The one who calls here for you?"

"Naw, the other one. Mother of my oldest boys. But I can't go back there."

"Why not?"

"Cause I thump her down, innit?"

"You what?"

"Thump her down. After me and her parted, she had all these weirdos hanging around the house. Night and fucking day. Kept on telling her I didn't want any fucking weirdos hanging around my boys. Know what I mean?"

"I think so. That's why you thumped her down?"

"Naw. She boxed me. And I didn't like that. So I just thump her down. She shouldn't have touched me. I was just telling her like it is. It was outside the house, see. Witnesses. Her friends. Went to court. Now I can't go within 500 yards of her home. That's why I haven't got any tools, innit. They're still in her house. Nuff fucking tools. Know what I mean?"

The following morning, he resumed working. He worked steadily through the morning on the ceiling, but it was clear that he had underestimated the amount of paint needed. At lunch time, I bought him a take-away from the Caribbean cafe on Allen Road. We talked over lunch.

"I haven't seen your mother in a while," I said.

"My mother!" he scoffed. "She's another one."

"You should be grateful to her. She kept this flat. Now it's giving you shelter."

"Let me tell you about my mother," he said vehemently. "For four fucking years, she let my father do whatever he wanted with one of my sisters."

I looked at him disbelievingly.

"Yeah, straight up. If I ever see that man again, I'd kill him. Fucking kill him."

"How old were you then?"

"Cunt left when I about twelve. Haven't seen him since. But it was all down to my mother, you see. She put up with it."

"Could she have done anything?"

"To be fair to her, she tried. But the bastard beat her up. Put her in hospital three times."

"That's rough," I said. "A rough childhood."

"Yeah, tell me about it. My mother says she was trying to protect me. Asked me whether he ever troubled me."

"How old are you?"

"Thirty-two, innit."

I did not believe everything he told me, but had no way of verifying what was true or false. It was the L-plate on the motorbike that suggested something had gone wrong in his childhood, left him with such a low level of literacy that he couldn't pass the written part of the test for a full road licence. He told me he had pretty much stopped attending school at fourteen and spent his early teenage years running wild, despite his mother's appeal for him to take his schoolwork seriously, something he now regretted.

I looked up at the ceiling and thought it needed another coat of paint. A large watermark was proving stubborn, despite the boy's efforts. Nonetheless, the ceiling was whiter and with the whiteness, the bulb and holder now seemed stained. I said: "You say you can do a bit of electrics."

"Yeah, a bit. My uncle's a spark. Taught me a bit over the years."

"Think you can fit a new lamp in this kitchen."

"Yeah, no problem. Should get yourself some spotlights with a dimmer. Nice up the place. Cost you extra, though. Know what I mean?"

"That's not a problem," I said.

We agreed on a price for the job.

That evening, I bought a simple three-headed spotlight and a dimmer switch. The following day, when he'd finished working on the ceiling, he fitted the new lamp and after a demonstration, I was satisfied that he knew what he was doing. "You seem to have quite a few skills," I said.

"Well, I've been in the building trade since I was sixteen. Pickup things, innit."

"Why don't you start your own business? Print some cards with your telephone number and put them in the local shops."

He thought for a moment, then said, "Not that kind of person. Always see myself working for somebody."

"Doesn't have to be that way. Just takes a bit of initiative. Lots of people do it."

213

"Yeah, maybe. Main problem's my baby mother. The one who calls here. Soon as she hears I am working, she's on my fucking case for money. I've got letters from her solicitor downstairs."

"Then give her something. In fact, you should give her fifty percent of what I'm paying you. Money comes and goes. Give it and it comes back to you."

"Yeah, maybe. I'll think about that."

The working day ended with only the woodwork remaining to be painted. That evening I had a dinner date with my dear friend Irma Benjamin in Stamford Hill.

★ ★ ★ ★

32. *Neville, taxis and the Inland Revenue, 1980s*

Neville had used his compensation from the British Boxing League to start a mini-cab company, and business was thriving. Located in a tumbledown building beside the railway bridge and Homerton station, K-Cars – its motto was "We'll take you there" – was a round-the-clock operation which drew its customers from the surrounding council estates, Homerton hospital, and the many nightclubs, some legal, others not, scattered throughout the area. Its drivers were mostly immigrants, men who had fled war-torn, coup-prone, corruption-riddled third-world nations. For many, cab-driving was one of several jobs, often combined with office cleaning and portering to support their families in London and the family network back home. There they had often enjoyed far higher statuses, as schoolteachers, students, civil servants, court clerks and office workers. Neville asked them no questions about their immigration status. A four-door, roadworthy vehicle and a current driving licence were all they needed – and it helped to own a copy of the London A-Z.

But when his mother, after a trip to Acton, complained that she felt she had been dragged to her destination in an old Toyota Corolla, its suspension so knackered that even on level ground the jarring sound of metal on asphalt was audible, Neville could no longer ignore the condition of the cars. But he still found it difficult to say 'no' when one of his drivers introduced a cousin, with a car that belonged on the scrapheap.

At one point Neville estimated that he had drivers from ten

African countries as well as Turkey, Iran, and several Caribbean islands. Political and religious debates in the backroom where the drivers rested were at times overheated. Neville put up a notice which read: "No rileigious or politikill discussions allowed." An Eritrean, an ex-primary school teacher, eventually corrected the boss's poorly spelled, though perfectly understood injunction.

Neville's business success was visible. He now lived in a house overlooking Hackney Downs, bought from a St Lucian returning home, and financed through a dodgily arranged mortgage. The house was a riotous place. The six children, even the youngest, wore the latest style clothes and brand-name trainers. Shirley who, like Neville, had ballooned in size, spared them nothing. Every toy craze was indulged. And if someone from one of the schools called up with a complaint about any of her children's behaviour, she went there and argued on their behalf. When she told Neville about such episodes, he took it as a sure sign that his children were in good hands; they had a strong mother.

Though Shirley did not like Lucas Bostock, Neville wanted the children to know their grandfather, who lived just twenty-minutes' walk away. Shirley thought him a miserable and mean old man because he ignored his grandchildren's birthdays and gave no Christmas presents. That he didn't acknowledge his own birthday cut no ice with her. And when Neville took the children to Carlisle Road, the house's graveyard quiet and the stern-faced old man with enormous, calloused hands and gruff voice, who only ever asked them what they were going be when they grew up, and met their uncomprehending silence with a disapproving glare, frightened them and they clung to their father for protection. The children were not keen on Rhoda, either – all that bible talk. They much preferred Shirley's easy-going parents who lived near Victoria Park and whose house was a smaller version of their own chaotic and riotously happy home.

They had a constant stream of visitors throughout the day: Neville and Shirley's families and the children's friends. Two large stainless-steel pots of rice and peas and chicken or beef stew were always on the stove, replenished whenever necessary. The deep freezer chest was never without pizzas, sausages, cuts of beef, chicken and fish. The wardrobe-sized fridge overflowed with pop and juice drinks in all manner of exotic flavours – guava, guanabara, mango, lychee, as well as apple and orange. During the evenings and at weekends, as many as four music systems and three televisions played at the same time in different parts of the house, with the adults enjoying reggae and r&b music from the remnants of a sound system – a massive speaker, a thousand-watt valve amplifier and a rare Pioneer turntable – which Neville had salvaged from an underground car park on the Homerton housing estate, where they had lived for many years. If on a Saturday night, a carload of party revellers mistook the music and dancing in Neville's house for a party and knocked on the door, they would be disabused of their mistake but invited in all the same. It was not uncommon for Neville to leave a full house, do an eight-hour shift as controller at the office, and return to find the same number of visitors at home, with a few new faces, a stranger or two among them. This habit of admitting total strangers to their home stopped only after Cherise, the oldest girl, complained that someone had tried to force his way into her top-floor room during the night, distracting attention from the fact – which would emerge later – that her teenage boyfriend was in bed with her at the time.

The partying continued long after the brown envelopes started to arrive, first monthly, then weekly. They were tax demands and Neville ignored them, stuffing them in a blue plastic bag in his office, like a dirty secret, to be discarded one day. His only care was that his family was happy.

He continued clinging to this consoling thought a year later when he found himself outside the Royal Court of Justice on a grim and grey afternoon in November. Its Gothic facade made no impression on him, nor its vast hallway through which men in suits hurried or stood about in groups, locked in solemn conversation. The court officer, a uniformed, middle-aged man, who reminded him of white men from the boxing game, directed him upstairs to the bankruptcy section with all the casualness of someone giving street directions. In the narrow reception area, he was greeted by the Inland Revenue lawyer, who quizzed him about his legal representation. He had none.

"You can't be serious about making me bankrupt for £15,000 pounds," Neville said.

"You've ignored all the Inland Revenue's letters, Mr Bostock," the young lawyer said.

"I have been so busy. I just haven't had time."

The lawyer sighed, as if wearily familiar with this excuse. "Well, it's too late now. We'll make you bankrupt. You can be sure of that."

Neville thought: I'm no big-time businessman. I ain't got no accounts in Jersey or Switzerland. I'm just a man trying to make a living. Keep my family happy. But his difficulty in voicing his thoughts came out as, "I'm just a small businessman."

"You can tell the judge that."

The proceedings in the court lasted only a few minutes. The judge wore a grey and black checked jacket, and had brilliantined hair, grey at the temples. He sat behind a desk, books and files tidily arranged. He listened impassively as the young lawyer made his case. "Your honour," he said, concluding, "Mr Bostock has consistently and wilfully ignored all our demands for payment. Indeed, I am surprised that he has bothered to attend this hearing."

The judge looked at Neville, and he, still unsure what was going on, returned his gaze with a half-smile.

"Do you have anything to say in your defence, Mr Bostock?"

Speaking slowly, Neville said, "All you had to do was come to the office. There's no need for all of this. Ask anybody at K-cars; I'm a fair man and a law-abiding citizen."

The judge shook his head, glanced at the folder on his desk and said: "Mr Bostock, I hereby declare you bankrupt."

Stunned, Neville asked, "What does that mean?"

"You will find out in the fullness of time, Mr Bostock," the judge said, without a trace of emotion in his voice.

Outside the courtroom, the young lawyer shook Neville's hand as if they had just concluded a pleasant and successful business meeting and pointed him towards a window. There he signed a few forms, and the court clerk instructed him to make his way to an address on Tottenham Court Road, where the next stage of the proceedings would happen.

He left the Royal Court of Justice still feeling puzzled. He remembered boxing matches when an opponent had delivered a powerful punch, but its effects were not immediately felt. A few yards from the court, it began to drizzle. Weaving his way through backstreets, the rain soaking through his clothes, he arrived at the Tottenham Court Road address. Here the receptionist directed him upstairs. He took a lift to the third floor and walked down a long narrow corridor lit by fluorescent strips.

He entered a numbered cubicle and waited. Eventually, a woman in an electric blue jacket appeared from the door opposite. Long brown hair, freckles, she reminded him of a girl he had liked in school but did not know how to tell her he liked her. She smiled and said: "Neville Bostock?"

"Yes."

She asked for the papers from the previous court and he fumbled in his jacket pocket to find them. He handed them over and she read through them quickly.

"I'll need details of all your bank accounts. If you do not have them with you, the name of the bank or building society will do."

He told her this.

"Do you have a cheque book, credit cards, or cash on you?"

"Yes, cash."

"You are required by law to hand it to me."

Neville took out a wad of notes, cash he had intended to give to Shirley for shopping. He handed it over, and some coins.

"Car keys. And if you can tell me the car's registration number and where it's parked."

He handed her the car keys and told her the car's location.

"I'm required by law to leave you with enough money for a single bus ride to your home. You live in Hackney, so that will be fifty pence."

She shoved the coin across the desk. Neville picked it and put it in his trouser pocket.

"Well, that will be all, Mr Bostock. You will hear from us in the near future."

Back outside, the drizzle still falling, covering the buildings in a grey gauze, he finally felt the blow. He walked away from the building slowly. He had fifty pence in his pocket. He had left his father's home at sixteen; he had fended for himself without ever brushing against the law; had spent three months in hospital and a year convalescing; he had lost his livelihood and found another; he had responsibility for six children and a wife.

Neville stopped at the office and told his team his fate. The business was insolvent. He did not know how much longer they could continue operating. They had to find work elsewhere. He asked Ashar, an Ethiopian, to communicate this to all the drivers as they reported for work.

The house was full when he reached home. Shirley's two sisters, Beverley and Portia, and their boyfriends were listening to music and chatting; the children were scattered about the house in their private domains. He greeted his in-laws in his usual affable manner, complimented one of the sisters on her new trainers and hugged Shirley. He went downstairs to the kitchen and helped himself to some food, sat at the table with it, but could not bring himself to eat.

Shirley came downstairs to the kitchen and took some beers from the fridge and a bottle of rosé from the rack.

"You okay, babes?" she said, "Wasn't expecting you back so early today."

"Yeah, yeah, I'm fine."

"Oh, I'm gonna need some shopping money. Fridge's nearly empty."

"Look, Shirl, you'd better ask your sisters to leave. Somethink's happened."

When they talked, he realised that the situation was worse than he thought. Shirley had not been paying either the monthly mortgage or the council tax for the past six months. Various family members had needed help. She owed money to her dressmaker, who had kept her ever expanding figure clothed, and smaller sums to various shopkeepers.

A terrible depression settled over their home. The music stopped. Visitors were discouraged. The mini-cab office was closed, its windows and doors boarded up, an insolvency notice plastered on the wood.

Neville tried calling in loans he had made to friends but got the same negative reply from those he managed to track down. When he received a pony, £25, from his old friend Boswell Anderson in part settlement for a large loan he had made after Boswell's famous and disastrous poker game with T-Bone Sterling, he almost wept with gratitude. That money soon went, swallowed by the children's demands. He managed to raise a generous sum from Samuel and an insignificant sum from Vincent, which he nonetheless received as a morale booster. He could not bring himself to ask his mother for cash, but when she heard about his crisis, she became a more frequent visitor, always bringing cans of baked beans, bread, juice and items of children's clothes. Christmas, usually a period of excess in the house, was the leanest they'd ever experienced.

In early January, with great reluctance and shame, he called on his father and gave him an outline of his plight. Hands knitted together and resting on his stomach, Lucas Bostock listened attentively and said: "Sounds to me like you're kissing the canvas, son. If I were you,

I'd take the count and while I'm down there, I'd think hard about why I didn't see that punch coming, or why I saw it coming but couldn't dodge it quickly enough."

From the side of the armchair his father produced a thick white envelope, handed it to Neville, and said, "No point writing you a cheque. Now, you don't want to hear this, but I'm going to tell you anyway: that woman of yours, she's no good. She's going to drag you down."

Neville handed back the envelope, saying "I don't want this." He had to exercise superhuman self-control to leave the house without flattening his father. As he walked up Carlisle Road, he swore for the second time in his life that he would never again speak to Lucas.

The eviction happened in early March. The two oldest children were shuttled between Rhoda and Shirley's parents, who were already accommodating three other grandchildren. Neville and Shirley, advised that this was the quickest route to secure social housing, took the other three with them into a homeless shelter on Dalston Lane. There, in two cramped rooms, their children taking breakfasts of baked beans, fried eggs and bread with scrofulous old men who always reeked of lager, he tried to make a new start. At night, he and Shirley fell asleep locked in each other's arms, the youngest child sleeping on a mattress on the floor.

Early one Sunday morning in April, Rhoda called at the hostel and persuaded Neville and Shirley to bring the children to church.

"Guess it'll make a change from spending Sunday with your parents," Neville said to Shirley. He had not had much sleep; using a friend's car, he had spent much of the night working as a mini-cab driver from an office on Morning Lane.

They set off expecting Rhoda to take them to her church on Chatsworth Road; instead, she took them to a Baptist church on Hackney Downs, five hundred yards from their former home. The service had started and the church was full; they took a seat at the back. Still sleepy, Neville listened to the service and stood and kneeled and sat at his mother's prompting. It was the singing that woke him. The choir, men and women, wore brown and yellow robes and there was something in their voices that touched Neville, made him alert, aware of a previously unrecognised region inside himself, a place he had never ventured into. As the choir sang, Neville felt himself borne aloft, as if he were floating and all his woes no longer mattered. He felt his eyes moisten.

The choir lowered their voices, and the Pastor, a huge dark man in tinted glasses and wearing a shiny grey suit, entered the pulpit and said: "If there is anyone here who has not been saved, come forward and give your heart to the Lord. Surrender your heart to Jesus our saviour, the son of God. He will carry your burdens and wash away your sins."

Members of the congregation went and knelt before the pulpit.

Neville stood up and took Shirley's hand. She said, "Neville what are you doing? We're only here for the service."

"That's right, you go ahead, Neville," Rhoda said. "Go with him, Shirley."

"We need to do this, Shirley," Neville said.

Shirley turned to Chad, the oldest of the children there, and told him to keep the other two seated. Neville led her down the aisle and at the base of the pulpit, crowded now, worshippers parted and gave them space. The choir's voices became louder, and Neville gripped Shirley's hand as the singing washed over him and the pastor intoned in a slow voice, "Yes, give your heart to Jesus Christ, the redeemer; only he can save you; give your heart to Jesus Christ, the son of God, the light everlasting, the way and the truth. Give your heart to Jesus."

The singing, the pastor's voice, the congregation shouting ecstatically, "Yes, Lord, yes My Lord, oh My Lord", and Shirley beside him, Neville felt a surge of energy rush through his body and a peacefulness settling on his mind. He had experienced a comparable feeling in the boxing ring after winning a fight and the crowd cheered him, hundreds of voices united in his praise. *Kumba, Kumba, Kumba!* This feeling was similar, but it had purity and goodness and light. And though it did not resound with his name, he felt that it spoke to something deeper and more personal than just a name. It spoke to his heart and his soul.

33. *Vincent meets Rachel, 1990s*

They met at an end-of-summer barbecue in Archway, at the house of one of Vincent's colleagues from *Urban Lines*. He had just begun to recover from another bout of self-recrimination. Rachel Whitby, two years his senior, had just returned from a three-month career

221

break which had taken her to Minas Geras in Brazil. She glowed with the well-being of the recently travelled and spoke with a breathless urgency that contrasted with his own slow, hesitant speech. It made him think of someone rushing to catch a bus while simultaneously commenting on the act. Vincent was swept off his feet.

Their early dates were rich in conversation as they explored their shared Caribbean roots, and the routes that had brought them to that house in Archway. Her parents came from Guyana and Jamaica, and she had grown up in Wolverhampton, studied Art History at Lancaster University, completed a master's on the Afro-Cuban painter Wifredo Lam, then got real and thrown herself into a career in local government.

When, less than a month later, he woke up in her brass bed of white Egyptian cotton sheets and wandered from the orderly bedroom to the living room with its huge blue-grey leather sofa, family photographs, vases of dried flowers, walls of framed prints, shelves of books and ceramics, he thought he was still asleep and dreaming. Their two-year age gap could not account for the different worlds they lived in. She owned her flat and had created a home. He was a tenant, lived in one room; he had been proud of his lack of possessions and puzzled by those who spent hours trawling through shops. Now, in refusing to shop, he felt he had denied himself a form of self-expression

Over the next few months, Rachel's self-discipline, focus, ambition, instant rapport with his father, made him see that he was still a sort of immigrant, his roots in the city were shallow, and so his most important duty was to strive. By opting out and wallowing in self-doubt he had betrayed that duty.

A year after meeting Rachel, as he witnessed their daughter's entry into the world – here was life, painful, bloody and screaming, without language or thought, vulnerable and defenceless – Vincent again experienced an overpowering sense of having cheated himself by withdrawing to a tower where he contemplated but did not participate. How innocent he had been. The courting rituals, the candlelit dinners and late-night conversations, the tender kisses, the mixing of body fluids, the sweating and grunting and sighs and groans – they all had one purpose; they were the means to one sole end. He wandered out of the hospital in a daze of stupefaction that lasted weeks and recurred at unpredictable and inconvenient moments for months.

While baby Kara was still in her pram, they moved into a cul-de-sac house on the north side of Finsbury Park. Vincent still kept the ninth-floor room, renting it out on short term lets by word of mouth. He had found a job on a new publication, *The Monitor*, and there were days when, as he walked back home across the park after collecting the rent, he felt gratified that he had at last entered adulthood.

It was not all domesticity and work. Occasionally, they went out into the city. One night they watched as a dancer, dressed in a dark green leotard with matching strips of cloth, suggesting seaweed, leapt two feet in the air, legs parallel to the floor, landed, then thrust out his trident and stood akimbo, his expression imperious, omnipotent and cruelly indifferent. The other twelve dancers rushed from the wings and threw themselves at his feet. Music from ceiling-high speakers climaxed with frenetic drum beats and the dancers remained frozen as the light faded. Poseidon had prevailed.

Vincent rose to his feet with the audience and clapped vigorously. The dancers, their smiles as muscular and healthy as their bodies, took a bow, then another and another. They filed off the stage, but the applause brought them back twice. He was among the first to sit down.

"Brilliant!" Rachel said.

Her swift and terse judgement sounded to Vincent both declarative and interrogative. He muttered "Great!" and wondered if "great" carried as much weight as "brilliant". Rachel had more than once accused him of being an ungenerous critic, a charge he was keen to avoid because Rachel's friend, Gayle Saunders, managed the dance company. He would have to work on his stock of hyperboles. "Brilliant and great," he said; if 'brilliant' suggested the ephemeral, it was complemented by the more enduring quality of 'great'.

"The choreographer worked with Merce Cunningham and Alvin Bailey," Rachel said.

He gave an impressed murmur. These were big names in the world of dance, but he was not a aficionado like Rachel. When they left the auditorium, they met Gayle in the lobby. Rachel showered her with praise – accepted with the grace of the professional fund raiser – before Gayle spotted a potential benefactor in the crowd, excused herself and wove her way towards a large woman in a multicoloured silk trouser suit with a beehive hairstyle.

They left the theatre and walked out to Euston Road, heading towards Kings Cross, where their car was parked. Rachel was talking about the enduring power of myth; Vincent's mind was elsewhere – the flowing traffic, the buildings. Passing a construction site, he wanted to pause and take a look, though he could see only the shadowy outline above the boarding. Rachel walked on, anxious to get home and relieve the babysitter.

"Poseidon, of course, personifies the power of the sea. Similar figures are found in many cultures, though only the Yoruba have, to my knowledge, a sea deity in the form of a female, Yemanja…"

Vincent glanced at St Pancras Station, its arches and gargoyles, its turrets and spires. Next to it, Kings Cross Station looked almost austere, as if between the building of one station and the other, architecture and by extension culture, had lost all belief in gods and saints and the otherworldly.

"What do you think, Vincent?" he heard Rachel say.

"I thought it was great… brilliant show."

"Vincent, you haven't been listening to me. I was talking about gods, deities."

Vincent's memory switched to rewind, and he recalled the gist of what Rachel had said. "Sorry, momentary lapse. I was listening to you. Actually, I was wondering about the extent to which all gods are born of human ignorance, the more sophisticated the civilisation, the more sophisticated the conception of god." It was a brave but futile stab at re-engagement. He felt Rachel bristle; she had detected his minor deception.

"That's not the point, and if you'd been listening to me, you'd know that."

That *was* just the point, Vincent thought; she'd fired her first arrow, and he didn't want this first evening out for weeks to end in a quarrel. He would appease Rachel, try to restore the easy companionship with which they had started the evening. "I wasn't arguing for or against the existence of god. In every culture religion inspires creativity. It doesn't actually matter whether the god worshipped is real. It's the effects that matter."

"Yes, I agree." In fact, if he'd had the mental alacrity, he could have connected his thoughts to Rachel's observations. A long and gruelling week at *The Monitor* had left him weary, unable to synchronise with this woman he loved and respected. And Rachel was probably just as tired. She ran the house and held down a demanding full-time job where she felt she wasn't taken seriously by the white, male masonic fraternity who ran the town hall. His inattentiveness was the most common source of friction in their relationship.

They reached the car and Vincent took the passenger seat. He could tell from the way Rachel put the car into gear, forcefully, jerkily, that his attempt at appeasement had failed. "We should go down Caledonian Road," he said. "There are road works in Camden Town."

Rachel did not reply, but he saw that she agreed. They drove clockwise through quiet back streets, and came out onto Euston Road, passing St Pancras again. As the car turned into York Way, Vincent thought he had glimpsed a familiar figure among the pedestrians. He sat upright and glanced back.

"What's the matter?"

"Nothing."

"Vincent, stop being so evasive. First you ignore me, now you're lying."

"I thought I saw Peter Caine from the office, that's all. And I wasn't ignoring you earlier."

"Why didn't you just say that? And yes, you were ignoring me."

They reached home in good time. After checking on Kara, Rachel paid the babysitter and the teenager went home.

Vincent also checked on Kara, hovered over her bed for a while, listening to her gentle breathing. He had missed reading her a bedtime story. In the living room, he put a cassette of Keith Jarrett's 'Koln Concert' in the stereo. He sat in an armchair in the bay window, and closed his eyes, as the ripples of notes built up into waves, and the pianist grunted and banged the piano as though he was in a shamanic trance. Was that her? Vincent wondered. Was she back in London? Don't think about it right now. You'll know soon enough. It was probably a trick of the light. He turned his mind to Phoenix House. His room had been empty for a month and he was paying the rent, something he could ill-afford and keep up his contribution to paying the mortgage for the house.

"Vincent, I'm going to bed." Rachel's voice yanked him back into this world and he opened his eyes. She stood in the doorway. She wore a gold-coloured, knee-length nightdress. Her hair was parted in the middle and two thick plaits curled from under her ears. A subtle fragrance tickled his nostrils.

"I'm sorry if I was a little sharp with you earlier. It's been a long week." As she came into the room, the audience at the Koln concert applauded, and she kissed Vincent on his lips.

"I'm sorry too," Vincent said. In a flash, he realised that Rachel's earlier mood was a signal. She had often expressed a desire for another child. It was that time of month. And she did look lovely. He followed her up the stairs and into the bedroom, illuminated by the bedside lamp and smelling of her perfume. Vincent performed dutifully, exerted himself manfully, and when it was over, he lay in the dark room until he was sure Rachel was asleep. Then he returned downstairs, searched for Bach's 'The Well Tempered Clavier', put it on the stereo and settled into the armchair, with the latest copy of *New Left Review*.

Between the music and the page, he thought about the evening. In all their rows, which were not as frequent as some couples they knew, his efforts at peacemaking were always rejected. Harmony was restored only when Rachel was ready. He realised he had not been attending to the music but to feelings of a vague and growing resentment. Since settling down with Rachel he had come to view his former way of life as an aberration. Now that he was a father, and somebody's partner he had seen more of Samuel, Neville and Maureen. Seldom a weekend passed when they – he, Rachel and Kara – didn't visit family.

Yet he could not rid himself of the feeling that he was dissembling, pretending to enjoy what the others enjoyed. In moments like these, he longed for his room on the ninth floor. He often stopped there on the way home from work, and luxuriated in its quiet and stillness, its view over the city. Yet he did not want to be alone again. There were many moments in this new life that gave him pleasure, as on Sunday mornings when, playing with Kara, he felt a powerful sense of peace, as if in helping to create a new life, he had fulfilled some fundamental purpose, beside which his disaffection paled into insignificance.

The music had stopped. He turned off the stereo and switched off the lights. He checked the front and back doors, used the bathroom, looked in on Kara, then went to bed.

The freshly laundered cotton sheet and duvet, the firm but yielding bed, a glimpse of Rachel's bare, smooth shoulder before he switched off the lamp, the soft pillow on which he rested his head, the knowledge that his daughter was sleeping soundly in the next room – these were all signs of the new purposeful Vincent. He willed himself to sleep, to accept his good fortune. But as he

lay there, comfortable and warm, it struck him that he had become
a character in Rachel's story.

34. *Vincent retreats to Phoenix House*

The next day, a delicate harmony restored between them, Vincent
left the house at mid-morning and entered the park on Green
Lanes. He was on his way to Phoenix House to attend a residents'
association meeting and check on the room.

A woman with a tennis racquet struck a ball for her overweight
Labrador and the dog, its pink tongue a flashing strip of colour,
padded after the ball at a lethargic pace. On the racetrack, a group
of hooded runners ran in silent unison under a cloud of steam.
The boating lake, its dark green water sluggish and faintly rancid,
played host to ducks scouring the surface for food.

As he walked, Vincent tried to shake off the suspicion that he
had sleep-walked his way into a trap, lost his freedom, and taken on
responsibilities for which he had neither the talent nor the strength.
He was an inadequate father, partner, breadwinner; somehow, he
had got himself into situation where the happiness of two other
people was dependent on him. Such feelings were not new, but he
had dismissed them by focusing on the obvious improvements in
his life. He had reconnected to his siblings and strengthened his
bond with his father, whose lectures on the duties of a man were less
frequent. But this morning, the arguments he had used to contain
his restlessness seemed less convincing.

He exited the park and crossed Seven Sisters Road. There was a
game on at Arsenal. Groups of supporters straggled along the road.
Finding himself walking behind a family of tourists burdened with
luggage and seemingly uncertain of their direction, he stepped
off the pavement and onto the road. He found himself staring
at a double-decker bus charging towards him like an enraged
behemoth. He leapt back onto the pavement as the bus sounded
its horn. The tourists did not appear to notice Vincent's near fatal
accident. They still blocked the pavement. Vincent barged through
them and cursed under his breath: "Bloody foreigners!"

He entered Phoenix House through the newly installed concierge's lodge, one of the most tangible outcomes of his years as

a member of the residents' association, as part of their campaign against the complex's sleazy reputation. The concierge on duty was a smiling West African. Vincent stopped and made small talk with him; he needed him on his side if he was to hold onto the room.

The meeting overran, and Vincent did not get to his room until mid-afternoon. Its shelves were empty of the books and files, which were now in the house. Vincent paced up and down. He had to find a tenant, ideally somebody who would stay longer than the previous one, who'd been there for only four months. He had considered handing back the keys to the landlord, but he knew how difficult it was to find space in the city. And it had come in useful. He had retreated there when Rachel and he were not getting on.

He lay on the bed, hands behind his head on the bare pillow. He would place an advert in a newsagent's window: 'To let, large room, own kitchen and bathroom, Finsbury Park...' Better still: 'Self-contained studio, minutes' walk from Victoria and Piccadilly lines station'. So far, he had only charged the actual rent, ignoring the chance to make a profit, but maybe he needed to charge something extra, which would be useful for periods when the room was unoccupied. He'd do that, he thought, closing his eyes.

He woke up to the glow of the city visible beyond the window and remembered in panic that he had promised to be back home by four p.m. to look after Kara while Rachel went to the gym. He gathered his coat and hurried out of the building. He joined a stream of football supporters making their way towards Manor House. Arsenal must have won; the supporters looked animated and there was much laughter among them.

"Where have you been?" Rachel hissed through gritted teeth as he closed the door.

"I'm sorry. I just lost track of the time. You can still go."

"No thanks to you. Kara needs a bath and her supper is in the fridge."

Rachel belonged to a women's gym and went twice a week. She gave Vincent a deadly stare as she left the house.

Over the next few hours Vincent busied himself with Kara. Feeding the child, trying to decipher the myriad sounds she made, discovering that he possessed a vast store of pre-language sounds that somehow managed to communicate and amuse, if not Kara, at least himself, absorbed him completely. He delayed her bath and spent time in her room playing with blocks of multi-coloured plastic. After bathing her, he put her to bed and read her a story, his voice low and soft as if she understood his every word. At eight o'clock precisely – Rachel was very strict about training Kara to sleep – he kissed her forehead, and looked into her eyes and saw what he believed was a love that matched his own. He switched off the light and tip-toed out of the room.

He sat at the kitchen table with pen and paper and tried to remember the wording for the adverts he planned. He made several unsuccessful starts and, frustrated, put aside the pen. A simple twenty-word ad and he could not find the words. No wonder he had not been able to write for *The Monitor* in months. Fortunately, the features editor was on extended sick leave and much of his duties had fallen on Vincent's desk. But the job, marginally better paid than *Urban Lines*, now felt less rewarding than he'd previously felt. In retrospect, he should have known that a newspaper which set out to challenge *The Voice*'s market could not be his natural home. Then there was the new computer system. He missed the act of loading up paper and the loud, musical tapping of manual typewriters. Now it was all screens and push 'send'; it sometimes seemed like a miracle that *The Monitor* made it to the news-stands every week.

He smelled soap and antiperspirant before he saw her. Lost in thought, he had not heard the front door open.

"Did she settle down okay?"

"She always does," Vincent said.

"Not with me she doesn't."

"Maybe because she knows I can't give her what you can."

Rachel left the kitchen and went upstairs.

He heard the creaky floorboard at the top of the stairs and was reminded that nailing it down was one of several repair jobs needing attention. He resumed his efforts to compose the advert and at last the words came to him: 'Large Self-Contained studio room in Finsbury Park. Less than five minutes' walk from Piccadilly and Victoria lines station.' He realised he could do no more because he did not know the going commercial rate for a comparable space. He would have to check newsagents' windows before setting a rent.

Rachel came back into the kitchen, and said, "She's fast asleep." She poured herself a glass of water and sat at the far end of the kitchen table. She took a sip of the water, put the glass aside and asked Vincent what he was writing. He told her.

"Don't you think it's time you handed back the keys?"

"I can't do that. I'm the secretary of the residents' association; they need me. Anyway, I'm sure half the block isn't occupied by the real tenants."

"We've been over this before, Vincent. That doesn't mean you have to do the same. It's unethical and probably illegal."

Vincent saw the local government officer charged with eliminating decades-long blockages in council services. She was no doubt a formidable figure in committee meetings – assertive, authoritative, frank; he could see her marshalling facts and figures in combat with white senior colleagues, complacent and indifferent, satisfied with their good intentions.

"If that's the case, then you're complicit in my wrong doing."

"Vincent, you know that the real issue isn't the room in Phoenix House. It's whether you want to be a part of our lives, Kara's and mine."

Vincent felt as if he had just been slapped. He was too stunned to speak. Here he was on a quiet Saturday, having spent three happy hours with his daughter, ensconced in a warm house, and looking forward to nothing more exciting than watching *Match of the Day* on TV. He shook his head and said, "Whatever gives you the idea…"

"Oh, come on, Vincent. You're hardly ever here. You're here physically, but not emotionally. It's as if you live in some ninth-floor room in your head, and every so often you deign to join us mere mortals on the ground floor. You can't build or sustain family life like that, Vincent. You've got to decide what you want and behave accordingly. This afternoon was a classic. Yesterday, after the theatre, another."

"I explained what happened today…" But his appeal fell on deaf ears. Rachel had donned her local government officer's hat, she was implementing the law, bringing change to an ossified bureaucracy; he was no better than the smug white males who kept Blacks out of jobs and gave them the worst services. After all, what did he know about real family life? Hadn't he told her about his grim, motherless childhood, his foul-mouthed, aggressive father? She was going to shake him out of his smug ignorance.

Vincent saw something else in Rachel, something which probably lay behind this unprovoked attack. Then he thought that he could not remember the last time he had touched her, initiated a kiss, embraced her. Ought he to do that now? Stand up, walk around the table and say, "Baby, I love you," and hug her with all the strength he could summon and lead her by the hand upstairs to Kara's room where they would gaze at the perfect miracle created by their love? He willed himself to move but some greater force kept him seated.

"That's not good enough, Vincent."

Rachel's voice, insistent and fierce, punctured his thoughts, dispelled the tenderness he wanted to show her. Suddenly he felt he was being reprimanded for failing to meet targets, for wilful neglect, disregard for a new legal framework.

"Sometimes I don't think I know who you are. And you know what really scares me? I don't think you know either. Because, if you knew yourself, you'd know what you want."

Vincent straightened his back and said, in almost a whisper, "Rachel, do us both a favour: back off, back off now."

Where do you start with answering a charge like that? Who am I? One person could write as many volumes as his lifetime allowed and still not give a definitive answer. Do you start with your ancestors, and if so, how far back do you go? Or do you start with your immediate family, your friends and colleagues, who all see different aspects of you; or do you spend years and a small fortune exploring your unconscious in therapy, knowing that the very words you use to say *This is who I am* are as slippery as an icy road. How could he give her an answer when she wasn't really interested in discussing who he was but who she would like to make him?

"Back off, or what?" Rachel stood up and pushed her chair against the wall.

Vincent rose and faced her and again felt an ambivalent desire that refused to inspire the positive action he knew could defuse this escalating row. Suddenly, Rachel lashed out and struck him on his chest with a flurry of blows, while shouting, "Or what, or what?" Vincent seized her wrists and urged her to calm down. There, I am holding her, he thought; I'm much physically stronger than she is. I should pin her hands to her sides and hug her and tell her what I know to be true.

Rachel's arms went limp but again he could not cross the chasm separating them. She hung her head and muttered, "Why are you threatening me, Vincent? I won't be threatened in my own home."

"Rachel, you should calm down. I'm going for a walk. Have the house to yourself for a while. Maybe when I get back you'll feel better and we can talk things over."

He brushed past her and got his coat and stepped out into the night, the cold air slashing his face and neck. He turned up the collar of his coat, hunched his shoulders and walked towards Green Lanes. As he walked, he thought of Kara, fast asleep in her bed, and he remembered feeding her as she sat on his lap that very evening and he shivered, not just from the cold but from another memory of waiting for his mother to come home and going to bed wondering where she was. He reached Green Lanes and turned towards Manor House, and thought: Will somebody please give me the strength to go back there. He felt a warm trickle on his cheek.

35. *Lucas and ghosts from the past, 1990s*

When Edna, Lucas Bostock's second wife, collected the weekly rent and banked it in her own account and claimed it was an oversight, the marriage was effectively over. Lucas had indulged her addiction, acquired while working as a maid in a media mogul's family home, for an expensive brand of Belgian chocolate that was only sold by an exclusive Piccadilly chocolatier – she possessed a shoe-sized box full of them. He'd tolerated her many visitors and their habit of laughing at the slightest hint of humour. But he could not forgive her theft of the weekly rent. For weeks afterwards he wandered around the house muttering, "It's the principle of the t'ing. All you had to do was ask me for the money." Edna got the message and began to move her things out of the house. The day she collected the last of her belongings, Lucas stood on the doorstep and called after her: "What Lucas Bostock own, 'im own."

With Edna's departure, Lucas moved his bedroom to a basement room and went through the entire winter without receiving a visitor. On some days, filled with an urgent need to escape the confines of the house, he rode around London on the buses, revisiting some of the buildings he had worked on over the years. His favourite destination was Waterloo; from there he would walk to the Southbank complex and, resting now and again to look at the river, wander up and down the walkways of these angular great buildings. They still managed, after all these years, to fill him with a sense of wonder for their size, and reverence for whoever imagined them into existence – but no curiosity to find out what actually went on behind their doors. He had been one of the army of men who had hammered the pine boards to make the shuttering for encasing the cement mix, had even spilled his blood when he drove a nail into the fleshy fold between his left thumb and index finger and his blood had mixed with the iron rods and wet, thick concrete. On one of these visits he had overheard two men describe the building as 'brutal' or something like that – like they were ugly eyesores. He had wanted to disagree, tell them that there was more beauty there than in all those fussy cathedrals. But he held his tongue because they sounded educated and he was only a retired carpenter from Jamaica. On other occasions, he might take a bus to the Barbican where he had also worked, and if the weather was mild enough he would sit on a bench overlooking the water and the school. The sight of the school children would remind him of his children and how they had disappointed him, because not one had chosen to follow him into the building trade.

In spring, he threw himself into a bout of house painting. He painted the brickwork at the back and front vermilion, and the window frames and doors yolk yellow. Some of the neighbours disliked his choice of colours. Carlisle Road had changed over the years, and the newcomers, young white professionals, preferred pastel shades and Venetian blinds. One neighbour, two doors away, even rang Lucas's doorbell to lodge a protest at his colour scheme because, he said, it would bring down property prices on the street. Relishing the fight, when summer came Lucas repainted the house in the same colours to underline his right to do as he pleased to his property. The neighbour moved on, and Lucas felt vindicated when he noticed that passers-by often stopped to look at his brightly coloured house.

That same summer, Lucas made an extraordinary discovery: the young spider plant – Florence George's departing gift – was flourishing despite his neglect. He could not recall having repotted it, but he must have done because it overflowed from a Grecian-shaped plastic pot. So, he began repotting its numerous offshoots and placing them around his living quarters. They in turn became as large and fruitful as the original. As the plants multiplied, Lucas repotted them in empty paint cans, old pots, cups with broken handles and jars, and placed them on surfaces until there were spider plants cascading from the tops of the wardrobe, the refrigerator top, the only surviving original Victorian mantelpiece in the house, chairs, the dining table and on wooden boxes placed beside the window for the sole purpose of accommodating these ever proliferating plants. Still they continued to grow, and each time a room became vacant, though he went through the motions of preparing it for occupancy by another tenant, he placed there instead a plant which in turn soon sprouted new plants, which, oddly, gave him more pleasure than the weekly round of rent collection.

When the last tenant left, a quiet professorial looking African, who moved with the stealthy silence of a man who craved invisibility, Lucas lost all self-restraint and threw himself into a frenzy of plant buying that sent him on many expeditions to John's Garden Centre on Stoke Newington Church Street and the Columbia Road Sunday morning flower market in search of new species. Now there were plants pressing against every window in the house, their healthy vitality maintained by their dedicated owner who kept the central heating on throughout the year, so the temperature never fell below 26 degrees centigrade.

Most days, he spent his time in the house tending his indoor garden. Climbing the stairs was not easy but he took each step slowly, hauling himself up with the help of the bannister. The stairs leading to the first floor were lined with African violets, mother's tongue ferns and money trees, their growth stunted only by his insistence on using broken cups and glasses as plant pots. In the first-floor rooms there were two begonias, three aspidistras, a yucca that touched the ceiling, an umbrella plant, and a Swiss cheese plant whose tendrils he invariably trod on as they trailed all over the linoleum floor. Their growth was no less vigorous for that. When he finished there, he rested on the bare mattress in the room where the Georges had lived for many years.

On the second and final floor, in the largest room, a room that still carried memories of Esther's betrayal, stood a six-foot tall avocado tree, which every year promised but failed to fruit, producing instead a marble-sized growth that shrivelled, turned brown, and dropped after a few days. In the next window was an equally tall banana tree, which made no promises beyond its tranquil beauty. He was less keen on the plant in the adjoining room – a Devil's ivy creeper that was out of control and swirled around the room, clung to the light cord, roamed across the wardrobe top and dresser, and entwined itself in the iron bedstead. He had already sheared it back, but this only seemed to encourage its growth, and he promised himself that next time, when he found the energy, he would attack it with a machete.

Some afternoons, having reached only as far as the first floor before succumbing to tiredness, he recovered his strength in the living room while looking out onto the street through the dense foliage of a cluster of plants. These included a euphorbia or pencil cactus, an unruly Boston fern, a rubber plant, and two echeveria. At least once a month he wandered from the back to the front of the house, his weak eyes searching for any repairs that were needed, though he was confident that the years of work he had put into the building would keep it sound for a long time. If, after stormy weather, a gutter needed to be repaired, he was still willing and able to take out the ladder and see to it himself.

He retired to his bedroom from as early as six p.m. most days. There, sitting up in bed surrounded by yet more of his silent companions – which included a magnificent elephants-foot plant – he listened to the radio and finished reading the morning newspaper. He still read the same newspaper he had been reading for decades, but no longer saw it as the fount of truth because it sometimes contradicted the radio reports and, more importantly, it was on its advice that he had, in a moment of madness, sold the second house and invested half the money in a new share issue scheme which crashed a few years later. Since then, he had restricted his investments to blue chip companies and their modest profits satisfied his diminished appetite for wealth.

His existence was not entirely solitary. He began receiving regular fortnightly visits from Velma Ricketts. An old flame and great grandmother of three, she had warned him that their relationship wouldn't last unless he changed his ways. Velma cleaned the kitchen and bedroom, and, if he was nice to her and moderated his crabbiness, she would give him a massage, which caused a flickering arousal like the rumbling of an extinct volcano. Velma shared her home with one of her daughters and a granddaughter and often expressed concern for Lucas's apparent isolation.

"It's not healthy, you living in a big old house by yourself at your age."

"You mean if I was younger, it'd be all right?"

"No, I mean people made to live with each other. It's human nature. That's how God made us."

"That's how God made you, and this how life made me. Me not complaining."

"Lord God, Lucas! What life do you to make you this way?"

It was not a question Lucas could answer but it was one he gave much thought to. And always his search for an answer brought an old memory: a little boy carrying a brown parcel under his arm as he made his way down a mountain road. He did not share this memory with Velma. Instead, he said, "Besides, I get plenty visitors."

This was partly true. Vincent came once a month and more recently Neville had visited twice within a month, bringing Lucas an audio bible as a conciliatory gift. The telephone was a vital link with the outside world, though it sometimes brought him news he would have preferred not to hear, such as the night Donnette telephoned from a prison in New York, and though she wanted nothing more than to hear her father's voice, she left him feeling ashamed to know that one of his offspring had become a criminal. On several occasions he was visited by Ken Beckford, the man whose life he had saved in Ladbroke Grove. Ken spoke with a strangled voice, the effect of the knife wound to this throat. But after a while, even these visits ceased. One day, Ken came to see him and told him he was going home. He was married to a Grenadian and they had bought an old colonial-style house set on land that had been used to grow spice – nutmeg, cinnamon, and vanilla – for over a century and he was going to make a go of becoming a spice farmer on an island not so long ago blessed with the benefits of an American invasion.

"Even if it doesn't work out," Ken said, "I'll have a sweet retirement. What about you, Lucas. Surprised you're still here."

"It's on my mind," he said. "Next year, probably. Definitely next year. Probably."

They parted with a firm handshake and Lucas closed the door, thinking that he did not really like the man whose life he had saved, but at least there was somebody in the world who wasn't cursing him. But Ken's visit left him feeling blue with nostalgia, thinking about home, sometimes with such intensity that he could smell the log fires where, in his youth, he roasted breadfruit with friends; could feel the sea breeze thrash his face; could reach out and touch the Bombay mango that he had watched ripening for months; hear the singing of the women on washday; watch the sunset over Port Antonio harbour. He wondered when and where he had lost his dream of returning home, whether his cousin Jean had stolen it in an act of vengeance, but he rejected this possibility because he knew only too well that nobody could steal from Lucas Bostock, and he had to conclude it had not been his dream. Then, one day, as he was watering a spider plant, clarity struck and he realised why, of the many things she could have given him, Florence George had gifted him this particular plant. His dream of returning home had never been strong enough because, since the day he was given a brown paper parcel and sent to join Jean's family, since that day, like a spider he had been carrying his home with him.

One day, he found the resolve to tackle the overgrown Devil's ivy on the top floor, and began his gardening routine with a machete bought from a Mauritian-owned hardware store on Church Street. He took his usual rest on the first floor, then, machete and watering bottle in hand, he climbed to the top floor. What he saw was a modest-sized and healthy plant with a few browning leaves, not the wild ivy of memory. He put aside the machete and was pulling off the dry, brittle leaves when he was startled by what seemed like a blinding flash of light over the bed. Where there had been an empty space, he saw Trinity Gordon.

"So, this is where you been hiding, Lucas Bostock. You ran away, couldn't face a rematch."

Lucas rubbed his eyes in disbelief, but the figure was still there. He wore a brown zoot suit such as young working men wore many years ago in Kingston when going sporting on a Saturday night. Lucas's lifelong refusal to believe in the supernatural and his famous courage abandoned him for a moment and he made to flee the room. But after grabbing the doorknob, he paused and looked the figure straight in the eye.

"That really you, Trinity?"

"Yes, is really me. Took me many years to find you, Lucas, many years of wandering. Thought you had gone Stateside, but you here in London all the time. Now I'm ready for that rematch anytime. Queensberry rules."

"Mahn, you must be out of yuh mind," Lucas said. "You know I'll only whip your behind again."

"Maybe, but we got to have a rematch. It's only fair. You owe me that."

"Name the date and time and me see you there," Lucas said.

But there was no reply and Lucas found himself staring into an empty space and the dead vine leaves at his feet. He decided that weariness had caused him to hallucinate. He abandoned his gardening efforts and retired to his bedroom, where sleep soon claimed him.

He woke up several hours later feeling hungry and thirsty. He made his way to the kitchen and warmed up some rice and chicken and ate contemplatively. He remembered the fight with Trinity Gordon, the braying crowd surrounding them as, stripped to the waist, they slogged it out on the waste ground. And he remembered the exact moment when he knew he had beaten Trinity, the counterpunch that caused his opponent's knees to buckle, the quick follow-up punch that connected so surely and powerfully that Trinity's head almost seemed to swivel on his neck before he crashed to the dusty ground. He had often wondered whether that second punch had been necessary. Damn, Trinity had picked the fight.

He left half the food on the plate and returned to his bed. He did not feel sleepy and so decided to check the performance of his shares. He had just identified one of the companies in his portfolio when he thought he heard a coughing sound. He looked up and saw standing at the door a figure whose identity puzzled him for an instant, before a name came to mind. It was Mr Norton, the sitting tenant who had occupied the basement when he bought the house.

"Did she come?" Mr Norton asked.

"Did who come?"

"Beatrice, of course."

Lucas could not answer this question immediately. But when he said yes, the figure vanished. Hearing the echo of his own voice in the empty room, Lucas decided that he had to get himself to the doctor. His mind was playing tricks on him.

36. Samuel's political ambitions, mid 1990s

In his quest for political office Samuel Bostock had found a staunch ally in Larry Haynes. They had met ten years before Larry became the MP for Walthamstow North and the older man had taken Samuel under his wing, vouchsafing his integrity and serious intent. But Haynes's support and encouragement had not yet yielded fruit. Samuel remained a respected a Labour councillor; the Commons eluded him.

In July, when Samuel had once again failed to win selection to contest a Labour seat, this time in the East Midlands, Larry Haynes invited him to a consolatory lunch at the Orinoco restaurant, which was owned by Haynes's brother. The restaurant's walls were decorated with New World images: framed old maps of West Indian islands, the Americas, and an Aubrey Williams original depicting a squat, grim-faced South American deity or spirit. Wooden barrels with rusting metal rings were suspended from the ceiling.

As soon as they were seated in a dimly-lit cubicle at the rear of the restaurant, Larry's mobile rang. While he answered the call, Samuel reflected that selection would have guaranteed him a parliamentary seat as John Carsons, whose sudden death created the vacancy, had secured a fifteen-thousand majority in the previous election. It would have taken an unprecedented swing for Labour to lose a constituency it had held for thirty years, and that was unlikely because the Conservatives, scandal ridden and directionless, were clearly exhausted.

Larry Haynes ended his call and switched off the phone. "Sorry about that. We won't be disturbed for a while. Only my PA has this number, and I've instructed her to field all my calls."

Haynes was a large man with a ragged, greying beard, narrow but bright eyes, and an odd, fixed smile, as if he had played some great trick on everyone and was waiting to be found out. The scion of a West Indian plantocratic family, Haynes had come to Britain on a Rhodes scholarship, spent some years as an academic economist, before entering politics through the trade union movement. In the process he'd reinvented himself as just another West Indian immigrant. His detractors whispered that his combination of abstract thinking, passionate idealism, and populist appeal would keep him anchored to the backbenches.

"Don't take it personally," Larry said.

"How else should I take it?" Samuel asked.

"Try to understand what's going on. The Conservative Party is a wounded animal. The new Labour dispensation is gearing up for power. They want their own people in secure seats."

"If you knew that beforehand, why did you encourage me to put my name forward?"

"Sam, when we first met at the '83 party conference and you told me of your ambition, I committed myself to helping you. But I also warned you that it wouldn't be easy. '87 filled everybody with optimism, but it was an exceptional year, unlikely to be ever repeated. The door has since been – how shall we say…?"

"Closed firmly?" Samuel suggested.

"Not exactly; the gap's certainly narrowed, but it's still ajar. Thing is to keep on trying. Put the interviews down to experience."

"What I understood is that my face didn't fit, again."

"If your face didn't fit, you wouldn't have got as far as the selection interview. Somebody at HQ likes you. And I know John spoke well of you."

"Really? I only met him a few times. Thought he didn't like me, actually. He always seemed so cold."

"He probably didn't," Larry grinned. "He respected the work you did with the Black Alliance in the '80s. You know we go back quite far?"

"Yes, I know you both started out as union men."

"Actually, we met many years before that, in Leicester, at the university there. I was using the university library for research and sometimes popped into the student union building to read the newspapers. One day, I wandered into the newspaper room and saw a young man reading Adam Smith's *The Theory of Moral Sentiment*. I was reading Marx's *Grundrisse*. I said to him, "You shouldn't be reading the enemy." He looked up at me and said, "Nobody tells me what to fucking read, mate," and stormed off. Next time I saw him, on a snowy day in late November, he was helping to clear the campus footpaths. His father was one of the campus maintenance team. He, John, couldn't afford higher education."

"I could never quite get a handle on him."

"No, he wasn't the most demonstrative of men, at least not when sober. You missed his heyday, before he settled for the backbenches and concentrating on his constituency work. He was an old working-class warrior, a dying breed. When the party removed Clause Four, he came close to resigning: he thought the party's leadership had been hijacked by unprincipled power-seekers, smooth-talking lawyers, good with the media, but disrespectful of the party's traditions."

"What surprised me is that he actually increased his majority in the last general election. Especially after all that fatwa controversy. Didn't they burn an effigy of Rushdie in John Carson's constituency? Wasn't his seat threatened at one time?"

"Yes, to both questions. You know, I have a fond memory of

John, years before all that fatwa business, at a TUC conference. A small group of us sitting up late, drinking and talking. This was before my medically imposed prohibition. We'd been arguing about something, and I vaguely recall Gramsci's name being bandied about. John's union background made it difficult for him to accept the importance of cultural sites of struggle, but we can ride that horse another day... As I said, it was late, John quaffed a double shot of vodka, stood up, swaying on his feet, face as red as beetroot, and said: 'Well, gentlemen thanks for the disagreement; I know I exist.'"

"That summed up the man. He fervently believed that to disagree and to keep on talking was the essence of a civilized exchange. So you can imagine his horror at that whole fatwa business. It made him aware that he didn't know a section of his constituents as well as he ought to have done. As you know, he defended Rushdie's right to free speech and it provoked quite a backlash from some of his constituents. He was more concerned with the politics of multiculturalism after that. Recognised its explosive potential."

"It's an issue Britain's been wrestling with since the '50s."

"Yes and no. When we West Indians came here, we were assimilated, held the same religious beliefs, spoke an English dialect. As the descendants of enslaved Africans, we were born with modernity, not a privileged position but an interesting one from which to watch other peoples, more burdened by tradition, engage with the modern. Our culture posed no threat to the status quo. John Carsons had to deal with people who had travelled with well-defined cultures which were not going to disappear in one or two generations, just because they're in Britain. Indeed, the very multiculturalism that we, West Indians and progressive forces, had fought for was being challenged by traditional cultures that clash with what defines our modern age. Carsons saw that clearly..."

"Visiting that part of England was an eye opener for me. It was as if the population of a whole Asian town had been transplanted there, women in burqas, men with hennaed beards, Arabic scripts on shop fronts..."

Just then the waitress brought their meal. Samuel had ordered steamed escoveitch fish, rice and peas and salad. The aroma hinted at black pepper and coconut. He began de-boning the fish and remarked on Larry's dish of boiled yams, vegetables and snapper.

"Still eating on doctor's orders, I see."

"Unfortunately, yes. No salt, pepper or oil. Everything steamed. Anyway, what were we saying?"

"Something about cultures."

"Yes, these cultures. Huge political implications. How do we balance respect for minority cultures and national cohesion? It was a question that taxed John Carson. Some young radicals dismissed him as a racist for recognising the problem, but they were wrong. He once said, "How can I respect a man who sees it as his divine right to stone an adulterer, cut off the hand of a thief, kill his daughter if she marries a non-believer? Am I racist for believing that is wrong? John agonised over these matters. You sensed a man fighting against his imminent obsolescence, resisting being swept aside by history. In his effort to understand, he read widely. He was an autodidact, an intuitive thinker, and he believed in the moral and intellectual superiority of Western civilisation, not least because of its self-reflexivity, its categories of thought. He thought that reflexivity helped promote tolerance."

"Isn't that rather Eurocentric?"

"Yes, yes, I put that to him – and this is one of the reasons I liked the man – and he said, 'I can only speak from where I stand'. But back to your point on Eurocentrism. It's a charge you'd have to level against me too, and, if you're honest, yourself. English is my mother tongue. My moral and political principles, the concepts I wield to make sense of reality, are rooted in enlightenment thinking. I am inescapably and irrevocably of the West. But – and this is where I disagreed with John – certain civilizational currents arrived in the west from elsewhere to help create what we call the modern. Take the ideal of freedom; it's no more uniquely western than gunpowder…"

Samuel felt he was being drawn into deeper waters than his own pragmatic cast of mind could negotiate. He concentrated on his meal as Larry discoursed on the Western debt to other peoples and cultures. During a pause he said, "I must say this latest setback has left me wondering whether I'm cut out for parliament."

"No, don't say that. You have admirers. But it's timing, timing. Be patient. You'll make progress. You may have to compromise your ambition, though."

"Meaning?"

"It's an open secret that a new Labour government will restore an elected authority to London. A mayor's office and an assembly. Things are still at the blueprint stage."

"And you think that could be possible point of entry?"

"Yes, it wouldn't be Westminster, but important all the same."

"That'd be a huge compromise, but it would be a step up. Right now I'm not sure I could face another selection committee."

"Well, let's wait and see. I'm owed a few favours and could, perhaps, be more useful to you if that comes about." Larry sipped his mineral water and glanced at his telephone.

Samuel sensed that the formal part of their lunch had ended. "Your advice over the years has been invaluable, Larry."

"Thank you, Sam. One tries. And how is your lovely wife?"

Yes, Elena, Sam thought. His failures and successes were hers too. She had polished his rough edges, groomed him for office. She had shown him that he was fluent in the language of confrontation and protest but hopeless in the language of negotiation and compromise. And she continued to believe in him – sometimes, he felt, more than he believed in himself.

"Oh, I told her we were meeting. She sends fond regards, said you must come to dinner again." In truth, Elena considered Larry Haynes bombastic, a devious political player. Sam's thoughts strayed to Sylvia. He was worried that she was, according to their sons, drinking heavily.

As lunch ended, Sam's PA called him to say his afternoon appointment had been cancelled, leaving him a gap in his day. He drove back towards central London and made a last-minute decision to drop in on his father. Sam was a rare visitor to Carlisle Road and though time had partly healed the rift between them, there were still issues that were unresolved, perhaps irresolvable.

He parked on Nevill Road and sat in his vintage Mercedes, still unsure whether to visit. Most of the changes in the neighbourhood were familiar from the occasions, usually at night, when he drove there to remind himself where he'd come from. He'd noted the shrinking number of windows with net curtains, aloe vera plants in the garden, scriptural notices in the windows, cars with Caribbean island flags, the front gardens used to grow vegetables – as if their West Indian owners couldn't abandon the habit of farming. Now, at least, he heard the sound of Bob Marley singing 'Waiting in Vain' coming from a house. A man and his daughter walked towards him, the man burly and tall, the child, dressed entirely in pink, bearing the unmistakeable stamp of her father. It was only after they had walked past that Samuel realised that the father was white, the child mixed-race – a common sight now, but in his own childhood rare. He got out of the car and walked towards Carlisle Road.

The appearance of his old house struck him as a strange combination of vigorous growth and stagnation. A grapevine planted in a barrel had reached above the ground floor window; it looked as if in years to come it would cover the house. The fading primary colours of the window frames and door made the house look gaudy, and whoever had done the work must have had shaky hands because paint streaked several windows. The metal railings were rusting, bars had lost their tops, and the gate released a creak that made Sam think of a dying animal.

The man who opened the door was smaller than he remembered, his jowls sagging to form a dark wattle under his chin; pepper-grain hair covered his head in blotches, but the face wore the same pugnacious expression.

"Who you want?"

"Dad, it's me, Samuel."

"Samuel?"

"It's me."

"Yes, yes, you look like him. That's true. You better come in. Your timing's not too good. We just about to eat."

"Sorry, I didn't mean to disturb your meal. I can come back a little later."

"Come back later? Bwoy, seems like you lose something. Any son of mine can always eat at my table."

Samuel felt the heat immediately. The central heating had to be on at maximum. Something brushed his face, the wispy leaf of a giant air plant. His father's slow movements and bowed posture stirred his pity. He saw more plants in small pots on the stairs, and leafy effusions emerging from the room at the top of the stairs he remembered as the tenants' kitchen. A reel of childhood memories unspooled in his mind and he realised why his previous visits to the neighbourhood, clandestine and nocturnal, had been unsatisfactory. Here was the heart of his origin, within these walls layered with wallpaper over the years, every dry-rotted, worm-ridden floorboard replaced by a man who worshipped in the temple of work.

"Never mind my other visitors," his father said, as he followed him into the backroom where, many years before, the family used to gather. Here, too, there were many plants. But the room was empty.

"Seems like it never rains but it pours. Been on my own all week, then today me have a full house. Fellahs, as you can see, I've got a visitor. Not just any visitor neither. Me son, me first born."

The table was set for four; beside each plate was a small potted cactus.

Samuel couldn't decide whether to point out the obvious fact that they were alone. No, better humour him, he thought, recalling some of the elderly constituents he had dealt with at his councillor's surgery.

"Now you sit there, Sammy boy."

Samuel sat at one end of the table and decided that the old man was mad. Why hadn't Neville or Vincent told him?

"Trinity and Mr Norton will have to sit together, eat from the same plate." He moved the cactus in front of Samuel and placed it next to another plate.

"Now that's better. What you saying, Horace? You like sitting next to Mr Norton? Well, too bad. Is not every day me firstborn son comes to visit me. We've to make room for him."

Refusing any help, his father brought a dish of rice and peas, stewed chicken and fried plantain, and placed it on the table – Samuel was relieved to see that though the table was set for four, there was just enough food for two and none was offered to the imaginary guests. Despite the lunch with Larry Haynes, he got stuck into the food before him, promising himself to go for a run that evening.

"So, what you doing this side of London?"

"I've been meaning to visit for some time. Sorry. But you know how it is – work, the children." He felt awkward and marvelled at this obviously demented old man's ability to reduce him to the status of a child.

"No need to apologise. As you can see, me is not short of company." His father looked around the empty table, then said: "How you children doing?".

Sam was relieved to hear this question, took it as a sign his father still had a foot in the real world. Sam updated him on his own children's progress and Lucas listened attentively and, satisfied that his grandchildren were not idlers, nodded with approval.

After a pause in their exchange, Lucas said: "Found a slate in the front garden. Have to go up on the roof soon."

"There's no need for you to do that. I can arrange for a roofer to mend it."

245

"A roofer? Not on my roof. Day me can't climb that ladder is the day me know me ready for me grave."

Samuel remembered the days when hammering resounded through the house. He had never wielded a hammer or paintbrush in his life.

"When you last see Vincent?" his father asked.

"Not for some time. No, I don't see much of him."

"Shame, shame. You boys should stick together. Help each other out."

"Vincent moves in a different world from me, Dad. He seems a bit lost to me, always changing jobs. Last time I heard he was out of work. Gone back to living in that room in Finsbury Park."

"A shame, yes. Mind you, me not surprised. That boy was never going to amount to much, at least not in any way I understand."

"How d'you know that?"

"A man knows his own seed. Vincent always seem like somebody who trying to work out what's going on without really wanting to find out. He always seemed disappointed when he placed the last piece in a jigsaw. Now you, you were different, you wanted to own the puzzles, used to keep them under your bed."

Samuel smiled. He had no memory of that childhood pastime nor any awareness that his father saw him and his siblings as being so different. His watch told him it was time to leave.

"Well, thanks for dropping by," his father said. "These fellows are getting restless."

"But, Dad, there's no one here," Samuel said, having abandoned his decision to humour him.

"Nobody here? Nobody here? Son, when you've lived as long as I have, when you've lived as hard as I have, when you've lived as mean as I have, you is never without company."

37. *Sam, Sylvia, drink and a little guilt*

A few weeks later, Samuel made a long overdue visit to Sylvia. For some minutes after being admitted to the house in Tulse Hill, he was left alone in the living room while Sylvia spoke on the phone in the kitchen. Seated in the highback wing-chair, once acknowledged as 'Daddy's chair', he surveyed the room in which Sylvia and his mother would be on the sofa, the boys on the Persian rug or bean bags. This seemed a lifetime ago, though the room remained much as it had been, though Sylvia had evidently acquired an interest in masks. Black African wooden masks hung on the walls, alongside glazed and painted ceramic faces with bulbous noses, thick lips and multi-coloured spots on their cheeks; their provenance was less obvious.

He readied himself for the purpose of his visit. Joseph had reported that Sylvia was on anti-depressants and drinking heavily. "Wine and strong lager," he had said. "Cheap lager, Tennents and Special Brew, the kind you see winos drinking outside Brixton Library." The boy had disdain in his voice, distress on his face. Sam recognised the appeal for him to do something. Busy with countless meetings and juggling various projects, he had also procrastinated because he didn't know what action to take. Since the divorce, Sylvia had behaved with punctilious politeness towards him when they were in the company of their children or in public. They'd had their disagreements about how their sons should be brought up, especially on how much and what kind of television they watched. He had won that argument, lost another on the boys' fondness for rap music. Sylvia had refused to impose a ban. Such negotiations he regarded as the stuff of parenthood, a role to which he remained committed. And he had worked hard to show that he still cared for her. After a day out with the boys, he would send them home with flowers for their mother; he never forgot her birthday, and several times each year, they all went out to dinner, like a normal family. Sylvia had met Elena, and Elena being Elena seemed to have charmed Sylvia into liking her. So, Joseph's report left him puzzled. Why had Sylvia taken to drink? Was it because the boys were no longer at home? He was here because of Joseph's concern, but there was also his political career. He didn't need a drunken ex-wife running loose in Brixton.

Sylvia's entry into the room ended his reflections. She apologised for keeping him waiting, offered him tea, which he politely declined. They discussed their sons for a moment and Sylvia laughed as she revealed that Joseph had brought a girl to meet her. She was always at her most attractive when laughing, her terracotta-coloured skin and white teeth in harmony, her large eyes blinking fast. It was sad they had so little in common now. He had continued growing; she had put all her energies into motherhood. He broached the subject of her health, mentioning the boys' now independent lives as an understandable reason for her to feel a little down.

"It's got nothing to do with Joseph and John," Sylvia said.

"There's nothing wrong with admitting that you're missing them. I miss them. But it's what children do. They fly the coop; it's a measure of how well you've done as a parent that they have the confidence to leave and the skills to survive outside the home." He cleared his throat. "I've been thinking, Sylvia, maybe you should take a holiday. What about Bequia? You've never been back. I'm sure it'd be good to see the island and your old friends again. I'll pay for it."

She narrowed her eyes and gazed at him intently.

"Bequia?" she said, in disbelief. "Look how long I left that place. I wouldn't know what to say to people now. Most of the people I knew, my friends, are not there anymore. They're in Canada or America."

"It's a popular holiday destination in the Caribbean now. But it doesn't have to be Bequia. The thing is to take a holiday."

"I don't need a holiday, Sam. I need a drink – my first of the day."

Sylvia left the room and returned with a half-full bottle of merlot. He declined her offer and watched her fill her glass, which she put on the mantelpiece and stood beside it. In her loose black lycra slacks and light-grey woollen top – which hung almost vertically from her shoulders over her flat breasts – she seemed somewhat asexual to him, as if time and the demands of motherhood had attenuated the femininity that had once entranced him.

"Tell me, Sam, are you trying to get rid of me?"

"Whatever gave you that idea?"

"Well, strictly speaking, you don't need me now, do you? Your sons are fine, on the road to being professionals."

"Our sons."

"Our sons, Sam. Yes, if you say so. Though I can't help thinking that I've just been a caretaker mother until they reached adulthood, and then you would claim them."

"That's unfair to me, the boys and yourself. You're their mother, always will be. Nobody can take that away from you. Sylvia, I know how you feel."

"You know how I feel, Sam? When did you become Samuel Bostock, the great empathiser? Where was your empathy when you walked out on me for that white girl?"

"I didn't leave you for a white girl, Sylvia. I left you for Elena, whose hospitality you have enjoyed, who has shown nothing but kindness to our sons, who is the mother of their brother."

"Half-brother. Yes, yes, of course. Her colour's got nothing to do with it. Elena's just Elena."

"That's right. And it wasn't a decision I took lightly. I've looked after you since then, Sylvia – give me some credit. This house, the boy's schooling. You've not wanted for anything."

"I've not wanted for anything? Aren't you the one who used to tell me that the big problem with your father was that he thought all a person needed in life was a roof, clothes and food. Am I not a woman? I have my needs, physical and emotional. Have you been thinking about them over the years? I died the night you left here. I told you that I would stand by you wherever you chose to go. I've done that. But the price I've paid… You've no idea, Samuel Bostock."

Sylvia picked up the glass and emptied it. She walked to the sofa, sat down, and released a weary, pained sigh. "And now look at me. I have nothing, nothing."

"That's not entirely true," Samuel said.

"Yes, it is, and you damn well know it, Sam. When I was young, I could have had any man; all I had to do was smile at a man and he would come running. Nowadays, men don't look at me; if they do, all they see is a middle-aged Black woman."

"Sylvia, I've never tried to stop you from remarrying." He leaned forward, his palms upturned, a gesture that was both pleading and appeasing, searching Sylvia's face.

"Didn't you? What man could I have brought in here? What man would have been good enough to have around your precious sons? Oh, I'm no saint, believe you me. I've seen enough hotel rooms in Victoria and Earls Court on the weekends you had Joseph and John, when you took them on holiday with your new family. But to bring a man here, I couldn't do it. Those boys worship you. It would have been a declaration of war to have brought a stranger here. Then there's the name you've made for yourself. Samuel Bostock, Black spokesman, future member of parliament. One guy I liked, and I knew liked me, just disappeared after I told him I was your ex-wife."

"I had no idea you felt inhibited about finding a new partner. I'm sorry."

"You had no idea! You're sorry! And you have the fucking cheek to tell me you know how I feel."

"There's no need to swear, Sylvia."

"I'll swear in my own home if I choose, thank you." She stood up and refilled her glass.

"Okay, okay." He shrugged his shoulders.

"You know how I feel! You know what it feels like to do anything, and I mean anything, for a man, and to have that man walk out on you for another woman."

"Whatever you did in the past for me, Sylvia, I didn't ask you to do it. I'll always be grateful for the help you gave me, but please, don't try to guilt trip me."

"Fair enough, Sam. I said to myself I would never mention our past. We both know it's there. And I take full responsibility for the decisions I made, for my own behaviour. So, I'm not holding that against you."

"Good."

"But I'll tell you what, Samuel Bostock, one day, if I ever get the chance, I'll make you feel something of what I feel, and it'll be just between you and me. Nobody else."

"Are you threatening me, Sylvia?" He would not be threatened or blackmailed nor live in fear of retribution and revenge. He was not some callous monster who had seized her in the prime of life and locked her away in a tower until, withered and aged, she no longer served a purpose. They had been little more than children when they became parents, and he had done the honourable thing. As soon as he'd recognised that Elena was no mere adventure across the race line, but somebody who ignited in him a belief and a purpose, he'd had the courage to be honest with Sylvia. Would she have been happier if he had chosen to deceive her, feigned happiness with her, continued living in a moribund marriage?

"Take it how you want," Sylvia said, tears rolling down her cheeks.

His surge of aggression abated. Drink no doubt had inspired her mean remark. Remorse returned with the realisation that he had failed to anticipate the effects of the boys' departure. They had been Sylvia's companions and links to his family, and in their absence, she had become isolated, and succumbed to melancholia. The bottle and pills had become her only reliable friends. But it wasn't too late, she could still be saved.

"OK, I won't take it as a threat, Sylvia. It's just the drink talking. You ought to cut down on that stuff, especially because you're on medication. The boys still need you. You're not helping them by behaving like a drunkard. You mentioned that Joseph had brought a girl home – a girl I haven't met."

He stood up, stepped close to Sylvia, took the glass from her hand, placed it on the mantelpiece, looked into her eyes, and said: "Sylvia, I didn't plan to hurt you, I didn't, honestly. You know that. We try our best not to hurt other people, but sometimes it's just the way things turn out. It could easily have been you who found somebody else."

"But it wasn't me. It was you, Sam. And I'm hurting so much inside, have been hurting for such a long time."

"I'll help you, Sylvia. I'm in the wrong. I've been so caught up in my career; I've neglected you. I have, and I'm sorry – should've been paying more attention to you after the boys left home. I'll correct that, I promise, but you've got to meet me halfway. You've got to stop this heavy drinking – clean yourself up."

"It's all I have," Sylvia said.

Samuel clasped her shoulders and said, "No, it isn't Sylvia. I'm still your friend and will be forever. I'm so grateful for how you've brought up our sons that words fail me. But you've got to look after yourself for the boys' sake, for your own sake. Find something to engage your time, take on a new challenge – maybe do an education course. I'll pay for it."

Sylvia looked steadily into Samuel's eyes, then pulled away. She inhaled deeply, shook her head, and picked up her glass from the mantelpiece. "Maybe you're right, Sam. I dunno, sometimes it all just seems so pointless, life I mean – that we're just here to produce more life and that's it, nothing else."

"You've done a great job with the boys, honestly, and there's still work to do; but now you've got to find some other purpose to fill your life."

"Guess so." She sighed.

She saw him to the door, and after he had kissed her cheek, she said coyly, "I'm very disappointed in you, Samuel Bostock."

He looked at her puzzled, and for a moment feared they were about to argue again.

She said, "You've forgotten I hate the sea."

"Sorry," Samuel said.

They laughed and parted.

Walking down Tulse Hill, Samuel realised he would soon have the opportunity to show Sylvia he meant what he'd said about ending her isolation. Elena was involved in The Camberwell Art Project, which had recently acquired capital funding for an exhibition space and cafe. It was due to open in a few months. He would make sure Sylvia received an invitation to the opening night, personally deliver it if necessary. He would talk to Elena. She would understand. Was he acting purely out of self-interest? No, he had neglected Sylvia's feelings and needs, and while he could not turn back the clock, there was no need to exclude her from his public life like some shameful secret. But he could not help thinking that Sylvia's occasional presence at public events could help raise his profile. He imagined a photograph in the newspaper of Councillor Sam Bostock flanked by his wife, ex-wife and their children. A portrait of a modern British family; a portrait of the times.

As he neared central Brixton, he switched on the car radio and heard, "Early indications suggest the Conservatives will suffer a massive defeat in this Northampton constituency..."

38. *Vincent wanders London*

Vincent passed Saturday afternoon wandering around docklands. These days the Canary Wharf tower, visible from the top of Finsbury Park's north slope, exercised an irresistible pull on him. He had spent many distracted weekend hours in its shadow. After resting in the green beside the Greenwich foot tunnel, he took a series of buses until he reached Mile End Road. From there he walked to Bethnal Green and along Mare Street to Lower Clapton Road, noting as he went the many signs of the dying summer: the yellowing leaves on the plane trees; a whistle with a red, green and yellow strap – a lost carnival souvenir from a week ago; shop windows displaying winter clothes, which he stopped to stare at until a pedestrian bumped into him, breaking the spell.

Nearing the Lea Bridge roundabout, he became aware of a ferocious thirst and decided to interrupt his homeward journey. He was by the White Horse pub, where he and Neville used to meet occasionally, to catch up on family news.

The pub was smoky, noisy, crowded. The round-bellied bespectacled barman kept overlooking him for regular customers, and it took him a long time to get served. From the bar, he drifted in search of a seat towards the rear of the pub. It was emptier there, dominated by two pool tables, one in use, and some small round tables with cast-iron legs and wooden tops. He leaned against a column and watched a pool game in progress.

The two players talked throughout the game. One was a strikingly handsome young man whose striped T-shirt fitted him like a second skin. He seemed to dance around the table, cuing with speed and panache but erratic accuracy. Vincent thought he was beautiful to watch in motion. His opponent was huge, with frizzy Afro-hair and a pimpled face. His game was slower, more thoughtful. While the Adonis sought to pot every shot, the big fellow was content to block access to the pockets. This strategy won him the game, and loser and victor shook hands. The stylish player promised to return for a rematch and the winner grinned and retorted: "Anytime. The result's gonna be the same."

Vincent watched a few more games until he was invited to play by a lanky lean player who had dispatched the big fellow and now lacked an opponent. He accepted, played and lost and returned to his spot beside the column and finished his drink. The front of the pub was now more crowded, and Vincent was surprised to see that it was approaching 10.30. He discovered that the pub also housed a nightclub in its basement. Its customers seemed mainly women, who stood about in groups and clutched tiny handbags studded with coloured glass.

He got a second pint of lager and returned to the pool tables, which were now both in use and surrounded by spectators. He sat at one of the small tables and gazed at his drink. He had promised to visit his mother the following day, and wondered whether he ought to get home, get a good night's rest. But the convivial atmosphere made that agenda seem less urgent.

"Never seen you in here before," a woman said.

He looked up and saw a stout woman with a broad face blemished by spots and small scars. She wore large Spanish-style earrings and a faint red lipstick. There was something vaguely masculine about her, as if her femininity was an uncomfortable uniform. She introduced herself as Angela and they fell into conversation, whose ease surprised Vincent because he had spoken only to shopkeepers and bus conductors since leaving work on Friday evening. He surmised she was a hooker, or a good-time girl looking to get him to spend money on her. Her request for a drink confirmed his suspicion.

"Sure," he said. It's what men like me do, he thought. Pay for female company. "The barman will probably serve you quicker, so you'd better get it," he said, and took out some pound coins.

"I wasn't serious," she said.

"I am. Go on, have a drink on me."

She took the money and went away. Vincent was sure he'd just been scammed; she was probably boasting about her conquest with her friends right now. His drink was almost finished. He would soon leave, hoping no-one was laughing at him.

"Here we go," she said, placing their drinks on the table. "Cheers… You don't look like the kind of guy who drinks in a pub on Saturday nights."

"Don't I? What kind of guy do I look like?"

"Dunno, like a schoolteacher, someone who works in an office."

It was what the barman had seen; he was not one of them.

"That's just appearances. I am a man of the people," he said.

"You even sound posh."

"Me? No. Born in Homerton Hospital, bred in Stoke Newington."

"Could've fooled me."

"Anyway, I was right about the barman. I'd still be standing there. Your feminine charm did the trick."

"S'pose it's useful sometimes. But after the week I've had, I could do without it."

"Tough?"

"You bet. My son's father came out of prison on Wednesday. Came round to my flat threatening to take my son away. Had to call the police on him."

"You're a mother?" Vincent said.

"A woman and a mother. That's me. I didn't always look like this, you know. Just ended up with the wrong kind of man."

"Sorry about that," he said, and a fragment of an exchange he'd had with Rachel strayed into his mind, "You're not the kind of man I can be happy with, Vincent."

"I'm sorry, too," Angela said. "Biggest bloody mistake I made having a kid with that bloke."

"So, what are you going to do about him?"

"Dunno. I've sent Giovanni – that's my son – to stay with my Mum until Leroy stops his foolishness. A good friend of mine is staying with me."

"Sounds like you're living under siege."

"Naw. This has been going on for ages. I'm used to it. It'll blow over. He'll probably be back in the nick soon, anyway. Either that or Frank will put him in hospital."

"Frank. Is that your boyfriend?"

"Naw, he's just a good mate. Anyway, I shouldn't be talking about him. Bloody hell, you're a right one aren't you. You've just got me to tell you my life story. What're you, some kind of nark?"

"You came over to me. I was sitting here quietly, minding my own business."

"That's true. I reckon you're alright. Look, I am supposed to be meeting some friends here, then we're going back to my place. Wanna to come along?"

"It's already way past my bedtime. I've got a busy day tomorrow."

"Sunday? The day of rest. You're joking. Look, I'm going to see if my mates are at the front. Back in a minute."

Vincent watched the woman disappear into the crowd. He had misread her; she was just another woman drawn to him by his solitary air.

Before he could finish his drink, Angela returned, her two friends in tow. Helen was huge, occupying enough space for two average-sized adults. She wore a black dress with a metallic shine, like mediaeval body armour and her straightened, reddish-brown hair seemed too perfect to be real. She gave Vincent a smile which prompted his hasty judgement that she was capable of great cruelty. Peaches, was dark and small, with an ectomorphic face framed by glistening, jerry-curled, shoulder-length hair. She wore an intricately embroidered black lace blouse that accentuated the swell of her stomach.

"Downstairs is dead," Angela said. "We're going back to my flat. Come along, Vincent."

He wanted to get outside, and he followed the women through the crowd and out into the night. Now all he had to do was walk away, resume his homeward journey.

"My place's on the other side of the roundabout."

"I've got to get home," Vincent said.

"Naw, come with us. We're not going to rape you," Angela said.

They were going in his direction, he reflected; he had time to make a final decision.

Above, a police helicopter flew in widening circles, its rotor blades sounding like the wings of a menacing giant insect. Cars packed with Saturday night revellers raced around the roundabout. The women were arguing about whether to cross the roundabout at the lights or use the underpass.

"It's not safe," Helen said.

"Don't be stupid; I use it all the time. Anyway, there's four of us," Angela said.

"What do you say, Vincent?"

She was testing his loyalty. "Makes no difference to me."

"That settles it; me and Vincent will meet you on the other side," Angela said.

She walked away, leaving her friends standing, and Vincent, alarmed at the thought of a woman using the underpass alone at this hour, went after her, catching up with her at the bottom of the steps.

"Aren't you afraid walking down here at night?" he asked.

"I am. But that's when I really need to use it."

"I don't understand."

"When I'm scared is when I need to walk in a place like this."

They fell silent. This was not Vincent's part of Hackney, but he had heard about the Lea Bridge roundabout. It was notorious as the hunting ground of muggers and men with pit bull terriers. Its walls were covered in graffiti.

Helen and Peaches were waiting for them at the top of the steps. "Fearless Angela," Helen said, shoving her playfully.

Vincent found himself walking beside Peaches and aware of her perfume. A vague and uncomfortable feeling of desire stirred in him. He slowed down, hoping she would join her friends, but she adjusted her pace. At the corner of Brooke Road, Angela stopped and repeated her invitation. Vincent saw no harm in accepting. He knew where he was, and half-an-hour with them would not do any harm. He often arrived home as late as 2pm from walking around the city.

Angela's home was a maisonette, clean and tidy, sparsely furnished, its walls painted magnolia. Holiday souvenirs from Jamaica hung on the wall: a map of the island, a two-dimensional varnished wooden carving of a male figure under a coconut tree. She brought out a bottle of Southern Comfort and a smaller bottle of whiskey, from which Vincent accepted a drink and, without touching it, asked to use the bathroom.

He locked the door and looked at himself in the full-length

mirror. His calf-length green raincoat, blue T-shirt and greying hair had given him away as an outsider. He splashed water on his face and remembered the moment when Rachel told him she was leaving him, taking Kara, and leaving London.

He gripped the basin and took a deep breath. A weary face, etched with grief, stared back at him and he guessed now that what had attracted Angela to him was his appeal to her maternal instincts. He had been spending too much time by himself, brooding, and a few hours among these women would lighten his load, give him temporary respite. He wiped his face with his handkerchief and left the bathroom.

In the living room, a sweet, cloying odour filled the air. Helen and Peaches, their heads resting on the back of the armchairs, were staring up at the ceiling. Angela, on the sofa, a small pipe in her hand, was leaning over the coffee table, on which were several foil-wrapped pellets.

"You were a long time, Vincent," she said. "Come and sit down beside me and relax. You seem so uptight. I've got just the thing to help. When I saw you in the pub, I thought to myself, There's a man who needs my help."

39. *Vincent encounters Pastor Neville*

Vincent's tongue felt furry and heavy as he staggered into a bright morning, felt a faint throbbing in the ground beneath his feet, shaded his eyes and smelled a bouquet of petrol, nicotine, and alcohol. The surrounding properties seemed to dance before his eyes, creating wavy, undulating lines like a Gaudi building. The shebeen where he had spent the night, drunk and high, swaying to music, was still going on. Angela and her friends were likely to stay there until noon. He had to get home, wherever that was. He must have walked here in the night with Angela, but his memory of the journey and route was hazy. He remembered laughter and a strange sensation, as if he had been wading through water.

It took him a while to get his bearings. He began walking and saw that he was in a mews. There were signs for motor-repair shops and he passed a car mounted on breeze blocks, its shiny wheel frames reflecting the sun. He paused and looked at it quizzically, trying to understand why the vehicle's square wheels seemed all wrong. At the end of the mews he recognised where he was. He turned left and then right onto Clarence Road, a 1970s housing estate on one side and a row of small shops on other. Several had empty windows and 'For Sale' signs.

Farther on, at a junction, he saw an open green space, the grass covered in dew. The suddenness of its appearance made it seem as if the smothering, oppressive fabric of the city had been ripped apart. He hastened towards Hackney Downs. There, a sudden exhilaration seized him, and he began running, filling his lungs with the moist morning air until exhaustion brought him to a standstill. He slumped under a plane tree, leaned against its rough trunk, and slept fitfully.

Rested and awake, his mind felt clearer. The sun was higher. He heard the ringing of church bells and saw a group of boys kicking a ball towards the railway arches. Behind a row of trees, the blue streak of a train sped across a brick viaduct bridge.

He had intended to walk home, but exhaustion made the journey seem too demanding. He would take a bus and walk back across the Downs, parallel to three tower blocks – grey concrete and glass monoliths that snatched at the sky like the fingers of drowning man.

At the other end of the Downs, people were gathered outside a church, others arriving in cars. He thought he saw his mother among them but quickly realised he was mistaken. He stood and watched, and felt pulled to be among them. He salivated, gargled and spat, hoping to be rid of the metallic taste and the stale odour of Saturday night's dissipation. He walked over and, without meeting anybody's eyes, passed among them through an arched doorway into the church, inhaling the smell of rosewater. A girl handed him a prayer book. He took a seat at the rear of the church, and no sooner had he sat down than he began to doze off. When he woke, all the pews were full, except where he sat, and the service had started. Worshippers were standing and singing and a choir, dressed in brown and yellow robes, seemed to float above them.

The singing stopped and the congregation sat down. A stocky man from among the elders walked to a wooden lectern. He wore a double-breasted green suit, his chin seemed to merge with his chest. He read out some announcements. His voice, though booming, was not clear at the back of the church. Then he called on another speaker. This man was taller, younger and powerfully built. He began reading a passage from the Bible in a slow, emphatic voice, which Vincent suddenly recognised.

He rose to his feet, stepped out into the aisle and shouted, "Neville!" The reader stopped and Vincent felt the eyes of the congregation on him. Two young male ushers appeared beside him. Neville raised his hand, as if commanding them.

"Let him be. He's my brother."

"He's drunk," somebody called out.

"Let him be, I say," Neville said. "Remember Proverbs, 'Give strong drink unto him who is ready to perish, and wine unto those that be of heavy hearts.'"

"No drunkards in the Lord's house!" somebody else shouted.

"No, let him be. He's my brother and he's in pain. Come and join us, Vincent. Come forward and place your life in Jesus's hands and you will surely know peace."

A murmur went through the congregation and when a woman started humming 'Amazing Grace', others followed and soon the whole church was filled with a wordless singing, like the susurration of a strong wind among trees. Vincent felt weak and tearful, wretched and doomed. Neville had stepped around the lectern and was standing at the edge of the platform, a towering figure, his palms turned upwards. "Put your trust in God," Vincent heard him say, "Come forward and put your trust in the Almighty."

Vincent found himself hesitantly walking towards his brother, as if the voices were a wave washing him ashore. It seemed to him that this was what his life lacked, this island of unified voices, this community of worshippers. Surely, he, miscreant, failure and loser, could find sanctuary here.

Neville was now on one knee, palms still outstretched. A few more yards and Vincent would be able to touch him. "Come, Vincent. The Lord will comfort you and wash away your pain. Give your life true meaning."

A memory of Kara flashed in Vincent's mind. He stopped and thought, "No, I can't, won't do this. I don't belong here. Yes, my life isn't working out. I am a failure. I failed to complete my studies, I failed to hold a down a regular job, failed to hold my family together. I have spent the night seeking oblivion in drink, drugs and music. Now I am being offered the consolation of religious tales. Enough! Drowning myself in this comfort would be my greatest failing, my ultimate act of cowardice. There is no

God, no supernatural guiding force, no transcendent being. I've transgressed, but I've harmed nobody but myself, offended only my own conscience. I've lost my family, my daughter. And I now recognise the depth of my pain, my sorrow. Kara is gone. I must take responsibility for my life and losing her. I will not seek solace here. I must live with my pain, my failure."

He turned abruptly, facing the two ushers, pushed them away and headed towards the door. He heard a woman's voice shout, "Was lost but now I am found," and when a baritone voice repeated the line in contrapuntal harmony, the humming increased in volume. Then someone else shouted, "Was blind but now I see," and another voice released an ecstatic "Hallelujah." These words echoed in Vincent's ears as he plunged back into the merciless daylight.

Close to Clapton bus garage, he leapt on the first Finsbury Park bus that came, climbed upstairs and took a front seat. The bus was almost empty. Images of Neville in the church were in his mind's eye and the haunting sound of all those voices was ringing in his ears. He could not remain seated. He paced the upper deck as the bus trundled down Northwold Road. On the High Road, he got off the bus and walked towards his home.

In the open air his agitation abated, and as he turned onto Church Street, his mind felt clearer. He had been static for too long – the pub, the blues dance, then the church. It felt so much better being on the move; each step brought him closer to himself.

Passing the Daniel Defoe pub, its windows dark and the author's portrait swinging in the breeze, he was struck by how often he had passed this landmark without really noticing it. Would Defoe, were he alive today, consider a city like London a more suitable setting for Robinson Crusoe? A man alone, stranded, forced to survive in an urban wilderness, his isolation due to his inability to connect with other people. Maybe he had misunderstood Friday's role in the story. Perhaps Defoe's cannibal was the projection of Crusoe's own base desires and the qualities that kept him isolated, silent, and destructive. Only when he had curbed and corrected those base desires could he be liberated from the island of himself. He really ought to reread *Robinson Crusoe*.

Lost in thought, he walked past the entrance to Clissold Park. Rather than turn back, he walked on to Green Lanes. He was tempted to find a tree, to rest under an umbrageous old horse chestnut tree near the ponds where he used to play as a boy, sleep with the earth, its texture and rhythm close to his skin, and wake looking up into the dense late-summer leaves.

He left the Park near Queens Drive. The prospect of reaching home, of closing the door to his ninth-floor bedsit, enlivened his steps. I'll sleep for the day, he thought. Sleep and wake and carry on, but carry on without the intoxication of alcohol and drugs or the idea of God.

40. *Lucas receives an invitation, and a family dinner*

Around mid-morning, as he watered the plants in the first-floor bathroom, Lucas became aware of the great silence and stillness of the day, as if the world had ended and nobody had bothered to tell him. He could not recall having heard a car pass down Carlisle Road, the chatter of passers-by, doors closing in neighbouring houses. He walked to the front of the house, the sound of his shuffling feet reassuring him that he had not gone deaf. Standing at the window, he looked out above and through the still fronds of the banana tree, which he had planted some years ago and which had grown as high the first-floor window. The curtains and blinds in the opposite houses were closed; nothing stirred, not even a leaf. He climbed to the top floor and took a brief nap in Esther's old room before beginning his slow descent.

Back downstairs, he scanned *The Daily Telegraph*'s financial pages. There had been no movement in his shares. Disappointed, he dozed off, then the doorbell woke him and while he was still searching for his slippers, it rang again, putting him in a tetchy mood. He shuffled to the door intending to give the caller, who was probably a canvasser or some mad Seventh Day Adventist, a good piece of his mind.

The caller was not a salesman or an evangelist. He seemed elderly, but his smart olive-green suit and open-necked white shirt, its collar flat on the jacket collar, gave him a youthful air.

"What you want?"

"I'm looking for Lucas Bostock." The man spoke with an American drawl.

"What you want with Lucas Bostock?"

"I've a letter for him from Jamaica." He held out a white envelope.

"Hmm. You better come in."

Lucas led his visitor to the living room and apologised for its disorderly state.

They sat opposite each other in highback club chairs, recently acquired because Lucas was tired of having to fight to stand after sitting down. Letter in hand, Lucas eyed the visitor and wondered why he seemed familiar, though he was sure they had never met. He did not know people who refused to dress their age.

"Kinda warm in here," the visitor said.

"That's the way my plants like it." Lucas put on his reading glasses and fumbled with the letter, regretting that the knife he used as an opener was beside his bed. He ripped it open, pulled out a small, folded sheet, and held the paper at a distance to read:

Dear Lucas,

Please come home.

Love, Jean

Lucas pursed his lips and straightened himself in his chair. He had mostly succeeded in putting Jean out of his mind over these past years. If she did cross his mind, he thought she had been claimed by the only certainty that remained in his life. Puzzled, he looked at his visitor.

The man raised his hands and said, "I'm only the messenger."

"And who are you, sir? How d'you know Jean?"

"You don't recognise me, Lucas?"

Lucas searched the man's face, but no name came to mind. He shook his head, then scratched a dry patch which tended to itch when he was thinking deeply.

"Name's Baker Woods."

Lucas did not recognise the name.

"Maybe you remember me as Trinity Gordon – my street name."

Lucas leaned forward in the chair. "Trinity? You can't be Trinity. 'Im dead, 'im dead long time. Me know that for sure. Is this some kinda stupid joke?" But even as he posed the question, Lucas was beginning to recognise in the creased face with its sagging cheeks and chin a younger more familiar face.

"This is no joke, Lucas. It's me, the same man you whipped years back. Older and, I like to think, a bit wiser."

"If you is Trinity, tell me how me beat you?"

"All I know is you gave me some punches to my head that kept me on my back for three months. I can't give you the details. I'm not that person anymore."

Lucas heard sincerity, honesty and remorse in the calm voice. He finally accepted that the person in his living room was the man he thought he had killed and whose spirit he had been communing with. There was something liberating in discovering that the hands he had used to build had not also been hands of death. Lucas thought of his long conversations with Trinity's spirit, and though he regarded them as nothing more than the harmless pastime of an old man, concluded that he'd been a fool.

Baker Woods said, "Think you knocked some sense into me, some foolishness out of me. I picked that fight out of jealousy and I deserved every blow I got."

He told Lucas that, on recovering, he'd joined his brother in New York. He'd worked in the building trade, married and had three children, two boys and a girl. After twenty-five years he'd returned to Jamaica with his sons and founded a construction company, which was still going strong, giving him a comfortable retirement and his grandchildren the best education that money could buy.

"How do you know Jean?"

"Miss Fraser? She's a neighbour. Tough old dame. Knew her for years before we learned that we both knew you. When she first told me about a cousin in London, she was as bitter as cola nut. But when I discovered that this cousin was the man who had knocked sense into me, changed my life, I told her that even if it was the last journey I made, I had to find you and thank you. She gave me the letter, sealed, the night before I left for the airport."

They talked for a while longer about the island. Baker Woods was interested in politics and told Lucas he'd been staunch Democrat voter and then a PNP supporter in Jamaica, and said, "I'd vote Labour if I lived here."

"Me is a Conservative supporter. Labour always just wants to grab you hard-earned money and share it out." Their difference brought the visit to a swift end. Lucas saw his visitor to the front door. After they had shaken hands, Baker Woods said: "And how's Rhonda?"

"Rhoda," Lucas corrected him, and said that as far as he knew she was still alive.

"See what a stupid young man I was. Always thought her name was Rhonda. Anyway, give her my regards."

Lucas stood and watched Baker Woods make his sprightly way to his car, a driver at the wheel. He closed the door, cleared his throat, and said, "Well fellows, looks like we're one less now."

Over the next month, Lucas made preparations to visit Jamaica. It would be just a visit, but the size of the trunk he bought in Dalston shopping centre told another story. In it he placed many tools: hammers, chisels, drills, saws, planes, screwdrivers, trowels, adzes, tape measures, levels, wrenches, pliers, a mallet, and an assortment of nails and Rawl plugs. An average-sized suitcase held his clothes. He spoke to Samuel on the phone, giving him instructions on what to do if, for any reason, he failed to return.

Samuel arranged a farewell dinner in a private room at a Caribbean restaurant in Camden Town. Neville, who had recently completed a theology degree, was already there when Lucas arrived with Samuel. Vincent came in soon after. Maureen had been invited but there was no sign of her. Whenever the dining room door opened, Lucas hoped it would be his daughter.

The waiter brought in the first course – pumpkin and fish soup. Neville insisted on saying grace, but Vincent plunged in straightaway, taking loud slurps. The others did their best to ignore him. Lucas wished Neville would end his long spiel, which seemed to thank a legion of people for the food, including the food distributor's second cousin. By the time Neville finished, Vincent's bowl was empty. As Lucas sipped his soup noisily, Neville announced that he had a going-away present for him. Lucas opened the present and saw that it was another audio bible, this time on CDs.

"Thank you, son," Lucas said. "I'm no great believer; you know that, but after the miracle that's happened to me recently, maybe is time I start paying more attention to such matters."

"The Lord's door is always open, Dad," Neville said.

Vincent laughed, and said, "Yeah, Dad, maybe you can make sure the door's hanging properly."

Lucas was not amused. He looked at his youngest son and saw that, unlike his brothers, he had not made any effort with his appearance. He was unshaven, his clothes dishevelled. He knew how estranged Vincent felt from his family, how much he missed his daughter. He felt worried for his youngest son.

"You shouldn't mock a person's faith," Samuel said.

"Oh, come on," Vincent said. "The guy's just spent ten minutes saying grace, and every word comes out of the bible. It's time we abandon all this talk about God and Jesus Christ."

"Faith is a private matter," Samuel said, "but if we must discuss religion, let's do it calmly and show respect to each other."

Lucas nodded in agreement.

"The fool hath said in his heart there is no God," Neville said.

"What kind of crap is that, Neville? That's respect, is it? You believe in a book that's a translation of a translation of a translation, a book that teaches people that some supreme being made the earth in seven days and made woman from the ribs of man, teaches people to believe in miracle healing and a man walking on water, and the sea parting, and you call me a fool? To hear you speak, you'd think that all the advances and discovery in knowledge over the past centuries hadn't happened."

Neville looked unruffled.

"And what do you believe, Mr Vincent?" Lucas asked.

"I don't believe in the crap Neville's peddling to uneducated and vulnerable immigrants, refugees and asylum seekers."

Samuel said, "Actually, from my work as a councillor, I know that churches like Neville's are doing a tremendous amount of practical work to orient and integrate new settlers here."

"Orient or disorient them?" Vincent scoffed.

"You haven't said what you believe in, Vincent," Lucas said. He was genuinely curious. He was an intuitive non-believer but the day when Trinity Gordon rang his door was forcing a rethink.

The waiter's entrance interrupted the exchange and Samuel and Neville swapped enquiries about each other's families, until the table had been cleared and the main course brought in. A family united in the presence of strangers. As soon as the waiter left, Vincent said:

"You asked me what I believe in, Dad. I can't give you a simple answer without sounding simplistic. Let's just say I don't believe in belief. I'm interested in knowledge not belief. And knowledge requires that you investigate reality, formulate theories, propositions, conjectures, hypotheses which can be tested, and if they are proven, they become part of knowledge; if disproved, they are abandoned. All genuine knowledge is tentative, provisional; there's always the possibility of being wrong. The Bible, on the other hand, is a collection of allegories and fables concerned with morality and ethics, fine in itself, necessary even, but many of those morals are not consistent with modern law, and its claims about the origins of life and the universe are, well, just nonsense.

"Einstein's theory of relativity, quantum mechanics, Darwin's and Wallace's discovery of natural selection offer us fascinating answers about the origins of life and the origins of the universe. We know that the earth is millions of years old, that homo sapiens evolved from earlier creatures and are relative newcomers to planet earth. The bible's just a fable written by priests and scribes in one of the parts of the world where written language first developed. They didn't and couldn't know what we now know, so they invented the existence of a supreme being, made in man's image. To worship God is to worship ignorance. Did you know that Galileo…"

"Scientists are only discovering God's will. The Bible is the word of God," Neville said. "Atheists and Satanists will always deny that."

"Please, Neville," Vincent said, "you're not with your congregants now, or your flock, as you call them – and they have to be sheep to follow you. Name-calling is the poorest form of reasoning. It leads to witch hunts, persecution – practices that your Christian faith is only too familiar with. You can't afford to accept that there's no god, because you have a vested interest in maintaining that belief…"

Lucas was only half-listening. He was eating the red snapper he had ordered, and the fried plantain – just right and delicious – was transporting him back in time. As the conversation carried on around him, he recalled his early days in London and the difficulties he had making himself understood, and the dawning realisation that he did not speak English. Decades later, here he was surrounded by his sons who, in Vincent's case, spoke an English that he could still barely follow. Even Neville, whose once halting tongue he had always felt concern over, had acquired fluency, even if he was only repeating biblical phrases. Maybe that was the useful thing about the bible, the entrance it gave into language.

"You're a peddler of intellectual poison," he heard Vincent say. Lucas did not know this Vincent, this aggressive debater, firm in his non-belief. But how much of this was the bitter words of a man grieving for the loss of his daughter?

"What about you, Samuel?" Lucas said.

Samuel looked thoughtful for a moment, then said: "Actually, Elena has recently rediscovered her Catholic roots. Began around the time of the Dunblane shootings. She's been going to mass every Sunday. I've been going along, too. In fact, I'm seriously thinking of taking Holy Communion."

Lucas looked at him wide-eyed. Vincent rubbed his forehead. Neville placed his hands in his lap.

"Yes, it's something about the rituals of the church. No disrespect meant, Dad, but our childhood lacked rituals and ceremonies."

"Oh, for fuck's sake," Vincent said.

"Bwoy, mind you tongue," Lucas said. Suddenly, he felt himself under attack from Samuel. "Lacked rituals and ceremonies? Son, me give you food, me give you clothes, me give you shelter." He held up his fork, a piece of fish and plantain on it. "And I'll tell you something else me give unnu. Me give unnu drive, yes me give you ambition. All of unnu. Yuh mother woulda drown unnu in love. But love not enough. No sah. You'd all be pushing dust carts now if she'd had her way. But I, yes I, Lucas Bostock, put some fire inna unnu belly. She woulda drown you in love."

"Some people would say it was Prometheus who gave us fire," Vincent said.

"As for you, Mr Vincent, me don't know what happen to you. All those years living in that whorehouse in Finsbury Park. Like you lose you way."

"Fantastic views of the park and city; that's what's kept me there."

"I wasn't implying you didn't give us something valuable, Dad," Samuel said. "I merely said that there are important things we didn't get. And the church is very good for that."

Neville started praying, "Heavenly father, who art in heaven hallowed be thy name…"

"Will you cut that crap," Vincent said.

Lucas fell quiet and ate the rest of his meal, tuning in and out of the continuing debate.

Desert – mango ice cream and sweet pudding – was too much for Lucas. He sat through it, lost in thought about the miraculous turnaround in his life – and hoping that Maureen would walk through the door and give him a chance to show that he was her father and that he loved her, rough and crude and hard as he was.

He did not hear what led up to Vincent's sudden outburst and departure, only the sound of the chair falling against the wall as Vincent said, "I don't have to sit here and listen to this moronic rubbish from you, Neville, a peddler of lies and myths to gullible vulnerable people. Pastor Neville Bostock – nothing but a modern-day shaman. Huh! And you, Samuel, you're just encouraging him.

Playing the politician, looking for compromise. There can't be any compromise between truth and falsehood. And the truth is that your political ambition lacks any moral object. You'll say anything to secure office. Truth suffers. Yeah, you guys belong together. I'm outta here."

He turned to Lucas and said, "Dad, I'll call you later tonight."

He slammed the door on the way out; the walls shook, the room echoed. Lucas concluded that he could do nothing for Vincent. He was a man, and a man has to carry his burdens and his pain alone. The evening continued in a sombre mood.

Samuel drove Lucas home. They sat in the car while Lucas went over the instructions he had already given him. If he chose to stay in Jamaica, the house was to be converted into flats – he gave Samuel the name of a builder – and part of the money remitted to him there. If he died out there, the will would take effect.

Father and son walked to the gate. Samuel asked Lucas again if he was sure he did not want a ride to the airport. Lucas confirmed that he preferred the arrangement he had made. A mini-cab would take him to Heathrow.

Lucas shook Samuel's hand and said, "Well, looks like you is the head of the family here now. Good luck. An' keep an eye on Vincent. Dat boy's in pain."

"We all know that, Dad. But he doesn't want anybody's help. He screens his calls. He only visits you and Mum. You can't help someone if he doesn't want help."

"True. He'll come through. Wonder what happen to Maureen."

Samuel shrugged and said, "I don't know, Dad, I don't know."

A few steps apart, Lucas called Samuel back. "By the way, tell your mother Trinity sends his regards. She will understand."

He opened the gate and looked at the banana tree and thought, "A banana tree in England. Raawtid. Wonders never cease." He walked gingerly up the steps and unlocked the door. He noticed a piece of paper on the door mat. He picked it up and saw that it was a note of some kind, but he did not want to take out his reading glasses. He brought the note to the bedroom, placed it on the bedside drawer. Washed and in bed, his glasses on, he opened the folded paper and read: *Unforgiven, unforgivable, unmissed. Maureen.*

★ ★ ★ ★

My friend Irma Benjamin lived in a grand old house in Stamford Hill, an area famous for its large community of Hasidic Jews. Irma had once joked that her success in purchasing the house from an elderly couple who were migrating to Israel was entirely due to her surname. Irma and I had the Caribbean in common – she came from Trinidad – and being brought to Britain as children. She was five years older than me but looked like a woman in her early forties. She had a dark brown complexion, kept her hair cropped short and had a fondness for large ivory earrings. She had started her working life as a nurse, gained a degree in anthropology through part-time study, while simultaneously moving into property ownership – her first purchase being her council flat at a hugely discounted price. Now she managed a handsome portfolio of properties in north London. She wintered – she was first person I heard use 'winter' as a verb – in the Caribbean and shopped in New York and Miami on her transatlantic journeys. Her home was tastefully decorated with paintings, ceramics, and sculptures in metal and wood. In her back garden was a fishpond with koi swimming about lazily.

She had heard me complain about my neighbour's son, and when, over drinks I updated her on developments in the house, she exclaimed, "That's a great thing you've done."

"That remains to be seen, Irma."

"Yes, but that's what community is about. We help each other, and he sounded pretty screwed up."

"Oh, he is, there's no doubt about that. Really fucked up childhood."

"You know, in all the years I've known you, and it must be twenty years, I don't recall ever hearing you swear."

"Maybe I've been spending too much time with that boy."

"You say he's thirty-two. Why do you insist on calling him a boy?"

"I've tried seeing him as man, which of course, he is – with his children – yet I can't shake the sense that I'm dealing with a boy. Maybe the problem's with me and not him."

"There may well be a problem there. After all, you're old enough to be his father."

"Irma, please. I have neither the skills nor the patience to help somebody like that."

"I understand. Knowing you as I do, I'm surprised you've even made the effort to help him."

"Help? All I did was give him a bit of work."

"Actually," Irma said, "I may be able to help him out too. One of my properties needs redecoration. I got a quote recently. If he gives me a cheaper quote, the job's his. It's at least two weeks' work. He could probably bring in a partner. Cash-in-hand work."

"Irma, that's wonderful. I'll tell him. But I must warn you, his manners are rough; he's spent most of his working life on building sites, not working in people's homes."

"I hear you. Still, give him my cellphone number."

"Your what?"

"Cellphone. Sorry, mobile number. I sometimes forget what language I'm in. Tell him to call me. You could make a bit of money yourself. Charge him ten per cent for finding him the work."

I laughed and said, "I'm no contractor."

"You have no business sense, my dear," she said, a coquettish smile on her lips, "which is why you'll always be poor, unless you find yourself a practical-minded wife. How are things on that side?"

One of the features of our relationship was a certain candour in matters of love. Age had not dimmed her flirtatiousness and when she flirted with me, it was always a cue for us to exchange notes on our love lives.

"Nothing on that front, I'm afraid."

"I know you're afraid. Afraid of love."

"Oh, come on Irma, that's unfair. I've a theory. I think all human beings are born with a finite capacity for romantic love. I used up all my – possibly very limited – capacity many years ago."

"That's one of the saddest things I've ever heard."

"My theory is yet to be verified, but if it is, it would also be further confirmation that the truth is often sad. And you?"

"Oh, nothing much to report. I nearly had brief fling with a rock musician I met on a day trip to a small Caribbean island – one of those exclusive resorts frequented by the rich and famous. He told me he liked brown sugar, and I said, 'the whole world knows that, but you do like dark brown sugar?' We arranged a tryst, but we knew it wasn't going to happen – besides I had to catch the boat back to Port au Prince. Frankly, it would have been like making love to a prune. The man is so wrinkled. To think I used to fancy him when I was a teenager."

We spent the rest of the evening sipping vintage Guyanese dark rum, nibbling on smoked marlin and fried plantain – she was a spare eater and preparing fried plantain was her only concession to a visitor – and listening to music from her massive music collection, slipping from jazz, to blues, to reggae, to folk to classical, renewing and reaffirming one of the bonds that held our old friendship together.

Fortified by Irma's company and slightly tipsy, I caught a bus back to Kingsland High Road. I deliberately took the short cut through the estate. Nearing the spot where I had once panicked, I felt inside my pocket for the pen I'd taken to carrying with me. I had no martial arts skills, but if somebody attacked me, I would do my best the injure my assailant with my pen.

I'd seen a man sitting in a white Volkswagen Golf, parked across the street, looking up at my window for three consecutive mornings. Initially, I thought he was part of the scaffolding team working on the neighbouring house. But he never left the car and his eyes were always trained on my windows. On the third morning, nearing midday, returning from the store on Allen Road, I saw him standing beside the car, still looking up at my window.

"Excuse me," he shouted. "Do you live upstairs in that house?"

"Yes, I do. Why?"

I saw right away that he was not a workman. He was slim and wore baggy, navy-blue linen trousers, pointed glossy-brown shoes, and a large Hawaiian-style cotton shirt. His hair, combed backwards, seemed to have been treated with either chemicals or a hot iron. His jet-black face was clean shaven, his skin glowed with health. I guessed that he was about thirty-five. He said his name was Paul.

"My mother died in that flat," he said, matter-of-factly.

"Pardon."

My mother used to live there. She died in her bedroom on the top floor." He pointed to it with a long smooth finger.

"How long ago was that?"

"Three years ago this month."

December would mark my third year in the flat. "I'm sorry," I said. I couldn't decide whether to invite him inside, and he saw my hesitation.

"I don't want to come in," he said.

I suggested that we go for a tea at a cafe on Albion Road. As we walked there, we exchanged names and shook hands. In the garden at the rear of the cafe, he said, "They killed her, you know."

"They?"

"That woman. That woman and her son. Persecuted her. Frightened her to death."

"What makes you say that?"

"I spoke to her on the phone a couple of days before she died; she was scared, terrified of the house, thought it was haunted, hated the woman in the other flat, thought she was evil, and was really scared of the son. I was living in the States, New York. We used to talk – once a week, if we hadn't quarrelled, once a month if had."

"Ghosts don't exist," I said.

"Should've tried telling my mother that. She was a born-again Christian. She believed in spirits."

"And the mother and son, what did they do to her?"

He told me that he had helped his mother move into the house. He'd then gone to join his partner in New York. He was gay, and this had been a source of acrimony with his mother. Shortly after he got to the States, they'd quarrelled on the phone and didn't talk again for three months. In every telephone conversation thereafter, she complained about Carmen Hillman's behaviour. Thinks she's the queen of the house was her most used phrase, he said. With her bedroom below his mother's living room, Carmen demanded that she give notice of visitors and limit the number of times she walked across the living-room floor. When his mother objected to Carmen's tyranny, Carmen called in her son as enforcer. The boy repeatedly threatened Paul's mother and carried out a campaign of terror against her. He spilt oil in the hallway, knowing that her room was carpeted, and she would trail the oil inside; he waited for her to open her flat door, then emerged scowling and swearing and abusing her; once or twice he followed her on the street."

"Did she go to the authorities?"

He sighed. "It's not the kind of thing she would do. She had a mastectomy when I was about twenty. The doctors warned her that the cancer could return. She'd always been a churchgoer, but after the operation she changed. She went to church at every opportunity and if her church was closed, she found another church to pray in. The doctors gave her the all-clear after six months. After that, well, she just believed it was the work of the Lord. So, when she started having trouble with her neighbour she took to prayer."

As he spoke, I remembered the biblical quotes scrawled on pieces of card stuck to the walls. The Sellotape marks were still on the living room and bedrooms walls, hidden behind paintings.

"I certainly believe what you say about the son. I've experienced some of that myself. You know, he's now living there, in the house."

"I didn't. Where's his mother?"

"I have no idea. She visits. But she doesn't actually live there."

"Well, now you know what you're up against."

"I do indeed."

There were a few minutes of silence between us, and noticing that he was wearing a large oval amethyst ring, set in gold, on his middle finger, I said, "That's beautiful ring you're wearing."

"Thank you. It's one of my earliest efforts."

"You made it?"

"Designed and made it."

"That's your line of business?"

"Yes. Have never done anything else."

"Fascinating. How did you get into that?"

"My mother. Before her…" he searched for the *mot juste*.

"Conversion, or reconversion?"

"Yes, something like that. Before, she was a great jewellery collector. Nothing expensive – semi-precious stones. We used to spend weekends trawling through markets – Camden, Portobello Road, Upper Street, those kinds of places. She loved amethyst, Brazilian or African."

"Didn't know there was a difference."

"Oh, there is. This is Brazilian – lovely dark, deep purple. African amethyst has a much lighter, more delicate colour."

"I am enlightened."

"Anyway, she sold her entire collection. I couldn't complain, as I got most of the money. That's how I got started in my business."

"Are you're living in the UK now?"

"Yes. For now."

"They say America can be a difficult place to gain a foothold in."

"It can be. But when you're in love, nowhere's difficult. My relationship broke up. And it's what took me there."

"Sometimes love is only about being elsewhere. Maybe if you give America a go on your own, it would work out."

He smiled and said, "You don't sound like a man who should be living in a house like… or at least not with those people, if they're anything like my mother described them."

"Thank you," I said. "Having had some run-ins with the boy, it's a thought that's often crossed my mind. But you know how it is. When you fall in this country there's a social safety net. And I fell, man, how I fell. Fell right into that net and got entangled in it and just haven't been able to disentangle and extricate myself. Never imagined I'd ever have to live in such proximity to somebody like that young man."

"I've seen the mother, but never the son."

"You don't want to meet him."

"It wouldn't bring back my mother, anyway. If only we hadn't quarrelled on that last telephone call. Stupid of me really. I told her she was being hysterical…"

He stopped and looked away and reached into his pocket for a handkerchief. He blew his nose and held his hands to face in a vain effort to conceal his tears. I reached across the table and touched his shoulder.

"You can't blame yourself, Paul."

"But I do. I thought about coming back to, you know, reassure her. But I was trying so hard to make my relationship work, and to make a living in that bloody city. Every time I spoke to her, she would say, "When are you going to give me a grandchild? Knowing very well that wasn't ever going to happen. It was her way of telling me she didn't approve of who and what I am."

"But from everything you've said it's clear that she loved you."

"Yes, yes, I know."

A few customers were looking in our direction. Paul suddenly became self-conscious, blew his nose again, and folded the hanky and wiped his eyes. He shook his shoulders and sat upright.

"You know, that's the first time I've cried since she died."

"Seems to me you needed that."

We settled the bill and walked towards Selkirk Road and home.

"So what are you going to do about the boy and his mother?"

"What can I do? I wrote to the housing department. Somebody wrote back saying that without any evidence my allegations were baseless. My mother died of a heart attack. End of story."

Outside my gate, Paul declined my invitation to come inside. We talked for a few minutes. I gave him my telephone number and told him to call anytime. He said he might call, then got into his car and drove away.

Two days later, a Friday, I got a telephone call from Paul on my mobile. He thanked me for giving him my time earlier in the week, then he said: "Last thing. What I said about the mother and son. Please don't repeat that to anybody. I've decided I was just trying to pass the buck. I'm sure their behaviour didn't help, but that's life… or death. My mother always saw enemies everywhere. This or that woman was always trying to do her in; this or that woman had given her the evil eye. It's one of the main reasons I didn't take on board her complaints. So, please forget what I said. Don't know why I said it, really. Maybe I was just trying to get your attention."

"Okay. I hear you. We'll leave it there."

"Thanks. Goodbye."

There was a tone of finality in that goodbye.

Within a minute of that call finishing, my mobile rang again. This time it was Irma. "That boy!" she said without preamble. "Don't ever recommend him to a friend. You'll lose your friends."

"Irma, please calm down. Remember I didn't recommend him. You offered to help. And I did warn you about him."

Irma had paid him well for the fortnight's work, though he had shouted and sworn at her, described his workmate as 'his bitch' to her face, and done such a poor job of retiling the bathroom – Irma invited me to see his shoddy handiwork – I felt bad for having mentioned his name, and relieved that my kitchen tiles remained untouched. She had warned him that if he ever saw her in the street, he should keep his distance and make no attempt to communicate, otherwise she would scream for help and call the police.

The boy said nothing to me about his experience at Irma's flat. He now wore a new pair of expensive Nike trainers, new, baggy black jeans and T-shirt, and had regained his old swagger, accentuated perhaps by the knowledge that he was wearing clothes that had never before touched the skin of another human being. Gone, too, was the old Nokia phone into which he used to shout as he approached the house, night or day. Now he shouted into a Blackberry. Once a week, a white bicycle was parked outside the house for about fifteen minutes. Somebody delivering something? And I saw at least three different girls leaving the house over the course of a week. But at least he did not play any loud music nor practise rapping for some time. This was while the boy found regular employment, but by early August he was out of work again and resumed his rapping.

I endured it for a week before complaining to him, and he agreed to turn down the volume, but he broke the agreement a few days later. There was now, I sensed, a new defiance in his behaviour. He was no longer as aggressive, but seemed determined to ignore my complaints, as if he had sized me up and was confident that, in the event of a fight, he was bound to win. I now regretted having admitted him into my home, tried to make peace with him or tried to help. I concluded that, having shared the story of his wretched childhood with me, he felt I should tolerate his behaviour.

In late August, I was informed that the property was to be painted, its bricks repointed. A week later, workmen had erected scaffolding and covered it in a blue net, dimming the light coming through the windows. From the street, the house looked as if it was wearing a blue dress. The boy kept quiet in the day, but as soon as the working day finished, he turned up the volume.

One of my encounters with the boy set me worrying.

"You didn't finish paying me for the work I did," he said.

"I paid you exactly what we agreed. Paid you more, actually. Bought you lunch twice. Even found you a well-paid gig."

"That woman paid me, but you didn't finish paying me."

"Are you trying to extort money from me?"

"I'm saying you didn't fucking pay me." He stabbed the air with his index finger.

I said quietly, "You can shout as much you want. You're not getting another penny from me."

"We'll see about that," he said.

The music not only increased in volume but went on late into the night. Most noticeable was the pattern to the music. He played for ten to twenty minutes. Then it went quiet for as long as half an hour, then it started again. Some evenings I would enter a quiet house, but as soon as I reached upstairs, the music started, loud and insistent. He was playing to harass me.

I resumed my complaints to the council. The noise pollution office sent me another log book. The police told me it was a housing matter.

By chance, one afternoon I encountered the boy's mother at a bus stop near Ridley Road market. After greeting her, I said: "Why have you inflicted your son on me? He's become a nuisance again."

She shook her head despairingly.

"Is there something wrong with him?"

"He's just a kid,"

"He's in his thirties; has three children."

"Yeah, but he's just a kid."

The bus came and we caught it and when we got off, we resumed our conversation. She told me the boy had helped to drive his abusive father away. He'd picked up the father and thrown him across the room. "That man put me in hospital four times," she said. "Don't know what would've happened without Junior."

"Why do you still call him Junior?"

"Cause he's got his father's first name, and I can't bring myself to use that name."

I said, "I really can't take that noise he's making."

"I've told him he should find a hostel. But he won't. What can I do? He's my son, my only son."

"Just get him to stop the noise."

"I can't. He's frustrated. Can't find work. He's just a frustrated kid."

She put a finger to her lips as the boy suddenly appeared in the doorway of the house, and she hurried towards him. For the next hour, his voice filled the house as he cursed and swore at his mother. I heard her leave the house that evening.

Later in October, at the end of what had been a busy day for me, I was driven into a frenzy by the boy's voice. I left the house and walked in the direction of the pub. Karen my neighbour was coming towards me. She said, "Something upset you?"

"That boy has turned the house into a hellhole. Do you never hear him?"

"Sometimes when I'm in the garden. But most of the time, nothing. The walls between the houses are thick."

I told her I'd been trying to get the noise witnessed for over a year.

"You've got to keep on trying," she said. "It took a colleague of mine over seven years to get her noise problem witnessed."

"Seven years?"

"But they got the person in the end. He was targeting her. Some people are like that. Don't give up."

I thanked her and went on my way.

The following week, on a dark, damp evening, as I left the house I saw behind me a hooded figure pushing a bicycle. Outside the Selkirk Pub, I looked behind me again and saw the hooded figure on the bicycle bearing down on me. I pressed against the railings of the pub, and he streaked past, laughing. When a similar incident happened a few days later, I went on the internet and ordered a spray can of mace. Until it arrived, I carried a small bottle containing a mixture of chilli pepper and salt. If he tried to attack me, I would aim to blind him, disable him long enough to deal at least one blow.

On the first Sunday in November, Irma and I met for a stroll in Clissold Park. She was preparing to leave for the Caribbean. I updated her on events in the house.

"Sounds as if he's completely out of control," she said.

"There's more to it than that, Irma," I said. I gave her a truncated version of my conversation with Paul, omitting any mention of his belief that the mother and son had contributed to his mother's death.

Irma was quiet for long time after I finished talking. We stopped by the lake, leant on the fencing and looked across the dark green water. She said: "You know, you have to look after yourself."

"I'm trying."

"That house just doesn't sound safe."

"I know it isn't. How unsafe is what I can't work out."

"And after all the help you've given him."

"That was months ago. He's spent or squandered all the money, on wine, women and, well, I am reluctant to call what he listens to as song – it would be an insult to what I know as music."

"Sometimes you sound as if you're enjoying yourself."

"Most certainly not. I've experienced fear and I don't intend to live in fear of that boy. I'm determined to reclaim my living room and silence him. I just don't want to be dragged into his pathological head space."

Irma said, "You know, one of the reasons I like you is that you're always reasonable. I've tried to work out what you want from life but gave up on that one because whatever it is you want, it's something that goes beyond what the vast majority of people want, something that goes beyond the material. And that makes me like you even more."

I laughed and said, "Irma, if I was the grasping type, I doubt that we would still be friends."

"True. But let's go back to your reasonableness. It's possible to be too reasonable. Remember, I've met the boy. That situation could turn very nasty if you choose to remain reasonable."

"Actually, Irma, I think it's reasonableness that's prevented any blood spilling so far. I believe he's capable of violence towards me. I suspect, in his muddled head, he's confusing me with the father he wants to kill. And there's an Oedipal aspect to this. For years, he was the man in his mother's house; she required him to play that role. Now he's back home, and there's another male in the same property, sharing the front door. I have refused to engage him at the level of violence, simply because I don't function at that level. That's compounding his confusion. Of course, I've had violent thoughts towards him. Thing is, I've stood my ground without threatening violence…"

"I don't buy all that Freudian stuff. A drowning man isn't concerned with the chemical composition of water. He's thinking how he can get to safety. Let me cut to the chase. The guy's obviously a little Hitler. You can't appease somebody like that."

"You think I ought to dismiss Chamberlain and summon up Churchill. I'm not going to start trading blows with him."

"I'm not suggesting you do, and wouldn't, even if I thought you stood a chance against him, which you don't."

"What are you suggesting?"

"Have you wondered how I've managed to keep my small collection of properties?"

"Well, you're a bright woman; it's one of the reasons I like you."

"Thank you. We're beginning to sound like a mutual admiration society. But let me continue… and please don't interrupt me, even when I ask a rhetorical question. In the early days, it was very difficult. Most tenants are fine, but I've had my fair share of troublesome tenants. A Nigerian couple who refused to pay the rent. A few years ago one of my properties was seized by Poles who changed all the locks. Took me eighteen months of legal wrangling to get that property back. When the Nigerians were giving me trouble, I used the services of a certain man. He sent somebody into the property, took off all doors, took out all the windows. They soon started paying. And the Poles, well let's just say he helped to oil the wheels of justice."

"Justice is personified as a female holding scales."

"So?"

"Oil the scales of justice would be a more apt metaphor."

"Oh, I see. You can be such a pedant. In that case, I meant oil the wheels of the law. The law's a creaky slow-moving machine. It works, but time, time. My associate, Cy, as I said, knows how to oil its wheels, get them in motion."

"Is that Sigh or Cy?"

"Cy. I'd like you to meet Cy. Tell him about the boy. He'll be able to help you. It will cost you though."

"How much?"

"That's between you and Cy. I'll let him know that a friend of mine is going to call. He'll give you a fair price."

"I don't really want to go down that road, Irma."

"You don't have to. But go and see Cy. That way, if all else fails, or you run out of patience, you'll have that option. That's all I am saying."

I punched Cy's name and number into my mobile's address book. Irma and I finished our walk and went our separate ways. She was due to leave London two days later and return anytime from late February to mid-March.

★ ★ ★ ★

41. *Rhoda, Vincent and Professor Khalid, 1998*

The months following Lucas's departure found Rhoda busier than ever. She was an organiser of her church's senior citizens' luncheon club, which met twice a week, each meeting requiring a day's preparation. And when death claimed a club member, as it did over three consecutive months, she and her church sisters loaned their catering skills to the bereaved family. So, she had little time to digest the news, relayed by Samuel, that Trinity Gordon was alive. And when she reflected on that news, she saw no reason to abandon the belief that some curse hung over her life and her family. It made her fervent dedication to the Lord, and doing good works, just as necessary. Her bad marriage, her separation from her sons, Neville's near fatal boxing injury, Vincent's and Samuel's broken relationships, Phil's car accident – these misfortunes must have been caused by something or someone and the only protection she knew of was the Lord Almighty's.

In late January, exhaustion and a lull in the round of funerals kept Rhoda at home for a whole week, during which she received a surprise visit from Vincent, for whom she had been praying fervently for several months because he, of all her children, remained indifferent to her potent and effective combination of love, God and Jesus. Look at Samuel and Neville; she had picked them up, given them new lives. If only Vincent would attend church with her. But he always gave her a blank look when she invited him, so she had stopped trying to convert him.

She cooked him dinner and invited him to stay as long as he wanted. He would stay for a few nights, and Rhoda was happy. She gave him a key to the house and said, "Keep it, Vincent. There's no need for you to be living alone in that room."

"I prefer to see it as my studio," Vincent said.

"Still one room."

They watched television together that night, and when Rhoda retired to her room, leaving Vincent alone, she knelt and prayed that he would stay longer than a few days. There were signs that their relationship was improving since the days when she felt that he, the most affected by the family's breakdown, was still resisting her maternal love. There was something fragile about him and that became all the more apparent when he insisted, as he frequently did, that everything was fine. He had his father's stubborn streak without his father's strength. At the end of her prayer, she decided she would invite him to come and live with her.

She did so over breakfast, saying, "There's plenty of room; I could do with the company."

"From what I know about your movements, you're hardly here, Mum. You don't need company."

"Everybody needs company."

"We'll see," he said. "By the way, those curtains look really old and shabby. I thought Sam would look after you better than that."

"I try not to trouble Samuel too much. He's so busy. I've got a new set, but I haven't put them up because it needs a different curtain rail." She had not entirely recovered from her disappointment with Samuel, but she did not want to stir that hornet's nest.

"Do you want me to fix them, the curtain rails?"

"A church brother promised to come and do it for me, but everybody's so busy these days."

"I'll do it. I've put up curtain rails a few times in my life."

"Thank you, son, I'd really appreciate that."

After looking at the new curtains, Vincent went out and came back with new curtains rails and screwed them onto the window frame. As mother and son worked together to hang the curtains onto the pole, they talked about family members and Vincent quizzed her about her life in Jamaica. The next day he went out and bought a freestanding wooden lamp with a high hat from a furniture store on Mare Street. "So you can read more comfortably," he told her.

After dinner, Rhoda made another effort to persuade him to stay. "Vincent, you know when I left you and Neville and Samuel with your father, not a day went by when I didn't think about you all."

"It's okay, Mom. I understand about economic migration. How it breaks up families. Always has, always will. And, of course, the old man wasn't the easiest person to get on with; I know that."

"That man…" She stopped. She had crossed an ocean for Lucas Bostock, had four children with him, and no amount of regretting could alter those facts.

That evening they went for a walk around the marsh. Rhoda told Vincent about the early years in London, and he listened attentively, asking questions and laughing at some of her answers.

He was still there the following Tuesday, a day she usually gave to the Luncheon Club, and she was convinced she had won a major round in her campaign. He even said, "See you later," as she left the house. But when she returned home, she found an empty house, and the keys she had given him were on the dining table.

That night, despite feeling tired, she struggled to sleep, worrying about Vincent. By morning, she could not shake a foreboding of imminent disaster. Although they spoke on the phone a few days later, when Vincent said he had left because he needed to get on with his work, her anxiety grew. Even Maureen's demands on her time paled into minor distractions.

One Sunday in February, Rhoda was among the faithful of the New Church of God milling about on the steps of the former Baptist Church. They were mostly middle-aged and retired women wearing sensible shoes and hats and long skirts and overcoats. Pastor Goodman had delivered a stirring sermon on Shadrack, Meshach and Abednego from the book of Daniel, and it formed the theme of much of the discussion taking place on that windy afternoon.

Rhoda had hoped to make a quick exit from the church, but she was detained first by Sister Bramble and then Sister Martins. Sister Martins was a slim brown woman from Montego Bay who was respected for her many rapturous conversations with the Almighty in languages that other congregants did not understand.

Voice lowered, she asked to speak to Rhoda in private.

"Sister Bostock, I've been watching you these past weeks and something tells me you need a little extra help. Sometimes, you know, the Almighty is so busy, only a special messenger can get through to him."

"The Lord has time for all his children," Rhoda said.

"A little extra help, that's all. I know somebody who can give you that help. When I lost my husband, Carlton, he saved me from going mad. Mad, I tell you. Take this, call him, he'll help to give you peace of mind."

Rhoda took the card but did not look at it until she got home. It read: 'Professor Idris Khalid, marabout'.

This Professor Khalid worked and lived in a sparsely furnished flat above an Asian-owned off-licence on West Green Road. His room smelled of vanilla and like its occupant had a quiet stillness. On each of its white walls were small, glass-framed parchments with the squiggles and curls and lines in a language that Rhoda guessed was Arabic. In the centre of the room were two plain stools and a round table, its surface a mass of carved swirls that she mistook for more strange letters until she sat down and recognised animals – elephants, lions and giraffes.

The marabout was bluish-black, tall, beanpole-thin, clean shaven and bald, his cheeks pockmarked. His voice, low with a rumbling bass quality, seemed as if it belonged to someone with a much larger, fleshier body. Following his instructions, Rhoda placed her hands palm down on the table. Seated opposite her, he also placed his palms down on the table. Rhoda noted the nails on his long thin fingers were cut short and two were as black his skin. He held himself erect in the backless seat and looked directly at her.

"You are troubled, Mrs Bostock," he said.

Rhoda glanced up but his blackened nails drew her eyes downwards and she felt a powerful urge to unburden herself to this stranger, to reveal all her secrets, her life story with all its mishaps and frustrations and disappointments. But she settled for saying "Yes", a choked whisper, which faded slowly in the silent room.

"We, all of us, are troubled, Mrs Bostock. We would not be human otherwise."

"Yes, but sometimes the weight seems so great. I asked the Lord to lighten the load, but every year it gets worse."

"Has something happened recently to make the burden seem heavier, the troubles worse?"

She told him about her anxiety for Vincent after his recent visit.

The marabout expressed sympathy for her distress. Then he rested his hands on Rhoda's. She flinched and had to remind herself that it was a church sister who had recommended this gentleman. She was in no danger.

Eyes closed, he muttered some words in a language she did not understand, and she felt, or imagined that she felt, a warmth flowing through her arms. Then, slowly, he removed his hands and placed them in their original position and opened his eyes.

"Yes, I can feel your pain, Mrs Bostock. Fear, too. You're afraid for your children, and grandchildren; you want to protect them."

"You can help?" Rhoda said.

"Yes, but first you must believe they will be safe. Life has weakened your belief in the munificence of the supreme being, the giver of life, creator of the universe. You must strengthen and deepen your belief."

He removed his hands from the table, placed them in his lap, fingers knitted, palms upwards.

Rhoda took this change in posture as a signal that the session was coming to a close. Her friend had not told her what to expect, only that Professor Khaled could help her. She had come with a mixture of scepticism and desperation. Now she was not sure what to think or feel. He had not done anything she could describe and yet, remarkably, she felt better for having made the visit. His advice that she needed to regain her belief echoed something she had read in the bible. Was it the story of Job? She would have to reread it.

"There is something else troubling you, Mrs Bostock," he said. "I sense something deeper, older. Something you need to say to find peace."

"Yes, there is," Rhoda said. "It's something that happened a long time ago, across the sea."

"Yes, tell me," he said calmly.

Could she tell this stranger? Before she could answer her question, she heard herself speaking. She told him how, as young woman, she had met Lucas Bostock, and how her aunt, with whom she lived, had encouraged their relationship because his large calloused hands showed he would work to maintain a family. She, though, was not convinced they had a future together. She told Professor Khalid how in a crowded Half-Way Tree, she had locked eyes for an instant with a stranger and seen courage and kindness in his eyes and admiration for her, and had felt certain he was the man for her, but she had already promised herself to Lucas Bostock. She told him how Lucas Bostock and the man had fought over her. She told him how, on the night of the fight, she remained in her room and prayed, prayed with fervour, that the victor would be the man known as Trinity Gordon, and he would take her away from the heat and dust and the noise and poverty of Kingston, away from the tenement yard, away from her aunt, who only saw in a man his potential to be a breadwinner, away from Lucas Bostock. She told this blue-black stranger about the rumours of Trinity's death and the years of living in fear of retribution. When she finished, she was crying, her palms covering her face in shame and regret.

He remained still and silent until she stopped crying. Then he said, "Take this and pin it on the door of your bedroom. It is for your protection."

Rhoda took a small sheet of paper with strange writing. It looked like a replica of one of the framed parchments on the wall.

"What is this? How much will it cost?" She was suddenly afraid again.

"It is called the prayer of protection, and it is written in Amharic and it is over a thousand years old. A condition of my gift and training is that I am not allowed to charge. But if you wish to make a donation…"

From that day, Rhoda visited the marabout once a month. They did little more than talk at the circular table with its carvings of animals. She would tell him about the difficulties she had faced and was facing, identify the members of her family she felt needed special protection. She always left with a newly acquired scrap of paper covered in strange writing, in Greek, Latin, Hebrew, Arabic, Mandarin and Sanskrit – all ancient prayers, all necessary, according to the marabout, because entreaties to God stood a better chance of being acknowledged when expressed in many tongues. Each piece of paper was pinned on her bedroom walls and door, a room that no visitor was allowed in. Each night, as she retired to bed, she prayed with quiet fervour for forgiveness for her past sins, and protection from evil for her family.

42. *Maureen meets an old friend, later that year*

One July evening, Maureen Bostock stood in the entrance of Queensway station looking out for her friend, Janet. Restless, she wandered down Queensway and stopped in front of a boutique selling accessories. There was nothing she needed, so she settled for examining her reflection in the shop window. She saw the blonde dreadlocks, some strung with multi-coloured plastic beads, the gold Indian nose stud, petal-shaped, the straw-effect gold earrings, the dark green crushed-velvet scarf, her black crushed-velvet, ankle-length tapered skirt and red Doc Martens. She decided with approval that she was a riot, a walking carnival.

She walked back to the station, just as a vast cloud reached the sun and everywhere seemed bathed in a crepuscular light. She clutched the large umbrella she had snatched up as she left the house, regretting that it would declare itself in bold Helvetica as a Cullen and Conway promotional gift when she unfurled it. She had worked for the supermarket chain until what she described as a personal crisis made her abandon the career ladder which she was scaling with some success. Suddenly, corporate targets, niche markets and the whole language of mass market retailing came to seem a criminal waste of time – something she had recognised was not finite. She had resigned as a divisional manager based at company HQ in search of a more meaningful existence. They had lived off their savings and when Phil, who had retrained as a software designer, had created and sold a computer game, working from the garden shed, it had made them comfortably off, though not rich. Maureen liked to think that his success was a reward for her loyalty and patience, and for his understanding of her needs, which were different from those of most other women.

"Want to play geisha?"

The woman who had uttered these words was slim, with an angular face and greying brown hair. She wore a black trouser suit with a waist-length jacket and tapered trousers – like a female matador.

"Janet!" Maureen exclaimed.

They'd arranged this meeting after many years of silence, both explaining how life's vicissitudes had prevented them from making contact before. Janet was due to attend a health conference in London – she worked for an NHS trust – so they'd seized this chance. They hugged, then held each other's waists at arm's length. Maureen took in Janet's elegant appearance but saw the crow's feet around her eyes, the slightly desiccated upper lip, which her make-up seemed to accentuate. Maureen was shocked at how different Janet was from the memory she had carried over the years. It was another reminder of time's finiteness.

"This geisha retired a long time ago," Maureen said, and they laughed.

They crossed Bayswater Road and entered Kensington Gardens. A light drizzle began to fall and Maureen unfurled her umbrella, and Janet took out a transparent plastic hooded poncho. As they walked, Janet recounted how, having fled back to the north, she had started a family and tried playing straight for five years before she was forced to confront the self she had been denying for years. Then she'd had to deal with the opprobrium of her family, an angry husband and puzzled and unforgiving children.

"And the woman you met was your first love?"

"No... You were."

"Me!"

"Yes. I can't tell you how often, when we used to play that silly game, that I hoped you would notice my performance was for you – laughing at those inane jokes, playing coy and submissive. I prayed you'd notice how well I was acting and, at the end of the performance, you'd kiss me in appreciation. Then that Marc Bolan look-a-like turned up. You were besotted with him."

"Is that why you left Birmingham?"

"Partly. I was so confused, hurting and not wanting to feel hurt for what I tried to dismiss as a mere crush, I went back home to lick my wounds, but they wouldn't heal. It wasn't just unrequited love; they were the wounds of someone who refused to accept who she was. I tried to be 'normal', tried really hard, and when I couldn't try anymore, I went from one extreme to another. Left my husband and children and joined a commune of radical feminists. Maybe I needed them after all those years of denial, needed to embrace a certainty found only in extremism. But after a few years, after few broken hearts, mine and others, I moved back to somewhere in the middle. I have found somebody and she's comfortable to be with, challenging in her own way, but we work as a couple. And you? I can't imagine you and Phil with two children."

"Oh, we're all right. Just about. And the way Andy, our eldest, is playing the field, I wouldn't be surprised if I became a grandmother soon."

"From geisha to grandmother!" Janet said.

They strolled aimlessly, and were now approaching the Albert Memorial, which was sheathed in scaffolding for renovation. They sat on its steps, looking towards the Albert Hall. Janet produced a packet of cigarettes and Maureen accepted one, though saying she should not, because she had given up.

"I wish somebody had taken me aside when I was younger and told me what to expect," Janet said.

"They did. It's called school."

"You know what I mean."

"I do. Just trying to be funny. Anyway, you wouldn't have listened."

"You're probably right. You said Phil's in a wheelchair. How did that happen?"

Maureen hesitated, then answered, "It was my fault. I told him I was leaving him and taking the children."

"That seems cruel, threatening to take the children."

"That's exactly what Phil said. Later, we worked out our differences, or learned to co-exist with them." Maureen fell silent. She couldn't reveal to her old friend why she'd wanted to leave Phil – the discovery, which came to her as though she had been woken from a deep sleep by having cold water thrown on her face, that she was black. No, it had not been so sudden – more the cumulative effect of countless small incidents and remarks: seeing Andrew in tears because a schoolmate had called him a starving Ethiopian, or the irate customer who had refused to accept that she was the store manager and stormed off after promising to write to Cullen and Conway's about employing ill-mannered darkies. The shield she had devised over the years had cracked and no longer protected her. It had once enabled her to insist to herself and the world that she was just Maureen Bostock, a person, an individual, a human being. Awake, she'd started to keep a sort of racism weather warning. What seemed like an unfriendly glance from a white person triggered a dark green, an explicit racial remark, amber, and racial abuse, red. And in the midst of this awakening, there was Phil, gentle and caring, with his pale pink skin, and the two beautiful children they had created. There had been nobody to talk to, not her mother who was taking ever greater refuge in God and all that stuff; not

Sam, who seemed so focused on his political career, or slow-talking Neville in those years when he was still damaged by his beating. She had come close to talking to Vincent, but his whispering voice and tormented expression made it clear he had enough troubles of his own. So, she had borne it alone, and the more she wanted to scream "Why didn't somebody tell me?", the harder she'd tried to keep up appearances. It was no easy act, falling apart, invisibly and secretly.

"I don't think I could've done it," Janet said. "Once I'd decided to be true to myself."

"I didn't think I could do it, either. Every day I'd wake up thinking I must end this charade. Maybe one day I will. But not right now."

"The children?"

"Partly. I didn't want to put them through what I went through. My parents splitting up."

"You survived it."

"Survive is the right word. I didn't want my children to be survivors. As simple and complicated as that."

"Maureen, I hope you don't mind me saying this, but you sound like one of those self-sacrificing Victorian mothers who committed living suicide for the greater good of the family."

"No, I don't mind. I hadn't thought of it like that. I made a choice, and for me it was the right choice. I couldn't insist on anyone else in my position making the same decision. Then, of course, there's Phil. Truth is, he's a friend, a dear, dear friend. He's understanding. He makes no demands on me. We've learned to live with each other's idiosyncrasies. Mine are probably more idio than most people's…"

Just then Maureen saw an elderly couple walking past. They walked close together, talking quietly, and Maureen wondered whether this was all she'd ever wanted, a companion. Perhaps she could settle for Phil in his wheelchair. She said, "Remember you used to tell me about growing up in a house filled with portraits of your ancestors? Going back five generations?"

"No, eight."

"I used to wonder about that. I didn't know a single grandparent. Not one. I used to wonder what it was like to have that as part of who you are."

"It's only recently I've come to appreciate knowing where I came from. I saw it as oppressive, the tyranny of the past. It probably made it more difficult for me to become me, to work out how it related to the me-in-the-present, how not to be burdened by it all."

"And did you work it out?"

Janet laughed. "No, I'm still working on it. Fact is, I don't think I'll ever stop searching for an answer. Maybe it's an endless quest, the eternal conversation between past and present as part of making your future."

"Well, you've got a lot of past to work with. I'd like to give my children some of that. So when the wind blows, they won't be blown over. They know Phil's mother, my mother. I'd like them and my grandchildren to have more sense of continuity."

"What about your father?"

"That bastard."

"Maureen!"

"Well, that's how I feel about him. I can't help it. I've tried, but whenever he comes to mind, which fortunately isn't a lot these days, I feel this uncontrollable anger."

"That's not good, Maureen. You were like that when we were younger. You should go and make your peace with him."

"That's not going to happen. He's left the country, gone home. Even if he was still here, I wouldn't make peace with him."

"I guess that's your choice."

"It's one I'm happy to live with. Anyway, you can talk. You told me on the phone you hadn't seen your folks for ages."

"That's different. They didn't want to see me. But they came round in the end – literally in the end. Within a year of our reconciliation, Mum went and Daddy followed a few months later. But I'm grateful that after all those years of denying me, they reached out to me."

Maureen remembered the last occasion when she and Lucas had talked. He had got her number from Vincent. She had lost her temper when he asked what her children wanted to be when they grew up, and went on to lecture her on the need to instil ambition in them – this from a man who had never seen her children, his grandchildren. She had told him never to call her home again and slammed down the phone. Had she been too harsh? No. As far as he was concerned, she didn't do forgiveness.

"It's getting a bit chilly," Janet said. "Let's walk a little."

Maureen felt pleased she had agreed to this reunion. Although she regretted that there was a part of herself she could not reveal to Janet, she welcomed the opportunity to share what she could.

Maybe if they continued to meet, she could admit Janet to this strangely powerful side of herself.

"Fancy coming back to my hotel for a drink?"

"Where's that?

"Lancaster Gate."

"Ooh, that sounds fancy. I haven't been into an hotel in ages. I'll come on one condition"

"What's that?"

"That you'll come and visit me and Phil. Bring your partner. Stay as long as you like. We have loads of room."

"Done."

They linked arms and Maureen thought, I mustn't lose this friend again.

45. *Vincent, Sylvia and a secret from the past, the following year*

Vincent had taken voluntary redundancy in January. His job had become intolerably boring, and he'd spent the next couple of months hustling for freelance work. This had so far yielded only one commission – an article on London's buskers for *Segue*, a new glossy magazine aimed at young male professionals. He had researched the piece in February – recording interviews with hoarse-sounding buskers in tube stations, markets and shopping malls – wrestled with it throughout March and submitted it, double the commissioned length in the hope that excess would be interpreted as enthusiasm, at the beginning of April. A fortnight later, he was still uncertain whether it had been accepted. The commissioning editor had not returned his calls. Meantime, he was scouring his notebook, a cornucopia of ideas inspired by long walks around London, for new ideas to sell. Canary Wharf remained one his favourite destinations, but he also explored landmarks closer to home – Hampstead Heath, Primrose Hill, and Alexander Palace were fast becoming new favourites for their views over London. He was unhappy with the rate at which he was converting inspiration into saleable ideas. Discounting payment for the recently completed article – even if it was accepted, he didn't know when he would be paid – he estimated that his small savings, if he nibbled at them like a mouse on a piece of cheese, would last until September. He was still writing letters as secretary of the Phoenix House residents' association. He was teaching himself to play the guitar – passing many hours on the minor pentatonic scale – and to speak Spanish and French using teach-yourself cassette tapes. He hoped – foolishly he knew – that fluency in another language might give him access to a new reality – one in which he did not know loss and sorrow, or that unappeasable longing for somebody or something to make him feel whole.

One Friday afternoon, passing a shop called Yemanja on Stroud Green Road, he stopped to look at its display of posters, cards, Makonde carvings, bronze jewellery, soapstone figurines. Although the shop had been there for many years, and he had bought items there, it now occurred to him that its existence and survival held some larger significance. He made a mental note to add the shop's name to his little notebook of ideas when he reached home.

As he turned away from the shop towards Seven Sisters Road, he saw a woman approaching who looked familiar. Middle-aged, slim, tall, with straightened hair, elegantly dressed in a beige raincoat, her name escaped him for a moment. It was at the opening of a gallery Elena was involved with he had seen her; she had stood apart from the crowd, with her two sons, his nephews, beside her. It was Sylvia, his elder brother's ex-wife.

They greeted each other with stiff formality. Sylvia was practically a stranger to him, though she was part of his memories of the years when his mother lived in Brixton. But she spoke to him now in a motherly way, enquiring after his siblings and his parents, as if they were her family too. Unsure how to relate to her, his replies were brief and unforthcoming.

She told him she had been visiting a friend in Crouch End, to borrow some lecture notes. Her sons had left home, and she was filling the time on her hands by studying for a degree.

"But you know all about that," she said. "I remember when you used to come to Brixton. You were such a serious and scholarly young man."

Vincent's discomfort worsened. It was like meeting one of those old Caribbean women from Carlisle Road who had known him as a child, perhaps used to pat his head or tell him to wipe his runny nose.

"I was just skiving," he said, dismissive and jocular, wanting to imply that she had never known him, did not know him now.

"I'm sure you weren't," she laughed. "Hey, maybe I can pick your brain on how to study. I'm finding it so tough. Can I buy you a cup of coffee? It's a such nice day and it's a Friday."

Indeed, earlier that day, while jogging around the park, Vincent had seen the golden flowers of large forsythia as an augury of better times ahead, and he accepted Sylvia's offer. They turned down Blackstock Road and saw Muslim worshippers wearing kaftans, roebuck trainers and embroidered skull caps emerging from two nearby mosques. They went to the Meeting Place, an Egyptian-owned bistro decorated with large Monet prints of water lilies. They found a table near the window. Vincent enquired about his nephews. Both were doing well. Joseph was still an accountant, John had left teaching to become a civil servant.

"You must be proud of them," Vincent said.

"I suppose I am, yes – especially when I see what other young Black men their age are getting up to."

Vincent wondered whether this was a dig at his failure to take advantage of the chances that had come his way. While he had floundered, London was changing, like some protean beast. The evidence was everywhere; the street beyond the cafe door was different from what he once knew. North African-owned cafes, patisseries, butchers, and grocery stores were ubiquitous. The English greengrocers with its seasonal Brussels sprouts, Granny Smiths and oyster mushrooms had long disappeared. He could not recall when he last saw his old school friend, Terry, who used to work there. He had achieved remarkable: inertia in the midst of change.

"Sam thinks our boys could have done better, though," Sylvia said. "He said I didn't push them hard enough."

"What did he want, a pair of astrophysicists? I'm sure that when he looks around at the knife and gun-wielding, drug-taking Black youngsters with their homophobia, misogyny and self-contempt, he must be proud of Joseph and John."

"Well, you know Sam; he's always pushing himself. Say, have you seen this?" Sylvia was carrying a large, bulging, red-leather shoulder bag, in which she rummaged, putting a compact case, mobile phone, lipstick, a small photo album on the table, while she searched for what she wanted to show Vincent.

There must be an entire lifetime in that bag, Vincent thought.

"Ah, found it." She pulled out a clear plastic wallet and from that a newspaper cutting. She handed it to Vincent.

It was a photograph, taken at a Downing Street reception for community leaders. Samuel and the new Labour Prime Minister were standing shoulder to shoulder, both smiling broadly into the camera. They seemed to be wearing identical dark suits and white shirts, only their ties differed.

"Sam's looking pretty good," Vincent said, proud and, he admitted to himself, a little envious. He handed the cutting back to Sylvia and found her looking at him with disconcerting intensity.

"It's funny, isn't it, how things turn out."

"What do you mean?"

"I remember the year your aunt Irene came to visit, and you came by one afternoon. Maureen and Neville were there too."

"Yes."

"And you were what, sixteen, seventeen?"

"Around that age. I certainly remember her visiting London. Mum was very happy."

"And we were gathered in the living room and you said you were going into politics and would become prime minister."

"Did I?"

"Yes, and Sam really jumped down your throat. Told you you were a dreamer, to be a more realistic."

"I don't recall that at all; sounds like Sam, though," he lied. He thought of the day he'd climbed a tree in Clissold Park, until fear stopped him from going further, and Samuel and Neville were shouting up at him to come down, their alarmed voices heightening his terror.

"And now he's rubbing shoulders with the PM," Sylvia said. "Funny, isn't it? Joseph tells me – I don't know how much truth there is in it – I hardly follow politics – that he's likely to get a safe seat at the next election."

"That's great. He deserves it; he's been trying for such a long time. It's incredible how he's pulled himself up. I often cite him as an example of what an ambitious person can do, no matter what his or her background. I'm a Labour voter, so I can't tell you how glad I was to see the end of seventeen years of Tory rule."

Her blank expression told him that she wasn't in the least interested in politics, and he began to wonder whether she had an ulterior motive in showing him the photograph.

"What exactly are you getting at, Sylvia?"

"Nothing. I was just making an observation."

"Maybe you think I ought to envy him?"

"No, no, really, Vincent, I just think it's funny the way our lives work out."

"I vaguely recall that day. It was probably after I'd been elected president of the Afro-Caribbean society at college and was thinking of running for president of the student union. I was young. I believed that anything was possible. If I'd been really committed to that goal, I'm sure I would have gone for it. I guess I wasn't."

Why was he justifying himself? Somehow, she had put him a corner and he had to defend both Sam and himself.

He added: "I'm sure you're not doing now what your teenage self thought she would be doing."

"Yeah, I guess you're right. I imagined I'd meet a handsome young man, fall in love and live happily ever after," Sylvia said.

"There you are then."

"And as you say, Sam's looking pretty good. We should all be proud of him. I certainly am. That's why I walk around with this picture." She put the plastic wallet back in her bag.

Was he being ungenerous concerning her motives? Whatever, he was relieved not to continue talking about Samuel. He walked his own path; comparisons with Samuel or Neville were invidious.

"It's a beautiful day, isn't it?" Sylvia said. "Looks like summer's here."

"You know what old English people say: Don't put your coat away until the end of May."

Sylvia held her forehead and grimaced.

"Something wrong?"

"I've suddenly got a terrible headache. I suffer from migraine and I don't seem to have my pills."

"There's a pharmacy round the corner."

"No, no. I have loads at home."

"I ought to be going," Vincent said.

"You live near here, don't you?"

"Yes."

"Could I rest in your place until this migraine passes? Then I'll head back to Brixton."

Sylvia's pained expression could not be refused, and he agreed, warning her that his room was probably in quite a mess.

In his room, Sylvia, eyes closed, stretched out on the foldaway sofa bed and Vincent sat at his desk, listening to her steady breathing. After twenty minutes of silence, Sylvia got up and asked for the bathroom. When she returned, she smelled of perfume and Vincent noticed that a button on her blouse had been undone, revealing a hint of cleavage.

"Thank you, Vincent. I feel much better," she said, smiling.

"You're welcome." He rose and picked up her coat.

Sylvia ignored him and reached into her capacious handbag and took out a silver flagon.

"I'm really thirsty," she said. "Want some?"

"No thank you, Sylvia. I think you'd better go now."

"Are you afraid of me, Vincent?"

"Yes, maybe I am. I think you need to go home, Sylvia. Go home and sleep off whatever is troubling you."

"You don't have to be afraid of me, Vincent. Let's be friends."

"We are already. But you should still go." He spoke as firmly as he could in a soft voice, and it seemed to work. Sylvia shook her head, as if she had woken up a second time and, unable to recognise her surroundings, was embarrassed and confused.

"You're right. I must go. But before I do, there's something I want to tell you about Sam. He didn't do it all by himself, you know; he didn't, as the saying goes, pull himself up by his own bootstraps. He couldn't have done it without me. You see, when we first lived together, not far from here…" And she went on to tell Vincent just how she had supported Sam when they were struggling for money.

Vincent walked Sylvia to a mini-cab office on Blackstock Road. As she was entering the cab, she paused, placed her left palm against his cheek, kissed the other, and said, "Thank you so much, Vincent. Thank you."

He stood and watched the car head towards Seven Sisters Road. As he walked home, he puzzled over why she had chosen to make such a disclosure. Was she just unburdening herself of a painful part of her life she needed to share with somebody? Then the penny dropped: she had been telling him how she had made Sam and in revealing that, how she could unmake him. I must warn Sam, he decided. That woman's dangerous.

Vincent's meeting with Sam, postponed several times because of Sam's busy and unpredictable schedule, didn't happen until early May, an afternoon of unseasonably hot weather. He took the underground and then walked across Clapham Common towards Sam's home. The common was littered with people, pink faces and pale limbs exposed, offered up to the sun as a ritual of worshipful gratitude for its surprising benignity. The air crackled with an almost electric dryness; the light was harsh.

Elena opened the door, greeted Vincent with a peck on the cheek, and said, "Sam's expecting you. I'm off to pick up Roy, then we're going to a meeting."

"Tell Roy Uncle Vincent says hello." He took in Elena's greying hair, shaped in a Beatles-style mop, and the way she exuded a subtle but distinct fragrance that suggested sincerity, warmth, and kindness.

"Will do," Elena said. She shouted for Sam and departed.

Sam emerged and invited Vincent into his narrow, book-lined study. While Sam went to make them tea, Vincent surveyed the room, his envy and admiration tempered by the suspicion that many of the books had not been read – their dustcovers looked untouched, the spines of the paperbacks were not broken. He noted on the wall above Sam's golden oak desk, itself a magnificent piece of ecclesiastical appearance, framed black and white portraits of Malcolm X and Martin Luther King. It set him thinking, for the first time in many years, about Levi-Straussian binary opposites. He turned back to the bookshelves and plucked out what looked like a virginal paperback copy of Ferdinand Dennis's *The Last Blues Dance*, an author and book he'd never heard of; he liked the title but wasn't in the mood for reading fiction.

They'd been talking for only a few minutes after Sam brought in the tea – regular for Vincent, jasmine for Sam – when the telephone rang. While Sam answered it, Vincent scrutinised him. He was again struck by his brother's preternaturally youthful appearance. He was wearing navy-blue linen trousers, a white, collarless cotton shirt and leather sandals. His dark skin glowed; there wasn't a grey strand in his thick, neatly trimmed hair; he looked as lean as a young man unsoftened by success or domestic bliss, and still in pursuit of both, but carrying himself with relaxed self-assurance. His brother's clothes made Vincent aware that the sudden change in temperature had caught him unawares. He was still dressed for winter, wearing a brown woollen jacket, a white shirt, faded blue jeans, frayed at the hems because they were slightly too long, and Doc Martens, the leather scuffed and the heels worn down. At least he'd left his greatcoat at home.

Sam updated Vincent on his various activities, the voluntary organisation he now directed and the many others on whose boards of trustees he sat. Then they talked about family: Neville, Maureen, their father in Jamaica. While they were laughing at how difficult it was to imagine the old man in retirement, Sam's phone rang again.

Vincent heard him say, "Yes, I know the programme. When is this live debate?" … "Who else are you inviting? … "The baroness. Good, good. Those are good people." Shaking of the head. …"By the way what's the fee?" … "Okay. Can I get back to you tomorrow? I'm in a meeting right now. Let me just take your extension number." Sam covered the mouthpiece and seemed in search of a pen.

Vincent pulled one from his inside jacket pocket and handed it to Sam who gave him a thumbs up and wrote down the number.

Putting down the phone, Sam said, "The bloody BBC, they expect you to work for nothing."

"Well, it is public service broadcasting, Sam."

"Do you know how much the channel directors and other corporations' leaders make a year?"

Vince shook his head.

Sam unplugged the phone, and they picked up where they had left off, talking about their father. Then Sam, as he often did, accused Vincent of neglecting their mother by failing to visit her often enough and Vincent found himself struggling to maintain the composure with which he'd embarked on this visit. While searching for the words to rebut this charge, he noticed a faint smile play in the corner of Sam's lips, and it reminded him that this was one of the ways Sam subjugated him, kept him in a permanent state of little brotherhood – loved, but inferior, lacking in purpose and substance, and plagued by irremediable feelings of maternal abandonment. To avoid an argument, Vincent excused himself and went to the bathroom and stayed there long enough to regain his equanimity. He returned to the study, and said, "Now, where were we?"

"We were talking about you and Mummy."

"Ahh, yes," Vincent said, dropping into his seat. "Correction, Sam: *you* were talking about Mum."

"Still angry with her, eh, Vince."

Vincent laughed dryly and said with icy calm: "That little trick of yours won't work. I've made my peace with Mum. How often I see her, whether I visit her at all, is my business, not yours. Fact of the matter, Sam, I didn't come here to talk about Mum."

"Fine, fine; you're quite right. Let me guess – you're having money trouble again? How much do you need?" Sam reached for a top drawer and opened it.

"I didn't come here for money either, so there's no need to pull out your chequebook."

"Oh, that's good to know. Especially, as you haven't paid me back the last loan I made you."

"Soon, soon," Vincent said.

"I've heard that before. Anyway, you seemed quite keen for us to meet. What's the problem, then?"

"It's Sylvia. I met her some weeks ago in Finsbury Park. She told me something I found really disturbing."

"Oh, yes. What was that?"

Vincent recalled in summary his exchange with Sylvia.

Sam sat upright in his chair, crossed his legs and folded his arms. "Sylvia told you that and that's why you want to talk to me?"

"Yes."

"You really shouldn't pay too much attention to Sylvia. She's never forgiven me for leaving her. She's capable of saying some terrible things. In fact, sometimes I wonder about her mental health."

"She seemed fine to me."

"But you're neither her ex-husband nor a psychiatrist."

"You're not a psychiatrist, either, Sam."

Sam laughed and graciously conceded the point, splaying his long fingers.

"Sam, I haven't come to argue with you. I've come to warn you. A man in your position can't afford to have such an allegation being bruited about. She'll ruin your reputation, bring you down."

"I'm hardly the incumbent of lofty political office, Vince. A mere local councillor and humble charity worker."

"Oh, come on Sam. Everybody knows about your political ambitions. You must be the most famous Black spokesman in the country outside parliament. It's only a matter of time before you're given an opportunity to contest a winnable seat. Sylvia could be biding her time, waiting for that moment."

"You're more optimistic about my political prospects than I am. I take that as a vote of confidence. Thanks. As for Sylvia, I know her better than you do. She probably told you what she did to hurt you and me. I very much doubt that she would dare to make such an outrageous allegation in public – for which there isn't a shred of evidence. But the most important consideration is this – something you wouldn't appreciate because you're not much of a family person. You see, Sylvia might be angry with me, but she knows we're tied together, inseparably so. To ruin my reputation would have an adverse impact on her children, her sons, my sons. I know that Sylvia wouldn't want to hurt our sons. Of course, it's unfortunate…"

"Sam, Sam," Vincent interjected, "You know, for years now I have held you up as an outstanding example of what's possible with discipline, ambition and so on. I don't know how many times I've recounted your story to people in support of my argument that a disadvantageous start isn't an insuperable challenge. So, let me put a direct question to you, and please give me a direct answer. "Is there any truth in what Sylvia told me?"

Sam shifted about in his chair uncomfortably, then stood up and walked to the window. With his back to Vincent, he said, "What does it matter, Vince? It happened decades ago."

"So, it's true, then. Basically, you lived off immoral earnings. You pimped, to put it bluntly."

"I didn't ask her to do anything like that for me."

"So, when did you find out?"

"Soon after she started…"

"Did you try to stop her?"

Samuel spun round and said, "Is that what you have come here for, Vince, an interrogation, an inquisition?"

"Inquisitions are conducted by religious bodies, interrogations by states."

"You really ought to have remained in academia, Vince. That's your natural home. All those years in that council block; those pathetic pieces of journalism for struggling little magazines read by marginal, disaffected people posing as self-important radicals – people as useful to the health of the nation as bedbugs are to a good night's sleep."

"You just don't get it, do you, Sam? For years, you presumed to know what was best for me, what was real and unreal, right and wrong. But you can't see that Sylvia has morally compromised you, rendered you unfit to stand for public office. I didn't come here to judge you; my own past is hardly spotless, but, then, I'm not a public figure. I came to warn you. But you still insist on trying to deride me as your naive little brother with his head in the clouds. Maybe I should take a page from your book. You seem to have a formula, if not for success, then certainly for an easy life. First Sylvia, then Mom, now Elena. Is that it, Sam? Is that the secret? Find a woman to carry you? Send her to walk the streets so you can live the lifestyle you believe is rightly yours?"

"You shit, get the fuck out of my house."

"Your house, Sam? That's rich. Don't worry, I am going." He stood up and added, "At least one thing about me, Sam, naive as I am, poor as I am, I stand or fall on my own two fucking feet, and there's no woman in the world who can say that she prostituted herself on my behalf; no woman's ever had to whore for me. None."

"Get out, you little bastard."

"That's more like it, Sam. Now we're seeing the real you. *Ciao*." Vincent made to leave room, but stopped, turned and said, "My pen, Sam, I'll take my pen back now."

Sam seemed momentarily nonplussed, then gathered himself, picked up the pen and thrust it at Vincent as though it were a dagger.

Vincent calmly took pen and said, "See you around, Sam."

Outside, his heart racing, Vincent walked through the falling dusk across the now empty common to the tube station, where, at the entrance, he hesitated for a moment. In his agitated state, the prospect of having to make the long descent on a creaky escalator to the station's dimly lit platform was unappealing. He would walk to Stockwell; from there he could catch a Victoria Line train to Finsbury Park. He walked on and as he walked, he realised that in discovering the truth about Sam's past, he had unwittingly entered into a compact of silence; the chance meeting with Sylvia had loaded him with a great weight which was bearing down on him.

By the time he reached Stockwell station, night had arrived, and, cloaked in its comforting anonymity, he decided to walk all the way home to Finsbury Park. Perhaps the city's nocturnal sights and noises would distract him from the mounting feeling of being crushed by truth and silence.

At this late hour the motorway traffic back into London from Watford was sparse and flowed unimpeded by road works or accidents. Neville Bostock, driving an MPV, was tired and eager to get home, but not so eager that he speeded. He drove in the slow lane, leaving it only to overtake even slower vehicles, articulated lorries and old cars. His companions, Kenton Coombes, who sat beside him, and Victor Carter, who sat in the back, were similarly exhausted. Victor, Neville sensed, was fighting sleep, not surprising given his performance at Ivor Jones's bedside. Victor had spoken in tongues for over an hour in an effort to expel the demons ravaging Ivor's body. Lymphatic cancer: six months to live, so the doctors said. But Neville, his brethren, and the dying man believed in the healing power of prayer. And how they had prayed!

The glow of the city was visible in the clear night sky. Neville's thoughts turned to the many other challenges facing him. Next week he hoped to sign a lease on a building in Morning Lane, a former fabric warehouse, for his new church. Would he get enough worshippers? It was a huge gamble. The Lord is with me, he intoned silently; I shall not fear failure. Other concerns rushed forth in his mind, crowding out his plans for next week. The next morning, he had to visit his daughter. The child – although she was the mother of two young children, he still saw her as a child – had a talent for attracting worthless men, shiftless, feckless no-gooders. Having thrown out the father of her youngest child, she wanted to change the lock on the front door of her flat. He, Neville, would, as he always did, go to her rescue, change the entire door if he had to…

"Think Brother Jones will come through it?" he heard Kenton say. Pulled out of his reverie, he became aware of the odour of sweat, aftershave and the car's own pine deodorant. He heard heavy breathing bordering on snoring from the passenger at the back.

"It's in the Lord's hands now," he said.

Kenton turned his shoulders away, as if the Pastor's apparent lack of optimism betrayed a weakness in his faith.

Neville wanted to quote a passage of scripture that would comfort and uplift his companion, but his memory refused to yield the necessary balm and silence was restored and in the silence it occurred to him that maybe Kenton Coombes was ashamed for having expressed doubt about the efficacy of the marathon session of feverish prayer and singing and hollering at the sick man's bedside.

His thoughts returned to his daughter's predicament. He should not be too harsh on her. She was almost a woman before the Lord entered their lives. Patience, forgiveness, prayer. The same, too, for his son, Chad. That boy had better mend his ways, start walking right, or he would spend many nights in prison. Imagine causing the police to visit his home, claiming that they had reason to believe that his son was involved in drug dealing. Of course, he had co-operated with them. Bible in hand, he'd given them a guided tour of the property, invited them to open cupboards and boxes, lift up the floorboards, if necessary, because he was certain that Chad, who saw himself as a wheeler-dealer in wholesale goods, would never desecrate the family home...

"When my time comes, when the Lord calls me, I hope it's sudden," he heard Kenton mumble. "A heart attack. Something like that."

"Don't know that we have any say in the matter," Neville said. He glanced in the rearview mirror, beyond Victor Carter's slumbering figure – head thrown back, mouth wide open. He eased the car into the middle lane, overtaking the slow-moving van he had been driving behind for some miles.

"Maybe you're right," Kenton said. "Look at Brother Ivor. Never touched alcohol, didn't womanize, prayed seven times a day..."

"The Lord works in mysterious ways," Neville said, aware that he heard fear in Kenton's voice.

"His wonders to perform," Kenton added.

Silence was restored. The glow of the city seemed brighter now; multicoloured fingers of light snatched at the cloudless sky. He rehearsed the itinerary for the rest of the journey: drop Victor Carter in Dalston, then carry on to Walthamstow where he and Kenton lived. Archway, Holloway Road, Highbury Corner. Then he remembered he'd loaned his toolbox to Frank Baines, another church brother. If he was to help his daughter change the lock, he'd need to pick up the toolbox. That could take the whole morning. Not enough time to see about the one hundred-plus second-hand plastic chairs he'd seen for sale in Tottenham. Home, dinner, sleep; then on the road early again. Must remember to have a good talk to Micah. Not happy with that boy's school report. No excuse...

As the car passed under the iron bridge over Archway Road, Neville became more alert. The traffic lights were in his favour as he entered Holloway Road, and this encouraged him to think again about the chairs he wanted to buy. A good deal. Must somehow get to Tottenham before the end of the day. Nearing the junction of Holloway Road and Seven Sisters, just beyond the Odeon cinema, he slowed down for the first red light for a over a mile. He noticed that the windscreen was murky, squirted water over it and started the wiper. For a second the windscreen was covered in an opaque mixture of soap, oil and dead insects. As it cleared, he made out cars speeding across the busy junction from Camden Road. A lone pedestrian passed in front of the car, illuminated in its headlights. Head hung low, hands in pockets, he walked slowly. Something familiar about his gait struck Neville; his clothes, too: the brown jacket, the too long jeans, the frayed cotton shirt. The man seemed to be talking to himself. His younger brother, Vincent? But doubt swiftly quashed that thought. The lights switched to amber as the figure receded from view.

Kenton Coombes, sensing Neville's agitation said, "Somebody you know?"

At the same time, Victor Carter woke and asked, "Where are we?"

Who should he answer first? The person who walked in front of the car has now been swallowed by the night. He wanted to answer yes, but said a choked no instead. The lights changed to green.

"In London," Kenton Coombes said.

No, that definitely wasn't Vincent. He pressed the accelerator and the car eased off and over the crossroads towards Highbury Corner. "Nobody I know," he said, certainty restored to his voice. A memory of when he had last seen Vincent began to jostle for space in his weary mind.

46. *Vincent runs in the park, a little later*

Vincent's slow, meandering journey home from Clapham Common had taken him along the south bank of the Thames and across Waterloo Bridge, along Kingsway up to Holborn, past Russell Square, to Euston, where he bought a drink in the station; from there he walked through the backstreets north of Euston

Road to Camden, and then headed to Finsbury Park. When he arrived home, his mind was buzzing with the sights, sounds and smell of the city at leisure on a hot night. Exhausted, he slept most of the following day, waking up in the evening to dash off a record review, which he went out to post. Then he had returned to his room and took to his bed. He drifted through several hot days, the result of a heatwave, and airless nights, ruminating on his own transgressions and those of Sam. On several occasions he concluded that there was nothing he could do but carry on, but a combination of regret for his own past and disappointment in Sam kept him anchored to his bed. Then one morning, after an especially close night, he woke up feeling he was coming down with a cold or the flu because his nose felt congested, his chest tight, his head muggy. It was this intimation of physical ill-health that finally roused him; he had to stop dwelling on the past.

In the morning, just after five a.m. he got out of bed, dressed and left his room. The elevator smelled of urine and beer and when its doors opened on the ground floor, he gulped down the fresher air. Uncomfortably positioned on two plastic chairs, the concierge was asleep and snoring loudly. Vincent's passage did not stir him. Somebody had vandalised the telephone kiosk opposite Phoenix House's entrance; glass was scattered on the ground. A car parked beside it had suffered a similar fate; its side window had been smashed, its stereo ripped out.

Seven Sisters Road was quiet as he made his way towards the underground station, passing the Esso petrol station and the all-night supermarket. An elderly Muslim, his white beard streaked with henna, passed him, then a younger man wearing sandals and an ankle-length gown. The Asian newsagent at the station was still unwrapping the morning papers when he arrived. While waiting, Vincent watched the early morning travellers rush into the station.

He read the paper over a cup of strong tea in an empty cafe on Blackstock Road. Arsenal dominated the sports pages; they had recently won two major trophies. He zipped through the quick crossword and got stuck on what seemed like an easy clue. He attributed this mental sluggishness to lack of sleep.

Other customers had arrived in the cafe, some familiar faces: the Turkish man with the bushy, unruly eyebrows and pock-marked face and a chain-smoking habit; the West Indian with fingernails that were so long they curled, and a penchant for two-tone suits a few sizes too small for him, the trousers legs stopping above his ankles; the red-bearded white man who always seemed to be quietly fuming at some ancient wrong. They were all probably like him, Vincent thought, the survivors of personal disasters, compelled to seek the silent companionship of strangers. He remembered mornings of waking up beside Rachel, with Kara snuggled up between them. He left the cafe.

He went for a walk around the park. He had taken up jogging since March but restricted it to the afternoons. The week-long heat wave, unusual for May, had turned the grass pale green, with patches of brown. The sky promised another hot day.

There was much on his mind: a recent letter from Rachel, with a photograph of Kara – they were now staying in an Ashram near Calcutta. A telephone conversation with his father, who, it was now clear, was unlikely to return from Jamaica, had left him with the impression that the irascible old man had at last found happiness in another family out there, with Donnette and her daughter and grandchild. His father had relayed Donnette's 'love'. Hearing that growl had made him realise how much he was missing him. Donnette was evidently there but they had not spoken directly.

He circled the park once, passing only one other early morning walker, then returned to his room and went back to bed. Some hours later, he began the day again. He was sure he had contracted some low-level bug, but he dragged himself to his desk. The last Residents' Association meeting had been noisy and heated, with several tenants calling for the building to be vacated and demolished as the only practical solution to its numerous and intractable problems. It was not the first time he had heard that argument, but he had never heard it put so forcefully. The burden of writing up the minutes had fallen to him, along with having to write letters on behalf of residents requesting housing transfers. He needed a proper computer and a mobile phone. He had to be ready for the new century and the millennium was just two years away. Money was on his mind.

He flicked through his ideas' notebook. There was the 'Robinson Crusoe in the City' idea, which had come to him one night, but he was not sure how to realise it or which publication to pitch it to. Still, it was one of several ideas gestating.

He remained at his desk until midday. After taking what was

supposed to be a brief break, the will to continue working deserted him. He picked up his guitar and music book and, sitting on the bed, ran through Franz Behr's 'In May' and Fernado Sor's 'Adante' a few times – two beginners' tunes he used to warm up. His sight-reading was improving, but his fingering was stiff and his tempo too fast. He ought to invest in a metronome. Money again. He did not have a healthy relationship with money. Here he was, almost forty years old, and he had no savings. He had removed his name from the titles of the house he'd bought with Rachel after it was clear they were never going to get back together. He put aside the guitar and lay on the bed. He recalled the occasions in his childhood when his father had sent him to ask for overdue rent from a tenant. He'd had to ask Uncle Horace several times. Then Uncle Horace died. Was there some connection between Uncle Horace's death and the wilful impoverishment to which he had subjected himself, working for small, obscure magazines dependent on charity-labour for their survival?

From his bed, he surveyed the room. The wall of books, the desk, the narrow wardrobe containing all the clothes he owned, the little black and white television seldom used, the wing table. How had he managed to live in this small space for such a long time? What perversity had drawn him back here time and again, undermining his effort to start a family? Maybe Rachel was right. He needed to spend less time looking out and more time looking in. But then he felt the room's walls narrowing, its ceiling becoming lower. He needed to get outside.

He entered the park through a hole in the fence. He walked straight up to the plateau and circled the boating lake. The sun was high, the sky a clear blue, the air moist, a hopeful sign that the heat wave had reached its climax. Customers sunned themselves on benches outside the park's cafe. There were supine bodies in the open areas, mostly women sunbathing. Couples sat under trees. Ten minutes of brisk walking made him feel better. He headed home.

As he neared the playground, he saw a child on the climbing frame. She was wearing a multicoloured, striped cotton jumpsuit. similar to one Kara used to wear, He leant against the railings and watched her climb the ladder to the slide. Her concentration, her unalloyed expression of joy, her whoops, all captivated him for a moment. He had not noticed the mother, but now she made herself visible and audible. Shouting the child's name, she ran to snatch the child off the bottom rung of the ladder, held her close to her chest, and shot him a hostile glance. He hurried away from the playground towards the park gates.

Back in his room, he finished the minutes of the residents' association meeting and knocked off two letters to the council. Then he turned over in his mind the call for Phoenix House to be demolished. Reluctantly, he agreed; it had become a dumping ground for single people who did not always remain single, its small rooms like cells. With that thought he drifted off to sleep. When he woke, he felt calmer, but thought the cold or flu he was coming down with was still there. But he did not feel he could afford to lose a day's work. His money was dwindling fast. He did not want to have to visit the benefits office, as he had done a decade before. He wanted to move forward.

He ate a light lunch and returned to his desk and stayed there for an hour. His agitation had returned, this time with an intensity that threatened his resolve to go forward. Clouds were gathering in the sky, the air felt viscid. He paced the room, considered going on one of his long walks, maybe up to Hampstead Heath via Highgate. He decided it would be too time-consuming. Better to go for a jog, run off the cold. The temperature seemed cooler.

He changed into his running gear, delivered the minutes to Mr Krishna's flat, posted the letters, and went back to the park. He intended to do two laps. He jogged at a gentle pace. He kept to the inner perimeter until he neared the Manor House Gate, where the park-keeper's lodge, a disused redbrick building, forced him onto the asphalt path. As he descended an incline shaded by plane trees on either side, their intertwined branches forming a cool canopy, he thought of his encounter with Sylvia.

Something good had come out of that encounter, despite her disclosure about Sam. When she was in his bedsit, passivity had seized him, but he had not allowed himself to be possessed, as he had with Donnette and with Rachel; both in different ways women who had sought his help. When had he ever initiated a relationship with a woman that was based on physical attraction or common interests? He remembered hearing his mother crying. He remembered feeling weak and wretched because he could not help her. When and where was that? Maybe he should go into therapy. Then his thoughts turned to Neville. He regretted the exchange they'd had at their father's farewell dinner. Neville had seen him at his lowest point and offered help, which he had rejected. Had Neville been goading him at dinner? He had to apologise one day, not for the views he expressed – that would amount to self-abnegation – but he'd been too aggressive. He must remember to mention the idea of science and religion as non-overlapping domains, a gracious compromise, different realms, different truths, the logos and mythoi. Was that too much of a compromise? Yes. Where is the morality in a belief system that threatens its believers with eternal damnation? Surely it robs them of the freedom to think, so they behave out of fear. Avoid all talk of religion. Bring some presents for the children. And Sam. Oh, Sam.

The path began to rise; to his right was the American garden and Endymion Road to his left. Another jogger seemed to glide past him. His thigh and calves were feeling the strain, and he envied the other runner's swift and effortless pace up the slope. His mind returned to Sylvia, and her reminder of Aunt Irene's visit. She had intended malice; he was sure now. But what if he had not been mocked, what if someone, even Samuel, had said, "That's a fine ambition"? Would his life have been different? He was half-way up the slope. No, he didn't have the perseverance, the discipline, the resolve, the focus Samuel had shown over the years. It had just been the fanciful dream of a teenager drunk on the myriad choices facing him in a city that gave the illusion that anything is possible. No more than that. He had been so young when he plucked that goal out of his imagination, so young. And it *had* driven him for several important years, propelled him out of Stoke Newington and through a degree programme. If only he'd clung to it, owned it, allowed it to own him. Instead, he had lost it. He'd never felt so alive since that time, spent years wandering aimlessly, all the while denying that he was lost. Why hadn't he revived that career ambition on returning to London? Did he lack courage? No. It was because Samuel had claimed it as his own and he had been seeking singularity, uniqueness. His courage was to carry on, though he had lost the only ambition he ever had. On that score Samuel was blameless; everyone knew Elena had pushed him into politics.

He was at the top of the slope, passing another gate, the boating lake, the cafe. Then the path descended again towards the Finsbury Park Gate. At the bottom, he turned at the old drinking fountain and readied himself to tackle yet another, though gentler incline.

The drinkers and hashish smokers were gathered on the grass. He felt their eyes on him. He no longer feared slipping into their company.

Halfway through the second lap, his thoughts returned to the women he had known, and he had to fight the temptation to stop jogging. Had he used them, used Donnette to explore sexual play, Rachel to experiment with fatherhood? Had he used them as means to an end, rather than engage with them as ends in themselves? If he had been more self-aware he could have avoided causing so much damage to other people's lives. How could he find redemption? No, only believers sinned and therefore sought redemption. Maybe, then, he could find a better balance in his life between his desires for solitude and intimacy.

His leg muscles hurt, his chest burned, but his mind was clearer than it had been all day. He refused to surrender to the pain; he claimed possession of it and ran on. He passed the Finsbury Park gate again and limped in jogging motion up the incline towards Manor House. He had done two laps, and never, in the weeks he had been running, had he felt so exhausted, so broken. He limped onto the grass and up a bank leading to a playing field. On the flat, he threw himself to the ground near the painted line of the football pitch and rolled onto his back. He was breathing heavily, his heart was pounding, his chest felt tight, his T-shirt clung to his back, sweat cascaded down his forehead. But he was happy that he had pushed himself to finish.

He thought he felt a drop of rain, colder than his sweat on his forehead. There was a break in the gathering clouds and the sky there was a vast patch of blue. He had never seen such an intense blue. It was as if shades of blue, azure, aquamarine and cobalt had united to create a fantastic and perfect patch of blue sky that expressed all the sorrow and beauty in the world. Then he imagined his mother wandering alone through her house and he felt like crying. He ought to visit soon, bring her some flowers, spend a weekend; explain why he had returned the house keys.

He became aware that he could not feel his legs, those legs that had minutes before ached, neither could he feel his hands. And he had no heartbeat and his lungs were still. He struggled to move but his body refused to respond. He had become a disembodied consciousness, a bundle of pictures and words, arbitrary and ambiguous words, their meanings elusive, always slipping and sliding away. The blue patch in the sky was shrinking fast, soon there were only the clouds, dark and pregnant with rain.

★ ★ ★ ★

The narrator meets Cy and winds up his story, 2020s

When, one weekday evening in late November, as I inserted the key into my flat door's lock, and I heard the boy shout out from behind the door of his flat: "I'm going to spill your stomach all over the floor," I decided to make an appointment with Cy.

Cy's kitchen was at the rear of the house. The dining area where we sat was a calm, clean space; a radio on the side table played what I thought was classical music, but I wasn't sure because the sound was barely audible. Cy was of medium height, slight, almost skinny. He wore a close-fitting, black, round-neck woollen sweater, black trousers and shoes that looked as if they were polished daily. On his right middle finger was a large signet ring encrusted with a small diamond. The *Daily Mirror*, opened to the horse racing pages, was spread on the table. A cigarillo, partly smoked, sat in a silver ashtray.

Everything about Cy seemed unhurried. I had been in the house in Archway for almost ten minutes. He had commented on the weather and enquired where I came from in Jamaica and volunteered that he came from Westmoreland. Came at sixteen, he had said, "Seventy next year." He had offered me a cup of tea, and having made it at a leisurely pace, now brought two cups to the oak table and carefully placed them on woven fibre mats. I was seated with my back to the window; he sat directly opposite me and relit the cigarillo.

"Is this BBC Radio Three? I asked, nodding at the radio.

"Yes. You want a different station?"

"No. I'm just a bit surprised."

"What were you expecting?" He smiled.

"Oh, I don't know," I repeated, feeling a little foolish. "That's a Roberts radio," I said, for want of anything better to say. "I've seen them in shops. Are they good?"

"Very good. Most prisoners swear by them. That's how I know about Roberts radio. Prison."

I felt a thorough idiot, but given the purpose of my visit, I thought it best not to ask what malfeasance had taken him to prison.

"Relax, man," he said. "As I said when you came in, any friend of Irma's is a friend of mine."

I had not been aware of my nervousness and now made a conscious effort to at least appear to be at ease.

"Irma tells me you have a little problem you want to deal with."

"Yes, I do have a problem. I am just exploring some options right now."

"What's the problem?"

I told him about the boy downstairs.

"Yeah, yeah. I know the type. The other day I was on a bus and came across one just like that. Black boy. In his school uniform. Giving another passenger grief. Had to go up and tell him, 'Bwoy behave yourself; go and learn some manners.' The most he could do was look at me and walk off. Bad man style."

"Except this guy's in his thirties."

Without varying his tone, Cy said, "I can arrange for somebody to fuck him in his arse; show him how powerless he is."

It took me great effort to conceal my shock at this suggestion. Cy clearly sensed my perturbation.

"Not your cup of tea? Not to worry."

"Maybe that's what he needs or wants," I said, "but I'm not the person to arrange that."

"Fair enough. Irma did say you're a reasonable man… Let me give you some other options, with prices. As you're Irma's friend, you'll get a discount. Ten percent on the quote. Is this guy right-handed or left-handed?"

"Right-handed," I said, hesitantly.

"To disable his right hand, smash up his fingers, break his wrists, elbow, we're talking about five hundred pounds. If you go for that option, you get the right leg done at a lower price. Thereafter, it's two hundred pounds per limb."

"Any other options?" I choked out.

"If you just want him to get a general duffing up. You're looking at about three hundred. That's the lowest priced service we offer."

"We?"

"You don't think that I actually do any of this do you? Look at me, I've got one foot in the grave."

"You look quite healthy to me."

"I'm trying; had a prostate operation last year. Haven't felt the same since. Anyway, back to business. I'm just fixer, an agent, a broker. You and me make an agreement, verbal. I take some details from you, ring around, see who's available, or wants the job. This time of year, close to Christmas, there won't be any shortage of takers; guys looking for a bit of extra money to buy something nice for the missus, take the family on winter break in the New Year. You'll never know who has the contract, never meet the person. It's all discreet. When it's done, done to your satisfaction of course, you pay cash. I take a twenty per cent commission. Pass an envelope to a man in crowded pub. And bob's your uncle. Simple as that."

"And what's the most expensive service you offer?"

"We can arrange for his disappearance. You'll never see him again. That's very expensive."

"How much?"

"Five, six,"

"Hundred?"

"Thousand. Depends on who picks up the job."

I was about to ask Cy a question when I suddenly became aware of another presence in the house. Somebody was coming down the stairs, and presently the person, a man, pushed open the kitchen. He was in his late thirties, and looked like a younger, but much taller and broader version of Cy.

"I'm going out, Pops," he said.

"When're you coming back?"

"Late, late. I'll phone if my plans change."

"Okay," Cy said.

The young man nodded at me, and I nodded back, then he was gone. When the front door closed, Cy said, "You wouldn't believe how much money I spent on that boy's education. Private schools, primary and secondary. Good thing I didn't have to pay for his university education. He's still living at home. Can you believe that?"

"I'm sure his mother appreciates his presence."

"Oh, she's living in Canada with his sister. Some years now."

This banal, commonplace domestic act, a young man bidding goodbye to a parent, was so unexpected that I completely forgot the question I wanted to put to Cy. We talked for a few minutes longer about inconsequential matters. I sensed that he was in no hurry for me to leave, but not because he wanted me make use of his unusual service. He sounded like a man who had lived a long and eventful life and wanted to talk. Had I met him elsewhere, under different circumstances, I might have listened. I made an excuse about having to complete several errands before the day ended. He walked me to the front door. As we shook hands he said, "Give me a ring if you decide to go ahead. And say hello to Irma if you see her before I do."

Out in the grey damp November afternoon, the pavements littered with sodden leaves, I walked along a quiet Archway street of redbrick Edwardian houses, windows flickering with the light from television screens, feeling that despite my advanced years and decades in London, despite being in a salubrious neighbourhood, I had just emerged from some hidden alleyway in the city.

Confined to my bedroom, now overcrowded with furniture – a double bed, a desk and chair, an armchair, a television, a dresser – I had a miserable Christmas. Several times, seething with resentment as the floor beneath my feet vibrated from the boy's music, I found Cy's number but not the ruthlessness to make the call that would bring a swift end to my suffering.

The boy now wore a black varsity jacket with the wording "Bad Dock" stitched on the back in large yellow letters. He was getting his shopping delivered by Tesco, and his mother had arranged for a new washing machine to be installed in the flat.

The New Year found me resigned to living in one room again, only being able to use my living room when the boy was away. I no longer bought my morning paper from the shop on Conrad Road. The sight of Zach Jr., a physics graduate, behind the counter in obedience to a father determined to escape from Britain back to the Caribbean, only made all human life seem more miserable and wretched. Now I bought my morning paper from Mehmet, an elderly Turk, a self-confessed repeat-deserter from the Turkish army – seven times, he boasted – and such a wizard at mental arithmetic that he rarely used the cash till. The sight of him behind the counter in his cramped little shop didn't seem so offensively a profligate waste of talent and education as Zach Jnr's.

It was in Mehmet's shop that I got an unforgettable fright one morning. I turned to leave, and there, standing in the doorway was the hideous sight of a woman with sunken cheeks and bulging eyes set in sunken eye sockets. The veins on her face were visible and her thin neck rose out of a coat that was stylish but too large for her. I recovered my composure; she moved aside, and I walked out of the shop. A few yards on, I looked back and saw that she was still standing outside, an arm outstretched. Mehmet's hand appeared and placed a coin her palm. When I next went into the shop, I asked Mehmet who she was. She was Turkish and had been brought to London as the young bride of a wealthy man. She'd had an affair, and the man had punished her by locking her up for three months and injecting her with heroin, then released her. Twenty, twenty-five years, Mehmet said. "And what happened to the man she had the affair with?" Mehmet pulled an index finger across his throat. I gulped. As I left his shop, he said: "Inshalla." After that day, I regularly saw the woman with the harrowed face walking with jerky determination along the High Street, sometimes stopping at a Turkish-owned shop, a palm outstretched. She was always given alms.

In late January, I received an email with an attachment from Irma. It read: "He name Chebeen and he propose." Irma had remembered the language she was in. The attachment was a photograph, taken aboard a schooner, of Irma, a broad smile on her face below a white sailor's cap, wearing starched white shorts, her long dark legs oiled. Next to her, a hairy arm around her waist, was a tall, powerfully built, brown-skinned man, dressed all in white, with a thick moustache. The background to this tableau was the blue sea. He name 'Chebeen and he propose'. I emailed back: "Congratulations. Looking forward to receiving a wedding invitation."

At the end of January, the house next door, the former squat, acquired new occupants, a Black family. My fate was now sealed, I thought, as I saw the size of the family, and the number of teenagers. Worse still, they were Jamaicans. I had lived in Brixton for two years and left because my home was sandwiched between two unbelievably noisy Jamaican-owned houses. Nightmare visions of losing even my quiet sanctuary on the top floor, as my bedroom walls shook with bass music, began to fill my waking hours.

But as the family settled into their new home, I saw that they were different. The oldest boy in the family, tall and lean, always had a hungry look in his eyes. He was attending college and planned to go on to university. Between 7 and 7.30 am, his seven siblings could be seen filing out the house in their school uniforms. And I became friendly with the father. His name was Eddie Gordon, and he wore thick black-framed glasses and rode a bicycle. He spoke with a Jamaican accent mixed with London cockney. He worked in the laundry of a children's hospital. That the family was nothing like the boy downstairs was confirmed when, as soon as the signs of spring began to appear, the father went into the back garden with a machete and cut down the weeds. The back garden of the house in which I lived had not been touched in three years.

Here were my people: aspirant immigrants and their British -born children. These were the people I had grown up among, people aware that bush was something to be cut, lest it reclaim, obscure and block their path to a better future for their children. The sight of the Gordon children coming and going imbued me with renewed energy for my fight against the boy downstairs.

One morning, the halogen bulb in my desk lamp blew, and I walked to MK Electronics. The eponymous MK was a dark, elderly St Lucian who had learned his skills in the British army. His shop had been on Church Street for over thirty years, and I had never been in there without seeing other customers. As well as selling electrical parts and goods, MK's also sold reconditioned electronic equipment, televisions mainly. While waiting for his Thai wife to find me the right bulb, I noticed a secondhand stereo-system for sale. It could play both CDs and tapes, had a FM and MW radio, and an auxiliary port for a turntable. At its loudest it could produce eighty decibels. My stereo at home was only capable of thirty decibels.

"It works fine. Could probably get two, three years use out of it," MK told me. I bought it on the spot.

Back home, I set up my new stereo in the living room, positioned in the alcove near the window. The speakers I placed on the floor. When the boy next played music, I turned on the stereo and gradually increased the volume. I established that thirty-eight decibels blocked out the sound of his music. Though I could do nothing about the vibrations under the floor, I began to use my living room again. As the weeks wore on, I had to increase the volume and reached the maximum of eighty decibels. The boy was determined not to be drowned out. His stereo was far more powerful. One evening, in frustration, having reached the maximum on my stereo without the desired effect, I once again took to banging the floor with the mallet. This went on for a few minutes. When I stopped, I decided to get some fresh air. I stood on the stoop outside. I had been there only a few minutes when the boy, whom I had not seen for many weeks, came out of his flat. He stopped in the doorway, looked down at me and said: "You're going to have to get used to your neighbour's noise."

I said: "My neighbours' sounds are the ordinary, regular sounds that people make as they go about their lives. What you are doing is a noise nuisance. I don't want to hear you in my home. You could be Jesus Christ, I don't want to hear you in my home."

My blasphemous retort seemed to stun him. "Now excuse me," I said and made to enter the house. Suddenly I found myself forced back and off balance. The boy moved at lightning speed to slam the front door and lock the dead lock, leaving his key in the lock, so I couldn't unlock the door.

Fortunately, I had my mobile phone in my pocket. I telephoned the police and said I had just been assaulted and was now being denied access to my home by the assailant. I was instructed to wait. I had no choice. As I stood outside, a couple walked past holding hands. Two of the teenagers from the Jamaican family came out and walked up the street. Life went on.

After some minutes, I heard the boy remove his key from the lock. I opened the front door and let myself into my flat.

A policeman came after another twenty minutes. It was now 9.15. He interviewed me in my living room, which was quiet. I gave him my version of events. He said, "Sounds as if he bounced you." He said he would have to interview the other person. He went downstairs and returned after ten minutes, saying that the person downstairs had made a countercharge of assault. I was furious.

"Officer, I was standing outside; that young man came out after me. He assaulted me."

"But yer not injured. There were no witnesses to the incident. It's your word against his."

"You say he's accused me of assaulting him? Okay. I assaulted him. Arrest me. Arrest me so I can stand before a judge and recount some of the things I've had to put up with in this house since that boy moved in downstairs. The threats of violence, verbal abuses, threats to burn down the house. I'll spend the night in jail. I don't mind."

The officer said, "I am not going to arrest you."

"I insist you arrest me. Just give me a minute. I'll put on proper clothes." I was wearing a track suit. I went upstairs and changed into trousers. Back downstairs, I picked up my shoes and put them on in front of the officer and said: "I'm ready whenever you are."

"As I said, I'm not going to arrest you. You don't want to spend the night in a cell."

"If it's the only way I can get this matter to court, I'm prepared to do that."

The officer's calm persuaded me that he wasn't going to arrest me. He left, saying, "You should take civil proceedings against your neighbour."

Some days later, I went for an interview with the antisocial behaviour unit. I left feeling despondent. Everybody seemed powerless; the boy had his mother's protection. But a few days later, I was woken around midnight by a loud banging on the front door, alternating with my bell ringing. I donned my dressing gown, went downstairs. Two uniformed policemen were on the steps.

"We want the guy in the other flat," one said.

"He never answers his bell."

"Can we come in, knock on his door?"

"Sure." I gave them access. As I locked my flat door, I heard the boy shouting in a loud voice, "I didn't hear the bell."

I went back to bed.

They came around at the same hour for about a week. At last, somebody in authority had taken my complaint seriously, and these late-night visits from the police had a salutary effect on the boy. He kept his distance. He stopped coming out of his flat the same time as I was leaving mine. He stopped playing loud music. But I had been there before and fully expected him to resume his noise once things had cooled off.

And, just as I expected, by early summer, the boy had started again. When he started rapping above the bass-driven music, I turned on the stereo's radio, permanently tuned to Radio Four, and left the room, closing the door. If the radio programme had a deep-voiced male speaker, the boy seemed to go into a frenzy of rapping. He could now be heard outside. On one occasion, I watched the mother of the Jamaican family standing at her gate looking disturbed as the boy spat out his musical profanities.

On one of my calls to the noise pollution office, I struck lucky. An officer brought round a recording device. She arrived at the house while the boy was performing and said she could hear it outside. She took a sound measurement and said his noise was borderline. But she would leave the machine for a week. She set up the recording device and turned it on. The boy's sound had increased in the interim. The officer made the first entry in the log as the floor vibrated: "Can't stay in the room", and over the next days, I recorded the boy's noise level. In one particularly noisy session, he shouted: "Numero Uno!"

The officer returned for the machine, took it away and within half an hour telephoned me to say that she had heard enough to warrant issuing a noise abatement order.

I sighed with relief. After four years I had finally proved my complaint. The music now stopped altogether, and I came and went from the house in peace. I spent a Saturday afternoon sitting in my living room reading a newspaper, and it seemed an utterly strange experience.

But within weeks, the boy had found a new way to disturb me. He triggered the smoke detector in his flat. Smoke filled the hallway, and the acrid smell of burnt food lingered for days. Then he started banging the doors. He had removed the Yale lock on the door leading into the ground floor flat. When that door banged, the sound travelled to the top of the house. Some nights, he banged it at such frequent intervals that I woke up the following morning with the drowsy feeling of one who had not had a proper night's sleep.

I complained. When I was told that nothing could be done about the door banging, I reluctantly conceded defeat and began searching for a new home. I had to leave that house, leave it to the boy downstairs and get on with my narratorial duties.

★ ★ ★ ★

47. Samuel, Larry Haynes and politics, 1998

The London Pride pulled away from its mooring on Embankment; Samuel and Larry Haynes sat at the stern, away from the late-summer tourists. Samuel was catching up with his old friend, advisor and mentor. He had instinctively held Larry's elbow as they boarded the boat, though he was enjoying rude health, his only sign of frailty the black walking stick with the brass knob top which he carried everywhere, which lent him an air of distinction and gravitas. He had recently returned from West Africa as part of an international election monitoring group.

"How was your journey, Larry?"

"Oh, air travel, even flying first class, always seems to bring out the misanthrope in me. And before you ask, the election was a bloody disaster. We gave it a clean bill of health, of course. Better

319

an imperfect democracy than rule by the gun. You could say we re-planted the sapling of democracy; let's see whether it takes root. Now tell me, how is your family coping with your brother's death?"

The boat was turning beside the Houses of Parliament. The view of the building, which seemed to rise out of the river, distracted Samuel for a moment.

"My mother's still mourning."

"That's understandable. A parent, especially a mother, burying a child is a profound disturbance to the natural order of things."

"I've promised to drop in on her later today. Needs some help with her garden."

"Good. I must say, I felt quite honoured to be invited to the funeral, felt like a member of the family."

"Well, you are in many ways."

Samuel remembered the telephone call from his mother and the haunting image of rain falling on Vincent's body through the night. A woman had found his body on an early morning walk with her dog and there had been a week between his death from cardiac arrest and the family finding out, because he had no identification on him. Samuel thought he was the last family member to see Vincent alive.

"And that was quite a eulogy you delivered."

"Nothing less than he deserved. Vincent had everything to live for." When he and Neville – who was uncharacteristically quiet throughout the funeral service and burial – had finally gained access to Vincent's bedsit, they found the large cheque he had recently earned, the letter from Rachel seeking reconciliation, the notebooks of ideas, occasional diary entries, scraps of writing, unfinished essays, the French and Spanish cassettes he used to teach himself those languages, the acoustic guitar with worn strings, the two-foot wide wardrobe in which he kept all the clothes he owned. Handling these mementos of Vincent's life, Samuel had been profoundly disturbed by the realisation that he had neither known his brother nor cared much to know him.

"It was the cruellest of deaths," Larry said.

During the long pause that followed, Samuel's gaze roamed across the riverbank. Two gulls wheeled in the sky, another pair bobbed up and down on the river's choppy surface, then took to the air as a speedboat rushed past. Larry Haynes broke the silence.

"The reason I wanted to see you, Sam, is this. I'm considering quitting parliament. Not immediately, but certainly before the government's served out its term."

"You… quit politics. What will you do with yourself?"

"I didn't say I was quitting politics – just parliament. I'm angling for a diplomatic post. The UN, South Africa, even a South American country, though that's unlikely. I've put feelers out. I'm owed a few favours. The point is that my resignation would, of course, trigger a bye-election. Now I can't promise you anything, but I'm prepared give you my imprimatur to get you on the nomination list."

"That's extremely kind of you. I feel honoured."

"You may not feel like that once the contest begins. The competition is likely to be very strong. The selection panel will choose the best person."

"Thank you. But I must confess that I've been having serious doubts about my own parliamentary ambition. I have yet to decide whether to even continue as a local councillor."

"Anything to do with your brother's death?"

"Everything. After the funeral, it dawned on me that I was pursuing something that was never really my ambition. One of the things I didn't mention, couldn't bring myself to say, is that the first person I heard talking about politics as a career was Vincent."

"Really?"

"Yes. He was. He was only a teenager and quite full of himself. Said he wanted to become foreign minister."

"I'm surprised. The impression I got from your eulogy was of a rather bookish person, not somebody cut out for the rough and tumble of politics."

"He certainly became that. But, shame to say, we – I – mocked him when he first revealed his interest in politics. Dismissed him as a fanciful dreamer. Years later, I met Elena and… Then you became a source of constant encouragement, advice and support. But I saw something at Vincent's funeral that stayed with me."

Samuel recounted meeting Vincent's friends from Phoenix House, the strangers who attended the funeral and stayed late into the night. The single mother on whose behalf Vincent had written letters to the borough council to seek more suitable housing for her and her son; the launderette workers who owed their jobs to Vincent's campaign; the lame, elderly Jewish man whom he sometimes shopped for; Mr Krishna, the chairman of the tenants' association, who told him of Vincent's tireless work, and many others whom Vincent had helped or offered small acts of kindness, acknowledging that they existed, that their problems could be solved. There was even some talk of a campaign to get a building named after Vincent Bostock. The gratitude of these ordinary folks had moved Samuel and triggered his reflections. Why had Vincent been so generous with his time, labouring through nights writing letters, compiling reports? He had not done it in pursuit of a career, no vainglorious ambition. Vincent had served and asked for nothing in return. His own work as an elected official was not rooted in such selfless motives. Vincent had treated people for themselves; he had seen his work as a means to an end: getting into parliament.

"It seemed somehow morally wrong to continue."

"I think you're being unnecessarily harsh on yourself," Larry said. "I'm not sure how many elected officials would pass your morality test. We live in a democracy. Thank goodness there are people who put themselves forward to serve the public. Personal advancement and public service aren't mutually incompatible. No, it seems to me that Vincent had imagination but lacked courage; you, however, had courage but lacked imagination. There are many fine public servants one could say the same of."

"Nonetheless, I'm seriously rethinking my future. Elena and I have talked much about the matter."

"She would be very disappointed, wouldn't she?"

"Yes, but she accepts it's my decision to make."

"Seems to me, Sam, if as you say Vincent identified politics as a career, you ought to carry on in his memory…"

"Yes, I've considered that."

"Look, Sam, take some time to think about it. I'm at home until around midday tomorrow, then I'm due in Paris on Saturday evening, UNESCO conference, for a week. You can call me before I leave, or after I get back. These are early days."

"Thanks. I do need time to think things through. I thought I'd pretty much made up my mind; but you're dangling quite a potential prize before me."

"I'm glad you recognise that."

Samuel glanced at the riverbank and shared the thought that he, a Londoner by birth, had never taken a boat ride on the Thames, had never seen the city from this vantage point.

"It's an experience I seek at least once a year. It's one of the reasons I make London my home." Larry's right hand swept the air in an arc.

The boat was passing under Waterloo Bridge.

"Tell me, Larry, is there any truth to the rumour that you were sounded out about a life-peerage and rejected it?"

"Yes."

"Do you mind if I ask why?"

"Not at all; something to do with the republican ideals of my youth; it's all a bit too feudal for me. If politics is the art of compromise, I've certainly done my share of that, having started out on the far shores of the left, but Lord Larry Haynes is a compromise too far – has a deathly ring."

Samuel heard weariness in Larry's voice. Or was it disillusionment? It was an open secret that he had hoped to secure a cabinet post in the second term, but the leadership had overlooked him.

"You've become a national institution, Larry. You'll be with us for a long time yet."

"Thank you. But I do sometimes wonder whether I've served any purpose other than perpetuating certain power relationships."

They had passed under Blackfriars Bridge. Samuel recognised Bankside Art Gallery. Some tourists, cameras and camcorders in their hands, had drifted to the back of the boat. A Chinese man looked at Samuel imploringly. He wanted somebody to take a picture of him and his wife or girlfriend. Samuel obliged.

"Yes, Larry, you were saying about power."

"Yes, I was. Where was I? You see, the average person sees political power as something that is held – even revolutionaries. But in fact, it's more often the case that political power thinks the holder and not the other way round.

"Aren't you rather denying human volition, agency there?"

"Not entirely. Remember Marx: "Men make history but not in circumstances of their own choosing."

"You remain an unreconstructed Marxist at heart."

"Not at all. I long abandoned any simplistic or indeed complex notion of economic determinism or seeing the proletariat as a modern-day redeeming force. I was never a supporter of the Soviet Union – a terrible advertisement for socialism, as somebody said. Thank goodness it's gone."

They were passing the Globe Theatre now.

"Perhaps you prefer Shakespeare's 'All the world's a stage and all the men and women on it are but actors'…?" Sam said.

"Both Marx and Shakespeare could be seen as pointing to the constraints on human volition. My own preference in this instance is for Marx because Shakespeare replaces God with the dramaturge. I'm afraid I'm still both a republican and an atheist."

"We forgive you your sins, Larry," Sam said.

Larry laughed. "Unfortunately for you, my sins are the future of the world. We like to flatter ourselves that we are free; the principle of individual freedom is fundamental to western civilisation and it is one to be cherished; and while I'm reluctant to go as far as those who see history merely as the configuration of different types of economic structures, I do recognise the need to pay attention to those structural constraints operating at any historical conjuncture. It's a necessary starting point for understanding reality. Take another example – language: are we prisoners of language? Take this city, are we its prisoners? The symbolic and the concrete constraining us, defining the nature and boundaries of our freedom."

"Yes, I see what you mean."

"I confess I'm sounding out some ideas I'm thinking of including in a lecture I have to give in a few weeks. Not that I have got much beyond its working title: 'Over the Wall: Progressive politics and ideas after the end of history'. We in the West like to see ourselves as belonging to the most developed, complex and sophisticated civilisation. But I often think that civilisation is just a thin veneer, beneath which our tribal instincts still dominate. Tribes fought over land and women, the former being one of the means of production, the latter the means of reproduction. Excuse my Marxism, here. Think of the Trojan Wars. Paris runs away with Helen, triggering a bloody and protracted war. Think of the fundamentalist Muslim's insistence on women wearing the veil. But I digress. Now, tell me, are you still on the management committee of War Against World Poverty?"

"Yes, just about. I haven't been to a meeting in ages, though. There don't seem to be enough hours in the day or days of the week to keep up all my commitments."

"Maybe you should consider putting more energy in that direction, now."

"Still encouraging? You have been such a staunch supporter of my political aspirations. Why?"

"We're not crabs in a barrel, son. I think you're sincere, honest, industrious, and that counts a lot for me. At your brother's funeral, I saw you surrounded by your mother, Elena, and your ex-wife – and that struck me. Back in the Caribbean, old folks used to say that God put women on earth to teach men responsibility. The presence of those women, the way they stood around you, protective, but also, seeking protection, was a vindication of my support for you. Besides, I wouldn't be where I am today without advice and support, sometimes from the most unlikely quarters. I see you as a potential successor, somebody who will continue championing the causes I championed. How we leave office is as important as how well we perform in office. But I'll respect whatever decision you make."

Samuel wondered whether he should now reveal the real reason why he was considering abandoning politics: his unshakeable feeling of guilt over Vincent's death. He remained silent. They were in The Pool, passing Capital Wharf on the left. On the right, behind Bermondsey's riverfront, was Jamaica Road. New apartment blocks and wharf warehouses converted into homes dominated the north bank, monuments to the river's renewal. As the greatest monument to that rejuvenation loomed – the Canary Wharf Tower, a plane soaring above it – Samuel remembered the drives through the city with his father and brothers on Christmas day, when the streets were ghostly quiet, and his father pointed out with pride the buildings he had worked on, as if he had built them singlehandedly. He recalled his father's admiration for the work of the architect, and it occurred to him now that his father had been saying more than just praising that role. At the outset, a person's life is like an empty space, a vacant lot, a plot of land, and the size of the architect's imagination, among many other qualities, plays a huge part in determining whether he builds a hovel, a house, a mansion, a castle or a skyscraper. Had he, Samuel, chosen to erect some grandiloquent edifice on the shifting sands of vanity, stolen ambition and youthful immorality?

Larry said, "To imagine that two hundred years ago, this city had a population of one million, and a century later seven million, and this river was the epicentre of that magnetic pull. People flocked here, people who had known the land and the timeless rhythms of its seasons and found themselves in a filthy and chaotic city without proper roads, sanitation, housing. Imagine the despair as dreams expired in the chaos and trauma of entering the modern. Many must have ended their miserable lives in this river. But look at it now."

Greenwich Royal Palace with its classical lines was the next landmark. Larry had arranged for a car to meet him in Greenwich; he contacted the driver while the boat moored. They disembarked at the pier and as they walked towards *The Cutty Sark*, Larry said: "Well, we've reached our destination on the river and there isn't a mad Belgian waiting for us."

He laughed, but Samuel did not understand the allusion.

48. *Samuel as a dutiful son, Rhoda, and a decision*

Later that day, Samuel, still turning over in his mind his conversation with Larry Haynes, parked his Rover outside his mother's house in Homerton. He remained seated as he tried to shift the focus of his thoughts away from having to make a decision that could transform his life and lead to the very prize he had been pursuing for years, to that of being a dutiful son. Dithering was not a part of his character; he might not, at the outset, have always known exactly what he wanted from life, but he prided himself on his ability to recognise an opportunity and act decisively in seizing it. Since parting with Larry, he had been telling himself that it was a simple choice: to compete or not to compete, though a favourable outcome was not guaranteed. Yet, a decision eluded him, like a greasy opponent in a wrestling match, twisting and writhing and slipping out of his grip.

Admitting himself to the house, he found his mother in the back room, sitting in front of the television. It was, as usual, tuned to a religious channel. A tall, handsome, brown-skinned preacher in a three-piece white suit strutted across a stage like a rock star, while cutaway shots showed the faces of the mesmerised and enraptured audience, mostly women. His mother sat on the sofa, a large red Bible on one side, the television's remote control on the other. She had lost a lot of weight in recent months; her face was gaunt, and the skin around her wrists hung loose. Sorrow and grief fed on her.

A few days before he'd had a disturbing telephone conversation with Maureen, who'd made the outlandish suggestion that their mother's mental health was less than sound.

"She's just lost her youngest child, Maureen. She's grieving."

"No, Sam. Something was going on before Vincent died. I just didn't know how to raise it with you. You need to visit her. Look in her bedroom and you'll see what I am talking about."

"Her bedroom? Anyway, when did you become a psychiatrist?"

"Look, Sam, I know my mother better than you do. There's something wrong."

He took a seat beside the dining table and surveyed the room. It needed a fresh coat of paint and new wallpaper. He would speak to Maureen. He no longer felt confident making suggestions to his mother. Since the rupture with Sylvia, he had often felt she was punishing him by accepting only the minimum help from him. And since Vincent's death she had a way of looking at him accusingly, as if he were responsible for his brother's passing.

"I'll start on the garden in a while," Samuel said.

"Before you do that," she said, "there's something..." She paused, lowered the television's volume and said: "Sylvia came here today."

"What did she want?"

"Nothing. Said she was in the neighbourhood."

"Didn't even know she had your address. Must have got it from the boys."

"I don't care how she got my address. Please tell her not to come to my home again. I'll always be civil to her outside. She's the mother of two of my grandsons. But please tell her not to come to my home again. I don't like the way she smiles at me."

"It's just your imagination, Mummy." Samuel recalled Sylvia's tears and apologies; her remorse for once threatening to wound him; her solemn promise to never again to discuss their past with anybody, her reaffirmation of the vow, made many years before, to support him in whatever he chose to do.

"Sam," Rhoda said firmly, "I don't want her in my home ever again. I told her that, and you must tell her too."

"As you wish, Mummy. I'll let her know."

"Thank you, Samuel."

Samuel excused himself and went upstairs to the visitor's bedroom; there he changed into gardening clothes: denim dungarees over a sweatshirt and wellingtons. Before returning downstairs, he looked in his mother's room and saw the wall covered with the papers she had been collecting. He looked closely at the small sheets covered in strange writing. He understood

Maureen's concern. How long had their mother been collecting those pieces of paper and to what end? He went downstairs into the living room and looked out at the street through the net curtains. Then he looked at the mantelpiece, at the photographs of himself and his siblings, his own children and all his fourteen nephews and nieces, and two great nieces from Neville's eldest daughter. Three generations of Bostocks was his mother's measure of her personal wealth and worth – not ambition nor property, not buildings soaring into the clouds. She had travelled far from the countryside, but it remained within her. He tried to imagine the pain Vincent's death was causing her, tried to imagine a mother's sorrow for a lost son. Vincent, he thought angrily, how ironic that you, who are no longer here to suffer with us, would have liked to take from her those ancient words which were her comfort and consolation in life. Had you succeeded, what would she have now? Blank, mute incomprehension? Damn you, Vincent, you were right, but you were also so damned wrong.

He went out into the back garden, a messy space with a wooden hut that had outlived its usefulness, a rosebush that had not been pruned in years, ankle-high grass and, at the far end, an apple tree whose red apples looked picturesque from a distance but were riddled with worms.

He began mowing the lawn, which took him into dusk. In the cool evening air, a half-moon faintly visible, he reflected that all his youthful wanting had led to this: Sylvia's implacable bitterness, Elena's disappointment, his mother's silent, accusatory glances. Here was his life now, and since Vincent's death it appeared to him like a prison, and he a prisoner of his ambitions and the ambitions the women in his life had for him. At such moments he envied the freedom he thought Vincent had enjoyed. But he knew that Vincent's life could never have been his. Where had Vincent's freedom got him? A premature death, which hung over the family like a vast and static rain cloud, a memory of a promise betrayed. There would be no less laughter and chatter at family gatherings, though; he would make sure of that, even if he had to play the clown.

There was still enough light, but he decided to stop; he would have to finish the job another time. He stood near the house, the sound of the television audible through the open window. He went inside and told his mother he had finished for the day and would either return on another weekend or send one of his sons.

"Stay with me for the night, Samuel," she said. "I don't want to be alone." Her voice sounded hoarse. She did not look at him.

This was the second time since the funeral she had made such a request; it was a privilege and a burden he accepted as her firstborn. The directness and simplicity of her appeal moved him. He glanced at his watch; Elena would be expecting him home soon, but he could not refuse his mother. He telephoned home and explained the situation. Elena understood.

His night was long and restless. Maureen's observation and what he had seen in his mother's bedroom troubled him; perhaps they should seek medical advice. He would speak to Maureen later, discuss a course of action, though he couldn't imagine what they could do about what looked like simple religious enthusiasm. Then there was Larry Haynes's offer. He would have liked to speak to Elena, but he was determined to be decisive on his own account; she would back his decision. Sylvia remained the unknown factor. Could he trust her to keep her promise? It was something Vincent could never understand, the complex loyalty of a woman like Sylvia.

He woke up much later than usual, ate the breakfast which his mother prepared and served with a briskness and lightness reminiscent of the days they lived in Brixton. Then he went out into the garden where the smell of freshly cut grass still hung in the air. Using a small chainsaw he had brought to the house some weeks before, he set about pruning the apple tree. Soon, he was standing on a carpet of fallen, worm-riddled red apples, with others still on the tree's lopped branches. He stepped back on and looked at his handiwork and decided there was no reason to stop at the branches. He sawed off the limbs, then reduced the trunk to a mere stump. Only then did he feel satisfied. Then, using a rake and gloved hands, he made a pile of the cuttings.

The sun was high in the sky when he finished and returned indoors. His mother was at her usual place in front of the television, watching an American church service. He bathed, changed his clothes, and came back downstairs and sat with her for a while, catching up on family news. It was eleven-forty-five. He went into the hallway, picked up the phone and dialled. It rang for a long while before it was finally answered.

"Larry…"

"Yes."

"It's Sam, Sam Bostock. I've made up my mind…"

★ ★ ★ ★

The narrator, signing off…

I no longer live in that neighbourhood, or in that house with the deep first floor windows which looked out onto the street, where a slim, dark-haired housewife skipped in and out of the house throughout the day, and the sun brought mothers out on the steps to exchange the latest gossip; where, at the back, from the kitchen, I watched three brothers bouncing on their trampoline for hours; and saw the two women cut logs with an electric saw and finish the job with an axe; where on quiet mornings you could hear the sounds of magpies and pigeons and a host of other birds – names unknown; and on summer evenings, young blonde-haired Bill, Karen's son, called out to his friend Dele to come out and play in the rough and tumble way of boys, rolling on the grass and clambering over each other; where I once watched a girl descend the stairs from the top floor of one of the houses opposite in her bathrobe, her legs pale and shapely, her hair falling about her face; and where Eddie Gordon ritualistically cut back the bush to keep the garden clear for his children to play and grow.

Sometimes, after quite some years, I miss the old neighbourhood. On one of my earliest return visits, made in response to a craving for the taste of egusi stew, and knowing it was the time of year when white yam from West Africa flooded Ridley Road market, I caught the north London line train to Dalston. I satisfied my palate with an egusi stew from the Nigerian restaurant on Bradbury Street, bought a yam, which I carried in my backpack, and wandered up to the Rio cinema, to see what was showing.

I was walking back down to the station, when I saw two familiar figures coming up the road. I stepped into an empty shop doorway and watched as Carmen Hillman, prematurely bent with age and using a stick, walked past. Following some yards behind, pulling a shopping bag, was the boy downstairs. He wore a leather jacket, plimsolls and grey jogging pants. He was obese and his movements were slow, deliberate, as if he was on medication. A few steps past me, Carmen turned and shouted at a volume above the sound of the traffic: "Hurry up, Junior!"

I watched him go by; schadenfreude, involuntary and brief, was quickly followed by an even stronger feeling of pity. I stepped out of the doorway and headed towards the station. It occurred to me that he had always belonged to his mother; that was his strength and his weakness.

My own weakness was revealed to me on a later visit. Having finished with the Bostocks, I began to feel that I lacked purpose; indeed, I started questioning my own existence. I could not identify a single family member or friend, apart from Irma Benjamin. I lacked distant memories. How did I acquire language, that most social of skills? Scouring my memory for details of my life before undertaking the long and arduous task of narrating the Bostocks' story led me back to Hackney, to a redbrick Victorian building on Dalston Lane. I had once lived there, that much I felt was true. But when, and for how long, I could not say.

That night I dreamed I was standing at the entrance of the building on Dalston Lane; questions assailed my mind, questions of such a profound nature that I doubted my ontological status, and I knew I had to enter the building to find the answers. I pushed open the front door, entered a small foyer with a large brown door at the far end. I pushed open that door and saw a figure seated at a desk. As I approached, he spun round and I said, "Who are you?" He laughed loudly and said, "I am your narrator." Horrified, I glanced behind me and saw there only a blank space, so I dashed forward through yet another door, into another room, with another figure seated at the desk, who declared himself the narrator of the first narrator. After what seemed like an eternity of opening doors, seeing seated figures – who all declared themselves the narrators of the previous one – I, your narrator, knew I was in deep trouble. At that point I woke up, stared into the dark, then fell asleep again. In the morning, I knew what I had to do. I had to find another story. So, I got an index card, which I intended to pin on the community notice board in the C.L.R. James library on Dalston Lane. And on this index card I wrote in large, black capital letters:

EXPERIENCED NARRATOR FOR HIRE,
MOSTLY RELIABLE, MOSTLY ACCURATE,
ALWAYS TRUTHFUL. AFFORDABLE RATES.
STORIES NEED YOU.
CALL: 0208020802070208.AAB

ABOUT THE AUTHOR

Ferdinand Dennis was born in 1956 in Kingston, Jamaica. In 1964, he came to London where he grew up. He has taught creative writing and is the author of the novels, *The Sleepless Summer* and *The Last Blues Dance*. His non-fiction includes *Back to Africa: A Journey and Behind the Frontlines*; *Journey into Afro-Britain* for which he was awarded the Martin Luther King Memorial Prize. Ferdinand Dennis lives in North London.